...AND THE CHICKENS DANCED

TABLE OF CONTENTS

Now here's something you don't see much in books anymore—a table of contents. I've included one because after you read these bite-sized chapters and recall them with a smile; some will be favorites. Others—well, you be the judge. You'll want to find them easily as you sit by the fire on cold winter nights, or the A/C on hot summer nights, click off the 60-incher, and laugh again as you recall my Dover adventures.

Greetings	7
The Gang of Five	11
Robicks	18
Dover Dogs	27
Emporia	31
The Studebaker	27
Koop	51
Abundance	60
Hayseed Santa	68
Harry	76
Monsters, Superheroes, and Cowboys	85
What If	97
Loogie Land	101
Clete	109
BB Gun Battles	118
Flatulence	126
And The Chickens Danced	136
Mean Streets	142
Death	155
Triple Crown	161
Freckles	170
Ride 'Em Pig Boy	177

Outhouses 185
A Train Runs Through It 195
Twin & Twin 204
No One Knew.. 215
All-Day Sucker 220
"Badder" Up.. 239
World's Greatest Pork Tenderloin 253
Discovery 268
Mr. Outdoor Movie Man 283
Lunchroom Legumes...................................... 294
Hot Dogs 302
Big-Ass Weddings 311
Big-Ass Wedding Dances 323
Sleeping With Dad 329
Easy (Going) Rider 347
My Old Man 364
Epilogue..374

GREETINGS

Welcome to Dover. My little red dot on the Rand McNally. Folks from real cities snubbed us as they passed through. *A wide spot in the road* they said. Our streets were a wreck, 80% potholes and 20% street, and conveyed more bare feet and bikes than cars. Our homes were humble, more about function than form and about as pretentious as an army barracks. Our hearts were big and checkbooks small. But our generosity...boundless. *Mi casa es su casa.*

Dover was down the road a piece from the county seat; home to the county courthouse, county sheriff, and the much-hated and equally feared county tax collector. The contempt that Dover folks held for the revenue-generating tax collector was ill-founded. Our piddly property taxes wouldn't even cover the county sheriff's donut budget.

Dover's population hovered around 173 souls. Our on-again, off-again procreation (pun intended) kept that tally in a state of flux. Every Sunday morning, depending on the hangovers, 173 butts (more or less) filled the pews in Dover's three churches. Our priests, ministers, and preachers urged their congregations to have bunches of babies. For the Protestants, God's instructions were optional. For us Catholics—not so much.

Dover subscribed to the social sensibilities common in most small towns. There were no big-city, over-achieving parents pushing their big-city, over-achieving children to aspire to lofty professions that focused more on finance than fulfillment. Our career paths were quite simple: grade school…high school…job. No Sam Walton or Bill Gates would ever rise Phoenix-like from the farm dust that swirled around Dover. Oh, we spawned a few standouts. Couple of lawyers, a doctor, and a few nurses. Even a writer, although most folks don't talk much about him. Over the years most of us scattered to the winds. Big cities and bright lights ya' know.

Dover Men were hard-working, blue-collar Joes who bought their shirts at Sears with the sleeves already rolled up. They worked in the fields and factories, stores and gas stations to put groceries on the table for their blue-collar kid-scrum. Brothers wrestled two and three to a bed, simmering in a near-lethal brew of testosterone and sweat. The lucky ones (older brothers like me), slept on the outside and wedged the youngest into the middle where they functioned as a barricade, separating the nightly onslaught of thrashing elbows and gnarly knees.

Dover was one big extended clan, a community nuclear family dealing with rivalrous siblings, crazy cousins, and drunken uncles. For those larger-than-life personalities that filled our town, bodacious was normal. They weren't show-offs mind you, but ordinary folks whose flamboyance was a natural part of their personality. They saw it as their responsibility, their duty, to needle the rest of us. Sewing another stitch into the fabric of our lives.

In the lavishly-embellished recollections that follow, you will be welcomed into our lives. The doors to our homes will be thrown open and our souls laid bare. Sit down a spell and share in our triumphs, our joys, our follies. And sadly—a few of our tragedies. I need to take a moment here for a little disclaimer: just like the name of the town itself, Dover Folks' names have been changed to protect their privacy. Some of you reading this might know "Dover." Like me, you may have grown up there. You might even remember some of these characters. If not, the fun's in the guessin'.

Before we go dancing down Dover's streets, I need to thank Sinclair Lewis and Richard Russo. Their books inspired me to write these stories. I make no allusion that I even come close to their literary skills. Dover is neither Lewis's Prairie Grove nor Russo's Empire Falls, but somewhere between. Not so much a Rockwellian hamlet filled with freckle-face kids and white-haired grandparents fixin' to carve that impossibly golden-browned turkey. What Dover lacked in urban chic it made up for with its homespun hoots and hollers. Sophistication supplanted by simplicity. A Dover mom's ready-to-wear dress wasn't high-fashion. But nothing could diminish the elegance of her unmakeuped face at Sunday morning Mass as she gazed upon her stair-step children with their spit-slicked cowlicks and unwashed eye boogers. At the other end of the pew her husband gave thanks with his folded, grease-creased hands.

Jump on this emotional roller coaster with me (the front seat is still open), and get ready for a ride you will not soon forget. Learn about the lunacy of our Hayseed Santa. The poignancy of the Pigboys. Our infatuation with flatulence. And the tragedy of Real Death.

Dover moms yelled out the backdoor at their kids before supper: *Wash your hands and git'chur butts up to the table.* Well, here's your invitation to get *your* butt up to the table and dig into this smörgåsbord of spicy adventures and savory characters. Oh, c'mon—this is Dover—you don't need a napkin.

THE GANG OF FIVE

In post-WWII baby-*bloom* America, our nation's population blossomed like wildflowers. GI's returned from the war, eager to put their lives back on a more conventional track and leave those awful memories "over there." They simmered with enthusiasm. And quite obviously, as demographers would soon discover—testosterone. From Connecticut to California, babies rained down from the heavens like Biblical frogs. Catholic babies, Methodist babies, Baptist babies—non-denominational babies. Black babies, brown babies, white babies—and somewhere-in-between babies.

Dover somehow missed out on that statistical *bloom*. Its population never really boomed—it *nudged*. When our post-war nudge reached its climax (pun intended), the sign by the road that connected us to the world read: *Pop. 173*. During those explosive growth years, when booming babies popped up around the nation like Whack-A-Moles, the number of souls in Dover fluctuated very little. Weary of the annual invoice from the local sign painter, the town council passed a cost-saving resolution: *Let It Hereby Be Resolved: That dang sign ain't to be touched until those horny GIs wear themselves out.*

The cause of Dover's population stagnation was pretty simple—for every birth announcement published in the *Every Wednesday—Come Rain or Shine* county newspaper, there was an offsetting obit. Like a lot of rural towns and villages, Dover was top-heavy with old folks. The cemetery, a half-mile north of town, sprouted a fresh row of granite slabs next to the corn field every year or so. 173 was a pretty much constant figure on the dangling *Pop.* panel.

Sometime in the early-nudge period of 1947 - 1949, *we* arrived. The Gang of Five. Little boy-bundles of joy from God's heaven. Our band of brothers by various mothers popped up at various times during that window of wonder. We wouldn't be joined by our fifth tag-along until 1951. One of our various mothers had back-to-back baby girl-bundles of joy and wouldn't get back on track and supply another brother for her Mother Hubbard home until then.

We were white boys. All five—Wonder Bread white. The only diversity that ever threatened our town was *"that bunch of Mexicans"* that migrated to our vanilla village when we were preteens (there will be more on this—much more—in a later chapter). However, at the end of our shirtless summers we nearly matched their coffee-colored complexion. By October we bleached back to Wonder Bread.

Chronologically, I slipped in somewhere in the middle of our gang. I was average height, average weight, and average I.Q. (A fact borne out by my grounded-for-a-month report cards.) When I was sixteen I started wearing Buddy Holly glasses. My nearsightedness was the result of having been shoved into an incubator within minutes of my birth. Family lore has it that my Bobblehead noggin was a bit bulbous to negotiate Mom's birth canal. Doc Hansen left me in there (the incubator…not Mom) until my powder-blue skin glowed powder-pink. As I grew I compensated for my vision issues by being a well-spoken (mouthy), outgoing (show-off) kid (punk). Oh—and filled with confidence (swagger). I'm still pretty much like that today.

Milo Deuter and I were born in the same year. Back then folks said we were *tight as ticks*. In today's texting terms he would be my BFF. In Dover-Boy profanity he was also my BFF. There was something special about sharing such close birth dates that bonded us. We were inseparable in grade school and would remain so through senior high. Sadly, a few years after graduation, we lost touch with each other. I probably wouldn't recognize him if I passed him on the street today. But back then, we were like brothers. Brothers without all the Neo-Freudian sibling issues. He was the yin to my yang. My leap-before-you-look offset by his tread-before-you-trip.

Arnie was Milo's brother. He was the delayed gang member that I mentioned earlier. Arnie arrived in the Deuter family *almost* three years after Milo. Did you catch that *almost* part? If Mother Nature had permitted it, Mr. and Mrs. uber-Catholic Deuter would have procreated two babies a year. Well, they came pretty close with Arnie. He trailed his two hairless sisters by only ten months—a Dover record. My folks came close. Eleven months separated me and *my* hairless sister.

By the time we were sixteen, Arnie's almost three-year age difference was not so apparent. He started burning through growth spurts when he was nine and was already two inches taller than Milo and me. The nuns at Saint Boniface grade school called Arnie assertive. We called him cocky. He was so cocky, he'd fight anyone that needed fightin'—fat guys, skinny guys, tall guys, short guys. He'd beat the shit out of all them. But under that tough guy façade, he was a pussycat. He never bullied anyone but wouldn't let anyone bully him either. Or us. Arnie was a guy you wanted in your corner.

Only two more members of our posse to tell you about and the roster will be complete. But first, I need to explain a little more about the Deuter boys—Milo and Arnie.

Before we banded together in a league of mavericks, the Deuter brothers and I were tight. Siamese triplets. It was about the time that they were eight or nine years old that their "house" burned down. The reason I put "house" in quotes is because, by any standard definition, they did not live in what most folks considered to be your standard domestic dwelling. They lived in a basement! Even before the energy crisis, which would come decades later and be responsible for the proliferation of underground homes from Maine to California, Mr. Deuter had his tribe living like post-apocalyptic subterranean survivalists. Where a framed house should have stood atop its basement walls, he laid down plywood sheeting and it became their roof. He rolled out a couple layers of tar paper on it and smeared the whole thing with buckets of black ooze. *Voila!* The Deuter "house" was ready for occupancy. No one knew for sure whether Mr. Deuter adopted his bohemian lifestyle because he was forward-thinking or just a cheap bastard. Most of us suspected the latter.

And occupy it they did—with gusto. Mrs. Deuter strung up a few blankets to roughly define the various rooms. It had four bedrooms as I recall. Mr. and Mrs. Deuter had the corner "suite" (Mrs. Deuter even blanketed off a little space and called it a closet). The other three bedrooms had three little Deuters each. Any squalling arrivals just home from the hospital slept with Mr. and Mrs. Deuter until they could make it through the night squalless. As I mentioned earlier, the Deuter darlings sometimes arrived in as little as ten-month cycles. However, Mrs. Deuter occasionally imposed a mandatory six-month cooling-off period on Mr. Deuter just to catch her breath. More importantly, she was running out of blankets to subdivide their ever-shrinking bedrooms. Had she not sent Mr. Dueter to his corner for a mandatory ten-count, he would have had to dig in a new addition.

Tragically their catacomb of blankets, beds, and mayhem caught fire one evening and the whole damn thing burned down. Well, more correctly—burned up. Mrs. Dueter liked to cook. Make that *fry*. Since there was no ventilation, their blankets, clothes, skin, and hair were infused with the ambience of fried something. Whenever Milo and Arnie came to school reeking of some sort of fried meat, Sister Mary Lawrence made them sit next to an open window. Town folks speculated that Mrs. Deuter was frying a couple of pounds of side pork for supper the night that it caught.

Dover's volunteer fire department (about as effective as that pack of dogs that pissed on Mom's petunias) finally squirted out the flame-flickers. But not until the charred remains of their basement home looked like a barbecue pit. The volunteer fire department chief—usually the guy who drew the short straw that year—condemned what was left, told Mrs. Deuter that reblanketing was not an option. So, they were forced to move. They landed in a rent house two doors down from us.

And that's how we became Siamese triplets. Milo, Arnie, and me.

Mickey Green was the oldest and, by Dover standards where age always trumped intellect, he should have been our leader. Our alpha male. But somehow, he was comfortable being just one of the guys. His old man never taught him how to be *assertive.* Like two-inch-taller-and-cockier Arnie. There were some Dover dads who apparently didn't pay attention in How-

To-Be-A-Dad School and, as a result, they displayed various degrees of child-rearing incompetence. But even as boys we somehow understood that none of our dads were perfect. When innocent kids grow up in a loving family environment they accept their parents' flaws as just being a part of their character with the barnacles and blemishes ignored. My old man drank way too much up at Tilleys. Milo and Arnie's old man neglected them and worked way too much overtime at the tractor factory. Riker's mom broke the gender barrier and chain-smoked way too many cigarettes. Mickey's old man liked other women way too much. I think Mickey sensed that his old man's character issue was a little more egregious than beer, overtime and cigarettes. In Dover, where everyone knew everything about everyone, he knew that we knew, and couldn't quite pull off his bravado. Thus, his reluctance to assume the mantle of leadership. But he was still a good guy. Affable, outgoing, *and* funny. Our gang's jokester. Comedy was his security blanket.

I saved Riker for last. He was the most flamboyant of the gang. If we were sparrows, he was a peacock. Ducks to his swan. Riker's folks broke Dover's baby-making mold and made a mere three. Yes! *Only* three! Riker and two sisters. As their young prince, Riker was (at least from our viewpoint) privileged. It was always a strange and wonderful experience to have a sleep-over at Riker's house and spend the entire night alone in a bed (something I would not do again until I got married). I awoke with a gentle breeze washing over my face, basking in the warmth of the sunshine streaming through the windows rather than the warmth of pissed-up pajamas streaming from my little brother Richie. I enjoyed a leisurely breakfast without the fear of losing an arm when I reached for the last piece of bacon. Riker's mom and dad actually listened to us at the breakfast table without having seven or eight brats fighting for face time. And finally, as if he wasn't already fortunate enough—Riker was cool. We were dorks compared to his Elvis-groove. But he never took advantage of it. It was just something that came to him naturally. We all wanted to be like Riker.

There was one concession our gang of five made to our exclusive membership. Whenever we were feeling particularly charitable we allowed Richie, my snotty-nosed little brother (he of pissed-up jammies), to tag along. Despite the near-generational gap (he was a whole two years younger than even Arnie), we gave him a pass. Sometimes he came in handy. Like when we scouted Dover's back alleys for pop bottles and came face-to-face with some snarling mixed-breed with strings of dog spit dripping from its fangs. When it went into attack mode and came after us like the hound of hell, being older and longer-legged, we easily outran Richie. We'd be several blocks ahead, wheezing and laughing as little Richie darted mere inches ahead of the beast's snapping jaws. It eventually caught up, nipped him in the ass, and pinned him to the ground. Just when Richie was about to become dog food, the mutt straddled his face and licked his nose. Apparently hounds of hell are addicted to snot salt.

So there we are. The Gang of Five. Or 5½—when we included Richie. An egalitarian mishmash of misfits. You're going to hear a lot about us as you navigate these pages. Some other Dover folks will pop up in various chapters and other boys will fade in and out of the narrative from time to time; but I will always circle back to our little gang and invite you run with us as we inflict our personal brand of hell on the mean streets of Dover.

ROBICKS

You may have figured this out by now—that *Pop.* sign in the last chapter was probably a dead giveaway—but Dover was not a vibrant retail hub teaming with commercial activity. Her streets were not bustling with consumers dashing from store to store blowing their non-discretionary income on stuff they didn't need. Every sweaty dollar was prudently, if not reluctantly, pried from purses and billfolds for life's essential commodities like beer and cigarettes. Oh…and food. So, with that in mind (the food thing), let's explore one of the vibrant spokes in Dover's retail hub: Robicks.

In today's fast-paced world we enjoy the fast-paced convenience of, umm, convenience stores. Quickie Marts. Bodegas. Mini-Marts. If you crammed all of them into one little Mom & Pop and plopped it down in the middle of Dover—you'd have yourself a Robicks.

  Behavioral scientists, when they're not telling us how to behave, conducted tests with lab rats and concluded that our most powerful memories are associated with our olfactory system. Our sense of smell. Robicks will be forever stored in my memory bank because of its orchestra of odors; a rich stew of aromatic delights that captured the pungency of a Middle Eastern spice bazaar. Shelves in today's big box stores are overstocked with hermetically-sealed, plastic-wrapped, chemically-preserved, artificially-colored, flavor-enhanced food *products*. Stroll—whoops, wrong word—*shove* your way down their jammed aisles and the only olfactory experience you'll have will come from the rich aroma of armpits.

Let's take a break from all that and step into Robicks. As you push the Wonder Bread sign screwed to the screen door, it hits you. No, not the screen door, but a friendly shout. A warm welcome that actually includes your name. But before you can open your mouth to shout *hey*, here it comes—the inquisition: "How's your_____?" (fill in the blank: gramma, aunt, dog). Your two-word response is all that's required: *pretty good* or *she died*.

With the social pleasantries dispensed, you're free to roam Robicks aisles to pick up whatever it was that you came in for. Most folks dropped in daily to buy their supper stuff. A lack of foresight (and fridge space) dictated their daily visit. Nobody bothered with a menu. They assumed that inspiration would strike and lift them from their grilled cheese and tomato soup doldrums.

Right about here—three or four steps from that just-slammed screen door—your nose goes on high alert. Queue the Klaxons! Swirling smells of real FOOD!

The loudest aroma, the one that shouted over all the rest like some alpha-smell, was always the bananas. Unlike today's bullet-proof green bunches hacked from the jungles of Guatemala and saturated with ripening-retardant chemicals, Robicks bananas were natural, yellow, and soft. And like my gramma's hands—speckled with age spots. The stalk was not carved into consumer-friendly, five-banana bunches. Mr. Robick hung his entire jungle-clump right in the middle of the store like an upside down Christmas tree. When the wholesale grocery delivery driver dragged it into the store, Mr. Robick fetched his step ladder and climbed up to tie it on a hook. Housewives picked however many they needed and stuffed them into paper sacks that had handy paper handles. Nothing like handy handles to hold your bananas.

Every morning Mr. Robick went about his routine of picking up the cans, boxes, and sacks off the floor to stack them back on the shelves. Persnickety Dover moms had ravaged them the previous day, searching for one *(just one, dammit)* un-dented can or still-sealed sack. When he finished, he stood back and proudly surveyed his little store. In his mind it looked once again like the pictures of the gleaming big-city grocery giants he admired in the Retail Grocery Association's monthly magazine. It was amazing just how much stuff Mr. Robick crammed onto the shelves of his three-aisle store. His dented can configurations and stacks of sacks challenged every geometrical principle known to man. Even the Pythagorean Theorem itself. Aisles were arranged in a more-or-less logical sequence that every kid in town had memorized by the time they were six years old. In fact, it wasn't uncommon for most of us to have Mr. Robicks shelves memorized before we could recite our ABC's.

As I mentioned earlier, this was before the widespread use of plastic wrap (except for Gramma's couch cushions and lamp shades). Meat was hacked from some carcass and wrapped in white paper ripped off a roll. Produce, like the bananas, got stuffed into a brown paper bag. Everything else was canned or sacked. Sacked rice, sacked macaroni (boxed Mac 'n Cheese wouldn't be invented for years), and sacked bread (that was actually sliced). Canned vegetables, canned soup, canned fruit, and canned beans. And of course—canned meat product. That's what it said in the small print on the back of the can—*meat product*. "Lips and assholes," the old man said. That always got him Mom-slap him on his bald spot that eventually claimed his whole head. He joked that her playful wallop sounded just like a slap on his ass, except his ass had more hair.

The departments along the outside walls simmered with most of those smells beginning with the produce department on the east wall. The meat department on the north wall ran a close second. Especially when Mr. Robick made up a batch of his head cheese. *Department* was a relative term. Actually finding stuff in Robicks was not unlike a treasure hunt. Whenever he got a hankerin' (or was bored) Mr. Robick rearranged his shelves. Mom squirted mounds of Burma Shave on her strawberry surprise dessert for supper one night.

Let's take a stroll through the produce department. As I already mentioned, the bananas enjoyed their own special position of prominence in the middle of the store at the junction of aisle two and the meat department. Kids were drawn to the bananas like the flies that dive-bombed them constantly. The intensity of the banana bouquet was directly proportional to the number of weeks they were past their prime. Mr. Robick called the bananas his *traffic generator*. He had read that term in the Retail Grocery Association's monthly magazine.

Ranking near the top of the National Fruit Grower's Macintosh Mushiness Scale were Mr. Robick's apples. They were so squishy, the applesauce companies rejected them. The marshmallows in aisle two were firmer.

Onions! That's what I remember most. The overpowering essence of onions. Yellow onions. Purple onions. White onions. And Green Onions. Every mom in Dover tossed fistfuls of onions into just about everything they fried, stewed, or baked. Frying was the preferred method of meal preparation. Pork and onions, beef and onions, chicken and onions, or fish and onions. No sandwich was complete without an inch-thick onion slice and mustard scraped from the jar. Yes—a jar! None of those plastic squeezy things that farted. No one liked onions more than the old man. Glorious, wonderful onions. Whenever he helped Mom with supper (which was like…never. Remember this was the 50's when cooking was women's work) he'd cut an onion in half and call it *sliced.*

Mom liked to play a game of chicken with Mr. Robick. She was an expert at produce department brinkmanship. She had the balls of a combat marine. She liked to engage in a deadly produce department standoff with Mr. Robick. I watched her many times as she stood her ground, daring Mr. Robick to blink first. It was a delicate strategy: how long would Mr. Robick allow his shriveled veggies languish? If he miscalculated, the resulting mush, formerly known as a potato or carrot, would be rendered useless and he wouldn't be able to salvage even a portion of his embedded costs. Every morning Mom stormed into his store and made a beeline for the veggies. She didn't even bother to return his *good morning* or *how's your _____*. Sniff, squeeze, and pinch were the only things on her mind. Then she turned around, shot Mr. Robick her Marine-balls glare, and walked out. She knew. They were getting close.

Nobody knew how he knew, but mere hours before that near-necrotic potato or shriveled carrot started oozing, Mr. Robick surrendered and marked them down. Mom rushed in, snatched them up, and boogied out of the store doing her victory dance. Shaved another 27¢ off the grocery budget.

Looking back, it really is quite bewildering just how Robicks produce department produced any income at all. Oh sure, Mrs. Robick (who oftentimes helped out with the produce department) had some pretty nice melons (wink wink), but their veggies paled in comparison to the backyard efforts of most folks. Everybody in Dover *put in* their own garden. Nobody planted—they *put in.* Some of them were so large, (the gardens—not the gardeners) that they could have been the backdrop to a John Steinbeck novel.

The Meat Department. Mr. Robick got more grocer pride from his meat department than anything else in his store. Sure, he had nice chops, but it was his big butts that built his reputation. Every morning, before he retreated into his world of sinew, gristle, and fat, he manned the front counter until Penny arrived to woman it. Mrs. Robick was nowhere to be seen at that ungodly hour. She pursued her beauty sleep (most folks said to no avail) until almost dinner time, and wouldn't make an appearance in the store until the late afternoon rush rushed in, when as many as two, sometimes three, shoppers would cram the aisles.

Penny walked into the store about an hour after Mr. Robick had unlatched the screen door and flipped "*Sorry, We're Closed*" to "OPEN". Over the years she had pretty much figured out that an hour was about how long it took him to get those dented cans and ripped sacks picked up and put back on the shelves. At 75 cents an hour, she wasn't about to do actual *physical* labor. Penny was the town's formerly-prized, very eligible, and (at one time, some folks said), very attractive bachelorette with her formerly-prized Barbie Doll face and formerly-prized curves. In Dover-speak, she had been 'quite a catch'. But after years of squandered opportunities, her eligibility status had been reduced to spinsterhood. So, while she checked out her men customers at the check-out counter, none of them bothered much anymore to check her out. A perfectly-coiffed Penny (at least she had her still-prized hair) put on her perfectly-pressed white apron with *Penny* red-thread-stitched above her perfectly-sagging left boob.

After an obligatory *Mornin'* uttered in Mr. Robick's general direction, she took up her position behind the recently-arrived one-armed adding machine. She had threatened to quit if Mr. Robick didn't get her the damned one-armed adding machine to augment her declining pencil and paper skills. It was hard enough just keeping up with those afternoon rushes when as many as two, sometimes three, customers would cram the aisles. Besides that, she was beginning to get a little embarrassed when folks snickered watching her lips move while she ciphered. Sometimes she forgot to jot down the nine and carry the four. The argument about that damned one-armed machine ended quite decisively after dinner one afternoon when the well-rested Mrs. Robick walked into the store and heard Penny bickering about quitting. Mrs. Robick, fearful of maybe having to forego her beauty sleep, stuck her fat nose in. Two women vs. one man. Mr. Robick didn't stand a chance as they pushed him over the brink of modernity.

Penny sat down on *her* stool and got all settled in. She rearranged the mess Mr. Robick had made of things and put her pencil and pad on the left (*where it's supposed to be*), and her one-armed adding machine on the right (*where it's supposed to be*). Then she pushed her penny plate—labeled *Penny's Pennies*—out front for folks caught short and sure as hell didn't want to break a dime for something as silly as two cents. Her always-present pack of Wrigley's Spearmint was nearby so she could annoy Mr. Robick all day with her incessant gum snapping.

After her fussin' was done, Mr. Robick donned his well-worn, *relatively* white butcher's apron that, by Wednesday or Thursday at the latest, would take on the splattered brilliance of some Jackson Pollock masterpiece. He turned around and walked away in silence. After so many years of working together, he had long since abandoned any thought of returning Penny's perfunctory *"Mornin'…"* He told folks, "Wasn't nothin' could make that old maid smile anyways."

Mr. Robick approached his sawdusted inner sanctum with the seriousness of a thoracic surgeon. His patients, cow and pig carcasses, hung in his walk-in cooler awaiting his skillful dissection. Not a single piece of fat or gristle would be wasted. A really good butcher could hide anything in head cheese. In fact so little was discarded, the sawdust on the floor hadn't been replaced in years.

Those who shopped early in the day oftentimes caught him gazing at some quarter-cow or half-hog, studying it like Da Vinci pondering a slab of Florentine marble; pondering exactly where the first cuts should be made to bring David forth in classic glory. Perfect chops and beautiful butts were but a knife stroke away.

Twice a year, our table was graced with the results of his considerable talents. His steaks for the old man's birthday and one of his big-ass hams for Easter. Mr. Robick hated Thanksgiving. Hard as he might try, there wasn't much he could do to a turkey carcass. Mom, ever the one to thumb her nose at tradition, ignored his turkeys and roasted a goose for our Thanksgiving feast. We drove out to Gramma's farm to watch her kill it. She locked us in the car while she lopped off its head as Polka Party Time blared on the radio. She didn't want us to hear its last desperate squawk or honk or whatever a goose does when it loses its head.

Always facing budgetary pressure, Mom bought what Mr. Robick disparagingly called *scraps*. He hoped that his reproachful term might dissuade our cost-conscious mom from such a bourgeois purchase and upgrade to a more costly selection. But not *our* mom. Anyone who'd engaged Mr. Robick in a vegetable war certainly wasn't about to spend frivolously for something so silly as a more identifiable cut of meat. Scraps would be just fine, thank you.

Lastly, let's visit the Mother Lode on the west wall—Robicks child-coveted, mom-cursed Candy Department. Perfectly arranged on the floor-to-ceiling shelves and spilling over onto Penny's check-out counter was a full complement of every kind of candy known to mankind and kidkind. Those shelves lured Dover kids in with their sugary-sweet siren-song: lemon drops, root beer barrels, Tootsie Pops, Baby Ruth, Snickers, Butter Finger, Good n' Plenty, Boston Baked Beans, Sugar Daddies, Malted Milk Balls, red and black licorice, jaw breakers, Red Hots, and an assortment of twofers that dazzled even the most hardened candy addict. And over there on the end was a place reserved for the *pièce de résistance*—the *crème de la crème* of confections—Holloway's All-Day Sucker. The caramel confection-on-a-stick that, according to the outlandish claim plastered on the front of the wrapper, would last a kid *All Day Long*.

Oh, the sugary sweetness that drifted from that glorious gallery. To a Dover kid it even overwhelmed the well-aged bananas, soggy veggies, and heady head cheese. Busting out of iron shackles would have been easier than escaping the iron grip of Mr. Robick's Candy Department.

DOVER DOGS

Everyone in Dover had a dog. You notice how I said that? Or, more correctly, how I *didn't* say that? I didn't say *owned* a dog. Owning a dog implies that some sort of retail transaction occurred. A purchase from a pet store, farmer, or friend. Old Man Peters was always trying to sell his coonhound puppies, but if you have ever lived next to someone who had coonhounds, you'd know why his sales were about a successful as selling ice cubes to Eskimos. No one in Dover ever bought a dog, so by extension, no one in Dover actually owned a dog. Shaky logic, I know, but logic and Dover behavior rarely shared the same bed.

Sometimes a dog might be given as a gift for a birthday, Christmas, or *some* kid's report card that (*just once, dammit*) did not come home littered with D's and F's (I'm not namin' names). The old man actually brought a coonhound puppy home as the result of a wager with Old Man Peters one night up at Tilleys. The old man lost. After two weeks curled up on our back porch, so did that coonhound puppy.

In Dover, dog acquisitions through any of the aforementioned means, purchasing, gambling, or gifting, were rare. Wandering mongrels just showed up one night and took up residence under some back porch or rusty yard sculpture, aka: Fords and Chevys. Milo and Arnie had a runty mixed-breed that folks in Dover called a Heinz 57. Milo traced its lineage to half the dogs in town. His old man said it was part possum because every time he kicked it, it hissed. Richie and I had a Cocker Spaniel-Collie mix. Mickey Green had three dogs—two Rottweilers and a Toy Poodle (go figure). No—he did not have a Rottweiler/Toy Poodle mix (think about it). You already know that Old Man Peters, Dover's crown prince of canines, had coonhounds. All five were direct descendants of Satan.

Everyone had at least one dog. And the really weird part—everyone knew the name of every dog that ever shit on the sidewalks of Dover. Dover dogs never shit in the woods or backyards like properly brought up mongrels. Always the sidewalks. Because of this no one in Dover ever set foot in their homes wearing shoes. They were always kicked off and left on the back porch. Except maybe their Sunday shoes. Sunday shoes remained pretty much shitless because walks to church were careful, methodical. Every step scrutinized and strategically set down like a Marine navigating a minefield. Father Hempel interrupted his sermon if so much as a scant scent of doggie poop drifted up to his pulpit. He stopped his scripted Sunday screed, sometimes in mid-sentence, just as he was getting to the part about the parish being broke or the hell fires that awaited our sin-drenched souls for all of eternity. He always made it quite clear that our sin-drenched souls would avoid those eternal flames if we went to confession every Saturday night or generously donated when the collection plate was passed. The latter always being the preferred method of escape. So right there, as soon as he got a whiff of canine crap, he paused somewhere between Ecclesiastes and Job, ripped off his bifocals, scanned the sleepy pews, and said that whoever had dog shit on their Sunday shoes was free to leave. He stood there pretty much alone after half of the families and three of the five nuns hit the door.

Dover dogs begat more dogs. Eight or nine at a time. Bitches with bloated bellies and parallel tit-rows dragging in the mud scoured the alleys and backyards for an abandoned car where they had their next litter. Locating an abandoned car in Dover really wasn't much of a challenge. They surrounded every house like Stonehenge sentinels. Pity the man that dared to call them *junk*. They were spare parts depots: carburetors, fan belts, headlights, windshields, and fenders that would certainly find some use some day. Just because an old Ford or Chevy was no longer drivable was no reason to throw it away. And if the owner was lucky enough it might fetch a handsome price from some out-of-town collector cruising the countryside for his next project. The old man got seven bucks for the rear end of our '51 Pontiac. Problem was…we were still driving it.

Darn near every week a fresh litter would pop up in some back seat or trunk and contribute to Dover's dog population. Some of you more adept students of American politics might recall when Hoover used the campaign slogan: *A Chicken In Every Pot.* Well, Joey Zimmerman, Dover's consummate political animal, ran on the campaign slogan: *A Dog In Every Yard.*

Even with all those tit-draggin' bitches throwin' all those litters Dover's dog population managed to more or less stay in check. No one knows how that happened for sure. It was as if they just disappeared. Somehow vanished. Many attributed this phenomenon to Old Man Peters, Dover's unofficial canine control officer. You're probably way ahead of me here (it's not that difficult), but many of us suspected that Old Man Peters took a few, shall we say, unauthorized liberties when he "discharged" his duties.

EMPORIA

One of the fundamental social foundations of what made Dover such a cohesive community was that amongst Dover folks, no one was rich, wealthy, or loaded. Class envy, for the most part, was nonexistent. Sure, some folks might have had better stuff than others. A couple of Schwins scattered in the yard that were not quite as rusty as the others in town. An extra couch on the front porch. A black & white Philco with a FULL 21-inch screen (19's were *de rigueur*…B&W mandatory). Some had a newer used car with a still-unripped backseat. But in spite of their possessions, Dover folks were an egalitarian bunch. Envy, greed, and materialism existed only in Father Hemple's every-other-Sunday Money and Materialism pulpit-rants (M&M's he called them). When he finished, everyone dropped an obligatory, guilt-reducing buck or two in the collection plate and rushed home to fried chicken, mashed potatoes, and a Cardinals game. Yup, egalitarian pretty much fits. Except for the story I'm about to tell you…

Generally speaking, wealth accumulation was not high on the agenda of Dover mommies and daddies. The daily struggle of keeping bellies full, feet shod, and babies dry took up most of their time. Sometimes though, Greed, the third Cardinal Sin (right behind Gluttony), reared its ugly head. Financial speculation would take ahold of some broke-ass wage slave when some charlatan's newspaper ad popped up on the back page of the sports section promising *unlimited* income opportunities and *untold* wealth (apparently charlatans liked *un-* prefixes). It would be scrutinized in a frenzied debate over a table of empty beer bottles up at Tilleys in the wee hours of the night. Broke-ass wage-slaves abandoned their cautious spending practices and tossed fiduciary responsibility under the bus. Someone would get sucked into one of those back-page schemes that almost always resulted in some degree of financial disaster. Keep in mind, by Dover's economic standards, even a couple hundred bucks lost in the blind pursuit of that elusive pot of gold could be devastating. And since everybody knew everything about everybody, the tongue-waggers would crank up the gossip mill and shred a man's reputation like a side order of Waffle House hash browns. Anonymity was a privilege reserved for big-city folks who lived in relative obscurity. In a town like Dover, every man's ass was always on the line.

And so it was that my old man fell victim to his first dance with the devil during one of his late-night beer binges up at Tilleys. Greed jumped up and bit him hard. He and Furlan McShane were teetering on that alcohol-fueled fine line that separates reality from pure ignorance. Furlan staggered over to the corner booth where the old man was working on a stack of empty Hamm's cans and sidled up next to the old man. He leaned in close and, with what he assumed would ensure confidentiality, cupped his hand over his mouth and whispered into the old man's ear.

Now, let's pause here for a moment to consider the absurdity of the scene I just described. There they were. Two grown men, Furlan, reeking of foundry smoke from the tractor plant, and the old man, reeking of gas and grease from his all-day dump truck deliveries, nuzzled side-by-side in the dark corner booth with Furlan whispering what could have been construed as sweet nothings into the old man's ear. Fortunately for them, most Dover Men had long since retreated to the place where men were supposed to be at that hour—home and family. Rumors of their midnight tryst were avoided. The only other person in Tilleys at that hour was Tilley herself, mesmerized by the flickering screen of her 19-inch Philco propped between a jar of pickled pigs' feet and beef jerky. Jack Parr, as he did every night at this time, was amusing late-night viewers with his wit and wisdom. Tilley understood roughly half of his jokes.]

Furlan continued whispering his thick-tongued proposition, "*My cousin went down there. Emporia, Kansas. He heard about it from some guy's brother who seen an ad on the back page of the sports section of the Sunday paper a month ago. So he drove down there and he seen 'em. He said they got 'em poppin' up all over the place. Damn near thick as telephone poles. Every flat-ass field and cow pasture is full of 'em. Bobbin' up and down like them plastic birds you see at the Ben Franklin that look like they're drinkin' a glass of water. Oil Wells! They're everwhere. Everbody's gettin' rich!*" Furlan got himself so lathered up, he started rattling off his words faster than some nervous eighth-grader (no names) spewing his sins in Father Hemple's confessional on Saturday night.

Well, right there it was. When the old man heard that last sentence, that was all she wrote. Even with Furlan slurin' he heard it. *Everbody's gettin' rich.* Checkmate! Bingo! Game...set...match!

By the end of the week, Furlan had extended the *opportunity* to join his surefire strategy to two more investors. Father Hempel had somehow got wind of the deal and summoned Furlan to the rectory. Furlan was sure that the venerable Rev. was going to chew his ass about greed and how he was following Satan down that slippery slope and all that. So you can imagine Furlan's shock when Father Hemple, a taker of the vows of poverty, wrote him a check. The parish priest was sure that this would secure his retirement, which, at that point, looked like it was destined to be spent in a falling-down house with a bunch of other elderly men in black who had been put out to pasture by the bishop. He had already resigned himself to pissing away his golden years with those old (ostensibly celibate) clerics playing euchre and drinking warm Kool-Aid. But this oil well scheme of Furlan's—well, this was a whole 'nother thing. This was Florida! Or at least Arizona. Eternal sunshine, five o'clock martinis, and Senior Specials at Denny's every night for supper. And who knows, if the damn thing brought in enough oil, say it was a gusher or something, maybe he could even afford a Grand Slam every other Friday morning.

The old man's brother, my Uncle Alf, would be Furlan's third sucker, err...investor. Uncle Alf and the old man were equally broke. And like the old man, he kept a second bank deposit book hidden from his wife for, you know, *incidentals*. My aunt and Mom had already "discovered" those little books years earlier and assumed that they were intended to take care of some family emergency, or dare to hope, their future retirement. Nothing escaped their scrutiny (read: snooping).

One night, about a week after the corner booth ear-whispering incident, the old man came home and parked his truck on the street in front of our house just as he did every night. He tiptoed through the back door (which is hard to do in steel-toed boots), set his lunch pail on the counter which (of course) fell to the floor, and headed straight for the only bathroom our family of ten shared. He was just zipping up when Mom swooped down on him like a tornado in a trailer park.

Earlier that day, just before *Stella Dallas* came on the radio and Mom's world ground to a halt as she made her weekly *inspection* of the heretofore undisclosed deposit book. There it was—a big fat zero! Her verbal assault was epic. Many nights in the past, when the old man stumbled in, we listened from our beds to their skirmishes that seemed to be as integral to their marriage as procreation. But tonight...this was different. This was not some simple border dispute where she rattled off her litany of the old man's minor violations. This was war: *Wat the hell is this?* She was wagging the little black book in front of his bleary eyes.

Mom didn't know it, but she was suckin' wind. Too late. Furlan had already cashed the old man's check along with Father Hemple's and Uncle Alf's and mailed the not inconsiderable sum to the guy in the newspaper ad on the back of the sports page who had a post office box in Emporia, Kansas. The mighty gears of greed had been set into motion. The four investors confidentially waited for the financial windfall that would surely make them and their families (except for Father Hemple...we were pretty sure) incomprehensibly, unbelievably, stinking rich. Oil! It was a sure thing! *Everbody's getting rich*!

A big chunk of the next year flew by and except for the occasional letter requesting additional funds, they didn't hear much out of the guy down in Emporia. In spite of the foursome's attempts to keep their *sure thing* on the q.t., they knew that everyone in town knew. Even the non-Catholics at the First Congregational Church knew. Father Hempel offered 300 (give or take) daily Masses which included 300 (give or take) supplications for his *special need*. Every Sunday the pews were packed with spiteful souls countering Father Hempel's supplications with their own selfish petitions praying that the four investors' would lose their asses. They simply couldn't abide the possibility that the old man, Uncle Alf, Furlan, and Father Hemple might upset the economic equilibrium that had taken decades establish in Dover. There was an unwritten rule that essentially guaranteed nobody would be better off (at least not *much* better off) than anybody else. Everyone knew the drill: *Nobody gets rich 'til I get rich first.*

It was late February when Furlan finally heard from the Emporia guy. Unlike the fuzzy mimeographed form-letters they normally received, he had actually sent what appeared to be a hand-written letter that updated them on the progress of their much-promised gusher. He rambled on and on about various oil patch minutia: mineral rights being negotiated, state and county drilling permits being filed, river pollution documents being prepared (even though the only river in flat-ass Kansas was more than a hundred miles away), county road commissioners needing to have their palms greased, heavy equipment permits being applied for, and how he was having a rough time finding roughnecks (whatever the hell they were). And right there, on the final line at the end of the last paragraph, above the scrawl that looked like it might be a signature, he inserted what he hoped would give the appearance of a relatively harmless appeal: *Please provide a $3000.00 cash infusion as soon as possible to cover these unanticipated costs that typically arise in projects such as this.*

$3000.00? Did he say $3000.00? He must have made a mistake and stuck in an extra zero. This certainly wasn't the usual couple a hunnnert bucks they had come to expect from the periodic fuzzy form-letters with the Emporia post office box address. $3000.00 was enough to buy two new cars! Four or five damn good used ones. Well, once Furlan read that, he immediately interpreted it to mean that their sure-fire, big-ass gusher was imminent! He sprang into action and called the old man, Uncle Alf, and Father Hempel. "Meeting tonight," he said. "My house. 7:30." When they plied Furlan for more information he whispered into the phone (thinking it would confuse the party-line snoops): *You know...our woil ell.* The town's most notorious gossip-monger just scratched her head.

They met at Furlan's at the appointed time. It was only Wednesday, but the old man tried to sneak in a quick shave anyway. Mom's radar screen lit up like a NORAD command center console up on the DEW line where bleary-eyed technicians kept their silent vigil on Khrushchev. Something was afoot and Mom smelled it right along with his Old Spice. Since she and the old man had recently brokered a peace treaty following the Little Black Bank Book affair, she gave him a pass. One of terms of the settlement included a clause where the old man promised to find enough extra work to replenish their rainy-day fund. He showed her his deposit book every Saturday night after confessions. There it was, in just a little under a year, most of the money had been replaced. If not for that, things might have gotten out of hand when she caught him shaving on that Wednesday. So she let it go. If the old man wanted to shave on a Wednesday, so be it. She laughed it off on the phone call that she made every night after supper to her aunt: "Can you imagine that?" she asked. "He shaved. And it's only Wednesday! Next thing you know he'll be taking a bath in the middle of the week too." They shared a good laugh over that last remark. Mom didn't hear the *click* near the end of the call. By 9:30 the next morning, everyone in town knew that the old man had shaved. And it was only Wednesday.

When the four investors arrived, Furlan escorted them down to his cellar to the *game room.* That's what he called it. His game room. It was nothing more than a card table and four folding chairs, a well-worn deck of cards with the jack of spades missing, and one of those green eye-shade things Furlan liked to wear on poker night. A bare light bulb swayed on an overhead cord. The table wobbled on the dirt floor as they sat down. Furlan glanced over his shoulder to be sure that Mrs. Furlan wasn't snooping from the top of the stairs, and once assured, took the folded letter from his pocket that had arrived by registered mail that morning. (In case you were wondering—yes, everyone in town was already aware of the envelope's arrival. Registered mail in Dover was a noteworthy event. Ranked right up there with surprise pregnancies and the acquisition of a newer used car).

Rather than waste the time it would take for them to read it individually, Furlan handed the letter to Father Hempel and asked him to read it aloud. But not too loud, "Use your confession voice," Furlan cautioned. "Don't want the old lady hearin'." After he finished, the Rt. Rev. Hemple laid the letter on the table and looked at his fellow investors who were staring in silence and sweating under the 250-watt bulb. *$3000.00!* he thought to himself. *That's more than four months of collection plates!*

Oddly, Furlan was grinning like a jackass eating cactus, "Don't you see, guys? This is a good thing. We been waitin' all year for this. This Emporia guy, he's got it all figgered out. All this stuff he said. Permits. Heavy equipment. And roughnecks—whatever the hell they are. Shit—whoops, 'scuse me Father—*hell*, we're gonna be gittin' our oil checks reg'lar as the Sunday paper in no time. We gotta send him this—what did he call it—this cash *in-fush-un*. That's all this is. Don't you see?"

Somehow, after Furlan explained it that way, it all made perfect sense to the league of dreamers gathered in his *game room* that smelled of not-quite-sealed jars of dill pickles. Perfect sense indeed. Dad went back to the bank the next morning. When he crawled back into his truck, his deposit book once again sported a big fat red zero. But this time that damn book would somehow manage to get lost and wouldn't reappear until it bulged with the incredible sums of that first month's oil check. Which surely couldn't be much more than a few weeks off. Oil! *Everbody's gettin' rich*!

The old man's 'few weeks' stretched to three months. Communication with the Emporia guy dried up—again. Furlan, although he would never admit it to the others, began to smell a rat. Not the one that infested his game room and was living large among the rotting beets, but the one in Emporia. So, trying to sound as nonchalant as possible, Furlan proposed that they take a road trip to Emporia to, you know, *maybe check up on things a little. See how their investment was doing.* They took a vote and everyone agreed. The trip would, of necessity, be a flying-ass weekend run (they were, except for Father Hemple, working men). The easy-street cleric, who never worked a day in his life, would have to stay behind. Two Sunday Masses and all that. Oh—and Saturday night confessions too. Almost forgot.

They arrived in Emporia Saturday night and checked-in to the Best Western Motel (which Furlan pronounced *MOW-tell)*. They booked *one* room, complete with orange shag carpet, a black & white television bolted to the dresser, two queen beds, and a shower! The tub actually had a real shower sticking out of the wall above the faucets! And since it was, after all, Saturday night, the old man would go first. He had read about these shower-things and was anxious to give 'er a try. They drew straws to see who got to sleep alone. Uncle Alf won. Which was a waste since he was more than familiar with that sleeping arrangement.

The next morning they walked across the parking lot to the Best Western Mow-tell's Wagon Wheel Diner complete with orange shag carpet and another black & white television bolted to the counter. The old man wondered aloud just how many televisions do places like The Best Western Motel have anyway? (Stuff like that always got him to thinking.) They ordered the Hungry Hombre (which Furlan pronounced *HUM-burr*) Breakfast: two eggs, two sausages, two pieces of toast (with plastic-wrapped grape jelly things in a bowl), grits (whatever the hell they were), and coffee. A way-too-bubbly-for-5:30 a.m. waitress who had *Sally Jean* embossed on her red name tag took their order. Sally Jean was resplendent in her powder-blue uniform, red name tag and matching red-rimmed glasses that hung from her neck on a sparkly chain. Furlan got all giddy as he ate his over-easy but still runny eggs because Sally Jean, who was bucking for a fat tip, kept calling him *Hon*.

The men supplemented their Hungry Hombre breakfast with five or six Camels or Chesterfields. As he got up to leave Furlan slipped a quarter under his greasy plate for Sally Jean. As they walked out he never heard it bang off the glass door behind him.

The three well-fed future millionaires jumped into the old man's Studebaker. Uncle Alf was the first to call shotgun. Furlan (just a little pissed off) crawled into the back seat. Everyone fired up a fresh Camel or Chesterfield as they headed for the Kansas prairie south of town. The guy from Emporia had included a county map in his registered letter asking for the $3000.00 cash infusion with a red X marking the spot where their much-promised gusher was being drilled. None of them bothered to notice that the map was nothing more than a fuzzy mimeographed copy of the county map that the Best Western Wagon Wheel Diner had on their menu cover.

The Studebaker bottomed out on the rutty road several times, damn near ripping the rear-end from its shackles. Furlan banged his head on the roof twice when the old man didn't see the wash-outs. When the so-called road came to an abrupt end, Uncle Alf got out and undid the chained gate. The old man eased the Studebaker through the door-handle-high weeds.

"Should be around them clumps of trees," Furlan said as he checked the map where the Emporia, Kansas guy had written: *Should be around them clumps of trees.*

Uncle Alf leaned ahead, as if that would help him see it better.

"Okay, keep your eyes peeled, Alf. Should be close," Furlan was starting to get excited and his voice went up half an octave.

There it was. Up ahead. Exactly like the map said, just past them clumps.

What?

Nothing!

That's precisely what they saw. *Nothing.* Just some scrub brush and falling-down fence posts with a *Keep Out* sign twisting in the wind.

They got out of the car and stood around kicking dirt clods and chewing on a weed when they heard the pickup approach. It stopped next to the old man's Studebaker where a grizzled old farmer—whoops—a grizzled old *rancher* climbed out.

"You boys lost?" he asked as he ambled up. Pointy boots and a tattered Stetson clearly identified him as being *different*. At least that's how the old man viewed him. Different.

"Don't think so," Furlan said as he fished the county map from his pocket. "We followed our map and it says it's supposed to be right over there." He pointed to the *Keep Out* sign.

The rancher took the map from Furlan and studied it for not much more than a few seconds. His grin exploded into laugh, which in turn exploded into a series of Marlboro coughs. That in turn triggered a couple of sympathetic Camel and Chesterfield coughs from the three investors.

They looked at him in bewildered amazement like a junior high kid after his first, err, kiss. Furlan started to shake his head. He wasn't the sharpest knife in the drawer, but apparently he was a little sharper than the old man and Uncle Alf. A few still-working neurons fired up.

"Sorry, fellers," the rancher said. "Didn't mean to laugh. I know this ain't gonna sound funny a-tall. Y'alls the third bunch I seen out here in six months. Ever one of 'em had a little map just like yer'n."

After the old man figured out that the rancher didn't say *urine*, a light bulb finally went off above his head too. Uncle Alf was the only one still, so to speak, in the dark. He just stood there and grinned. Uncle Alf grinned a lot.

"I reckon y'all musta seen his Sunday paper ad sommers…"

"Yup," Furlan said. "My cousin's brother's buddy seen it on the back page of the sports section." By now Furlan had taken his disbelief off suspension. He finally got it: they'd been swindled by some flim-flam man. But something in him refused to give in completely. He put up a brave front in an effort to retain a bit of his dignity while the rancher was still around.

"Well, I know you fellers came out here 'spectin to see some big-ass derrick spittin' oil ever wheres like in some Rock Hudson movie, but them fence posts and scrub brush is about all you're gonna see around these parts. The oil you read about's been took out years ago. Most of it 20 miles south a here."

"What the hell?" was all the old man could say.

"What the hell?" Uncle Alf chimed in (with a smile).

"You mean all of this. That ad? The letter? This map? All that and we ain't got nothin'?" Furlan finally capitulated. Screw dignity.

"'Fraid so, mister," the rancher said as he put his hands in his back pockets. "Hope that feller didn't take too much from ya's. Sonofabitch's 'bout as slippery as goose guts on a doorknob. We ain't seen him for better'n a year now. Folks been speculatin' he's clear down in Mexico or sommers. Chasin' whores and drinkin' tequila. You fellers musta been his last bunch."

It took a while, but eventually Mom and the old man (as they always did) worked things out again. When he walked in the door after the long drive back from Emporia she saw the beat-dog look in his eyes. There wasn't much he could hide from her. And except for that deposit book with that fat red zero, there was nothing he ever *did* try to hide from her. He loved her and she him. And that was all that really mattered.

Sure Mom was upset, but she knew. She knew that his heart had been in the right place. She knew that it was nothing more than a desperate attempt by a good man trying his damnedest to make things better. Wanting to pull his family up a notch or two.

The old man was no Joe Kennedy, but he and Joe did have a few things in common. They were both Catholic. Both raised an army of kids. And they both wanted the best possible life for their families. The only difference was Joe Kennedy got lucky and ended up with more money. A whole lot more money.

As for the old man—he's still the richest man I've ever known.

THE STUDEBAKER

Dover Men, when they weren't off on a "toot" which was a colloquialism for getting "tight" which was a colloquialism for getting drunk, pretty much behaved like real men. Self-assured. Responsible. Macho. No quiche-eating tea-sippers in Dover. Chesterfields and coffee in the morning. Chesterfields and brewskis at night. Maybe didn't eat quiche, but those self-assured, macho men unknowingly fell into a niche.

Just like dang near all of us today, Dover Men were identified by their church, job, and of course—beer. Catholic farmers and Methodist factory workers gathered together in a harmonious (for the most part) fraternity at Tilleys to drink their character-defining beer. Mostly Schlitz. Lotsa Schlitz.

However, even more than jobs, church, and beer, Dover Men were defined by the automobile they drove. The majority of Dover Men drove General Motors *products*. Not cars, mind you, but products. Chevys mostly. Old Man Peters was an Olds Man. There were a few Pontiac aficionados. To qualify for a big-ass Pontiac, one of the pricier GM products, one had to have a big-ass income. Well, at least a somewhat higher income than the average Dover Man. Not a Cadillac-higher income. Just a Pontiac-higher income. Teddy Giesenburg was one of those.

Dover Men speculated up at Tilleys on Saturday nights that he *musta made a tonna money* to drive his Big-ass Blue Bonneville. Midnight blue. You see, Teddy owned the Deep Rock gas station and could have taught the folks at Kerr-McGee in their shiny corporate headquarters in Oklahoma City a thing or two about marketing. When his cross-town rival (*cross-town* in Dover was any home or business more than two blocks away) was charging 28¢ a gallon, Teddy sold his for 32¢. Teddy understood the bargain-hunting (read: cheap) Dover Men better than any other retail merchant in town. To lure them in he gave away a *free* bottle of pop with every fill-up. Fifteen gallons gave Teddy an extra 60¢ profit. Well, the wholesale price for a bottle of RC Cola was about a nickel. Giving away five cents worth of brown fizzy water in order to rake in a 60¢ windfall was a tradeoff that Teddy was glad to make. So, every two years Teddy drove over to the county seat and bought a shiny-new Midnight-Blue Big-ass Bonneville courtesy of all his cola-guzzling customers.

Here's what really set Teddy apart from the herd and distinguished him from the other Dover motorheads. He actually parked his shiny-new Midnight-Blue Big-Ass Bonneville in his garage! In case you missed that, let me say it again—in his garage. A most uncommon practice in Dover where Fords and Chevys rusted away out on the driveway.

Even though Saint Boniface was only two blocks away, Teddy piled his family into the white fake-leather interior every Sunday and drove it to church. He, his wife, two daughters, and three sons walked out into the garage, took off their shoes, slid into their pre-assigned white fake-leather seat, put their shoes on their laps and their stockinged feet on the newspapers Teddy had spread on the white rubber floor mats that protected the white fake-wool carpet, arranged their freshly ironed dresses about themselves (the daughters...not the sons), and slammed the doors shut. Then one of them got out, put his or her shoes back on and opened the garage door. All set, they finally drove up to Saint Boniface. In the time that it took them to go through all those sequenced gyrations, they could have easily walked to church. Twice. Teddy always made sure that they arrived half an hour early so he could park near the front door where everyone would be consumed with envy as they walked past. Which was his primary motivation for buying the damn thing anyway. Everybody knew that.

Chevrolets were the G.M. product of choice and were parked in the driveways of most Dover Men. As I mentioned earlier, rarely were they tucked away out of the elements in their garages. The garage was crammed with stacks of bent-spoke bicycles, three or four lawnmowers (one might actually run), and a plethora of garden tools, lawn darts, badminton sets, and rusty lawn chairs which, just like the family that owned them, hadn't been in the backyard ever since they bought that damn 19-inch black & white Philco.

There was a good reason that Chevys were the preferred wheels for most Dover Men. They were tough. Sherman Tank tough. Even blistering hot summer days or a bone-numbing Siberian winter nights wouldn't affect their reliability. Note that I said *reliability*…not longevity. To ensure that the quarterly sales charts always went in the right direction and kept the Detroit CEO's and their bonus checks fat, automobiles back then were engineered to wear out in 50 or 60,000 miles. Somehow that abbreviated life span didn't bother Dover Men. They'd stand around in Tilleys with their Chesterfields and Schlitzes and brag how their car was damn near five-years-old. If properly maintained, which meant changing the oil maybe once a year, that five-year-old Chevy might make 70 or 80,000.

Meticulously maintained models, where the owner actually greased the tangle of couplings, bearings, and tie rods that made up its drivetrain, sometimes made 90.

Milo and Arnie Deuter's old man had a '53 Chevy Bel Air. He plopped his industrial-grade ass into the driver's seat and fired that sucker up every morning for his commute to the tractor plant. It exceeded the expectations of even Detroit's best engineers. Mr. Deuter's Bel Air had racked up an incredible 132,653 miles. Articles were written about it the newspaper. Channel 7 wanted to run a spot about it on TV but the producer killed the piece when the audio engineer had to insert more bleeps than there were actual words. Old Man Deuter liked to, shall we say, embellish his vocabulary with colorful expressions. If you got behind him at Saturday night confessions you knew that the *Gunsmoke* rerun would be long over by the time you got home.

His '53 Bel Air was a mechanical marvel and was the topic of many barber shop and beer tavern debates. In fact, after the party that Tilley threw when it racked up 100,000 miles (a heretofore unheard of milestone), the Dover Men started a pool. For a dime you could guess when the Deutermobile would finally be laid to rest under the tree in the Deuter's backyard. She threw a rod one Siberian January morning when he was about half-way to work. Old Man Peters won the pot—$27.53. Because she had such a generous heart Tilley had tossed in that odd three cents from her little penny jar next to the cash register.

Some Dover Men drove Fords. Ford-men were, by popular consensus, less car-savvy. Even when the Chevy Men harassed them with their good-natured *Fix Or Repair Daily* (F-O-R-D) disparagements, they smiled and bought the backward-thinking

Ford Man a beer anyway. After all, this was just good-natured fun. Wasn't it?

Dover had a few Plymouth Men, Dodge Men, and a sprinkling of DeSoto Men. My old man was none of the above. In nearly every social and political arena, he staked his position way out in left field somewhere. It was not a conscious decision on his part. Bucking traditional viewpoints was as natural to him as firing up that first Chesterfield before he got out of bed. For instance, when it was Quaker Nixon vs. Catholic Kennedy, the old man ignored Father Hempel and picked Nixon. Cardinals vs. Yankees? Yup—you guessed it. Even in the very epicenter of Cardinal Country, the old man went for The Mick every time. And of course (as you will hear countless times in the following pages) the old man, while surrounded by sea of Schlitz sippers, drank Hamm's. That last one was perhaps his most egregious offense. However, no Dover Man ever uttered so much as one scornful word about another's choice of adult beverage. A Dover Man could ridicule another for his car, politics, or even his cigarettes with impunity. But the unspoken Dover code of conduct was quite clear on one point: no one ever gave another man shit about his beer. Never. Everybody knew that.

So, knowing that about my old man, it won't shock you when I tell you that, even in the midst of all those Chevy Men and Ford Men, my swim-against-the-current old man was a Studebaker Man. Many nights they mumbled : *Hell, the damn things aren't even 'Merican. Come from sommer's up there in Canada.* They even stumbled trying to say those four whole syllables—*Stew-duh-bay-cur*! Nobody drove a car with a name that required damn near a college education to *pernounce*. Everybody knows that.

Oh, the ridicule. The ostracizing. The social embarrassment. The mean-spirited taunting. And that was just for me and my brothers and sisters on the Saint Boniface playground. But the old man, he didn't care how much the Ford-men and Chevy Men jabbed him. He blew off their half-drunk guffaws as he sat at the end of the bar sipping his Hamm's, dreaming of the day when Nixon would run again while he watched The Mick hit another homerun on Tilley's 19-inch Philco.

The old man taught me and my four brothers well. Today, when I make my Walmart run, I proudly park my grasshopper-green Kia among the acres of Fords and Chevys and the occasional Dodge. It does just fine, thank you very much. Three of my brothers are Isuzu Men.

Our other brother, the one who lives in San Francisco and we don't discuss much—he drives a Beemer. Not everyone knows that.

KOOP

Except for the old man and his Nixon thing, Dover politics were mostly local. Town council, town mayor, and for the more advanced voters—county commissioners—were the only elections we cared about. None of the others got much of a turnout. Most Dover residents couldn't tell you the names of their state or national office holders even if they had been listed on a multiple choice question: Wonder Woman, Goofy, Chuck Grassley, or Donald Duck. But come on, aren't we all like that to some extent? Can you name your state representative? See what I mean?

Dover held a city council election every six years. The town fathers, per state law, were free to establish the interval for local elections. As a cost saving measure, they set it at every six years. Printing all 87 ballots with the five names of the five candidates for the five city-council positions was expensive. Obviously the outcome was never what you would call a nail-biter since all five candidates ran unopposed. But state law is state law. There was even talk of extending the exercise in futility to 10 years. After a heated debate, that required a time-out when Old Man Peters got himself all worked up and his consumption started acting up, the resolution was tabled. Four of the five councilmen were octogenarians and a 10-year term seemed pretty silly.

All five of Dover's wards had a councilman to represent it. A ward consisted of two blocks except for Ward Five which had three because it included the town dump. For as long as anyone could remember, it had always been a *five-councilman* council until Old Man Zimmerman experienced what the paper called "an untimely death." (You really don't want to know…let's just say it was an "intestinal" issue). The day after his funeral, even before his body was cold, Mrs. Old Man Zimmerman was appointed to take his place and was officially sworn in. They seated her in her dead husband's folding chair at the folding table that they always set up next to the town firetruck in the town hall. She had the distinction of being the only lady, well, make that *woman* on the council.

A typical agenda at a typical town council's monthly session might include such politically charged issues as repairing Old Lady Green's sidewalk cracks. Canine issues were oftentimes on the agenda, what with Dover's ever-expanding dog population. Rewriting the noise ordinance to increase Old Man Peter's fines for letting his coonhounds yelp all night came up at least once a year. It was pretty much a waste of time since he never paid anyway.

Garbage was always a touchy issue. Well—not so much the actual garbage, but the collection of such. Other town councils often became embroiled in heated discussions regarding trash pickup schedules, route alterations, or the exclusion of certain items such as dead animals or human waste from the list of allowable contents. Dover, if you hadn't guessed by now, was not typical and as such had no official trash pickup…*per se*. I say *per se* because Old Man Peters, part entrepreneur and part just-too-damn-lazy to get a real job, smelled opportunity (pun intended) and decided that he would go into the trash pick-up business. He had noticed how folks' trash was piling up in their backyards, making it difficult for him to pick through it as he mined for "treasures" (which he cleaned up and sold in his *Junk-tique)*. His bold business plan came to him one rainy Tuesday morning as he was digging through Old Lady Green's can (well...not *her* can...her *garbage* can). After she finished yelling at him from her porch to get his ass out of her trash, they struck up a conversation and started talking in a more civil tone. As they talked he discovered that she was actually willing to pay him to get rid of it for her. So he tossed her junk in his trunk to take to the dump (except for her busted toaster that he put on his front seat). In just a few short years he had expanded his business empire and became Dover's garbage czar. For this convenience, he charged everyone fifty cents. With tax (which he kept) and handling charges, that came to 68 cents a month.

In the spring of 1956 the town council addressed a political hot potato the likes of which Dover hadn't seen since Mrs. Old Man Zimmerman was a little girl. In those days, dang near every town hosted some sort of annual festival that honored an aspect of their cultural heritage. Protivin had Czech Daze. New Hampton—Petunia Daze. Decorah's Nordic Fest was always a big hit. Still another—Bill Town (I swear that's its real name)—celebrated End-Of-The-Month Payment Daze. Clever...I guess. Apparently a little *too* clever. Nobody else got it either. So as you can see, all around the region, our summertime was quite hectic what with all of our rich cultural celebrations and various *Daze*.

What the heck..., Old Man Peters wrote in his petition (nearly all of the petitions brought up before the council began with the preamble: *What the heck...*) that addressed Dover's *Daze* deficiency. As recorded in the official minutes that night in

Peter's Petition # 1378, it read: *What the heck, we need to get off our dead asses and get us one of them Daze.* Various Daze names were discussed and rejected for various reasons. Mostly because Dover's homogenized population couldn't lay claim to any specific European heritage. Those Czechs and Norskis mentioned above pretty much thumbed their noses at us. Said we were a bunch of ethnic mongrels. So, in keeping with the mongrel theme, the best that Old Man Peters and the council came up with was Dover Dog Daze.

As you might suspect, Dover Dog Daze was not one of your *must-see* events. That first year it attracted one family from out of town. Turns out they got lost looking for Bill Town, which, through some bureaucratic snafu, held its weekend-long End-Of-The-Month Payment Daze on the same daze as Dover Dog Daze.

After a year or two of struggling, Dover Dog Daze finally gained a little traction and enjoyed moderate popularity. The annual Dog Daze Fetch Competition was a big hit until Old Man Peters, a little too enthusiastic or (more likely) drunk, accidentally threw the official "fetch stick" into the woods and his coonhound came back with an actual human leg clamped in its jaws. Nobody ever figured that one out. Channel 7 came to town one year to do a piece on the Dog Daze Dog Whistle Symphony. The cameras rolled as an ensemble of grinning smart asses walked out on stage with little tin dog whistles and started blowing. Even I knew that little tin dog whistles resonate so high on the frequency scale that only dogs can hear them. Most folks got it. They knew we were just spoofing. Everyone, that is, except the Channel 7 News producer. He aired the silent piece anyway, just to justify the cost of dispatching his news crew all the way to Dover. He told his sound engineer insert an audio track from one of his wife's *Scottish Fife Band* albums. The *Bury a Bone in a Backyard Con*test was a hit until, yup—

you guessed it—Old Man Peters coonhound dug up an actual human leg. Crowd attendance pretty much petered-out after that.

In the waning years of the festival a family or two sometimes strayed into town from somewhere. They'd stick around for the Fetch-A-Stick contest and maybe the Dog Whistle Symphony (just to hear the Dover dogs howl). Except for those one or two out-of-town stray families, the streets were empty. Dover folks never bothered to attend any of the festival events. They treated it like any other Saturday afternoon and gathered up at Tilleys, toasting themselves and bashing Nixon and Fords. Eventually, when the windfall profits that should have been generated by the thousands of tickets sold failed to materialize, the town council suspended Dover Dog Daze. Old Man Peters filed Peters Petition #1379: *What the heck, since ain't nobody comin' to the Damn Dog Daze thing anyways, let's just cancel the sonofabitch.* It passed unanimously.

Hubert Kooper was called "Koop" for as long as anyone could remember. Some said since he stopped wearing knickers . No, that's not right. No kid in Dover wore knickers. Dover boys wore jeans or overalls. Maybe trousers. But knever knickers. He was still a kid when folks started calling him Koop and has been Koop ever since. Although, after he was elected mayor, a lot of folks called him a lot worse. In towns like Dover, mayors got about as much respect as the town cop. Which, in our case, Koop was both. Hizzoner Koop ruled the roost with a pretty much a laissez faire policy and let the Dover Town Council run things. With Old Man Peters always proposing petitions and resolutions and such, it wasn't like he had much of a choice.

Everyone knew that the day would come eventually, so they weren't shocked the night Koop stood up in front of the Dover

Town Council and made his historic announcement. He walked into the city hall cum fire station and, as was his custom, sat in the folding chair closest to the door. He laid his hands on top of the agenda sheet that Old Lady Zimmerman always typed up and nobody ever bothered to read and announced that, even though he had just been elected to his fifth six-year term, it was time for him to retire from public service. His resignation would be effective immediately! Koop, one of Dover's most eligible and way-overdo bachelors, married Mrs. Koop only a few months earlier when he saw her at one of his campaign speeches which was pretty easy since she and her sister were the only ones in attendance. Mrs. Koop (Katherine) wanted to get started putting his equally way-overdo testosterone to work and make some little Koops. The clock was ticking and she had read that all that backed-up testosterone would eventually, err…peter out. She told her husband to stop playing mayor and find himself a real job. After all, a houseful of little Koops would eat way more groceries than the piddly mayor's salary could provide.

After Koop finished with his historic announcement, Mrs. Old Man Zimmerman and the rest of the city fathers (a title she abhorred, although her moustache was a bit more pronounced than the other city fathers) looked at each other in confusion (which happened a lot). "What the heck?" Mrs. Old Man Zimmerman remarked, "You don't do nothin' around here anyway. Everbody knows we're the ones wear the pants in this outfit." Which was pretty much a true statement. Mrs. Old Man Zimmerman hadn't worn a dress since she was that little girl we were talking about. (Both of her aunts pleaded with her to wear a dress for her wedding, but she, of course, refused.) Hank Thompson, representing ward five, was always careful to leave his Wednesday-night dress hidden in the back of his closet where his wife would never find it when she came home from her Wednesday night Saint Boniface Ladies Altar Society euchre tournament. So, being the de facto Head Councilman ever since she ousted Old Man Peters in a power struggle months earlier, Mrs. Old Man Zimmerman opened the floor for a discussion as to whether or not they would accept Koop's resignation. Certainly none of *them* wanted his job. They knew, with a great deal of certainty, that even if they ran around beating the bushes until the cows came home (dueling cliché's), they'd never scare up anyone willing to step up and assume the mayoral mantle of responsibility that had been borne by Koop for so many years.

Koop didn't give them a chance to debate their acceptance of his resignation. He stood up and walked out after he finished his little farewell address, which later, upon reflection, many would compare to Washington's farewell address. No, not *that* Washington. Alfred Washington, the former mayor of Bill Town who had resigned in disgrace several years earlier after he got caught up in a scandal concerning his son—the town maintenance man. Seems his boy was siphoning gas from the Bill Town town tractor and selling it to teenagers. He and Alfred split the proceeds.

Koop had been gone maybe five or ten seconds when he stuck his head back in the door and added that he'd be across the street at Tilleys if they needed anything. The Dover town council members batted a few ideas around, racking their brains (it was a pretty small rack) for some (any) semi-viable solution. Mrs. Old Man Zimmerman was the first one who noticed it. Old Man Green wasn't in attendance that night. Old Man Green rarely contributed more than a phlegm-filled cough or two at the Dover Town Council meetings so his presence had little if any effect on the outcome of the evening's deliberations. Most nights he just stayed home and watched reruns of *Gunsmoke* hoping to cop a shot at Miss Kitty's cleavage.

"What the heck…" she stood up and proclaimed… (Okay, get ready—you're going to love her logic). "Look…guys," she boomed. Mrs. Old Man Zimmerman never just spoke…she always boomed. Everyone in church at Saturday night confessions knew every one of her sins. "Koop still had five years and nine months left to go…" She took a dramatic pause to look around the table.

"…And since there ain't no way this town can function that long without a mayor—why, I don't know—but anyway, since our bylaws say that the town council hasta appoint somebody to finish out any unexpired term…

"And since we all know that we could beat the bushes 'til the cows come home and ain't none of the chicken-shit folks in this town'll step up and run for the job…

"And *since* Old Man Green ain't here tonight…

"Well then, by God, let's make him our mayor *pro tem*."

You follow that? Neither did they.

When she finished booming, she sat down, quite pleased with her political savvy. Hearing aids squealed all around the table.

She considered opening the floor for discussion, but decided against it when she saw Old Man Peters struggling to stand to deliver his two cents worth. Whenever Old Man Peters got up to give his two cents worth, it pretty much insured that whatever was being discussed would devolve into not much more than a series of incomprehensible rants. So she quickly moved that they skip the discussion and asked for a voice vote. Since no one knew what the hell *pro tem* meant (and were afraid to ask), it was unanimous. *Gunsmoke*-watching Old Man Green would be Dover's next mayor. Pro tem.

Mrs. Old Man Zimmerman pounded her fist on the card table much the same way Koop did (the gavel had been stolen years ago) and the meeting was adjourned. They folded up the chairs and shoved the table back to the corner and loaded it down with six firemen's suits with DFD stitched above the pocket, five firemen's helmets, and one walkie-talkie (its mate had been stolen years ago...same night the gavel went missing). The male town fathers lined up behind the female town father and followed her across the street to Tilleys where they spent the rest of the night toasting Koop's retirement.

Since all the toasting was an "official" Dover Town Council function, Mrs. Old Man Zimmerman put all the Schlitzes on her "official" town council expense account.

ABUNDANCE

Gramma always said, "*You can't miss something you never had.*" I'm sure the big city kids thought there were a lot of things we country bumpkins were missing out on. From our viewpoint, when we were growing up in Dover we were blessed with an abundance of just about anything a kid could want. Sometimes we even got more than we bargained for.

Our first and most familiar abundance was our pack of brothers and sisters. In the 1940's and 50's rural America was beginning to transition to a more urban lifestyle. However, young post-WWII couples continued to cling to the cultural ideals ingrained in them by their rural parents. From the time this country was founded until the mid-20th century, large families were not some novelty borne of reproductive ignorance…they were essential. They ensured that plenty of cheap labor was coming up through the supply chain. (My old man and his brothers were a five-boy supply chain. He claimed that when he was growing up, farm boys like him worked from sun-up to sundown…*sloppin' hogs, milkin' cows, plowin' fields, and pickin' corn*.) Even after their rural exodus, the newly urbanized couples were simply unable to break those cultural chains of making continuous chains of babies. When they migrated from the family farm to sprawling metropolitan areas like Dover, Mother Hubbard families soon filled their homes to the rafters. Even though they were now city Catholics, they still adhered to the moral imperative imposed on them by the pope just like their country-cousin Catholics. In case they forgot, Father Hemple was always around somewhere, waving the hellfire flag at them. They didn't realize that those hairless pink things crawling on the floor and climbing the curtains were no longer an economic asset but a liability that required massive infusions of groceries and diapers. Lots of diapers. But in spite of their inability to provide meaningful contributions to the economic viability of the family unit, most of those kids showered their parents with loving affection and hours of giggles and kisses. In my case—I was a pain in the ass. I know this because the old man told me so every day. However, in my own defense, by the time I was 22 I started helping out around the house. I gave Mom a break and even mowed the yard once.

Another abundance we had in Dover was a variety of recreational opportunities. As every Dover Boy knew, a recreational opportunity's enjoyment was directly proportional to the amount of trouble he got his ass in. We got into trouble playing our after-school softball games—broken windows. We got into trouble during our back-alley war games—more broken windows when the intended target (*someone's* pain-in-the-ass little brother), ducked. We even got into trouble playing grab-ass on the living room floor. Once again when *someone's* pain-in-the-ass little brother slipped out of a full nelson and pushed *someone else* into an end-table and shattered Mom's cheesy porcelain collie that the old man won wagering way too many nickels on county fair milk jugs. My head gash was still bleeding when the old man stepped in and convinced me that getting my ass up to bed was probably a better alternative than the blistering belt he was in the process of pulling from his beer gut. The old man thrived on theatrics.

School provided our best *opportunity* for trouble. None of us were what you would call model students. The nuns at Saint Boniface tried their best to sow the seeds of intellectual curiosity. They got down on their knees every night to petition the Lord: *Please God, some kid, any kid…can't just one of them blossom?* God was apparently distracted helping all the starving kids in China so their prayers went unanswered. That new electronic marvel—the television—invaded Dover living rooms and trumped teaching every time. Alas, their seeds fell on fallow ground. Unfinished homework was *de rigueur*. To Sister Mary Lawrence (aka: Sister Mary Larry), half-assed assignments were damn near a mortal sin and she came down on us hard. The sentence for such egregious offenses was standing in the corner for an hour or two regardless of the status of the offender's bladder. She jammed us into those corners especially during arithmetic class. (Long division was brutal and made about as much sense as when the old man sat me down and tried to have his sex talk. Words always failed him when he came to the part about insertion. So we talked about the Yankees.) Sister Mary Larry harvested more math-challenged offenders than there were corners, so she shoved six or seven of us in each one where we pushed, pinched, and scratched any warm flesh within reach. Even spit in the hair on the head in front. Especially if it was a girl. We spat with impunity, enjoying the safety of the herd. Like gazelles huddled on the African savanna fearing the stalking lions, we knew that

Sister Mary Larry's ruler would only taste the flesh of those on the perimeter.

Recess was a relative Garden of Eden for transgressors. Even the really-good kids got into trouble at recess when we not-so-goods lured them into our den of iniquity. We introduced them to the dark side of recess life with our bootleg copies of *Playboy* "borrowed" from some dad's stash. Those bountiful, silicone-enhanced, store-bought tits hooked 'em every time. Sister Mary Larry was on constant centerfold patrol from her third-floor bunker that overlooked the playground. With her military-surplus field binoculars she searched for gaggles of prepubescent 12-year-old boys huddled under the teeter-totters, getting themselves all *heated up* over the jugs of Miss Whatever-Month. When she spotted us passing pages of boobs around like plates of chicken at a picnic, she'd throw her military-surplus binoculars on the floor, lace up her military-surplus combat boots, and fly down three flights of stairs like a raging black-and-white banshee. She lined all of us up (even the aforementioned really-good kids) in a perp walk and marched us over to Father Hempel's office in the church rectory. He didn't have a home like everyone else—he lived in a *rectory*. Whatever that was (sounded anatomical). After he suggested that she leave his office (no one, not even Father Hemple, ever *told* Sister Mary Larry what to do…just *suggested*), he closed the door and locked it. She had been known to burst back in to make sure that Father Hemple was doing, you know, the *right thing*. He walked behind us and patted our buzz-cut heads (which was always a little creepy whenever he closed his eyes) and went back to his desk and sat down. He smiled at us and delivered another of his less-than-heartfelt lectures on those centerfold *breasts*. That's what he called them—breasts. We had no idea what the heck he was talking about. Breasts? Weren't they one of the pieces on our plate of picnic chicken?

These weren't breasts. These were tits. Jugs. Boobs. Even pre-pubescent 12-year-olds knew that. After he chastened us about the perils of porn, he played the Satan card on us. Sort of his grand finale'. In *Beelzebub 101* back in seminary he was taught that anything pleasurable was inextricably linked to Lucifer. "Now boys..." he admonished with his weakly disguised grin. After he made us kneel down and say three Hail Marys he released us to go back to class. We tried our best to look penitent as we filed past Sister Mary Larry.

To help us avoid what our Baltimore Catechism called *the near occasion of sin*, Father Hempel put our *Playboy* in his desk drawer along with our other previously confiscated copies. You know—for safe keeping.

Dover had another commodity in astonishing abundance. More than anything—even dogs—we had snow! Beautiful, wonderful, school-cancelling SNOW! They say that Eskimos have 73 words to describe snow. White snow. Gray snow. Vertical snow. Sideways snow. Crunchy snow, slushy snow, even feathery snow. Dover kids had just one. *Thank-You-Jesus* Snow! Dover parents had another word for it that Jesus probably didn't appreciate.

The folks in Phoenix liked to say, "*Yeah—but it's a dry heat.*" Dover folks, sometime around mid-March, after having suffered through 5½ months of snow up to their armpits, whined, "*Yeah—but it'll be gone by April.*" It never was. No matter how hard nor'easters ripped through the Midwestern prairies like some Third Reich Panzer division bearing down on Paris, no matter how high our hard-packed Himalayan snow banks soared, no matter how deep the bone-crushing temps dropped, Old Man Peters always bragged up at Tilleys how bad it was back in _____ (insert any year beginning with aught).

Blizzards were the big enchilada of snow storms. When our Thank-You-Jesus snow finally arrived and Sister Mary Larry looked out her window and saw the snow flying sideways, she closed the school. On our kid-calendar one day of school closure was one week on a mom-calendar. To our glee, those arctic blizzard conditions would sometimes last for days. While the wind howled and raged outside, Mom howled and raged inside. Sometimes, around the third or fourth day, we heard her banging something against the wall behind her locked bedroom door. When she finally came out, her bruised forehead left little guesswork. By 10 a.m. of yet another not-school day we got a little, shall we say…restless. Captain Kangaroo was over. Mighty Mouse with his near-perfect Pavarotti tenor had become passé. Four or five bowls of Cheerios had been spilled on the linoleum floor in front of the 19" black&white Philco. Essence of pissed-up jammies wafted throughout the living room and began spilling out to the kitchen. Within three minutes of the last Looney Tune sign-off with Bugs Bunny's iconic, *Bedaah…bedaah…bedaah. That's all folks*, boredom crept in. So, we did what we did best. We went to war. We kicked, scratched, and gouged until we begged our sisters to let us go. Calm was restored only after they strutted away to go play with their dollies. After Richie stopped screaming that his left eye wouldn't work, we heard Mom, still in her bedroom yet to make an appearance that morning, shaking her little bottle of pills. A few muffled cuss words. Then she cracked her bedroom door open to sneak a look. Seeing no sharp objects in our hands (she considered giving each of us a scissors and telling us to run around and play), she came out.

She marched Richie and me to the kitchen and lined us up to begin *the ordeal*. The ordeal was an elaborate process that Mom printed on a check-list and taped to the fridge door. She checked off every line item as she layered us in two pairs of blue jeans, five shirts, cheap JC Penney rayon parkas with itchy fake-fur hoods, and two pairs of brown cotton gloves. And lastly—our five-buckle, black rubber boots. But first she stretched two pairs of socks over our feet, inspecting them closely to ensure that the holes were not lined up on top of each other. Frostbite was serious stuff. She grabbed a spoon from her kitchen drawer and wedged our two-socked toes into our everyday shoes. Woe to him who dared to wear his Sunday shoes inside his five-buckle, black rubber boots. But no matter how diligent the wearer, snow always found its way inside the five-buckle, black rubber boots, leaving both pairs of socks and the everyday shoes soaked.

She finished us off by wrapping itchy scarves around our hooded faces. We looked like Siberian Sheiks. Only then, after we were swaddled tighter than baby Jesus lying in the ¾ life-size nativity scene set up next to the altar at Saint Boniface, would she send us forth. Even with the gale-force winds howling around our cheap JC Penney hoods we heard the door lock behind us. Richie and I dug out the old man's snow shovel in the garage and, like intrepid arctic explorers, set out in search of the perfect snow bank that we'd transform into a frontier fort that Hopalong Cassidy himself would have been proud of. We had our entire afternoon planned: locate the perfect snowbank, dig and tunnel away for hours until that frontier fort emerged, cover the floors with rugs and blankets from the old man's garage, and establish a defensible perimeter. We wouldn't finish until supper time. And heck, since there was *definitely* no way Mom was going to stick her head out the window into the arctic blast to yell at us to get out butts in the house for supper, well, we might even stay out there until dark.

Twelve minutes later…Richie had to pee. Okay…me too.

After beating the back door with the old man's shovel for what seemed like hours, Mom unlocked it. We stomped into her kitchen looking every bit as abominable Himalayan guy. We stood on the kitchen linoleum dripping a river that flowed all the way to the living room linoleum. We not-so-patiently did the pee-pee dance while our not-so-patient mom unbuckled our five-buckle, black rubber boots and jerked away (rather roughly, I might add), our two pairs of blue jeans, five shirts, cheap JC Penney rayon parkas with the itchy fake-fur hood, and two pairs of brown cotton gloves as she mumbled something under her breath that sounded more or less like a Hail Mary (her words were slurred). I noticed her little pill bottle laid empty next to the dirty dishes.

We were half-way into our fourth day of blizzard *vacation* when every kid in Dover called the convent to plead with Sister Mary Larry to please unlock those doors. She would not answer her phone.

Abundance. With all of our huddling under the teeter-totters getting all worked up over Miss July's big bountiful jugs, our after-school softball games with a never-ending supply of back-alley windows that needed breaking, and those also-big-bountiful blizzards, none of us Dover kids knew that we were missing out on anything. But it would have been nice to have a JC Penney rayon parka with *real* fur.

HAYSEED SANTA

Every year, as regular as the changing of the four seasons, Dover kids underwent a tectonic shift from being naughty to nice. Rumblings of our transition were triggered by the release date of the Sears and Roebuck Christmas catalog. The Sears and Roebuck marketing geniuses were under a competitive threat from the sneaky JC Penney marketing geniuses who, every year, moved up their Christmas catalog release date earlier and earlier. So the Sears and Roebuck marketing geniuses responded much like the Pentagon did to the Russian threat. Except this was way more serious than some silly nuclear arms race. This was a battle to control the spending habits of Baby Boomers who would one day wield such awesome economic power; they would shake the very foundations of capitalism and make the heretofore unheard of Jeff Bezos the richest rich bastard in the world. So, what in years past arrived in the mail after Thanksgiving eventually found its way into our Easter baskets. A banner screamed across its cover, *Forget the stinking Easter Bunny...Christmas is Only Eight Months Away Kids!* That annual avalanche of brick-thick wish books buried the Dover post office and overwhelmed Milly Parker, the town's postmistress. (I always liked her civil servant job title...*mistress*. It sounded naughty to a boy teetering on the brink of puberty.) When the truck backed up to her loading dock, spilling over with bales of Sears and Roebucks, she'd be MIA. Yup...fishing with her sister up in Minnesota. She had a second-cousin who worked on the Sears and Roebuck shipping docks in Chicago and he called her (long-distance, even), and tipped her off. She called her boss (again...long-distance, even) down at the state capital and scheduled her federally-approved vacation to coincide with its arrival.

The ever-expanding number of pages in the magnum opus provided all the incentive we needed to get right with Jesus. But more importantly—to get right with Mom. The Sears and Roebuck layout artists crammed Visions of Christmas margin-to-margin. All the toys, games, and dolls known to mankind (and kidkind) were splashed on those pages in four-color-printing-process brilliance. There were a few pages with pants, shirts, and shoes, but we tore them up before Mom and Gramma saw them and got some silly notion in their heads. Whenever my brothers and sisters and I spotted yet another gotta-have toy, game, or doll that we just hadda have, we ripped that page out and taped it to our side of the headboard so we could drool on it as we fell asleep. By Thanksgiving the remains of the dog-eared relic had been reduced from its biblical thickness to a few tattered pages that had the *stocking stuffers* on them. The "Under A Buck" crap that didn't even require the not-included batteries.

As our headboards morphed into virtual scrapbooks, we got nicer and nicer. While normal kids had visions of sugar-plum fairies dancing elegant minuets in their heads, we had John Travolta strutting at a disco party. We'd say "excuse me" even *before* we pulled our sister's hair. And "thank you" for no reason at all. In the final weeks running up to Christmas we stumbled around with glazed eyes, looking like the Offenheimer twins whose mom gave them little white pills to make them sit still at school.

Yes sir, those marketing geniuses at Sears and Roebuck hooked us hard. Glorious, splendid, magnificent toys, games, and dolls. Big yellow trucks that sliced little pink fingers into meaty shreds. Wooden cars that rendered some little brother comatose if he had the misfortune to be sitting in the trajectory of one of them heaved across the room simply because that idiot Santa brought the wrong color. Spring-loaded gadgets. Battery-powered gadgets. Even gadgets that didn't do anything (discerning kids always read the small print: *This gadget doesn't do anything*). The Sears and Roebuck marketing geniuses made us toy junkies. We curled up in the fetal position on the couch jonesing for a toy-fix and went into withdrawal if we couldn't thrash the pages of the catalog at least once a day. As Christmas got closer and closer we tore through them with reckless abandon, fearful that we may have somehow overlooked some car, truck, or battery-powered, sharp-edged steel gadget. One year, overcome with toy lust, I accidentally taped a page with pants and shirts on my side of the headboard. Mom and Gramma *both* saw it. It was the worst Christmas I ever had.

There were dollies too. Pages and pages of dollies. Dollies that cried. Dollies that walked. Cute little dollies that actually pissed their dolly diapers after they drank some sort of liquid from little plastic bottles shoved into their puckered plastic lips. Dollies that blinked their eyes. Dollies that thrashed their arms around in an apoplectic fit, groping for the affections of some six or seven-year-old mommy. There were even anatomically correct dollies. (Okay—full disclosure—I looked.) One year I smeared some chocolate chips on one of their dolly diapers. My sister still laughs about it. No—not the smeared diaper (although it was pretty cute), but how I spent the rest of that Christmas day pounding mercilessly on my locked bedroom door. It probably didn't help when I yelled at Mom that it was too bad that Santa didn't bring her a sense of humor.

Christmas morning. 6:30. We had been awake since 5:00. Pre-Christmas niceness was history. Naughty was the order of the day. We had conned Mom, err, Santa, another year and we scored big. Our living room was littered with Erector Sets, robots, cars, trucks, (maybe a dollie or two—I don't remember) and guns that looked real. There were entire fleets of wind-up toys whose metal-fatigued springs busted after the old man's twenty-third *I-said-don't-wind-the-sonofabitch-so-tight* went unheeded. Their coiled springs flailed through the air like a pissed-off rattlesnake, catching some unsuspecting little brother upside the head, making him the first Christmas casualty. By noon our bathroom looked like an emergency room. But with more blood.

My stupid sisters had their stupid dollies laid out in neat little rows like a hospital maternity ward. They were nice. Not my sisters—the dollies. I guess.

1955. It was a big year for Chevrolet and their sleek design break-through with the '55 Bel Air. The Brooklyn Dodgers won their first ever World Series when they beat my old man's Yankees. But it was an even bigger year for the annual Dover Christmas extravaganza. By early December Dover adults finally caught up with us kids and shifted into Christmas overdrive. The holiday spirit filled the air.

Harold was the town's maintenance man/dog catcher/pot-hole filler. Being the town's maintenance man/dog catcher/pot-hole filler meant that he was the only *paid* municipal employee (except for Mrs. Old Man Zimmerman, whose well-padded town council expense account supplemented her income rather handsomely). Just to be cute (read smart-ass), every year about this time, whenever Harold stumbled into Tilleys for a beer after catching a dog or filling a pothole, the tavern crew of holiday revelers (read: drunks) filled with holiday spirit (read: Schlitz) would sing out, *Hark the Harold.* It was also one of Harold's job responsibilities to string up Dover's paltry Christmas lights and moth-eaten decorations. There were atheist villages in Russia that probably had more elaborate Christmas decorations than Dover. Both strands of the tennis-ball-sized lights that he tied to the telephone poles on Main Street had, at most, a half-dozen red, green, or yellow bulbs that still worked. Koop, the town mayor, always officiated at the official "lighting ceremony" on the first Saturday night of December. With well-worn, well-scripted theatrics (that he never deviated from and every kid in Dover knew by heart), he delivered his well-worn, well-scripted Santie Speech and threw the switch. Then he threw his silly Santa hat in the air and declared that Dover was officially Santa-ready. Mr. Robick had his cheap plastic record player set up outside his store and blasted Gene Autry's *Here Comes Santie Claus* at DEFCON-3. The cheap 4-inch speaker rattled with tinny absurdity. Mr. Autry's voice could barely be heard over the howling dogs tortured by Koop's squealing megaphone. Mr. Robick played that damn 45 rpm record every year until eventually its scratchy grooves yielded not much more than white noise.

On the Saturday before Christmas Dover's Very Own Town Santa Claus would make his much-ballyhooed appearance. It was an event that had become legendary over the years. For as long as anyone could remember Dover's Very Own Town Santa arrived in the middle of Main Street under one of those strings of semi-operable Christmas lights. Not in some gleaming sled stacked with gifts for nice little boys and girls with Rudolph snorting in his harness, but on the back of Dover's Very Own Town Fire Truck. A converted 1954 Ford F-600 with "BFD" embossed in gold letters on both doors. (Dover had purchased the converted 1954 Ford F-600 firetruck from Bill Town. In spite of Father Hemple's fussing about the "BFD's" implied message, Harold still hadn't gotten around to painting over it with "DVOTFD".)

Our Dover Santa looked amazingly like Old Man Peters. He had Old Man Peters nose, Old Man Peters rheumy eyes, and Old Man Peters ruddy cheeks creased by the way-too-tight string that sort-of secured his beard, keeping it, for the most part, in place. And since Dover's Very Own Town Santa Claus Suit lacked the requisite white gloves, he even had Old Man Peters age-speckled hands and yellow fingers. All of us Dover kids, hanging on hard to our willful suspension of disbelief, saw nothin' but Santa. With his nicotine-stained grip Dover's Very Own Town Santa hung on hard as the BFD firetruck rounded the U-turn at the end of Main Street. Screaming kids and yelping dogs streamed in his wake, trying their best to out-scream the siren. Koop was in the BFD cab with Harold flipping the siren's switch, convinced that its unrelenting wail somehow heightened the drama of Old Man Peter's...err...Santa's arrival.

The truck slid to a halt in the slushy snow and nearly threw Santa off the hose rack. After Harold smacked Koop's fingers off the siren switch, the kids and dogs settled down. Old Man Peters wobbled down off the truck and took a crack at Santa's iconic "Ho-Ho-Ho." After 37 years of three-pack-a-day Chesterfields, each "Ho" was complemented by two or three *lung-rattlers* (you know...coughs).

Several men from the Dover Commercial Club (a forerunner to today's Chambers of Commerce) hovered around Santa with baskets of brown paper sacks loaded with Christmas goodies for all the nice little boys and girls. When all the nice little boys and girls spied those baskets, nice got nixed. The crush was on. They screamed and shoved like teenagers watching Elvis on *Ed Sullivan*. The Commercial Club basket holders un-hovered around Santa and tried to shield him from the hoard. Man-sized elbows collided with kid-sized eyeballs.

Old Man Peters, terrified at the onslaught, let go a series of lung-rattlers. His glasses, which were stuck together with a strip of white tape, fell apart when some teenager, standing on the sidewalk by Mr. Robicks cheap record player, tossed a snowball that smacked Santie right between his eyes. Split bifocals dangled like earrings.

The men with the baskets lost their footing and fell, spilling the *millions* (maybe more) of brown paper sacks everywhere. Old Man Peters lost his footing when he was smacked up side the head with that snowball and went down in the slush. Crawling kids scoured the ground for the busted paper sacks. Adults standing back on the sidewalks were bent over with hysteria. Old ladies were aghast at the ridicule being cast upon Dover's near-sacred Christmas tradition.

It was all over before Gene Autry was half-way through his second verse. Richie and I marched home victorious. Our pockets stuffed with partially-sucked linty Christmas candy, stale peanuts, and bruised apples. As we pushed our way through the crowd we stuck our fingers in our ears to block out the crying brats who, because of their small size, got nothing.

After the last Dover Mom collected the last brat crawling through the slush looking for just one missed piece of candy or stale peanut, Mr. Robick unplugged Mr. Autry and the street cleared out. Harold jumped back in the F-600 and ground the

Ford's starter until the battery was dead and had to get a jumpstart from some old lady in a Buick. He and Koop drove off with a pack of yelping dogs in hot pursuit of Koop's screaming siren.

In all the confusion, they forgot Santie.

A dazed Old Man Peters, wobbling on his gouty knees in nearsighted dizziness, of course, didn't see them drive off. Some kid, trying to suck up to Santie and score one of those long-gone bags, helped him to stand up. Gouty knees creaked. Beard sagged. Busted bifocals dangled. Bleary eyes squinted. In an act of pure desperation, he *felt* around for the BFD F-600. When he realized that he missed his ride, he grabbed onto the belt loop of one of the men who had been holding the baskets. They all, of course, filed into Tilleys. The men at the bar cheered "Ho-Ho-Ho" as they slapped him on the back. All Santie could manage was—you guessed it—a lung-rattler.

Several years ago I took my own sons to see Santa at the mall. My youngest, having inherited his mother's skepticism, questioned the legitimacy of the mall Santa: "Daddy, did you see his beard? It was crooked?"

I just smiled.

HARRY

Some folks are an enigma by choice. They prefer to remain shrouded in a veil of mystery. Unfathomable. Aloof. Others are a mystery because we make them such. We stand back, reluctant to engage them; unwilling to figure them out. Are we somehow intimidated? Or just plain lazy?

   I'm not sure that I know enough about Harry to weave much of a story. Not really sure that anyone does. Everyone knew *about* Harry, but nobody really *knew* Harry. He was one of those folks who shunned the limelight and flew under the community radar. Without the racism, Harry could have been Ralph Ellison's protagonist in *Invisible Man*. Oh, I suppose I could have weenied-out and cast him as some cartoonish figure, fraught with more eccentricities than Mr. Magoo. But that would have been a disservice to Harry. As I pondered Harry in preparation to put my remembrances of him down on paper, something tugged at me, telling me that floating somewhere in that aloof pool of genes was a dignity that belied his eccentricity. That *something* inspired me to characterize him with a sense of honesty and poise that (hopefully) does him right. Perhaps not a tribute, but for my meager skills…close.

Men like Harry somehow carved out their little lives in little towns like Dover. He was like that stubborn piece in a jigsaw puzzle, refusing to fit in no matter how you flipped it around. At one moment reclusive and alone. Lost in ponderous solitude. (I would like to believe that he was caught up in some sort of personal introspection, but that would be attributing an intellectual depth to Harry that probably didn't exist.) Then suddenly...*Click!* Harry'd explode in a burst of laughter and reel you in. His court jester antics mystified the casual observer: was something going on back there behind the curtain?

Harry kept that curtain drawn pretty tight. He was, you see, an alcoholic.

Like a lot of alcoholics, Harry rarely related to folks much deeper than the superficial. He did not belong to any of our social groups, clubs, or organizations. And he sure as hell didn't connect with any of our churches. His flock included the hardworking, hard-drinking members of the only congregation that Harry ever joined—Tilleys Tavern. To continue the analogy, while Harry lacked the ecclesiastical skills to be their preacher, he did a hell of a job leading the choir.

None of us made much of an effort to penetrate the fog. Sure, we'd chit-chat: *How 'bout them Yankees? Think it'll rain?* Shoot the shit was about all we did. Why didn't some of us, maybe just *one* of us—even if it would have been more out of curiosity than sincerity—step back and engage? Beneath that boozy mist had to be a heart that cried out for...for *something*.

About all you're going to get here are my recollections of the external Harry. The things I remember about the part he played for anyone willing to pull up a stool and buy him a beer. I will offer a few insights (guesses, really) about the private side of a man who's guarded sincerity made a lasting impact on everyone he met.

Harry was born…well…sometime. It's really not safe to assume that it was the early 20th century. Might've been late 19th. No one really knew for sure. Not even Harry. When I first saw Harry he appeared to be in his sixties. Fifties maybe. But then, anyone over thirty looked to be fifty or sixty to a twelve-year-old. Age assessment skills are not a kid's strong suite. My first recollection of Harry is one afternoon (where else?) up at Tilleys. I was nine, maybe ten years old. I squirmed around on the barstool next to my dad, twirling circles and watching the Hamm's "sky blue waters" ripple in the electric beer sign Tilley always plugged in first thing after she opened up. At any given moment on any given day, whenever he felt the urge, the old man stopped his truck in front of Tilleys and dropped in for a *short one* (that's what Harry and the choir called a ten-cent six-ounce draft). The old man, who pegged the nice-guy meter harder than anyone, naturally struck up a conversation with Harry. In the early-afternoon doldrums, while farmers farmed and factory wage-slaves slaved, they were the only ones bellied up to the bar. I eavesdropped between sips of RC Cola as they bantered back and forth in their game of verbal volleyball. Harry tossed in snippets here and there about whether the weather would change while the old man took his shots at Kennedy and the Democrat bastards.

Harry lived alone on the south edge of town in a ramshackle house that, using the kindest description I can come up with here, was surrounded by his not-so-discerning collection of other people's abandoned treasures. AKA…*junk*. His horde was heroic, having been accumulated over a lifetime. Most of it scrounged. Some actually purchased. Much of it nocturnal donations (drive-by drop-offs). Stacks of those treasures were temporarily dispersed amongst the weeds in maze-like patterns until eventually they ended up on his back porch. The good stuff made it to the living room.

After a night of hard-drinking (soft-drinking was rarely practiced in Dover), when the state-mandated 2 a.m. closing time rolled around, Tilley *encouraged* Harry to go home. But tonight Tilley couldn't leave Barbara Stanwyck alone to fend for herself. So Harry got himself an extra beer. On the house. As soon as it became apparent that Ms. Stanwyck didn't have a prayer with that lyin' sonofabitch, Tilly showed Harry the door. He stumbled through the streets apparently lost, but always amazed himself when he somehow found his way back home.

During the third week of the month, when his check arrived in the mail and he didn't have to rely on the hit-n'-miss generosity of others, overconsumption was in order. He'd pass out with his pickled head cradled in his arms on the bar. Whenever that happened and even stumbling home was not an option, some semi-sober Samaritan poured Harry into the backseat of his car and drove him home.

Harry got up every morning like a lot of us—groggy but filled with expectations. Ready to begin anew the sequential banalities of daily life. There was a certain sense of innocence about Harry. He was baggage-free and didn't lug life's accumulated barnacles around like so much emotional ballast. Every day was a neat, book-ended experience that was to be gathered in and played out like a hand of cards in a euchre game. Winning never considered. Playing to win was for the tormented slobs who turned out like me. Deadlines. Meetings. Schedules. To-Do-Lists. Sometimes, maybe, he'd pause a moment to reflect on his life. Then again…not. Harry probably pondered his soul about as much as you and I do—not much. Unless you are lying on some shrink's couch once or twice a week, you probably have no clue who that is staring back at you from your bathroom mirror every morning. (Be honest.)

Is it possible that the world of an alcoholic is to be, in some perverse way, envied? They suffer existential angst only for a few relatively lucid moments. Then—POW—anxiety is locked away in some dark dungeon as they're swept away to comfortable oblivion. A happy place where everyone they meet is their friend. Everything they say is near-genius. Or so damn funny they *should'a been a comedian*. A place where there is no hidden agenda and everything they do is true and faithful and genuine. I wonder.

As Harry woke up in sheets he had wrestled into knots (the crack of dawn having long since cracked), he untangled himself and swung his feet to the floor. He glanced down at his feet—holy shit!—shoes. He scratched his head and wondered how the hell he got there. *Oh well*. The mid-morning symphony was already into its fourth or fifth stanza with songbirds singing, roosters crowing, and hogs snorting. Once, deep into a bullshit session with some of his cronies, I heard Harry joke that he never woke up with a hangover or a…wait for it…woman! (Harry timed a punch line better than Henny Youngman). I heard many Dover Men chide him that, had he actually woken up with a real woman, he'd a shit his pants. We assumed that, after years of abuse, his body had somehow developed an immunity of sorts. To hangovers that is…not women. Or more likely, he lived in a pretty-much perpetual hangover. He just didn't know the difference.

He attended to his morning ministrations while he still had a relatively clear mind and could focus. We all run through one—a morning routine—prioritized and sequenced. Deviate from that routine and the rest of your day doesn't seem to sync up. Coffee, newspaper, dump. Then toast and more coffee. Maybe (if you didn't hit snooze a couple of times) a shower before you run off to race with the rats. I don't know what Harry's morning routine consisted of, but one thing is certain—it didn't take long. By 9:30, ten o'clock at the latest, he'd be waiting on the bench outside Tilleys, contemplating the cracks in her sidewalk, until she threw wide the doors to paradise. His patience was legendary. Harry never hurried. No time clock to punch. No boss to suck up to. Tilley's timing, always delayed…never exact, depended upon how long it took her to push her broom across the floor to rearrange last night's cigarette butts and peanut shells. Sometimes, if she was reading an interesting piece of gossip in the paper (all that lip movement took time), the delay got delayed. When he heard that magic *click* as she turned the key, Harry jumped up and danced through the door. He climbed up on his stool without a word and waited for Tilley to bring him a short one.

By noon, certainly no later than one o'clock, time started to get fuzzy on the edges. While Dover's wage-slaves watched the tractor-factory clock, Harry teetered in his five o'clock world. A small pile of lose change was scattered on the bar in front of him. Maybe a few more coins were in his pocket purse. One of those red plastic things he squeezed to make its lips open up to reveal (hopefully) a few more quarters and dimes. They were his sustenance and got him through the day. Should he somehow drink his way through his stash (unlikely at a dime a glass), Tilley would mark it down on his bar tab—which somehow got wiped clean at the end of the month. The benefactor, if not Tilley herself, always anonymous.

When the *real* five o'clock arrived Tilley flicked on the light over the pool table and pulled the chain on the Hamm's Beer sign hanging in the window, setting the evening stage with neon ambience. By 5:30 the regulars drifted through the door, having survived another day of the same-old same-old. As the night rolled on a Chesterfield fog rolled in. Beer flowed, spirits soared, and bullshit prevailed. Game on. By eight o'clock, the hardcores skirted the fringes of rational thought. They already missed supper (again), so figured *what the hell...* Inevitably, someone transgressed that thin line which separated ribaldry from insult. The potential for retaliation escalated. Rarely did such a break in social protocol result in physical confrontation, but make no mistake, if anyone tossed out a few recklessly chosen words, he'd catch a fist the size of a picnic ham upside the head. There were two topics that Dover Men considered *verboten*: Mothers and wives. But football teams and cars were take-your-best-shot targets. TV shows and politics—always fair game. It was all a matter of perception. And perception was a rare commodity in late-night Tilleys.

My trove of Tilleys-trivia is so profound because Riker and I could oftentimes be found in her back room, shooting eight-ball (there was no kid-discrimination in Tilleys). Riker always beat me. He'd let me win just enough games to keep me subsidizing his allowance. I knew he was doing it, but I shelled out all of those nickels anyway. My strategy was to use him to help sharpen my shooting skills until one day I could turn things around and develop a little positive cash flow myself. Then, after I cleaned him out, I'd move on to the Deuter Brothers and eventually Mickey. And when I got really good, I'd take on the big guys. The Brylcreem boys who hot-rodded their fender-skirted, fuzzy-mirrored Fords up and down Main Street until Koop cracked down and warned them to slow their asses down. After I burned through all of them, I'd take on Roger, Dover's very own Minnesota Fats. A god. But, alas, none of that would ever happen. My eight-ball skills, like my batting skills, pretty much sucked.

I mention all this because, oftentimes, while Riker and I stroked away at some near-impossible double-bank side-pocket shot with talcum powder up to our elbows—we heard it. *The laugh!* Harry's unmistakable laugh.

As the night pressed on and all those stand-up comedians pressed in, Harry found himself at the center of attention. He was charming, lighthearted, and high-spirited. A court jester holding forth. They bought him beers. They slapped his back. Gave him a hug. <u>Whoa!</u>...stop the bus! Hell no. Dover Men didn't hug. Maybe their old ladies on Saturday night. But certainly not each other. Invariably somebody told Harry a joke that he had heard earlier that day out on the factory floor. After the not-so-well-timed punchline was tossed out, everybody stood back and waited for it. *The Laugh.* It was unmistakable, singular, iconic. And decibels louder than the bar-talk rumble.

How can I possibly describe that laugh? Here's all I got: It was, well, a kind of a one-syllable squawk. Sorry, that's the best I can do. No, wait—try this: imagine a rooster's crow choked off halfway through. That one-syllable squawk abruptly terminated. If you were in Tilleys and you heard that strangled rooster somewhere in the smoky din, you knew that Harry was in the house. And dang it...you couldn't help but smile!

That's about it. That's Harry 101. I hope that my little sketch somehow painted a tribute to him. Some of my remembrances probably conflict with the reality of Harry; but don't we all do that? Recall our most treasured memories with a touch of emotional ambiguity? Writing about Harry was challenging. He was like a Picasso that challenges definition. How much easier it would have been to have stayed focused on my other characters and moved on and just left Harry out. But he demanded a presence in these pages. Actually...he deserved it.

You still don't *know* Harry, but now, at least, you know *about* Harry. Not to know about him would be not to know Dover.

I pray that someday when Saint Pete checks off my name and throws wide the pearly gates to that other paradise, Harry will be standing there with Tilley to greet me. I pray he smiles at what I had to say about him.

And if I'm lucky… maybe he'll crow.

MONSTERS, SUPERHEROES, AND COWBOYS

Don't let them fool you—The Daughters of the American Revolution, the Republicans, and the National Fireworks Association. They will tell you that the 4th of July is America's greatest holiday. Madison Avenue and *Toys-Used-To-B-Us* contend it's Christmas. Mothers swear it's Mother's Day (except mothers do not swear…most of 'em). Dover kids know better. The Republicans, Madison Avenue, and yes—even Moms—they got it all wrong. America's greatest holiday is Halloween. Americans spend more than $9 billion every year on Halloween. You get that? Nine cavity-causing, belly-aching billion! That's more than the defense budget for over half the countries in the world.

For us—Milo, Arnie, Riker, Mickey, me and even Richie—Halloween was anticipated with more wide-eyed, sugar-addicted drool than Christmas *and* the 4th of July combined. Our mania for Milky Ways was shared by Doctor David Mohlar, the dentist in Bill Town who drooled all over his patients as he merrily drilled away, dreaming about Halloween and his Florida vacation home. He paid for it off the backs…err, teeth…of

Dover kids. Every weekend, starting in July, he drove over to Dover to nail his flyers on telephone poles, stop signs, and church doors (he had read how Martin Luther had done that with wild success). His whole reason was to remind us that Halloween was only four months away. He retired in '63 at the age of 36 to his 6,336 square foot ocean-front dream home.

Halloween represented everything good and wonderful to Dover kids. The object of our good and wonderful affections? Confections! Chocolaty, sugary confections. And the best part was that it required little if any effort to get it. No false finger-crossed promises of good behavior. No scrounging back alleys for pop bottles. And no stealing from Mr. Robick's candy shelves while Riker diverted his attention at the meat counter telling him how beautiful his butts looked. Guilt haunted us for weeks. Well, okay—hours.

Our costumes were not the elaborate store-bought affairs that Walmart mommies blow entire paychecks on nowadays. We ransacked Mom's sewing room for rags and remnants to create our very own custom costume. If our pillaging came up empty, we raided our closets and, after that, Mom and Dad's closet. Jimmy Slidell—he lived on the south side of town not far from Old Man Peters—scrounged through his sister's closet for his costumes. He lives in San Francisco today.

I generally went for the monster motif. Some soot under my eyes and a little ketchup on my neck and I was good. I was the only monster in Dover who wore Buddy Holly horn-rimmed glasses. I've been as nearsighted as a rhinoceros since I was nine. *Four-eyes...coke bottles...*I've heard it all. I still bear emotional scars deeper than the Grand Canyon.

Most of the guys went with the superhero thing. Superman, Batman, and Spiderman (Jimmy Slidell was Superwoman).

They were pretty much all we had. Today's glut of superheroes had yet to make their debut on the pop culture scene. A few years later Stan Lee would create Ant-Man, but he didn't make any sense to us Dover Boys. Spiderman…okay. But Ant-Man? What the hell was he? Cockroach-Man's little brother?

Then there was my easily frightened little brother Richie. Richie always dressed in some benign creation he'd conjure with towels and blankets. Nothing more frightening than a cowboy or the little people on *The Wizard of Oz* who represented the Lollipop Guild. His aversion to scary costumes may have had something to do with all those nights I crawled under his bed to pound the floor with the old man's boots. It also may help explain his bladder control issues.

So there we were, all dressed up in Mom's living room; twitching in front of the couch while she licked dozens of Kodak flash bulbs hoping that some of the *sonsabitches* (Remember that swearing thing? I said *most* moms) would flash. She fired off two or three Nevada-nuclear-test-site flashes like we saw on Walter Cronkite. When she ran out of spit and was satisfied that maybe one of the damn pictures would turn out, she sprayed Bactine on her blistered fingers (those nuclear-flash flash bulbs were damn hot). She kissed our masked-lips and released us to march off on our candy safari. The Deuter Brothers had been pounding away on our front door for twenty minutes, impatient to get started. They were all decked out in their Batman and Superman costumes which were nothing more than a safety-pinned bed sheet draped around their necks and a Ben Franklin Dime Store mask with a too-tight rubber band clamping it to their faces. Mom double-bagged a couple of Robicks paper sacks for our booty (not landfill-choking plastic…it hadn't been invented yet. At check-out Mr. Robick always asked, "Paper or paper?"). In two hours those paper bags would be spilling over with enough sugar to rot every molar in

Dover. Monsters, superheroes, and cowboys disappeared into the night.

One thing was sure about a Dover Halloween: it was either freeze-your-nuts-off cold or sweat-your-ass-off hot. On the cold years our ensemble of rags and remnants were stuffed inside our JC Penney fake-fur-lined parkas. On the hot years our masks dripped with sweat and chocolate spit. The eye holes were the only ventilation our Ben Franklin Dime Store masks had. The dime store mask factory that Ben Franklin subcontracted somewhere in China or Japan always cut the eyes in the wrong place—too high or too low. We constantly jockeyed with them to more or less see where the heck we were going. Arnie broke his nose one year when he plastered his face right into Old Lady Green's porch post. Blood dripped down his chin and neck. For the rest of the night he was peppered with smart-ass questions from smart-ass old men: "How the hell come Batman's bleedin'? Ain't he s'posta be some kinda superhero? Superheroes don't bleed."

The night wore on and, like plundering Huns, we descended on any structure that held even the slightest possibility of yielding so much as a morsel of candy from behind their shut, locked, and darkened doors. Did you notice how I used the term *structure*? Over the years we figured out which toolsheds and garages the cheap-bastard Old Farts hid in to avoid us. No door went unknocked. Nor window unrattled or doorbell unrung. With hungry eyes we peered into blacked-out windows scanning for the cowering inhabitants. We knew all the cheap tricks that the cheap-bastard Old Farts used in past years. Turn off the lights. Pull down the shades. Close the curtains. Duck tape the dog's mouth. Toss a pile of mail and old newspapers on the porch. With our heads cocked to one side like coyotes stalking a bunny, we heard them with their smelly slippers shuffling on the linoleum; watching *Gunsmoke* in the dark with the sound off. Undaunted, our door pounding was relentless. We, by God, were not to be denied. *Open your damn door and give us anything: half-rotted apples, last year's left-over Three Musketeers, or stale Fig Newtons.* Anything. Dammit—booty was booty.

We lined up on the porch with Richie front and center (he was our token cute-kid). Riker and Milo stood on each side. The Deuter Brothers and I hung in the rear. Riker stepped up and dropkicked the door. He assumed the terrified occupants would appreciate the dramatic haunted house effect. When the pissed-off homeowner jerked the door open we launched into our well-worn chorus: *Trick or Treat.* The Old Man or Old Lady held their candy high over their heads as if they were tempting their stupid Chihuahua with a doggie yum-yum. They refused to fork over so much as a Tootsie Roll until we let them see our sweaty faces. It was essential that we be properly attributed to some Dover family: "Ain't you a Deuter-kid? Ain't you a Rausch-kid?" None of us had proper Christian names. Just surnames with a -kid suffix.

Old Man Zimmerman played the smartass card better than any other smartass Old Man in Dover. Most folks (more or less willingly) handed out treats, but only after a proper family attribution. But not Old Man Zimmerman. He tested our ability to come up with the *trick* part. This year Mickey was ready for him knowing that his challenge would (once again) be issued.

Old Man Zimmerman always jerked his door open on the first knock. He always thought that scared the bejeesus out of us. He always lost his arthritic grip on the doorknob and always banged himself in the head. We always laughed. That always pissed him off. With all those *alwayses*, Old Man Zimmerman was pretty predictable and Riker was loaded for bear.

"Okay, you kids wanna treat?" he grinned, looking scarier than we did with his gnarly yellow teeth, three-day whisker patches, and freshly-bumped bleeding forehead. "First you gotta do me a trick."

Mickey, stepped up and cleared his throat. We held our breaths, waiting…waiting. We knew what was coming. Through his mask he unleashed his well-rehearsed retaliation, "You wanna a trick? Get one from your Old Lady. Everybody else does."

Old Man Zimmerman got so pissed off he started rattling his plastic punkin candy holder like a Mexican maraca filled with two-for-a-penny jaw breakers (he *always* gave us ONE). He cussed enough to fill five or six "normal" confessions with Father Hemple. He ranted and raved, about as threatening as a hamster, until the plastic tube from his roll-around oxygen tank slipped out of his nose. When Mrs. Old Man Zimmerman heard all the ruckus, she got up from *Gunsmoke* and came out on the porch with a rolled-up newspaper and smacked her old man upside the head. After she gained control of the situation (it required several smacks), she chewed his ass, "Dammit Old Man, give these sweet children one of yer damn jaw breakers, ya cheap bastard. And don't you give me no backtalk."

Then she looked down at sweet little Richie standing up front and wrinkled her nose, "Say, ain't you a Rausch-kid?"

Nine o'clock. We had Dover sucked dry of every Snickers, Baby Ruth, Tootsie Roll, and Holloway's All-Day Suckers. Every door kicked. Every darkened window glared into. Every backyard toolshed battered. That is every door, window, and toolshed except one. *Old Man Peters*. Because there was the promise of that majestic morsel behind his door, we reluctantly trudged up his porch steps with our spit-soaked masks and saggy sacks. Notice I said *reluctantly*. Just like Dover folks who crossed to the other side of the street whenever they saw him coming, we avoided him as well and saved him for last. He smelled like wood smoke in a moldy cellar. He spit when he cussed. And the worst part was, the reason we saved him for last—it was near-impossible to break away from him as he ranted about everything from anarchists to queers. If we hit him up early in the night, the rest of the Dover kids would have the entire town cleaned out.

I know you're probably thinking what's one more house? Just let it go. Well, it was greed made us do it. We were too weak to stay away. We knew he was hording them. He always did. Halloween's Holy Grail: *Hershey's Milk Chocolate Bars*. And, as an added incentive to lure us into his lair—*With Almonds*!

Old Man Peters lived alone. Mrs. Old Man Peters had up and left him one July night in 1958. God knows she probably had a whole litany of reasons, but the one that the Dover gossips talked about most was his relentless smoking. Old Man Peters smoked like a '55 Ford. The only way she put up with him all those years was by establishing a few ground rules, threatening the wrath of God should he violate even one. Rule number one: the dogs. She drew a line in the sand at five. No more than five coonhounds. If another dog (coonhound or whatever), came along by way of natural birth or got dumped off in the middle of the night, it had to *removed* (don't ask).

Rule number two, her most cherished rule, the central tenet of her unquestioned code of conduct: absolutely NO shoes in the house. She threw a Hamm's beer case on their back porch for him to deposit his dog-shit-crusted boots every night before he came in to supper.

Rule number three, of equal if not greater importance: NO SMOKING in the house. Old Man Peters was reduced to supporting his three-pack-a-day habit in his toolshed with his five coonhounds. Doc Johnson, the town vet, said two of his coonhounds succumbed to his secondhand smoke and died an *almost*-painless death. Before they died, folks would drive from as far away as Bill Town just to hear those two coonhounds bark. They actually coughed after every yelp. They always got a lot of laughs.

So, as I was saying, by '58 Mrs. Old Man Peters was long gone and took her silly-ass rules with her. But even though he hadn't seen her for years, Old Man Peters couldn't break the chains and go back to his old habit of wearing his dog-shit-crusted boots in the house. He'd dutifully undo his doo-doo boot laces, jam their heels into the little *BOOTIE-OFF* thing that every Dover home had bolted somewhere on its back porch, and walk around in his house in his socks. And, as crazy as it sounds, he never violated Mrs. Old Man Peters rule number three about not smoking in the house. In fact, after he replaced his two dearly departed coonhounds with two new coonhound pups he caught sniffing his boots on his back porch one night and didn't want them to suffer the same fate as their predecessors, he quit smoking completely. To satisfy his nicotine urges, he started chewing chewing tobacco. Hence, he had spit cans in every room so one of them was never out of range. He had them everywhere: on the TV tray beside his La-Z-Boy, under his bed, and next to the butter on his kitchen table. There was even one alongside his new-fangled indoor toilet with a little card taped to it: *Same Spit…Different Day*. Every time he went into his new-fangled indoor toilet to…err…*sit*, he'd look at that little card and smile. He thought it was pretty cute.

We stood at tense attention in his parlor like Ulysses' voyagers lured by the sweet siren song of Hershey's Milk Chocolate—

WITH ALMONDS. We stared at them through our Chinese or Japanese cockeyed eyeholes. Right there on the TV tray beside his La-Z-Boy, fanned out like some card trick in their iconic brown wrappers in front of the spit can were the Hershey's Milk Chocolate—*WITH ALMONDS*. He gum-smiled at us (his teeth were on the kitchen table between the butter and spit can). He knew it. He had us. Every year we'd stand there like sheep, waiting…waiting. Who would it be *this* year? No matter how much he stalled, no matter how much he glared, no matter how much the suspense mounted, and no matter how much we fidgeted, no matter how much…okay, okay, you get the picture. We, by God, were not leaving without them. All that remained was for Old Man Peters to decide who would be his sacrificial lamb this year.

We listened to his rants on everything from Nixon to "them California queers." His invectives were punctuated with language more appropriate for the bunkroom of some merchant marine freighter sailing for Hong Kong than the tender ears of five *innocent* Dover boys.

No ethnic, religious, or political group escaped his decrees: Jews, Catholics, and Republicans. Then Mexicans, colored folks, and just for good measure, a couple more shots at them queers. Then he raged about how bad the Cardinals sucked. Well, right there—that's where I drew the line. Oh hell no, not *my* Cardinals. How dare he mess with my Cardinals. And by God, I'd let him know it. I summoned my courage and peeled the sweaty mask from my face. I even said a little prayer: *Please Lord, don't let my voice crack*. I took one step forward, opened my mouth to retaliate and, of course, the first syllable out of my mouth cracked like a third-grade girl. "Do *not* trash-talk my Cardinals," I squeaked. "Jews, Catholics, colored folks…that's fine. Queers even. But *not* my Cardinals!" Old Man Peters looked at me and waved his hand in the air as if he were shooing some fly off his dog shit-crusted boots. I stepped back in line. Dismissed but not defeated. Next time I'd clear my throat first.

We stood there, thinking to ourselves, *Here it comes. Any minute now.* It appeared that he was winding down, having exhausted his litany. Then to our surprise, he launched an entirely new outburst which apparently he had read about in *The National Enquirer* or something—transvestites. Whatever they were. It sounded as though they might be related to the queers—only a lot worse. He stopped to cough up a hawker which he sent sailing into the spit can on the TV tray next to his chair. It splashed down like an Olympic diver. Barely a ripple. The Hershey's Milk Chocolate—*WITH ALMONDS* were spared.

With Old Man peters' attention temporarily diverted towards the spit can, I nudged my brother closer. Richie turned toward me and bared his fangs. He knew it was coming too. I made a motion with my head towards the TV tray with the fanned-out Hershey Bars, hoping to convey to my dumb-ass little brother: *Ya want em' or not?*

Old Man Peters looked back at us as he wiped his chin with the back of his hand. Like one of his coonhounds sensing the dying heartbeats of a bunny shaking like a rag doll in its jaws, he moved in for the kill. Here it comes...wait for it: "*You boys like a Hershey Bar?*"

Nobody said a word. Nobody moved. First one flinches loses.

"Well...do you? They...got...almonds." His voice went up an entire octave.

Nothing. Silence. Finally, I couldn't take it anymore. My nose was itching from a sweat drop that had been perched there since his *Nixon v. Satan* rant. I reached up under my monster mask and scratched my nose.

Right there. That was all she wrote. Game over.

"Alrighty then, Billy Rausch. (How did he know? My voice-crack must have given me away.) Getcha' ass over here. Looks like yer the lucky one this year. Go ahead—you know the drill. Dump it off the back porch."

Thought I was gonna die. I jerked my mask into submission until it gave me a relatively useful line of sight and crept forward. I saw it through my right eye hole first. There it was. The Mother of All Spit Cans. The #2 institutional-sized Lima Bean can he scrounged from the town dump. It simmered with Copenhagen spit. Black as coffee and thick as glue. His recent hawker floated on top like a turd.

I stumbled over to his chair, jerking my mask, struggling to see. Just a little further. I reached out. I felt it—the #2 can. I had it in my grip. The surface shimmered like a moonlit swamp. A streak of slime dribbled onto my fingers as I picked it up. One wrong move, one miscalculation, and a couple of cups of Copenhagen crap would cascade all over the Hershey's Milk Chocolate—*WITH ALMONDS*.

I picked it up and started for the backdoor.

What the hell was that? I didn't see it!

As I stepped out onto the porch I tripped over something.

A coonhound had pulled one of his dog shit-crusted boots from the Hamm's beer case and dropped it right in front of the door.

I went down with a splash. You catch that? *A splash*. Five Imperial U.S. quarts soaked my rag ensemble. *Fight it, Bill. Fight it.* I struggled for control. I ripped off my mask just in time. I felt something churning in my eat-as-you-go *ButterfingerTootsieRollandSnickers* gut. Without warning it geysered. I opened my mouth and hurled.

I picked up the can and wobbled back into the house. *What the...?* I looked back at three coonhounds lapping up the spill.

Old Man Peters snorted as he tossed Hershey's Milk Chocolate Bars with Almonds into our paper sacks.

When we got home I gave mine to Richie.

WHAT IF...

Mickey and I met up on the corner by Old Lady Brown's house on one of those unseasonably warm October Saturday nights. A scrum of moths clouded the street light with their death-spiral. Frogs that should have already checked in to the Hibernation Hotel were croaking like the men's section of the Saint Boniface church choir. He and I were going to meet the Deuter Brothers at Riker's house. The night was young and adventure beckoned. We never knew what we'd do on any given Saturday night. In our live-for-the moment lives, planning was a novel thought reserved only for adults. Whatever tonight might bring, we were certain that it would be epic. *We hadn't yet learned that anticipation and results are all too often inversely proportional.* (There aren't many pearls of wisdom in these lavishly-embellished tales, but that right there is one of 'em. I put it in italics so you wouldn't miss it.) Something as simple as sitting in Riker's basement watching fuzzy episodes of *Gunsmoke* fell into our epic category. Getting lucky and copping a cleavage shot of Miss Kitty's tittys was beyond epic (Amanda Blake...I still love you).

As we stumbled in the dark (Dover's parsimonious street lights were a block apart and what little illumination they provided was far from seamless), Mickey seemed unusually animated. He did that a lot. Got himself all *animated.* The silliest things would set him off and he'd go all goofy on us. Mickey, you see, was the comedian of our gang of five. Jokester, clown, smartass. Always ready with a quip, a wise-ass remark, or some corny joke he had memorized from *Reader's Digest*.

Mickey (remember…he was the oldest of us) was 18½ when he graduated high school. Less than a week later he received a nice little invitation from our local draft board to come and have a free, tax-payer-paid physical. He flunked. The 4-F fallen arches thing like Clinton and Trump. It wasn't his fault. He wanted to go, he really did. But alas, he missed out on the Vietnam party McNamara and the boys threw for us young, dumb, and full of cum blue-collar kids. So Mickey lowered his sights and followed his old man's footsteps to the tractor factory.

Fast-forward one lifetime. He forfeited thirty-four of the best years of his life to that tractor factory where, like so many Dover Men, he carved out a living. Sweat his balls off. Made a paycheck. Pick your favorite cliché. He punched that damn time clock every morning at 6:58 and wasted the next eight or ten hours doing some repetitive assembly line bullshit. The industrial engineers had it all figured out down to the second. String together enough boltings, weldings, and wirings and…BAM…a tractor pops out at the end of the line every 12.37 minutes. As he manned his station fitting fenders or mounting motors, I think he dreamed a lot: *"What if…"*

  He was the kind of guy you hoped you'd run into at a house party. Squeeze next to in a crowded booth up at Tilleys. Or throw gutter balls with on league night. He was the guy that always had a running repertoire of jokes. An inexhaustible supply of ad-libs. A seemingly endless stream of one-liners and zingers. I think he spent a lot of time dreaming about *"What if…"*

What if he had been somehow encouraged to develop his comedic talents by some mentor or crazy uncle? Or even us guys. Really—he *was* funny. Hilarious sometimes.

But after so many jokes, gags, and one-liners he wore us out. With damn near every sentence couching some cute quip or punchline…well, you can see what I mean. Right? It got to the point where all we did was toss him an obligatory laugh or two. More like a chuckle, actually. And sometimes (it hurts me to say this), we shouted, "Hey, Mickey…stop already."

In our gang-of-five days, years before the second shift beat him down like a dog and sucked every ounce of aspirational juice out of his marrow, Mickey was tenacious. Sometimes he'd stop to pick up a stick in the ditch and hold it next to his mouth like a microphone, imagining the spotlight shining on him in some smoky comedy club in Chicago or Dallas—crackin' 'em up. Killin' 'em with his shit-your-pants shtick. I think he even heard their applause. Maybe saw them elbowing each other in the ribs as they doubled over in laughter. *"What if…"*

So, back to that unseasonably warm October Saturday night. We met on the corner in front of Old Lady Brown's house. Moths spiraling. Frogs croaking. For whatever reason he bubbled with more enthusiasm that usual.

As he approached, his trademark grin flashed in those pissy streetlights. That was usually a warning that he had probably just made up a new joke. He didn't steal all of them from the *Reader's Digest.* Some of his stuff was original. Some of it actually pretty good. A lot of it—not so much. Regardless of merit (or lack of), we should have done better by him. We should have laughed more. More chuckles. More snickers. We didn't have to be so mean.

We were a tough crowd. Tough crowd.

No—change that.

We were little assholes. We were mean.

"Hey, Bill," he looked at me with a straight face. The corners of his mouth curled up like the Mona Lisa. Beguiling. Ambiguity holding back a punch line that was waiting to explode.

"Hey, Mickey," I muttered, trying my asshole-best to stifle his enthusiasm.

"Hey…how come the witch couldn't get pregnant?" Mona Lisa morphed up a notch.

I knew the drill. Play along. Like I said, he *was* tenacious and wouldn't surrender until, by God, he got a laugh. So I shot back a pretty-much mirthless reply, "Okay, I'll bite…how come the witch couldn't get knocked up?"

"Because her boyfriend had a Hollowiener!" Then the explainer, "Get it. *Hollow…wiener?*"

I figured that was probably one he made up. Okay—not too bad for a 12-year-old.

It was usually right about there that, if we were all hangin' out together, all hell was supposed to break lose. We'd chuckle a little and shove him around a lot. We'd tell him to go away and shut up. He'd wobble around as he rolled with the punches and laughed at his own joke.

We were a tough crowd. Tough crowd.

And even though we didn't realize it at the time, we were the meanest joke of all.

What if…

LOOGIE LAND

Every boy in Dover knew every other boy in Dover. We were brothers, buddies, or cousins. There were a few outliers that somehow never seemed to—you know—fit in. *They* were the ones that developed proper social skills. *They* had decorum. *They* conducted themselves within the boundaries of behavior appropriate for our age group. In situations that called for social skills, decorum, and boundaries, *they* cut the mustard. But could they cut a fart? We could. Could they ride a pig? We could. Could they tip a shithouse? We could. (You'll have to wait a few chapters to read about our farting, pig riding, and shithouse tipping skills. This is what we writers call a *teaser*.) But the question we have to answer right now, more than anything else—could they launch a loogie? We most certainly could. You'll see what I mean…

Boredom rarely bored its way into the lives of Dover boys. However, I will be the first to admit that, every so often, an insidious vacuum crept into our lives. A lack of *something* more or less constructive to kill time with. However, *constructive* certainly was not a prerequisite. In fact, it was rarely even a consideration. We were innovative little bastards. Maybe cunning is a better word. When we couldn't come up with something constructive to do with our time (which was like...never), we deferred to the devil. Like the never-ending cuppa joe that flowed from the *Mother of Perpetual Brewing* coffee pot at the Saint Boniface Ladies Altar Society meetings, we percolated with a relentless brew of trouble.

One summer (we were about nine or ten) the devil introduced us to something that was, shall we say, *fiendish* to fiddle with. *Body fluids*. No, not *that* body fluid. I assure you, the fluid we played with was innocent. Innocent, but nonetheless repulsive and socially unacceptable. So, if you have a problem with repulsive and socially unacceptable (or have a weak stomach) you may want to skip this chapter. We're going to peg the yuck-meter pretty hard with this one. You'd be well advised to just jump ahead a few pages. But if you have a relatively decent set of cojones, hang around. This is gonna get good.

After we figured out that we could actually play with it, we invented a game of sorts. A competition. We set up a few rules along with a scoring system. And of course, a method to declare a winner. It was always about the winning. We never played just for fun. Simple enjoyment was a foreign concept. Cut-throat winning was all we knew. And if we didn't win, we did what Republicans did...picked up our toys and went home.

Competition is everywhere. Ancient Rome had gladiators. Greece had the Olympics. Spain—bullfighters. Channel 7—fake rasslers. But Dover boys—we had *loogies*. Hawkers. Okay, for those of you who like medical terminology—phlegm.

Most summer afternoons we went skinny-dipping in the quarry, hunted pop bottles, or built forts down by the tracks. But after we discovered the wonderful world of loogies, we added a whole 'nother deviancy to our repertoire. We lined up on the sidewalk out in front of Robicks and squatted on the curb like a gaggle of geese. When folks walked by and heard us gurgling and hacking away, they'd shake their heads; wondering what those little bastards were up to now. To us it was perfectly obvious. We were working up one of those aforementioned hawkers, aka: a loogie. Anybody could see that.

We growled and gurgled until we summoned a milky-white loogie from deep in our windpipes. Arnie claimed that he could break a loogie lose from his lungs. (We challenged him on that one, but he couldn't prove it.) After the loogie was brought forth, we rolled it around in our mouths like a peeled grape for a few seconds to filter the superfluous spit. We worked it around until it was distilled it to its core essence—a well-defined loogie. After we were satisfied with its texture, mass, and consistency; we sucked in a deep breath, puckered our lips and let 'er fly. Whoever launched his loogie into the street the farthest won the round. It was that simple. No elaborate rules or regulations; although we occasionally awarded style points for flamboyance. It was not about finesse or accuracy. Distance was the only metric used to determine the winner. We were usually good for eight or nine launches before we had our wind pipes sucked dry.

We played softball on the softball diamond and basketball on the Saint Boniface playground half-court. But loogie competitions were held exclusively on the sidewalk in front of Robicks. Mr. Robick swept his sidewalk off every morning and it was one of the cleanest in town. He ran a tight ship and told us we were welcome to hold our contest in front of his store as long as our trajectories splashed down on the street and NOT his clean sidewalk. By allowing us to use his always-swept sidewalk, his thinking was that someone in the gathering throng might step into his store and actually buy something. Mr. Robick was a marketing genius.

Riker was the widely-acclaimed and much-envied Lord of the Loogies. He could fire one off with the explosiveness of a Howitzer. I will never forget that day in early June, just a few weeks after school was out for the summer. I was actually sitting right next to him on the curb when he set the Dover World Record. We competed all summer long, rain or shine, trying to beat Riker's mark but always fell short of that stellar performance. So, with his seemingly impossible mark established, there was no way any of us could have known that Riker's world record would be shattered by some unlikely challenger in the waning days of that endless summer.

School would start up again in less than a week. Riker caught one of those awful summer colds. That's what our moms and grammas called them—*summer colds*. None of us ever questioned their extensive medical knowledge concerning pulmonary afflictions. If mom said it was a summer cold then certainly somewhere in one of Doc Hansen's medical books, right after consumption and whooping cough, her seasonally-adjusted term must be listed. Riker arrived late at our weekly competition on that infamous August morning. His mother had yelled out the door and made him come back into the house to get a snot rag, aka: hankie. She didn't know. She had no idea that we'd rather get caught talking to a *girl* in the Saint Boniface lunchroom than using a snot rag. Everyone knew that when your nose backed up, you just sucked it in and swallowed.

The ailing Riker finally showed up with his ironed and folded snot rag tucked into his back pocket—where it would stay. He sat down next to me on the edge of Mr. Robick's freshly swept sidewalk and wrinkled his backed-up his nose and sucked a few times. *What's this? He didn't swallow it.* Milo was the first one to figure it out. He was saving it! Riker was actually holding it in his mouth. He was working up the mother lode of loogies. This was not to be one of your run-of-the mill throat-phlegm hawkers, but a sucked-in, nose-snot loogie!

Loogie launches were always about timing. There was a narrow window of opportunity. A sweet spot where the mass, consistency, and density were optimal. Hold it too long and some insidious spit would creep in from the cheeks and dilute what might have been the perfect wad. Suddenly, he had it! Those three conditions had been met. Riker stood up and spread his arms wide. "Schtand blaaack guys," he gurgled, "I feel it comin'. Gimme room."

He held his lips tight and fought the urge to breathe. He would not succumb to premature *hackulation*. His cheeks ballooned. Droplets oozed from the corners of his mouth. He leaned back and took a deep breath. The Howitzer was primed. Mikey and Arnie grabbed his shoulders to steady him. This was a special moment in time. Could lightning strike twice in one summer? Was Riker about to shatter his own world record? The earth stopped rotating. The cosmos froze. The skies darkened. Thunder rumbled in the distance. Cecil B. DeMille was probably shitting his pants. This was going to be Biblical. Old-Testament Biblical.

Suddenly, without warning—Riker exploded. **KA-BLEWEY!!** His Richter-Scale eruption likely registered on a seismograph somewhere in Hawaii or wherever it was they kept them.

His loogie-launch catapulted in a spit-spray that actually cast a little rainbow in the sun. It arched high into the sky and sailed over Main Street. We heard it splash down just shy of the town park. Milo reached into his pocket and whipped out his old man's tape measure that he always brought along in case, you know, disputes arose. I grabbed the end of it and stretched it across the street.

Milo looked down at the tape when I had the other end squarely on the epicenter of the splash-down, "21 feet 8 inches!"

"No way!" the crowd shouted from behind us.

So we measured it twice.

"Yup…21 feet 8 inches," Milo verified the results.

Some of the folks across the street who had witnessed the launch heard our carrying-on gathered in the growing crowd behind us on Mr. Robick's just-swept sidewalk. "What's all the buzz?" someone whispered in the back. "Shut up," two women hissed. "Cant'cha see them little bastards got a world record in the makin'?"

Stone-cold Easter Island faces froze all around us. They were overcome by awe at what they had just witnessed. It would be an event that would be forever etched in their minds and set down in the chronicles of Dover folklore. Riker actually did it! He smashed his own world record! Someday aging raconteurs would gather their grandkids at their feet around the fireplace on cold winter nights and recall this historical event, "I'm a-tellin' you, I was there. I saw it all. Remember it like it was yesterday. Them skies, they was a-gittin' dark…"

Riker stood there in a post-launch daze, as much amazed as anyone. We pummeled the conquering hero with back-slaps. Two mommies stepped up and tried to hoist him up on their shoulders like he had just scored the winning touchdown in the conference playoff against Bill Town. Just like Dover Football players (who never won a conference anything) they fumbled him like a greasy football as they struggled to lift him. They had his left leg slung over the shorter mommy's shoulder and scratched her nose with his zipper when it happened. A dark figure pushed through the crowd and elbowed for position. *Old Man Peters!*

"That ain't nothin'", he grumbled as he wobbled to the front. The crowd cheer petered out from a full-afterburner F-16 roar to Saturday night confessional silence. Babies stopped squalling mid-squall. Dogs stopped barking mid-bark (which was pretty weird). The two mommies dropped Riker. "Move aside boys and I'll show you how she's really done," he said as he stepped onto Mr. Robick's fresh-swept, crowd-covered sidewalk. The exact same spot where only minutes earlier Riker had re-ascended to even greater legendary eminence.

You'll probably remember that Old Man Peters was a 37-year veteran of a three-pack-a-day love affair with Chesterfields. He smoked for a living. When he filed for Social Security and the lady asked him for his occupation, he said "smoker". Now, I don't care who you are...but that's some serious smoking. 72 cigarettes got sucked into his lungs every day. His fingertips radiated with a golden glow that was yellower than Blue Bonnet Margarine. But somehow Old Man Peters wheezy lungs just took it in stride. Doc Hansen said that his chest X-ray looked like a gunnysack of rotten spuds.

Old Man Peters elbowed us aside as he stood on the launch pad. He shoved one mommy so hard, she dropped her baby. (It just laid there, squirming on the sidewalk next to Riker who was still squirming too.) Old Man Peters braced himself as he assumed his pre-launch profile: arms extended, knees slightly bent and head cocked sideways toward the sky as if he were searching the clouds for that F-16 that just shut down. He wobbled as he gulped for air. His eyes bulged. His left one—the one that never looked straight at you—started to flutter.

How the hell can he do that? everyone in the crowd thought to themselves. *How long can he suck in air?* His barrel chest bulged. Man-boobs sagged. Legs tottered on those creaky bent knees. Face faded to blue. Holding. Holding. Waiting…

Suddenly, just like a fart you never saw coming, he let 'er rip. Riker's Howitzer was a firecracker compared to Old Man Peters Atlas Rocket.

KA-WHOOOOOOOOMY!!

A catarrhal crap-ball catapulted from his mouth. Higher and higher. It arched over the entire span of Dover's main street. A pack of butt-sniffing dogs on the opposite side scattered when its shadow darkened their path.

SPLOOSH! Everyone heard it. No mistaking that sound. Like a busted water balloon. We rushed to point of impact. It lay there in the weeds, quivering like my Aunt Caddie's green Jell-O at our family reunion. Laced with black streaks of whatever it was that a 37-year, three-pack-a-day career does to lungs.

"37 feet, 8 and ¾ inches!" Milo uttered with no joy in his voice. No joy.

Riker stood up, leaving the baby to fend for itsel, and stepped over to Old Man Peters and took his defeat like a man. He stuck out his hand and offered it to his challenger. Dover's new Champeen of the World wiped the post-launch slime from his mouth on the back of his hand and stuck it out to shake.

Good old Riker—jerked it back just in time.

CLETE

Remember Floyd? No, not the Pink one. You know...the *other* Floyd. That bumbling Mayberry barber who mumbled. Andy and Barney never knew what the hell he was going on about. With his beady eyes and toady expressions, doesn't he remind you of your 8th grade P.E. teacher who liked to get you alone in the gym to ask you what kind jammies you slept in last night? No? Maybe that was just me. There I go again...rambling off the subject.

In Dover *our* Floyd was Clete. Nobody called him Cletus. Always Clete. Truth be told, even Cletus wasn't his real name. When he was born his mother named him Delphin. She claimed that she had read it in the Bible. Some book in the Old Testament. Deuteronomy maybe. Where Sheebob and Nebazooka (or something) and *Delphin* were slaughtering calves for their annual Stick-A-Cow-Head-On-A-Spear Festival. Anyway, she liked the way it sounded as it rolled off her lips. *Delphin*. She secretly prayed (whenever she had her Old Testament opened to Deuteronomy) that one day his buddies would call him *Delphy* or *Delphie* or something. She thought it sounded cool. *Delphy* or *Delphie* or something.

Well, little Delphin wasn't having any of it. At the tender age of eight he announced at supper one night, right after his burnt meatloaf and just before his burnt apple spice cake, that his name from thence forward shall be called Clete. And under no circumstances shall anyone ever invoke the name Cletus or he (shudder) would run away from home. That's what he would do, he'd run away. Well, since Delphin, I mean Clete, was her only child and, short of Divine Intervention, there was no prospect of a 57-year-old post-menopausal woman giving birth to another, and since the last thing she wanted was for little Delphy or Delphie or something to run away from home and leave her stranded with her no-count husband, she caved. And that's how we got Clete.

Clete was Dover's barber. But you already knew that. No one ever figured out what motivated him to become a barber. Some suspect it was his inability to develop other Life Skills. This is what happens to little boys whose mothers let them dork around the house all day watching reruns of *I love Lucy, Gunsmoke,* and *National Geographic* documentaries on African tribal customs with natives flopping around the fire. (Of course Clete was focused on the topless tribal women…not bottomless tribal men. I think.) He never learned how to saw a board, dig a ditch, fix a car, or plow a field. Things that Dover Men called "working with your hands." Backbreaking, knuckle-bustin' physical labor befitting farmers, factory workers, and truck drivers was not for Clete. For him, working with his hands meant cutting hair. And, as you shall see, it perhaps wasn't really the profession that he was (sorry) cut out for.

Most folks cut him some slack (so to speak) and assumed that Clete, at some point in his life, *possibly* attended a real barber college. This assumption could not be verified either by a diploma (that should have been displayed on the walls of his barber shop) or by the results of his efforts (that should have been displayed on the heads of smiling customers as they walked—sometimes ran—out). Rumor had it that he dropped out of some store-front barber college in San Diego when he was discharged from the Navy and blew all his G.I. Bill money on tuition. Dover Men up at Tilleys speculated he blew it on blow jobs from San Diego hookers. Hard (sorry again) to say. Dover Men were too busy practicing their Life Skills and working with their hands to ponder Clete's peripatetic wonderings.

After he blew through his G.I. Bill Money for whatever reason (nefarious or otherwise), he eventually returned to Dover and moved back in with his mother. With questionable barbering skills and unquestioned hope, he bought a falling-down building on Main Street that had been abandoned as long as anyone could remember. After he gave the resident rats their shotgun eviction notice he hired a couple of jackleg carpenters to nail cheap imitation-wood paneling on the walls, lay down the cheap imitation-tile linoleum floors, and run some pipes for the running water as required by the State Board of Barbering and Cosmetology. Apparently the folks at the State Board of Barbering and Cosmetology were not concerned whether Clete had a diploma or not. But by God, they would have their linoleum floors…and running water! Then he hired one of the jackleg carpenter's brother, a jackleg sign painter (who apparently couldn't spell), to paint **CLETE'S BARBAR SHOP** on the window. For two dollars more the guy painted a scissors that looked more like a hedge clippers which, as it turned out, was just about right. Clete painted red stripes on an old porch pole he took off his mom's house and nailed it next to the door. His red runs and drips made it look like it was bleeding which, as it turned out, was just about right. He taped a Now Open sign in the window just below *BARBAR* and started shearing any Dover head that walked in with a warm body attached to it.

Clete plastered his barbershop walls with expired calendars he found in his dad's garage. He liked the outdoorsy ones. Montana mountains, Minnesota lakes, Maine fishing villages. And his fave…snarling traffic fading into the distant Los Angeles smog. Clete said it reminded him of his days in San Diego throwing his GI Bill money at all those hookers. He wanted to hang a few, shall we say, more provocative calendars like my uncle Pete had plastered everywhere in his gas station, but his dad told him to keep his damn hands off those. Besides that, he had to consider the prudish mommies and Father Hemple, our ostensibly prudish parish priest, who dropped in every few weeks to spend a few hours perusing Clete's *amazing* magazines. Sometimes he actually got a haircut. (More on those amazing magazines coming up.) And right up there, between Montana and Minnesota, in the middle of the wall opposite his chair-contraption with its levers and pedals and things was a poster the size of a kitchen table illustrating the most popular men's hair styles. Styles that customers would wistfully point to knowing that in less than seven, maybe eight minutes tops, they'd be freshly shorn with a cut that wouldn't remotely resemble their carefully considered selection.

The poster had illustrations of several Norman Rockwell-like young men who looked more like frat boys than salt-of-the-earth Dover Men. Their perfectly coiffed locks brought tears to our eyes. Oh how we longed to look like them. Their elegant hairstyles: *The Ducktail, The Flat Top, and The Crew Cut* filled us with false hopes of what would never be. I always pointed to *The Ducktail*. Even at the age of nine I yearned to be cool and look like James Dean or Elvis in all of their Duck-Tailed glory. It was a yearning that, even to this day, would remain ever unfulfilled.

Before we get to the rest of the story, you should know the age progression of Clete's customers beginning with *moi*. Mom started dragging me to Clete's little shop of horrors when I was three or four years old. In all fairness to Clete, *horror* is not an accurate reflection of his little shop. It was simply the perspective that three or four-year-old Dover boys had for things like barber shops, dentist offices, and monsters under our beds that crawled out after midnight to stare at what kind of jammies we were wearing.

Clete kept a plywood board behind his counter that he flopped across the armrests of his chair-contraption for us "little guys". (He called me that until I was 18—*Little Guy*. Still haunts me). After mom smacked my butt a few times and I was subdued into submission, Clete slung a belt around me that he took from a hook on the wall and strapped me to his board. He reassured Mom that it was for my safety. "We can't have the little guy falling and messing up my floor," he smiled. Well, that was a stretch. Clete swept his floor maybe once a week. Usually on Saturday nights. He was always in violation of the State Board of Barbering and Cosmetology Code that was displayed on the wall where Clete's diploma should have hung: *Hair clippings and various other scalp residue (?) shall be disposed of after each customer has been shorn to the standards as illustrated on the official State Board-provided frat-boy poster.* In small print at the bottom (so as not to alarm the public) they said it was a disease thing.

Mom explained to Clete exactly how she wanted my impossibly-cute curly locks styled. She pointed out various bumps and dents on my noggin as well as my lavish network of spirals and swirls that she called cowlicks. When she forgot to comb my hair in the morning, I ran around all day with my towheaded head looking like a fuzzy dairy cone. In no uncertain terms she specified length, shape, and contour in the hope that somehow, please God—just once—please help Clete even come close.

As Mom rambled on with her instructions, Clete just stood there. Clippers buzzing in his right hand and comb clamped in his left, his eyes glued to the clock. He tapped his foot while he waited for her to finish. I was already four minutes into my allotted seven or eight-minute time slot. When she finally wrapped up, Clete told her to go sit the hell down in a chair under the frat-boy poster so he could go to work.

Two minutes later I emerged from a flurry of clippers and comb—crying. My neck bleeding from the nicks and cuts that *I* caused (Clete was a Republican and never took the blame for anything) when *I* kept hunching up. "*Voila!*" Clete exclaimed. I slouched on my plywood perch sporting a fresh, Eastern-European-immigrant-looking Buzz-Cut. My prickly scrub-brush head tingled. Mom's vision of parading her impossibly-cute, curly-haired child down the church aisle at the 10:30 Mass on Sunday morning was shattered. She threw 50¢, mostly nickels and dimes, at Clete and we stormed out. Both of us crying. Seven weeks later, we'd do it all over again.

So, continuing with our age-defined progression, by the time I was eleven, Mom gave me a handful of nickels and dimes and I'd walk "uptown" to get my haircut all by myself. She finally figured out that her Clete-pleading was an exercise in futility so she stayed home and listened to *Stella Dallas* on the radio. I was left to fend for myself like some early Christian thrown to the lions.

Eleven years-old. On the very cusp of manhood. I was finally tall enough that I didn't need the plywood booster-board. I sat down in Clete's chair-contraption with the levers and pedals and things and pointed to the heavily-Brylcreemed frat boy in the middle of the poster sporting a James Dean Ducktail. Even though I pretty much knew what was coming, I made a token effort. The old man taught me to speak up for myself and always said, *"The squeaky hinge always cries wolf."* (The old man was the Mix-Master of metaphors.) Clete ripped a little paper napkin thingy from what looked like a Kleenex box and coiled it around my neck per the State Board of Barbering and Cosmetology rules—yup, a disease thing. They said that all that *scalp residue* lying on barber shop floors are swarming with germs and viruses that are eager to infect un-Kleenexed necks. He snapped a cape in the air that released a swarm of hair from his last victim and it immediately mingled with the swarm of germs and viruses. He hooked it around my neck with some sort of stick pin. In spite of my sanitary paper napkin, it immediately drew blood. I felt the germs and viruses breach the barrier.

So there I sat in Clete's chair contraption, looking like a tent with a Roman-collared head on top. Seven or eight minutes later I emerged with a fresh Flat Top. My nearly-hairless head tingled. However, my usual round-as-a-punkin' scrub-brush was now a scrub brush with a horizontal top. I had age-progressed from Buzz Cut to the way more elegant Flat Top. Dover boys' ages were defined by Clete's barbering skills. Folks knew that if the *little guy* had a Flat Top he had to be at least eleven.

Dover Men were in a whole 'nother category. On Saturday mornings they packed Clete's shop, most of them suffering the effects of their Friday night Tilley-binges as they sat in his assortment of kitchen chairs, yard-sale chairs, and steel folding-chairs (with *Saint Boniface Church Hall* stenciled on the back).

Sunburned farmers with cream-colored foreheads and coffee-colored cheeks sat alongside factory wage-slaves with cream-colored everything.

In spite of their hangovers, the farmers and factory men grinned like Cheshire cats as they pleasured themselves oogling Clete's stash of those *amazing* magazines I was telling you about. He kept them out of plain sight, tucked away in a box in the corner. Dover Men rifled through those dog-eared editions, blissfully unaware whether or not they were oogling the same Miss March or July that they oogled only three months earlier. They covered them with copies of *Sports Afield* or *Life* so they could oogle in privacy, without fear that some prudish Dover Mom would wander in with her little guy and, you know, take offense.

Clete called up his customers by their Christian names rather than, say, "Number 13" like they shout in today's strip-mall hair emporiums. Clete usually had to shout the Christian name two or three times before the semi-excited oogling Dover Man heard it. The dog-eared *Penthouse* or *Playboy* was stuffed back in the corner box, and the next victim stepped up to be papered, draped, and shorn. After he pointed to the frat boy of his choice, he leaned back, clenched his jaws and closed his eyes for his allotted seven or eight minutes. Clete was egalitarian that way…regardless of the age or size of the noggin, everyone got their seven or eight minutes. It was really just a diversionary tactic designed to make us feel like we got our money's worth. When the clippers stopped buzzing and the hair and scalp residue stopped flying, the Dover man opened his eyes to a slap of rosewater on his cheeks. For an additional dime though, Clete would slap on the *good stuff.* It lingered all the way through Sunday Mass the next morning. Dover Men had to pay Clete double for *their* seven or eight minutes than what we Dover Boys paid for *our* seven or eight minutes. Apparently it required more barbering skill to leave a little semi-combable hair on the top. For his hard-earned dollar another Kim Jong Un look-alike emerged with a haircut that would easily last another three months. The white-wall tire engineers at Goodyear would have been proud.

    Five o'clock. Clete's last customer escaped and his hectic Saturday finally came to a close. All but three of the seven or eight-minute time slots had been filled. Scotch-taped dollar bills and piles of nickels and dimes filled his till. After his end-of-the-week sweep, he locked up and rushed across the street to Tilleys to join his customers in a haze of Chesterfields and rose water.

Today I smile when I recall my hair-raising haircuts. I yearn for Clete's barber shop with its colorful bottles of hair tonic and rose water. I yearn for his tubs of Butch Wax and tubes of Brylcreem. I yearn for the frat-boy poster with its Flat Tops and Ducktails. I yearn for the Dover streets buzzing with buzz-cut *little guys*. And I yearn for all those Dover Men oogling those *amazing* magazines.

But more than anything—I yearn for my hair.

BB GUN BATTLES

Paintball was all the rage when I was raising my sons. Many Saturday mornings we'd drive out to the edge of town to the industrial-grade metal building in the industrial park where industrial-type businesses were supposed to do industrial things. Outside of the paintball business that moved in when some guy thought he was going to get rich manufacturing electric blankets for air mattresses to help people get more use out of their swimming pools late into the cold Autumn days (he died giving it the first test run), about the only (kinda) industrial thing that ever happened out there was some Chinese company came in and manufactured Halloween masks. Yup, you guessed it, they went tits up when their design engineers couldn't get the eyeholes right. Our industrial park soon became overgrown with weeds and beer cans. Anyway, I digress. We stood in line all those Saturday mornings with all the other dads and their boys. Before we were allowed to wage paintball battles, we had to sign a twelve-page disclaimer in triplicate. This supposedly *legal* document protected The Paintball Owners Association of America from the bloodsucking lawyers lying in the weeds. *Figuratively* speaking…err not. After our signatures were secured (in triplicate) we walked into the industrial-grade metal building and suited up in NFL-grade helmets, goggles, face masks, padded gloves, padded shirts, padded pants, and protective NFL-grade cups. *Cups? Really?* All of this was designed to protect us from the plastic balls filled with FDA-approved paint. By making us suit up in Arnold Schwarzenegger *Terminator* outfits, the members of the Paintball Owners Association of America slept well at night, knowing that the blood-sucking lawyers didn't have a chance.

As vicious as they were and as lawyer-proof as they claimed to be, Paintball Wars, in spite of all the helmets, goggles, and padded pants, couldn't compete with the lethal combat fought by Dover Boys on hot summer nights. Dover streets raged as we waged BB Gun Battles!

Before we were allowed to shoot real rifles like Remington .22's, Dover Boys were armed with Daisy BB Guns. Our lethal (if you were a sparrow or some old lady's kitty) weapons were equipped with genuine hardwood stocks and foundry-forged Pittsburgh steel barrels. Deadly things that had to be *cocked*. We liked that word. *Cocked!* And we spit it out with gusto. It was one of the few times that saying a dirty word wouldn't result in a foam-filled mouth.

"Cock yer gun, Milo."
"It's cocked. Cock yers."
"My cock's stuck and won't cock."
"Uncock yer cock and cock it again."
"It's already uncocked and jist won't cock."

Cocked. It still resonates with me. We wore it out. The word. Not our *cocks*.

We planned our battles for days. Offensive tactics and defensive positions were laid out like Marines storming some South Pacific beach. We picked a new platoon captain before every battle using rock-paper-scissors. After we picked the new captains they picked their troops by shouting our names in order of preference. One's pickworthiness was directly proportional to one's popularity. The lower on the list—the more you sucked.

After platoons were picked, we spoke the last friendly words we'd utter for the entire night and wished each other luck. We split up and settled into the least chigger-infested patch of weeds we could find to hunker down and make our plans. In a typical night's battle, Riker, Milo, and I fought Mickey, Arnie, and Gary (the new kid) who had recently moved to town when his old man got hired by the tractor factory. Richie was too little to be trusted with a BB gun, so, to make him feel like he was part of the gang, we used him as a warm-up target.

We huddled with our platoon captains on opposite sides of the town park, a more-than-generous term for the vacant lot between the beer taverns that somehow survived greater downtown Dover's urban beautification projects. Which meant that Harold, the town maintenance man, never mowed it. My team huddled in the weeds along the backside of the park while Mickey, Arnie, and Gary the new kid hunkered down in the weeds along the front. In hushed tones we laid out our strategy, assigned positions, and checked our weapons (just to make darn sure they'd, you know, *cock*). Each combatant was allowed to carry one BB gun and two tubes of BB's. The marketing geniuses at the Daisy Corporation packaged their BB's in red paper tubes that resembled (no, they looked exactly like) 12-gauge Remington shotgun shells. It was not unlike the candy industry marketing geniuses who created candy cigarettes (complete with candy red tips that made them look like they were lit). They looked just like real Camels and real Chesterfields. *"Can't Start 'Em Too Young"* was printed on the front of every package. They were packaged in exact reproductions of the major brands just like mommy's and daddy's. Lacking self-control (which would pretty much set the pattern for the rest of my life) I soon developed a three-pack-a-day habit just like the old man, and smoked, errr...ate Chesterfields. Just like the old man.

Our battles always started out Civil War style...with a Yankee whoop and Rebel holler. We sprang from our bunkers and scattered like cockroaches. To the casual observer our chaotic dispersal defied logic. To us it was all part of an elegant plan to confuse and overwhelm the enemy. We executed it with such speed that we even confused and overwhelmed ourselves.

The Dover city limits defined the perimeter of our battlefield. All twelve blocks. Thirteen if you included the town dump. Nothing was off-limits. Except for the church grounds around Saint Boniface. The previous summer, one of us (I ain't sayin' *who*), shot out Saint Peter's left eye in the stained glass window above the altar. It depicted a scene where Jesus was handing Saint Peter the keys to his car...I think. Father Hempel, always short of funds from the meager collections that were so "generously" given by the parishioners, had already pretty much burned through his contingency funds on a new carburetor for the Saint Boniface Briggs & Stratton lawn mower. With no money left for this unbudgeted repair, he just glued an orange cats-eye marble in the hole where Saint Peter's eye formerly glared down upon the unwashed masses. During the 8:30 Sunday Masses, when the sun struck that orange cats-eye marble just right, some said it was sorta spiritual the way old Saint Pete seemed to wink at them. Others said it looked creepy.

I was not allowed to leave home for combat duty with my BB gun until drill sergeant Mom drilled those words of warning into me that every gun-toting kid had memorized by the time they could cock their Daisy—*Yer Gonna Shoot Yerself In The Eye*. Now, stop here and think about that. It's pretty much impossible—anatomically speaking. It would be like trying to kiss your elbow. Try it...go ahead and kiss your elbow...I'll wait. In order for a boy to shoot his eye out, he'd need orangutan arms (or very dexterous toes) to pull the trigger *after* he jammed the end of the barrel into his eye. I think she meant to say *Yer Gonna Shoot Somebody Else In The Eye*.

The rules of engagement clearly stated that we were only allowed to target arms, legs, chest, and ass. The whole point was to inflict a sting. Maybe raise a welt. Never cause an *actual* injury. Occasionally, somebody caught a BB in the face. Okay—sometimes in the eye. Which obviously went unreported. *I Told You So's* were always accompanied by weeklong groundings. I don't know if it was metal fatigue of the Daisy's spring-loaded cock (still lovin' that word) or the resilience of Dover Boys, but the result was pretty paltry. We'd shove our finger in and dig it out like an eye booger.

Remember Murphy's Law: *If something can go wrong it will*. Well—it did. The whimpering was faint at first. A little voice crying out in the darkness, seeking consolation. We heard the cry coming from behind Old Lady Greene's trash barrel. It was one we didn't recognize. We never cried. It was better to cut off your arm and eat it than to actually cry in front of your fellow soldiers every time you caught a BB in the ass. When the little-voice blubbering escalated to full-out wailing—we knew. It was the new kid. *Gary!* He actually did it. He shot himself in the eye. Being a new kid he (obviously) had a new gun with a cocked spring that still packed a punch.

Have you ever heard someone try to talk while they're crying like a little girl? Not only is it pathetic, it's incomprehensible. Words, spit, and gulps of air get all stuttered together. It sounded like he said he was aiming at what he thought was

Arnie's ass. It turned out to be one of Old Man Peters coonhounds. In fairness to Gary, in a dark alley, Arnie's ass and one of Old Man Peters coonhounds had a certain similarity that easily could have caused his confusion. Especially him being the new kid and all. We spent hours shooting at Old Man Peters coonhounds on hot summer afternoons as they followed us around treasure hunting in the Dover town dump. Just to hear them yelp whenever we nailed one brought immeasurable joy to our twisted hearts. But to score a yelp we had to hit them in their ribs or bellies. Head-shots were futile. Their coonhound skulls were so thick that BB's bounced off like hailstones on a Buick.

Apparently Gary's shot did exactly that. It hit Old Man Peters coonhound's head at just the perfect angle and it ricocheted right back at him. SPLAT! He did it! Mom was right. He actually did it. He shot himself in the eye.

We all watched Audi Murphy do field dressings in *To Heck and Back* (yup—that's how we had to say it. Cock—no problem. But no Hells.) So we did field finger-digs. But crybaby Gary slapped his hand on his eye and wouldn't let any of us come near. The platoon captains declared a truce and combat was temporarily suspended while we led the squalling, semi-sightless Gary back to his house. Riker took him up to the front porch, pounded on the door, and then ran off and left Gary standing there alone. We all crouched in the weeds across from his house to watch the unfolding drama. We took out our candy Chesterfields and "smoked" while there was a break in the battle (just like Audie).

Gary's shrieks cried out in the night. His mom had a cow. "I told you that you'd shoot yourself in the damn eye," (apparently she had been talking to my mom). His dad had a cow. Well—maybe a half-cow. I think most dads expected us to shoot ourselves in the eye once in a while. In a half-cow show of solidarity with his wife, he said the same thing. The "I told you so…" thing. Except he chuckled while he said it. Gary's mom didn't much appreciate it and slapped him upside his head.

He tried. Gary's dad. He tried to dig that BB out. Nothing worked. Tweezers, Q-Tips, a ballpoint pen. Nothing. Even our tried-and-true finger-dig came up empty. Gary's dad thought he was being a smart ass when he pulled his Barlow out of his pocket and snapped a blade open. Gary's mom didn't appreciate that either and slapped him upside his head. "Ya damn idiot, Norbert. Cancha just once in yer damn life be serious?"

Nothing would dislodge that BB, so Gary's mom did what every Dover Mom did when their *Mother's Book of Medical Stuff* provided no solution to the malady *de jure*. She threw him in the back seat of their '54 Plymouth and hauled him off to Doc Hansen's house/office.

Doc Hansen met them at the front door of his house/office combo in his jammies. Actually, he wasn't wearing jammies at all. It was a "borrowed" hospital gown (country doctors didn't make a lot of money). He dug around in his doctor bag for his doctor-light-on-a-headband and strapped it on. He shook his head and threw his doctor-light back into his bag. "Ain't much I can do. Appears someone's been pokin' around in there with a ballpoint or something and shoved that damn BB deeper."

"Ya damn idiot, Norbert," Gary's mom started in again as she slapped him up the *other* side of his head. When he stopped snickering Doc Hansen told them that, as far as knew, the nearest eye specialist was down at the state capitol at Our Lady of Expensive Care Regional Hospital. Well, Gary's mom reassured Doc Hansen that there was no way she could afford that. Like most broke-ass Dover families, Gary's folks didn't have a lot of discretionary funds (like the old man used to say, *they didn't have a pot to piss in*). Affordable Health Care was still a distant dream that Nixon and the Republicans blocked like linebackers. So poor Doc Hansen did what every country doctor learned in Country Doctor Medical School: *When in doubt—cut it out.*

A week or two later, after Gary's eyeless socket stopped oozing and was more or less healed, Doc Hansen did the only thing that Gary's piss-potless folks could afford. He dug around in his kid's toy box and found a marble. It was an orange cats-eye (you probably already saw that coming). He wiped it off with some alcohol and shoved it in the formerly eyeless eye socket.

Remarkably, Gary adjusted quite nicely, thank-you. His cats-eye glass-eye fit like a glove. Little tears even trickled out whenever he cried. Which, as you already know, was quite often.

For many years after that, whenever the sun struck Gary's orange cats-eye eye at just right angle, some said it looked like he was winking. Others said it looked creepy.

FLATULENCE

Last Tuesday morning, after I drained the last cup of Folgers from the Mr. Coffee and got bored sitting at our kitchen window mindlessly watching the neighbor's dog sniffing the south side of our dog; I went into my man cave to mindlessly watch HBO. The entertainment value of both was roughly equivalent. I was all set for a couple of hours of mindless viewing pleasure. I had been waiting for the folks at HBO to run one of this year's Oscar winners, which, because life somehow always seems to get in the way, I missed at the 12-screen mall movie bunker. I sat back, beat my La-Z-Boy into submission, and clicked the vibrator setting to "*I Like It When You're Rough With Me*". I picked up "The Brick" (our NASA launch-control remote), and randomly poked a bunch of buttons until something happened. Through some cosmic mystery known only to the cable guy and my nine-year-old grandson, our 60-inch flat screen flashed to life. Glorious high-def colors danced across the screen.

   Allow me to indulge your patience with this rambling lead-in because what happened next is relevant to what you are about to read. Preceding the movie, HBO showed the artsy-fartsy logos of six or eight production companies, three or four studios, and the Academy of Motion Picture Arts and Sciences disclaimers. And finally the MPAA (Motion Picture Association of America) stuff. As self-appointed guardians of my scruples (as if I had any), the MPAA posted their rating boxes with an array of consonants like *V, N, and C&S* designed to warn me that what I was about to watch *may* contain scenes of *Violence, Nudity, Cussing & Swearing*. Whenever I see any of those letters in the rating box things (especially the *N* one), I turn up the volume and shove my La-Z-Boy even closer. In the last box—way at the bottom of the screen—there they were. Two letters that are especially germane to this story: *MC—Mature Content*.

Unlike the MPAA's *MC*, this chapter is rated *IC*. What you are about to read contains *Immature Content*. You might even find it disgusting. So there, consider yourself warned. If by some chance, these events are an affront to *your* scruples—chill. Take a deep breath and go back to a time when your youthful enthusiasm stooped to such deviant depths. What we Dover Boys are about to do in this story has been practiced by prepubescent hooligans (even postpubescent hooligans) since the beginning of time.

Of course, I'm talking about *Farting*!

I'm not sure where our Gang of Five's infatuation with flatulence got started, but I'm pretty sure it was in church. Sometime around third grade. Maybe fourth. For Catholic kids, our school day started with a pre-class Mass.

I especially remember one pre-class Mass. It was an April Wednesday morning Mass and it was running longer than usual. Father Hempel was waxing nostalgic in his sermon about the time when he was a little boy sitting in a pew just like us. He droned on and on with his eyes closed and an eerie smile on his thin lips (probably too much coffee). You may not know this: the Catholic Mass is a very dynamic production where parishioners are choreographed to sit, stand, and kneel at various (and quite precise) times. The exact sequence of the alternating positions is known only to Catholics. It's in our DNA. When Father Hemple finished waxing, we resumed our ecclesiastical dance. Somewhere between the Nicene Creed and the Offertory, just as we were making one of those dynamic transitions from kneeling to standing, Riker couldn't hold it any longer. His sauerkraut supper from the night before reached critical mass and deep in his gut he felt it. A fart was brewing. What else could he do? Holding it back would only delay what would later be a catastrophic disaster. Change-your-underwear catastrophic. So naturally— he let 'er rip. A silent one. Since it went forth into the world concealed in its shroud of silence, the fart's origin was known only to its creator. It slithered down to *her* end of the pew. The essence of sour sauerkraut was so sharp it curled Sister Mary Larry's nose hairs like when Mom got to listening to *Stella Dallas* and left her Toni Home Perm in too long. Riker looked over at me. I looked back at him. I recognized his expression immediately. *Guilt.* Actually, more like pride. That fart was his and he wanted me to know it.

I risked a glance at Sister Mary Larry. I couldn't tell. Was she pissed or nauseous? She had an expression that I had never seen before. Even without the curly nose hairs it was somehow…different. Then I saw it. Too late. Holy shit! *She knew*! Riker and I had just screwed up. Screwed up bad. We had cast caution to the wind and she caught us exchanging glances. After Mass we'd surely taste her wrath.

We were sitting at our desks, ripping open our little brown paper sacks, getting ready to eat the breakfast our moms had packed for us. In those days, Catholics fasted if they were going to receive communion. I was just about to dig into the egg sandwich Mom packed for me. I always said a little prayed before I ate: *Please Jesus…let the yolks be runny.* I hated Mom's egg sandwiches when the yolks had the consistency of yellow chalk because she forgot about them while she listened to *Stella Dallas*. I cautiously peeled back the wax paper. Bingo! Thank you Jesus. It was a runny yellow-yolk morning! I was about to clamp down with my first bite when Sister Mary Larry clamped down on us like a black-and-white Rottweiler. She jerked Riker by his left ear and me by my right and dragged us into the much-feared *cloakroom*. I looked back at my desk. Mom's perfect egg sandwich oozed all over my arithmetic homework. The Dueter brothers were already hovering over it like vultures.

The cloakroom was a place where no kid ever wanted to be. It was not just a place for wet boots, wet mittens, and wet JC Penney parkas with fake fur hoods; it was an evil, sinister chamber where evil, sinister nun-things happened. So, there we were—two of Saint Boniface's most notorious bad boys and Sister Mary Rottweiler…err, Larry. She towered over us, her face burning red in stark contrast to the white thingy that covered her cheeks, chin, neck, and forehead. The only facial features any nun ever displayed for public view were eyes, nose, and mouth (I still have nightmares). And *she* was pissed. "I know that one of you little bastards did it," her publicly displayed mouth hissed as her publicly displayed eyes distorted into narrow slits. "I don't know which one and I really don't give a shit. *Assume the position.*"

Riker and I looked at each other, eyes bulging, trembling even more than we did in Father Hemple's confessional on Saturday nights when masturbation loomed large on our litany of egregious offenses. We knew what was coming. Resistance was futile. Slowly, we took up *the position*: down on our knees, back erect, arms outstretched, palms down, fingers fanned. She reached under her robe thingy and fumbled around for her leather sheath. It took her quite a while. (Apparently nuns store a lot of stuff under their robe thingys.) She finally found it—*The Ruler*. She unsheathed it and whipped it out like Sister Mary Zorro. Her white knuckles quivered with anticipation.

She flailed away on our fanned fingers until Riker and I were certain that we'd never be able to rifle through the pages of beautiful bras in the Sears and Roebuck catalog again. When she finished, she was gasping for breath just like she did when she was all bent over in her sweaty habit at the finish line of the Dover Dog Daze Fun Run. She returned *The Ruler* to whence it came. With bared teeth she hissed, "If I ever catch either of you fouling the air like that again in the House of the Lord..." She stopped mid-sentence. I think her pulsing neck veins made it hard to go on.

Her ominous warning backfired and inspired us to new heights. After that morning, Riker, Mickey, Arnie, Milo, the new kid Gary, and I put ourselves on a rotating schedule. We perfumed our pew at every morning Mass, somewhere between the Nicene Creed and the Offertory. Our farts were like the gossamer angel wings fluttering around the statues of the saints on the altar. It drove Sister Mary Larry crazy. She never had a clue who.

By the end of fourth grade, we were fart aficionados. We even developed an entire glossary of terms for everything associated with the fine art of farting. We classified most of them by their sound. We called the barely audible ones *Squeakers*. Higher up on the decibel scale were the *Boomers*. Finally, the pièce de résistance, the pinnacle of achievement, the rare and much-envied *Ripper*. In my entire fart career I've only had two.

A few years later, near the end of eighth grade, we were at that transitional time when innocent boys (like us) emerged from our childhood cocoons and morphed into behind-the-school playground cigarette smokin', hip-gyratin' teenagers. We were on the cusp of bidding farewell to church farts, Looney Toons, and centerfolds. No…not centerfolds! (I was just testing to see if you were paying attention.) But before we made that *giant leap for mankind*, one last adventure awaited us in the wonderful world of farts.

Mickey's aunt sent her son to Dover that summer from the big city to spend a few weeks with his country bumpkin cousin. He was a high school sophomore and really impressed us when he told us how he had been suspended from school for six weeks, had already kissed two girls, and actually touched a training bra. After we started breathing again, he proceeded to take us to fart school and taught us things we had never imagined could be accomplished with farts. He told us how he was goofing off in chemistry lab one afternoon when he paged ahead to the lesson on page 178 of his lab book and saw it: *Human Farts Contain Methane*. According to the equations at the bottom of the page, human farts: …*if ignited properly, will generate a blue flame the intensity of which is directly proportional to the volume of the intestinal tract, the diameter of the anal orifice, and the applied pressure*. (Remember that…the part about the pressure. It will be important later on.)

He told us that his personal experimentation pretty much proved that those equations on the bottom of page 178 were correct. However, his terms weren't quite so scientific. Basically he said: "You light a big one and she'll burn the hair right off yer ass." That got our attention, even though, as prepubescent Dover boys, our asses (and other body parts) were yet to sprout postpubescent fuzz.

A few days later Mickey's cousin's country vacation was abruptly cut short. Mickey's aunt came to fetch him back to the big city. Over coffee and cigarettes she told Mickey's mom that her husband's lawyer was "full of bullshit" and his promised early release never happened. He was still being *detained by the authorities*. She needed to get her son back home to mow lawns and sack groceries at the Piggly Wiggly and help make ends meet.

As we were dorking around behind her station wagon and saying our goodbyes, Mickey's cousin told us, "Pigs' always bustin' my old man for public intox and the man puts his ass on ice 'til he gets his shit straight." We had no idea what he was talking about.

With our newly acquired insights to body chemistry we planned our first fart burning. We decided to put his cousin's theory to the test on Friday night. We had to be extra nice to our moms so they'd give us permission to camp out in the fort that we built down by the railroad tracks. We all agreed to sneak two cans of Van Camp's Pork & Beans from our moms' pantries and wolf them down up in our bedrooms after supper. Remember, this wasn't our first fart rodeo. We already knew what worked in the church pews.

Friday night. We met up at the fort after supper as planned. Our two-can Van Camp's strategy was fully implemented and already beginning to rumble. We wanted to get the full visual impact, so we dorked around playing grab-ass in the crab grass until it started to get dark. Anticipation was running high. With everybodys ass properly grabbed and the chiggers starting to come out, we started to un-dork. I noticed it first. Gary wasn't acting quite normal. He seemed nervous. Going-to-confession nervous. We figured it was just new-guy jitters. Still trying to fit in and not sure of what he was supposed to do. As we settled into our fort some of us began to doubt Mickey's cousin. After all, he *was* a bullshitter. C'mon…kissed two whole girls. I mean…he was, after all, ONLY a sophomore. *Two?* He was probably sitting back home laughing his ass off about how he had convinced us that farts would actually burn. Throw a flame even.

But we had come this far, so what the hell. I drew the short straw (like always), so I had to go first. I was shaking like a sacrificial lamb as I got down on the dirt floor. I pulled my pants down and squirmed around until my, err, *orifice* pointed out the door in a relatively safe direction. Before I left the house, I snuck into my old man's bedroom and "borrowed" his prized WWII Zippo from his underwear drawer. He only took it out after Mass on Sundays for his Sunday Chesterfields. He had an everyday lighter for his everyday Chesterfields. By Saturday afternoon I would have it safely back under his underwear before he even noticed that it was gone. I handed it to Arnie and he flicked it to life. I spread my legs as he inched it closer…closer…but not *too* close. Mickey's cousin warned us that was the trickiest part.

I have always had the unique ability to work up a fart the way most boys belch on demand. I strained and pushed. Couple of misfires. On my fourth push, everything clicked. My butt muscles relaxed and my pucker unpuckered. My gas valve was wide open. FARRROOOMPH! It worked. It actually worked. Blue ambience. We giggled like a bunch of girls. The Deuter brothers harmonized: *sonofabitch*. Riker dropped an f-bomb. Mickey's cousin…he was right! It wasn't bullshit after all. I shot blue flame that lit up the fort all the way out the door. Dover Boy shadows danced on the walls.

Riker and Milo went next. Milo amazed us with his orange glow. He later confessed that he had wolfed down an onion with his beans. I'm no chemist, but I'm guessing that the onion's acid or something added that dramatic effect to his pyrotechnics.

Next up, Gary the new guy. He maneuvered into place and adjusted the patch over his left eye that his mom made him wear when he was outdoors: *We don't want that cats-eye getting scratched now, do we?* His nervousness escalated as he pulled down his drawers and settled into position. Turns out he wasn't really nervous after all. That grimace I thought I had noticed earlier was jaw-clamping pain. He had a really bad stomach ache. He forgot all about our two-can strategy and would later confess that he downed *three*.

Well—here's pretty much what happened:

Arnie flicked my old man's Zippo and maneuvered it into place. He shot Gary a thumbs up. Gary bit his lip. Spread his legs. Closed his eyes. Mumbled a Hail Mary. Stomach muscles cramped. The Zippo glowed. But…but…he couldn't unpucker. "Lighten up, Gary," we shouted. "Relax."

He strained and moaned. Nothing. Grunted. Still nothing. He pushed down hard. Then harder. Stomach muscles spasmed.

Then (how do I say this delicately?)…he *way more* than farted. His flame was so brilliant, so intense, that we didn't actually see what happened next. *Something* (sort of) firm blew the Zippo right out of Arnie's hand.

Gary the new guy was awesome. He was our newest best friend. A few weeks later, after he healed, we even let him look at our *Playboys*.

I told the old man that I lost his prized WWII Zippo. I got an ass-whippin' for it, but I was pretty sure he wouldn't want it back. We just let it lay in the weeds where it landed.

...AND THE CHICKENS DANCED

Psychologists tell us that our earliest childhood memories start getting burned into our little noggins somewhere around the age of four or five. At that age our synaptic networks have blossomed and our cerebral cortex is capable of storing and recalling visual, auditory, and olfactory events that have been etched onto our near infinity-sized *tablula rasa*.

Everyone's Way-Back Machine is unique. Different events impress different people in different ways. Some things stick. Others slide off like goose guts on a doorknob. For me, my earliest memories are Mom's hugs. The old man's ass-chewings. Christmas toy orgies. Birthdays with sugary birthday cakes. And sugary aunts with their wrinkly dollar bills stuffed into cheesy Hallmarks.

But more than any of that, more than Christmas, birthdays, and ass-chewings, my most unforgettable memory, the one that sticks like gum on a Sunday shoe, is cowering behind Gramma's apron to watch the Chickens Dance.

Way back in time, before sliced bread and televisions, even before Safeway and Walmart; men were manly and women weren't a whole lot different—they just had a little less hair on their backs. Pioneer men did manly things. They climbed trees, threw rocks, and if they didn't feel like it—skipped their bath. But by far, the manliest thing they did—they killed big beefy animals. Warm-blooded mammals mostly, with meat hanging everywhere on their bones. They did all that killing because they ate a lot of meat. They had meat for breakfast. Meat for dinner (Manly men didn't eat no stinking *lunch)*. They ate meat for supper and meat for dessert. They ate meat for appetizers to make them hungry for more meat at supper. They had their man-friends over on Saturday nights and ate meat snacks and drank fermented swamp water as they sat next to the fire to watch their kids beat each other's brains out. Television and football hadn't been invented yet, so they couldn't just turn the channel if they wanted to watch a different game. So they had more kids.

Pioneer men combed the hair on their backs, put on their manly leather shirts and pants and donned their gutted-out-coonskin cap. (Tilted at a rakish angle, of course. Tail in the back, of course.) They *aimlessly* roamed the prairie *wantonly* killing anything with four legs. (They did a lot of things that required adverbs.) Buffalos, boars, goats, and deers (I know…I know—no "*s*"). They dragged their dead carcass home, hung it up in a tree, and stuck it in the neck so all the blood squirted out. In order to get at all that meat, they first had to butcher their dead carcass. Their little pioneer kids watched from the dirt-floor porch of the dirt-floor cabin as their manly dads butchered away, splattered with blood and guts. It wasn't pretty.

While menfolk killed, stuck, and butchered their dead buffaloes, boars, goats, and deers (again…I know, dammit!) their womenfolk decided that they wanted a piece of the action and wanted to do more to help feed their entertainment systems, err…kids. Womenfolk were quite proficient doing manly things like plow pulling and stump digging. But those things somehow didn't satisfy their blood lust, so they started killing and butchering too. But the only meat-bearing animals that still roamed the prairie after the menfolk pretty much decimated the buffalos, boars, goats, and deer (got it!) were prairie chickens. But before they could decimate all the prairie chickens, they first had to quilt a bunch of quilts and trade them for their own guns at (where else?)—the trading post. Then they hollowed-out their own coonskin caps (donned them at rakish angles), and went out and killed and butchered chickens.

Those pioneer womenfolk passed on their chicken killin' skills to future generations which would eventually include Dover Womenfolk. And no one was better at chicken killin' than my gramma and my mom and her sisters. Every spring Gramma's brooder house (think of it as a kind of nursery for baby chickens) chirped with broods of toddling chicks. Cute yellow fluff-nuggets. After spending their summer eating $500 worth of oats and high-protein chicken feed, they transformed into $237 worth of chicken meat. By late September their transformation had turned them into peck-you-in-the-ass descendants of dinosaurs. Feathered T. Rexes. If a four-year-old strayed too far from gramma's apron, he risked getting the hide ripped off his bones by some razor-sharp chicken beak.

   As the lazy days of summer came to a close, Grandpa's hectic field work was winding down. He cultivated the corn for the third and final time and put up his second crop of hay. In a few months it would be plowin' time when Grandpa would put the fields to sleep for the winter so they could rest up for spring. Then Mother Nature would gently warm them so they could wake up and begin the whole wonderful cycle again. Just before the leaves started to turn, as she did every year, Gramma called my mom's party line from her party line to tell her that it was time to "twist some necks". Gramma loved euphemisms; although to her they weren't euphemisms…it was just the way she talked. If you didn't pay attention when she spoke, she'd lose you by the third sentence. She didn't have to waste her time calling my aunts; they were listening in on mom's party line. So Mom and her sisters (none of whom had what you would call "conventional" names…Caddy, Duffy, and Rosie), gathered their knives, galvanized tin pails (for guts, heads, and feathers if you were wondering), and galvanized tin dishpans (for the $237 worth of meat if you're wondering). They rounded up their brood of four-year-old, impressionable, emotionally-insecure, easily-frightened kids and we all went over the river and through the woods to Gramma's farm for the annual Chicken Dance.

By the time we arrived, Grampa had already corralled Gramma's cackling horde into a makeshift coop he cobbled together in their front yard. Gramma sat on one of her kitchen chairs next to her corralled feathered friends, all set with her buckets of boiling water, sharp knives, and a pile of old rags (you know…for the blood bath).

"Bout time ya get up here. We're burnin' daylight," she barked as we tumbled out of the Studebaker. She corralled us four-year-old, impressionable, emotionally-insecure, easily-frightened kids next to her corralled feathered fiends (I intentionally dropped the *r*), sharp knives, and piles of old rags and told us to stay the hell away from her boiling buckets. "Don't want nobody gettin' hurt."

She and her daughters left us alone with the sharp knives and mini-T. Rexes and walked over to a shade tree where they huddled together like a high school football team. We heard

Gramma mumble as she went over their game plan (in case Mom and her sisters forgot). Grandma always quarterbacked (spoiler alert: things get pretty gruesome from here on out. No one will criticize you if you chicken-out and move along to the next chapter). So, as quarterback, Gramma did the neck-ringin' and cuttin'. She grabbed whichever unlucky bird happened to be closest to her and cracked its neck like a stale pretzel. *Snap!* Audible confirmation. Then, with its rubbery neck in one hand and butcher knife in the other she sliced that sucker's head clean off. *Plop*! Second audible confirmation as she tossed the bug-eyed head into the gut bucket. Later, after the dance was over, Grandpa would empty all the gut buckets into the hog trough. He made us four-year-old, impressionable, emotionally-insecure, easily-frightened kids go with him to watch his pigs chomp their way through the piles of bloody guts, feathers, and heads.

Next up...Aunt Duffy. She grabbed the headless chicken from Gramma and choked it for all it was worth. You know...so blood wouldn't spray all over her dress. (Yes, I said *dress*. Women in pants wouldn't become *de rigueur* until the mid-60's, after all that women's lib stuff). She carried her choked chicken a safe distance away from Gramma and us four-year-old, impressionable, emotionally-insecure, easily-frightened kids and threw it into the yard. And then...and then...*the chicken danced*!

It flopped around in Gramma's front yard for several minutes (hours to us). Spraying blood like a lawn sprinkler. Some of it splattered on our snow-white tee shirts. All of us four-year-old, impressionable, emotionally-insecure, easily-frightened kids cowered under Gramma's table stacked with sharp knives. The bloody carcass eventually collapsed on the lawn. Its dance over. Every ounce of life drained from its veins. The ripping beak that still quivered in the gut bucket was rendered harmless. Every squawk squeezed from its throat.

Mom was up next. She grabbed the limp chicken with her rubber gloves and dunked it into a bucket of boiling water. Properly scalded, it was ready for plucking. Mom could pluck a clucker quicker than Colonel Sanders. When she finished, it looked like the scrawny rubber chicken my smart-ass uncle always brought to my birthday parties. Sometimes, before she passed it on to Aunt Caddy to be gutted, she wiggled one of its naked wings, making it wave at us four-year-old, impressionable, emotionally-insecure, easily-frightened kids huddling behind Gramma.

As the day wore on, if Gramma thought that they were burning too much daylight, she pushed the envelope and decapitated as many as she could grab. Sometimes there'd be as many as five or six chickens rockin' and rollin' out in the yard in a crimson fountain.

The mass slaughter continued all afternoon until the two hundred or so formerly cute little fluff-nuggets were reduced to fifteen or twenty dishpans of meat. And an equal number of buckets of guts. Happy hogs licked their pig lips all night long.

Gramma and her crew had finally burned all the daylight. The evening sun faded to an orange glow over Grandpa's fresh-cut hay field as the last bird performed the finalé to the annual chicken dance. By now Gramma's front yard was a bloody slip n' slide. Come October, the autumn rains would wash away the ruby-red remnants.

Next summer we'd do it all over again.

MEAN STREETS

B.C.—Before Cars. Streets were not much more than trails etched by the wanderings of beasts and nomadic humans that crisscrossed the little patch of dirt that would eventually come to be called Dover. Wandering German immigrants beat out the wandering Polish and Irish immigrants and settled down there first. For several years the population never climbed higher than a dozen or so. The little settlement, either by design or just bad luck, resisted growth. But then it happened—a wandering German Catholic priest settled down with them and set up shop. Well, that was all she wrote. After he converted those wandering Germans into Catholic Germans—BOOM!—the whole village crawled with babies. Lots of babies. Those babies grew up and begat more babies. With folks poppin' up like Whack-A-Moles, things started to get out of hand. They started bickering over who the hell's weed-infested yard all those kids were running around in. Free-range goats and cows ate some neighbor's weeds that he was saving for his own free-range goats and cows (which were down the road eating someone else's weeds). As tensions escalated and things started getting out of hand they hired a surveyor to stake out a checkerboard pattern that would make up the blocks, streets, and alleys of their growing community.

From that framework, our little patch of dirt grew to a village. And from that village—a town. And before you know it, our little community boasted three churches, three beer taverns, and (for a while) three grocery stores. But just one barbershop, one hardware store, and one blacksmith shop, which, with the advent of electricity, became a welding shop. And of course, the constitutionally-mandated, federal-tax-financed post office.

Over the next several decades Dover continued to evolve—sort of. Farmers farmed. Retailers retailed. Tractor-factory workers worked. And baby boomers boomed. In a span of 40 or 50 years our little Camelot expanded outward in all directions. Urban sprawl brought on the addition of 26 more houses with their 26 outhouses. Dover's population exploded, pushing its city boundaries farther and farther into the surrounding prairie until it consumed an entire 11 or 12 blocks. Well, those dirt trails soon proved to be inadequate for the transportation needs of the increasingly mobile Dover residents. Garages and driveways overflowed with four and five Fords and Chevys (sometimes as many as two actually ran). And so we have the makins' for a tale that links Riker, the Deuter Brothers, Mickey, Richie and me to Dover's urban renewal plans that would transform those dirt trails into a modern-day mass transit system.

Dover, even to this very day, never had a traffic light. However, one intersection, where the state "highway" and the county road bumped into each other, had four stop signs. Other than that, even stop signs were a rarity. Venture away from that "controlled" crossroads and Dover's streets were a free-for-all where none but the bravest would risk fate and fenders. Only when the county sheriff dispatched his deputy to patrol Dover for jaywalkers and public intox (both offenses usually occurring simultaneously) would those four stop signs be respected. So, with the sheriff's deputy usually nowhere within miles of Dover, vehicles (*vehicles* being anything with two, three, or four wheels and a motor) entered the four-way intersection with little regard for conventional traffic rules (like actually stopping). As you might imagine, mayhem ruled.

So with nothing better to do and being just plain hard-up for entertainment, Dover folks gathered there at various times of the day or night with cold six-packs and folding chairs to watch the near-endless game of chicken. Like Romans screaming in the Coliseum at Christian-killing gladiators and Christian-eating lions, Dover folks screamed at devil-may-care *vehicle* drivers, daring them to throw caution to the wind and just get on with it. It was not unlike you sitting there in your living room today watching some NASCAR event on your 60-incher. Be honest, you're not watching just to see them run around in circles for hours and hours; you're watching (and secretly hoping) for a big-ass pile-up. Dover folks didn't consider it to be a successful outing unless at least one fender-bender resulted. Drivers' flying fists and flying profanities were a bonus.

Civic pressure mounted to get something done after Dover registered its first vehicular fatality. One of Old Man Peters' coonhounds got itself run over by Old Man Green's tractor. Some said Old Man Green did it intentionally since he steered a considerable distance north of the intersection just to hit the damn thing. (Even on his death bed, Old Man Green maintained his innocence.) Old Lady Sturdavant was Dover's cat lady (every town's got one) and happened to be sitting in the front row of the folding chairs on that fateful day. She had a stable of forty-three *named* felines and never, not ever once, let any of them out of her house for fear something like this would happen to them. She jumped up out of her downwind folding chair (folks always made her sit downwind) and wagged a finger at Mayor Koop and the Dover town council, "See...I told you something like this was gonna happen." Since Old Man Peters' coonhound didn't go easy, so she had to yell to be heard above its last yelps. With all of her yelling, all of that dying coonhound's yelping, and all of Old Man Peters ranting it was pure pandemonium. "You bunch of laggards need to get something the hell done before a more serious incident claims nine innocent lives." Folks knew what she was referring to.

Right there Mayor Koop and the Dover town laggards, err...Dover town council, fearing that Old Lady Sturdavant would go and get herself all lawyered-up, passed a resolution. Mayor Koop scribbled it down on the cardboard of an empty six-pack he and the laggards had just polished off: *We, the members of the Dover Town Council, do hereby pass a resolution to get something the hell done.* They signed it and drew straws to see who would walk downwind and show it to Old Lady Sturdavant to get her to shut the hell up.

Over the next several months, Mayor Koop and the Dover Town Council embarked upon an urban renewal project the sheer size and cost of which Dover hadn't seen since they bailed out the dismally failed Dover Dog Daze fiasco with the hundred and fifty bucks they sort of "borrowed" from the senior citizen coffee fund (seniors, as we all know, drink a lot of coffee). They bickered back and forth for weeks over the financial analysis (read: wild-ass guess) until Mrs. Old Man Zimmerman, who had taken her dead husband's seat on the city council and, much to the dread of the all-male town council, had somehow got herself reelected, brokered a settlement between the two opposing camps with rock-paper-scissors. After they agreed on the final estimate they realized that the meager post-Dog-Daze town treasury could only absorb the cost of replacing the stop sign that Old Man Green demolished when he took a victory lap around the intersection on his tractor after Old Man Peters' coonhound yelped its last yelp and he had *accidentally,* after backing over it five or six times, had ground the expired canine into a greasy spot.

So the town council did what any broke-ass town council could do. They lied. Well, *embellished* is what Mrs. Old Man Zimmerman preferred to call it. On the form that the State Highway Department mailed back to Mrs. Old Man Zimmerman they sort of overstated (in triplicate) the number of *outrageous* accidents that had occurred at that dangerous intersection of the state highway and county road. All pumped up with their inflated statistics, they piled into Koop's station wagon with enough ham sandwiches and RC Colas for both dinner and supper and took a trip down to the state capitol. They did a little political arm-twisting (Mrs. Old Man Zimmerman didn't know that it was a euphemistic term and actually twisted one engineer's arm. He barely made it back from the ER for the conclusion of the meeting). Koop and his entourage of ham-breath councilmen were feeling pretty cocky. They felt quite sure that all of their political arm twisting and badgering was what brought the state DOT engineers to their knees and convinced them to rebuild Dover's *entire* main drag. But it wasn't that at all. The seasoned DOT engineers (nearly as seasoned as the horseradish mustard Mrs. Koop slathered on their ham sandwiches) were not that easily duped by those inflated figures that were being tossed around. No indeed. The State Highway Department budget was stuffed with a shit-pot of money that came from a most unlikely source—the governor himself. It was left over from the illegal reelection campaign contribution made by the governor's brother-in-law (who just happened to own one of the biggest road construction companies in the state). After his landslide reelection, the guv transferred the money from his illegal campaign fund to his illegal slush fund. He told his campaign finance manager to make it disappear before the Federal Election Commission came snooping around. For the Dover town council, it was a classic example of being in the right place at the right time. On their drive home from the state capitol, Koop told the council members if he had known it was going to be that easy, he wouldn't have bothered to wear his fake-silk tie. The one with Mount Rushmore hand-painted on it that was imported all the way from Japan. He was always sure to get that part about Japan in there. It made his two-dollar tie sound expensive. He thought.

The highway engineers finished their survey and had the plans drawn up in a matter of weeks. Compared to overpasses, bridges, and interstate highways, the "Piddly Dover Job" (the official project title) was a slam dunk. Bids were let and some outfit in Texas was awarded the contract. The governor's brother-in-law went ballistic and threatened to go public with the campaign contribution thing. He changed his mind when his wife (the governor's sister—of course) slapped him upside the head for even thinking about ratting out her brother.

Dover merchants were giddy with enthusiasm anticipating the explosive revenue growth that would surely fall into their pockets when all those Texas construction folks would arrive and consume whatever it was that Texas construction folks consumed. Mrs. Old Man Zimmerman even converted her spare bedroom into Dover's first B&B. (Bed&Blankets—she wasn't about to cook no damn breakfast.) In spite of the Dover merchants' dreams of all explosive revenue growth, it turned out that the only businesses that actually benefitted were the beer taverns.

It took two and a half months for the "Piddly Dover Job" to be completed. The DOT engineers had estimated three weeks. But they didn't know Dover folks. Dover folks never experienced a project like that before. To them it was anything but piddly. So, being just plain hard-up for entertainment (which you already know) they unfolded their folding chairs on the right-of-way to watch the D-9 Cats crawl all over town. Progress was delayed several times when the Dover folks refused to fold up their folding chairs and get the hell out of the way. The D-9 Cat drivers hurled empty beer bottles at them to no avail.

My goodness, what an impact those four blocks of newly-built roads had on Dover. The old dirt streets were dug down to a depth of six feet and replaced with tons and tons of crushed rock. *Actual* concrete curbs were poured. Dover folks had seen the actual concrete curbs that surrounded the courthouse in the county seat, but never dreamed that they would have them in their town. After trenchers trenched the drainage ditches, 150 feet of 18-inch concrete culverts were connected to the curb-side concrete drainage boxes. Everything was paved over with the blackest blacktop anyone had ever seen. The good folks at the state DOT were even generous enough to paint a white center line but they might as well have saved some of the governor's ill-gotten campaign funds. Center lines were meaningless in Dover. Traffic engineers will tell you that painted white center lines are simply *suggestive* barriers that are only effective when responsible drivers respect them. The DOT essentially wasted 132 gallons of white paint.

With all that being said, let's get to the nitty-gritty of this story. Remember those drainage facilities I mentioned? 150 feet of 18-inch concrete culverts that connected to the concrete drainage boxes to divert rain water away from the Dover Expressway? 'Twas those 18-inch concrete culverts that made a lasting impression on me. Makes me go all Freudian-like just thinking about them; reducing me to a state of existential angst. Even today it still gives me the willies.

Those newly-constructed concrete drainage boxes had six-inch slots cut into the curb to allow rainwater in where it collected and ran off in the 18-inch concrete culverts. Those culverts were just too much of an attraction for Riker, the Deuter Brothers, Mickey, Richie, and me to resist. I think it was Milo who came up with our little game that would prove to be my undoing.

Milo's brilliantly conceived plan was actually pretty simple. Here is how it was *supposed* to go: The first order of business was to draw straws. The concrete drainage box, which had been redefined as a WWII pillbox, could only hold three of us. Four if we included Richie. According to Milo's plan (bordering on sheer genius we thought), the long-straw winners would slither on their bellies through the 150-foot, 18-inch concrete culverts like combat Marines, inching their way to their mission objective—the concrete pillbox. The first one to arrive would take a stick with a hankie tied to the end and poke it out of the six-inch slit to signal their safe arrival. The short-straw guys served as combat observers and would crouch in the weeds to wait for the action to begin.

When a vehicle approached, the guys in the pillbox were supposed to wait until they saw the tires outside their little slit. Then, at just the right time, they'd scream like my sisters watching Elvis on Ed Sullivan.

The unsuspecting vehicle operator, more than likely listening to Frankie Yankovic on Polka Party Time on his radio and not focusing on the Dover Expressway traffic, would hear the screams. Once he realized that they were actual screams and not Frankie Yankovic yodeling, he'd jam on his brakes and screech to a halt and have a *Holy-shit-what-did-I-just-do* panic attack. He'd jump from his two, three, or four-wheeled vehicle, convinced that he had just made a major contribution to Dover's population control program. Some (we hoped) might even get down on their bellies and desperately search under their truck, tractor, or occasional car for the squashed body, sweating about how would they ever come up with the twenty bucks they'd have to shell out for the fine. Maybe more—depending upon whose kid they'd run over.

Per Milo's plan, while all this drama played out, the short-straw guys would be lying in the weeds, laughing their asses off. It was a classic! We were sure that we'd enjoy hundreds of hours pissing-off hundreds of Dover drivers.

That was how it was *supposed* to go...

It was one of the most tragic events that would ever rock Dover. Before it was over yellow police tape was deployed as flashing red lights streaked through the panic-stricken night. I still have the old newspaper clipping in my scrapbook where some cub reporter described, in shocking detail, the entire thing: *It all started out innocently enough one late October afternoon...*

After school, Richie and I rushed home and tossed our school clothes and mostly unskidded school underwear in a pile on the floor next to our beds where we could easily find them the next morning. After we wolfed down a peanut butter sandwich and glass of milk, we ran back to our room and jumped into our everyday clothes and everyday underwear which were also lying in a pile on the floor next to our beds—jeans with holey knees, shirts with holey sleeves, and socks with holey toes. And nicely-skidded underwear.

Richie and I kicked the screen door that, once opened always stayed open. Over the years, eight kids and 13,500 drop-kick daily openings took a serious toll on the spring. We ran out of the kitchen like lifers in a prison break. We were so excited, we barely heard mom yell: "Supper's at six, getchur your butts home. Then she added her familiar addendum, "...*or else*." That we heard.

It was our inaugural run of Milo's game. I actually drew one of the long straws. I was accustomed to losing at just about everything, so I was shocked when it happened. For once in my life—I really did it. I actually drew the long straw. With my big mouth and soprano scream that rivaled even the sweetest Italian *castrato*, I would be a perfect belly crawler. I'd show the guys what a real scream sounded like. (If only I had known how prophetic my thoughts would turn out to be.) I knelt down and flopped on my belly like Robert Mitchum in *The Longest Day* and started crawling through the 150-foot, 18-inch concrete culvert. The distant pillbox loomed large as I squinted into the dark tunnel. My date with destiny waited.

For the past month or so I had been having one of my infrequent growth spurts. Pre-pubescent boys know when growth spurts hit because the long bones in our legs and arms ache. Can't-sleep-at-night ache. Arnie and Milo had two or three growth spurts a year. Me—maybe once every two years or so. Growth spurts, according to Mom's *Reader's Digest Book on Medical Stuff*, not only made pre-pubescent boys longer—they made us bigger around as well. All that gravy in our Low Country Germanic diet didn't hurt. We put gravy on everything from taters to tacos. I was barely a body-length inside when I noticed that the 18-inch tube felt a little, shall we say, "cozy" but I soldiered on anyway. I was nearly halfway to the pillbox when it happened. One of the concrete sections had apparently settled just enough to make its alignment with the next one a little off-kilter, causing a bit of a dip. My head and shoulders made it through just fine, but my butt got stuck. Forward progress halted.

I gasped for air. *C'mon, you can do this, Bill.*

I kicked. I squirmed. *Oh jeeze!!* Then I kicked some more.

Panic poured from my pores. My fingernails clawed the concrete.

I kicked and squirmed harder. I was still stuck. I wiggled like a worm. The more I kicked, squirmed, and wiggled the stucker I got. I tried to look ahead, but I could barely tilt my head enough for a front view. Darkness swallowed me whole like that guy in the bible who ended up in a whale's belly. I lost the distant dot of October twilight coming from the pillbox. In my now-terrified mind it did a zoom-out like a Alfred Hitchcock dramatic effect in the late-night movie on Channel 7. It was thousands of feet away. Maybe miles. I heard Riker and Mickey's muffled voices behind me, "Get your ass movin', Rausch."

I was stuck. Stuck hard.

The sun was going down.

Everything…darker.

Can't…breathe.

I was sweating. Sweating hard.

My arms were pinned under me. Pinned hard.

I couldn't budge.

I was stuck…*oh shit*…I was stuck! I was stuck. I was stuck. I was stuck. My head had a broken record in it. I was stuck. Dammit…I was stuck.

Mickey's voice died.

Riker's voice died.

Silence.

Thought I was gonna die.

Die alone.

Then I panicked. Panicked hard.

I actually felt (well, I *thought* I felt) the 18-inch concrete culvert squeeze me like those Chinese finger trap thingys we won at the ring toss at the Saint Boniface church bazaar.

By now I was wrapped in total darkness. *Did I black out? Is this how it all ends? Am I dead? Did I remember to hide that half-eaten Baby Ruth under our bed so that little shit Richie doesn't find it after my funeral? Oh crap—I got my everyday underwear on.* Morbid thoughts filled my head. Then…suddenly…I felt it. Something jerking my feet? I prayed, *Dear God, let it be human.* What's this? He actually heard it? God heard my prayer. It was Richie. I heard his familiar whine. My dear, sweet, loving, good, kind brother Richie. I think he (Richie…not God) said, "Hold on, idiot. I'm trying to tie a rope around your ankles. Stop yer kicking. That was my face, idiot." Sweet, loving Richie. He's such a kidder.

Then, everything got quiet again. He was gone. I was alone in my private prequel to hell. That stupid little shit-idiot Richie abandoned me to die a slow death.

Suddenly, just as I heard angel wings flutter, I felt it. Richie's rope tightened. Just a little twitch at first. Small jerks, like a fish nibbling on a hook. Then, forceful, painful, powerful yanks. I thought my legs were going to be ripped right out of their sockets like Sunday-chicken thighs.

Voila! (cue the cork pop)—I busted free. In a matter of minutes I was reverse-hauled out of the culvert. Moonlight flooded in my eyes. Croaking frogs echoed in my ears. Frogs? Mikey, Riker, and the Deuter Brothers had reeled me in like a weed carp and I was flopping around in the putrid ditch water. Adrenaline, I guess

As I laid there with a coil of muddy rope wrapped around my legs, the town cop's pissy red light with a magnet holding it to the roof of his pickup added extra drama to what could have been a fatal scene. He even had his roll of yellow *Do Not Cross – Police Crime Scene* tape lying on the hood, ready to deploy just in case the incident had escalated to a, you know…a fatality. He had called Channel Seven News at Six hoping for a little TV face time and had even gone home and changed into his clean, Sunday cop shirt and shaved and everything (even though it was only Thursday). He practiced saying *We suspect foul play was at work in this tragic incident and we will want to question that little shit Richie* as he shaved. When the news folks failed showed up he went home and put his everyday cop shirt back on.

I was free. I was alive. I was happy. But my euphoria didn't last long. Doc Hansen had to splint my left leg. He told the old man it was nearly dislocated, what with all that jerking and pulling. The old man gazed at Doc Hansen and then me with teary eyes (which I mistook as an overwhelming emotional reaction that his first-born son was alive and safe). All he said was, *How much this gonna cost?*

Even after all these years, with that fateful night now safely in my distant past, I still get the heebie-jeebies whenever I find myself in a tight space. Psychiatrists have a word for this syndrome—*imprinting*. My shrink, Dr. I. Emma Nutt, explained it to me. She theorized that within days of that *experience*, claustrophobia imprinted my subconscious with an indelible code that took root in my pre-frontal cortex. She helped me to cope by identifying the source of my existential angst. I gazed at her with teary eyes (which she mistook as my overwhelming emotional reaction) and asked, *How much this gonna cost?*

DEATH

We were lucky. *Real Death* never set foot inside Dover. Real Death always happened to other people. Somewhere else out there in the world. It made for lively tavern talk or party-line gossip. Brutal traffic accidents, catastrophic weather, or violent big-city streets. That's where Real Death happened. But never Dover. Maybe we were just lucky. Maybe God always smiled on Dover. But then something happened and our luck ran out. God forgot to smile.

I probably need to qualify that term in my opening statement. *Real Death* (call it Tragic Death or Wrongful Death), was the kind of death that set mothers to crying and fathers to cursing. It wouldn't find Dover until I was well into my teens. Our Real Death experiences came in the form of Newspaper Deaths and Television Deaths that took anonymous lives from anonymous people. Faceless folks who didn't amount to much in our good-luck lives. To us they were just an inch or two of obit ink or a news bite on *Channel Seven News at Six*.

Of course our old folks, they died. But that was different. That was Natural Death. Anticipated Death. In some cases, I'm sure,

Longed-For Death. But Real Death—the Death that did those heart-breaking things to Dover Moms and Dover Dads—it cowered in the dark shadows. Patiently waiting. Waiting.

This chapter will be kept (necessarily) brief. Brief because I don't deal with this kind of stuff very well. Call me chicken—I just don't like to talk about it. So let me warn you right here, if you're expecting some protracted discourse detailing the emotional suppression we summon to help us cope with tragedy, it ain't gonna happen. Don't dive into my words expecting to discover some philosophical insight into our cosmic karma. Just move along. There's nothing here for you to see. Hollywood directors and high-dollar writers much more talented than me have already beat Death to death.

Dover kids lived in an idyllic Camelot, swaddled in innocence and smothered with love. Our lives were a never-ending book where the final chapter would never be written. From our perspective, life was an undisputed proposition: *We live. Old People die.* Simple, I know. But that's the way it was. To us they had always been old anyway. When they *passed on* (I always did and still do have a great distaste that euphemism), adults said some Hail Marys, put them in a box, and buried them. Then they, the living, *moved on.* Oh sure, we'd hear about them—the dead ones—being memorialized in stories and jokes (just the good stuff, thank you). They were missed—for a while. But after a few weeks, maybe a month or two, Dover folks picked up life right where that old person had interrupted and they *moved on.* Our moms and dads put their heads down and pressed their noses against the proverbial grindstone. Memories faded and the stories died. Tavern talk and party-line gossip returned to more mundane things: "Who's that fella Lisa's sleepin' with on *As The World Turns*." Or, "You see how much Teddie Giesenberg give for that new Bonneville?"

Then, something happened. Over *there* somewhere. A funny-sounding name, really. Dover kids only spoke American. The first time we heard it, we weren't sure what it was. Walter Cronkite called it *Vietnam*.

Many Brave Young Dover Boys got shipped there. Big brothers, cousins, boyfriends, husbands, sons. Most of them went willingly. Eagerly, even. "Gonna shoot me some Gooks," we heard one bragging as he stood on the sidewalk outside of Tilleys. He beamed in sharp contrast to the sullen Dover Men gathered around him in their sea of faded overalls and boots with crooked-worn heels. He towered in the middle of their denim scrum, a sharp-dressed soldier in his sharp-pressed uniform. He had a couple of everybody-gets-one basic training medals pinned above his pocket. His shoes glassy as Cinderella's. The wary father watched his son carry on, trying his best to look proud. "Ain't he somethin'," he'd say. "That's my boy," he'd say. "He's a man now." If anyone had bothered to stop gawking at that newly-minted piece of cannon fodder standing in their midst and glance over at *its* father, they might have noticed how his eyes betrayed him. He knew. (Dad's always know.) After a few more chuckles and grunts from the Dover Men, the father threw his arm around his son's shoulder and walked him inside where Tilley had a cold Schlitz ready for the shiny new soldier. Somehow, even though he wouldn't celebrate his 18th birthday for another year, he had become one of them—a Dover Man. If he was lucky.

Even *we* sensed that something was different. We saw the way the Dover Men looked at him. We heard his *shpiel* about *them Gooks*, repeated for the third time, as much to convince them as himself. We understood his excitement. Sharp-pressed uniform, glassy shoes, ribbons. But what was this strange thirst to kill? Dover Boys didn't talk like that.

Everyone in Dover was talking about that place called *Vietnam*. "It's yer goddamn duty to join up," a Dover Man shouted one night up at Tilleys at some long-haired *hippie* (another new word for us to absorb) who had come home from college that summer. "Just like we done." But the hippie never would. He never bought in to that false sense of obligation from those Greatest Generation Dover Men whose honor it was to have fought in a *just* war in defense of liberty and freedom. Our generation of young Dover Boys went off to fight in defense of Standard Oil and Dow Chemical. Our Dover Boys went off like other Brave Young Boys from Selma to San Francisco. Some signed up. Some got drafted. Regardless of what motivated them to go to that faraway jungle, enlisted or drafted, patriotism or adventure, by the time they completed basic training—with screaming D.I.'s and hours of indoctrination—they were convinced that they did the right thing. The Truth that drives the reckless abandon of youth is not the same Truth that tempers late-in-life wisdom.

They all came back home. Some alive. No sugar-coated euphemisms here. Those boys didn't *pass on*. No one *lost* their son. They were slaughtered. They were dead.

After that first flag-draped coffin rolled down the aisle at Saint Boniface, Real Death became a bitter reality for us Dover kids. Disney-World dreams died. Endless summers shattered. Our big brothers were dead. Our uncles were dead. Our dads were dead. Dover Men up at Tilleys dropped their bullshit bravado. *He was just a kid*, they mumbled up and down the bar.

No, it wasn't *some Gook done it* like they all said. What killed them was far more evil than a random bullet burning through the jungle. Real Death ambushed those Brave Young Dover Boys.

What the hell were we thinking?

MEANWHILE...BACK TO OUR STORY

Take a deep breath. That was the most haunting chapter that you'll have to read. I felt compelled to get that off my chest. Thank you—you're off the hook now. You may now remove your seatbelts and roam about the rest of the pages...

TRIPLE CROWN

You've no doubt read those surveys that chamber of commerce folks publish from time to time: *The Ten Most Popular Places to Live in the United States*. Google it and you might be surprised by what you see. Some towns are included due to the business and industry they attract and the job opportunities they create. On a more social level, some cities are recognized for their churches and schools. Others for their parks, lakes, mountains, and valleys. And some for their hiking and biking trails. All of these are significant components that contribute to the quality of life. Well—according to those chamber of commerce folks anyway. Ask anyone in Dover, and they will tell you that the most *significant components* that enriched the fabric of our community came from a whole 'nother source.

Before we get going on this chapter, let's get some of that chamber of commerce stuff out of the way. We had three churches. Not necessarily one on every corner like the folks who lived in *The Ten Most* had…but damn near. You already know quite a bit about Saint Boniface—*my* big fat Catholic church. And before you finish you'll learn a lot more. There will even be an entire chapter on Big Fat Catholic Weddings. All three of our churches opened for business *almost* every Sunday. I say almost because one of them, the one that had just a handful of *non-Catholics* (that's what Sister Mary Larry called them), had a roamer-preacher. A roamer-preacher is not unlike the roamer outfielder they have in sissy slow-pitch softball who runs around screwing up the real outfielders and screws everything up. And if he or she is a ball-hog—he or she screws up the shortstop too. The harried roamer-preacher tried his (sorry, no *hers* back then) best to cover three or four churches. Sometimes less—depending upon how well he sucked up to his bishop. Some Sundays he wouldn't show up. We assumed that his no-shows had more to do with scheduling conflicts than with sobriety. Maybe.

For many years we had two schools: Saint Boniface and P.S. 146. Due to budgetary constraints, the public school board consolidated our P.S.146 with P.S. 162 that was up at the county seat (they renamed it P.S. 154—the average of 146+162). Our Saint Boniface School hung on for as long as it could. Eventually it shrunk from K-12 to K-8. Finally—K-K. Father Hemple was apparently more adept at squeezing funds from his tight-fisted flock than the school board was at raising the school millage from tight-fisted tax payers. "Guilt's a helluva motivator," Father Hemple liked to brag. But in the end, with a K-K student population of five, the economic model proved to be unsustainable when we had more nuns than students. Sister Mary Larry closed the doors for the last time and rolled into the sunset in her wheelchair.

Farming was the economic backbone of Dover. Back then, coaxing a living from the soil challenged most farmers' attempts at wealth accumulation. Success was directly proportional to the number of cows in the barn, pigs in the pen, and mouths at the supper table. And rain. Too much rain…you're screwed. Too little rain…you're screwed. Weather was the second most popular topic farmers bitched about up at Tilleys. First? Well, Nixon. Of course.

And lastly, let's talk about Dover's industrial infrastructure. Okay. Did I mention that we had three churches?

All those *significant components* aside, Dover folks used a much different metric to gauge our success as a thriving, vibrant community. Sure, we had our churches, schools, and farming infrastructure. But they offered little, if anything, to help Dover land a spot on the list of *The Most Popular Places to Live in the United States.* If anyone had considered relocating to Dover, our chamber of commerce had one recruitment tool that hooked 'em every time: Beer Taverns! We had three. Yes *three,* big, beautiful beer taverns. Tilleys, Charlies, and Bonfigs.

What say we take a look at those three jewels that made up our *tipple* crown? Err…Triple Crown.

Let's face it, when you boil it all down, beer's beer, right? There's little you can do to distinguish one tavern from another based solely on its beer. Schlitz (in Dover, always pronounced *Slits*), Miller, and Blue Ribbon were the most asked for. Budweiser has always been the *King of Beers* and enjoyed national market dominance even back then. Not so much in Dover. No one drank Bud in Dover. Budweiser was a big-city beer for big-city tastes. So, if Schlitz, Miller, and Blue Ribbon in one tavern are the same Schlitz, Miller, and Blue Ribbon in another, how the heck did Dover's taverns differentiate themselves? It all came down to one thing—institutional identity.

Tilleys was my old man's go-to tavern. It was owned, operated, and sometimes cleaned by, errr…Tilley. She had her name painted on a sign that hung out over the sidewalk that lit up at night if she remembered to turn it on and her old man remembered to change the light bulb when it burned out. *TILLEYS.* No apostrophe—Tilleys. Tilley was an affable woman. She was also a large woman. For Russian-village *babushkas* and American-village barkeeps, affability and largeness went hand-in-hand. Think of Jabba the Hut with big hair. Big silver-white hair. Her age was somewhere between 29 and 60. Nobody asked because nobody had the balls. You try and that affability thing went right out the window. But overall, Tilley was a gentle soul. Warm, grandmotherly almost. But make no mistake, if anyone ever crossed the line (its location on any given night dependent on Tilley's temperament, tolerance, or time of month), she'd rip them a new one.

Her booming personality had no equal. She never cussed or uttered what was called back then an "off-color" joke. She was the nightly master of ceremonies. Some said more like a ringmaster trying to keep all the clowns in line. She ruled her realm with benevolence, enthroned on her lofty perch behind the bar, nestled between the industrial-sized jars of pickled pigs' feet and pickled polish sausages.

Within an arm's length of her perch was an array of colorful beer taps that were connected to a grid of pipes, hoses, and tubes that snaked their way to her backroom cooler. Every morning, before he went to the tractor factory, her old man switched out however many kegs the Dover Men drained the previous night. If anyone asked for a beer that was not included in her colorful array, that request fell upon deaf ears. Tilley was an ardent subscriber to Newton's First Law of Motion: *A body at rest tends to stay at rest.*

With her perfectly-coifed silver-white big hair, affable demeanor (for the most part), and always dressed in a dress, Tilley was the quintessential small-town barkeep.

Charlies was owned and operated by Chas. Brown. Said so on the sign he had painted on the wavy glass in the front window. Like Charlie, the wavy glass was old. Real old. Charlies was (indisputably) the oldest tavern in Dover. Along with that claim, it also claimed (indisputably) the oldest beer drinkers in town. Given their gittin'-up-there-in-age distinction, they were actually beer *sippers*. Guzzling went south about the same time that the last dribbles of testosterone dried up and left them with near-soprano voices and man-boobs. Canes and crutches were *de rigueur*. Walkers and wheelchairs were for the diehards (pun intended).

Charlies, in addition to being Dover's most established establishment, also boasted one other distinction: it housed (taverned?) the town's only *billiard* table. Not some cheesy Sears and Roebuck 7 ½-foot *pool* table, but a *jen-you-whine*, handcrafted, slate-topped, nine-foot, big-ass billiard table. It weighed as much as a Buick. As Charlies clientele succumbed to the ravages of time, the rarely-used table suffered the indignity of being not much more than a place to stack beer cases. The old beer sippers lacked both the eyesight and endurance to showcase their once-mighty skills. Whenever Riker, Mickey, the Deuter Brothers, or I went in, which sadly wasn't often, Charlie gave us permission to actually touch it. It would have been easier to get a private audience with the pope than permission to actually play a game on it.

Charlies majestic bar was an architectural masterpiece that could have been taken right out of some Dickensian English pub. While his billiard table rivaled the hand-carved altar that adorned Saint Boniface church, his bar matched any armoire that might have adorned the halls of some medieval Rhine Valley castle. It was a paragon of old-world craftsmanship with its handmade details and rich wood veneers.

Charlie was a cool dude. Well, a cool Old-Man Dude. Even in the days before anyone knew what cool was, Charlie was already there. His slow, even drawl suggested to the casual listener that he hailed from the hills of Tennessee or the plains of Georgia. He always sported dark glasses. Always. Not exactly your lay-on-the-beach stylin' sunglasses but a bit more, shall we say…*staid*. They were a testament to his vision issues rather than his coolness. Nonetheless, they added to his aura.

I really liked Charlie. I liked him a lot. Sadly (but pretty normal for a kid when you think about it), I did not have the gumption (maturity) to express it. Here's the deal. Here's why I liked him so much: Until Dover boys reached the age of 13 or 14, Dover Men blew us off like a pesky fly whenever we tried to join in their simple conversations. Their go-away-kid-you-bother-me attitude kept us at bay. But not Charlie. He took time to actually engage us in back-and-forth repartee. He seemed to care what we thought and delighted in our youthful perspective (read: naïveté).

I loved Charlie. Still do.

Everol Bonfig was born to be a bartender. It was in his DNA. Some folks have genes for blue eyes or curly hair. Everol had bartender genes. Folks said that when he was a toddler he toddled around with a bar rag in his hand. No blankey for him. His personality made him the perfect barkeep. Engaging but not obsequious. Conversational without being overbearing. Like a ship's captain in the iceberg-infested North Atlantic seas, he helped his, shall we say, less lucid customers navigate the treacherous waters that separated fact from alcohol-fueled fiction. He always impressed the listener with his bartender banter (read: bullshit).

He was the consummate gentleman. Ladies were treated with the respect that they deserved in his bar. And if they drank to a point where they didn't deserve his respect, he gave it to them anyway. I once watched him refuse to serve a falling-down-drunk mother of eight. By the time he finished reasoning with her; she gushed with admiration. She came back the next morning and thanked him for shutting her off.

Bonfigs was the crown jewel of Dover's taverns. By far the largest, it boasted two—count 'em—two sections. Each with its own bar. The two sides were separated by an actual wall. Not some cheesy wooden bannister or beaded curtain, but a real wall. It provided an architectural barrier that separated the beer and bullshit aficionados on one side from the cheeseburger and RC Cola aficionados on the other. Dover's only nickel-eating pinball machine was on our cheeseburger side. Scantily clad, big-titty girls gazed down from a carnival of lights with an expression on their faces that said they'd date any of us any time, any place, anywhere. Obviously, we spent a lot of time in front of it. Sometimes actually playing it. Something about those flashing tittys.

When Riker, Arnie, Milo, Mickey, and I grew from being snotty-nosed kids to being snotty-nosed teenagers, we widened our circle of friendship to include Everol's kid. Riker pilfered adult magazines from his old man's stash. The Deuter brothers pilfered chocolate oatmeal cookies from their mom's kitchen. Mickey pilfered jokes from *Reader's Digest* and *Sex to Sexty*. But Everol's kid had the ultimate pilfering gig. He had damn-near unlimited access to the backroom where his old man maintained mountains of beer. Hamm's, Schlitz, Blue Ribbon, and Miller. Even Blatz. He became our best friend ever. Thanks to him our Saturday nights, which would have otherwise been spent in somebody's boring basement playing boring ping-pong and drinking R.C.'s until our back teeth floated, now had focus.

Real meaning. Real beer! We were, for the most part, tapped out after two beers. Richie went straight to La-La Land after he drank just one and became a near-endless source of entertainment. You ever watch an eight-year-old fall off a stool? Ten or twelve times? Our wonderful Saturday nights were basic training for the day when we'd take our place beside the Dover Men and belly-up to the bar.

I'm quite certain that the layout of Dover's main street was accidental. Not much ever happened in Dover as the result of some grand plan or organizational focus. Dover's serendipity gave a whole new meaning to the adage: *shit happens*. Tilleys and Bonfigs just *happened* to pop up on the more forward-thinking south side of the street. Charlies just *happened* to spring up on the not-so-much north side. Clete's barbershop and Koop's hardware stood shoulder-to-shoulder alongside Charlies. It was darn near impossible to determine which of those north-side establishments generated more excitement. Watching Old Man Peters suck on a bottle of Schlitz for three hours while he and Charlie listened to the Cardinals game on the radio or buying a bag of ten-penny nails from Koop.

Customer loyalty was nonexistent amongst Dover's beer-drinking population. Bonfigs and Tilleys customers flip-flopped their affections like loveless whores. Sometimes several times a night. Again—like loveless whores. This vacillation would be triggered when some sobriety-challenged, smart-mouth drinker talked back one time too many. Neither Everol nor Tilley tolerated their brain-numbed defiance. When it happened, as most assuredly it would, the rejected barfly would wobble across the street only to find Charlies closed. After all, it *was* 7:30! Charlie was long-since home, sitting on the couch in his jammies watching a Cardinals game on television.

Dover's taverns were more than a place to drink. They were old-world social gathering places where strangers became friends. Friends became enemies and, before the night was finished, went back to being friends again. Our great beer halls provided a welcoming atmosphere where relationships were reinforced, sometimes reinforcement coming in the form of simply buying the next round. (Bodily contact between Dover Men was quite restricted. Relationship reinforcement was never accompanied with a hug. Hand shake, maybe. But never, not ever, a hug!) New-world problems were debated, and disagreements resolved (mostly without incident). Occasionally, some stranger just passing through town stopped in for a beer at one of Dover's taverns. They walked in not knowing anyone, but if they didn't screw up and ask for a Budweiser, they soon found themselves surrounded by five or six new best friends.

And if they bought a round—they'd be family.

FRECKLES

Lucy and Desi. Peanut butter and Jelly. Fibber McGee and Molly. Little boys and Dogs. Some combinations are just meant to be. This collection of well-embellished boyhood memories would be incomplete without a tale about my first love—Freckles. I poured every ounce of affection in my little-boy heart into Freckles. You'll have to wait a few chapters to read about my misadventures when I transferred those affections to my *second* love.

Freckles was *my* dog. My hairless sisters and sweaty brothers would try to claim her as their dog. Or, at minimum, our *family* dog. But her affections were all mine. Her dog DNA was a curious recipe: four parts cocker spaniel, two parts rat terrier, and one part of whatever came sniffing around the backyard on the day that her mama went into heat. Most Dover dogs sprang from similar rogue lineages (except the purebreds—the yappy lap dogs old folks locked in their bedrooms so they could hear *Gunsmoke* on TV). Freckles' coat, full-white, half-curly, was cockle-burr Velcro. They'd stick so thick we called her a *cockle* spaniel. She stood about as high as the old man's knees. Except when she pranced around on her hind legs like a circus poodle to panhandle for Doggie Yum-Yums. When the old man came home at night, smelling like Chesterfields and trucks, she was the first one to greet him on the back porch where she sniffed her way all the way up to his crotch. She sniffed everybody's crotch. Two aunts tried (halfheartedly at best) to make her stop. She had a black spot in the middle of her chest about the size of a donut, which led us to believe that the last depositor to her gene pool was Father Hemple's black lab. Oddly, she didn't have a freckle anywhere. So...her name? Who knows. It was a boy-thing.

It was a cold and stormy night... (come on, you didn't think you'd get out of this book without me using that line) when the old man slipped into Mom's kitchen dripping puddles on her linoleum floor. He was cradling a shivering bundle of pink skin in his hands that looked like a baby rat. It was a smelly puppy with barely-open eyes that he found lying on the side of the road. It had just started to rain when pulled his truck over to smack the tail lights with his fist. That's the only way they'd come on. He always said he was going to fix them someday, but as it turned out, I was glad he didn't.

Dad, the maker of metaphors, smiled, "Look kids, it raining puppies and dogs."

I took the peach-fuzz puppy from Dad's hands and held her up to my face. She squeaked. She squirmed. She pissed all over my tee shirt. Then, to set the hook in my little-boy heart, she licked my cheek. That was all it took—game over. Freckles and I bonded like superglue. From that moment on we were inseparable. Well...except at night. Mom would not allow her to curl up at the foot of our three-brother bed and sleep with us. "Proper dogs sleep outside on the porch. Or in a barn," she said. "Dogs don't sleep in *my* house. S'not proper."

Mom knew all kinds of stuff about all kinds of animals. She grew up on gramma's farm. Whenever she had coffee with her friends she liked to say: *You can take the girl out of the country, but you can't take the country out of the girl.* Mom was proud of her heritage and raised us with that same sense of pride. "Never forget your *roots* (rhymes with *puts*)," she always told us.

Two years later, when I was eight, she got pregnant. Freckles…not Mom! Wait a minute, now that I think about it, one of them was usually pregnant. Sometimes both. Anyway, we never knew who the daddy was (this time I am *definitely* referring to Freckles). Like all Dover dogs, Freckles was a dog-whore and did not discriminate when it came to choosing her sexual partners.

Young Freckles was the victim of teen pregnancy (I warned you she didn't discriminate). This would be the first of what would turn out to be many pregnancies in her life. She was barely thirteen human-years old (two dog-years) the first time she came into heat. Old Man Peters used that word—*heat*—when he talked about his coonhounds' lusty behavior. "Women get horney—dogs get heat," he told me one afternoon when we were sitting on his front porch watching one of his bitch coonhounds getting it on with some rascal who sniffed his way into his yard.

In the span of her life she brought 45 or 6 puppies into the world. I wrote em' all down in a tablet I kept in my dresser. Names, birth dates, discriminating features, everything. She dropped six to eight pups at a whack. One summer she actually had a twelve-pup litter and got her picture on the front page of the paper. I horned my way in next to her until the newspaper guy shoved me away and said, "Get 'chass outta the way kid." He grabbed Richie and pushed him next to Freckles. Said Richie was more adorable.

After Freckles weaned her pups, they got to where they gobbled half a bag of puppy chow a day. That's when the old man stepped in and told me it was time to get rid of them. Mom's approach was much more benevolent. She took me in her arms and whispered, "Bill, every mother dreads the day that she has to let go and cut her kids free. Sweetie, Billy honey, those damn puppies gotta go. They're eatin' half my damn grocery budget." So, I became a one-boy adoption agency. I somehow managed to always find a home for her kids. Depending upon their daddy *du jour*, the farmers loved them. Remember, Freckles was two parts rat terrier. If the daddy's DNA didn't dilute those genes too much, they made great rat cops. They kept lots of corn cribs vermin-free. Occasionally some laggard daddy would introduce such a gnarly tangle of genes into the mix they'd be pretty much worthless and just lay under the porch all day. (I always suspected one of Old Man Peters coonhounds whenever that happened.) When they had the rat population under control they chased the chickens around the barnyard. Until they chased one egg-laying, revenue-generating chicken too many.

I was 12 or 13 when Freckles was getting close to the end of her reproductive life cycle. It was right about then that it happened. The old man was out on the back porch gazing at the stars as he fired up the day's first Chesterfield, listening to the birds rustle the sleep from their feathers. He saw her crawling out of the weeds, tail dragging, eyes drooping like Betty Davis. Frazzled and worn out. She had been out running all night with the Dover dog pack. "Knocked up again, ain't ya?" he scolded as she curled up on her stinky rug next to his stinky boots. Somehow the old man could always tell.

Two months later, 63 days to be exact, and…whoops…there they were. The old man was pissed when he got up that morning and saw her laying there in the birth-den she always dug in the back yard. He was right again. In spite of her getting up there in dog years, Freckles actually broke her own record. Thirteen! Cute. Squeaky. Hairless. Blind and pink. Thirteen.

I still had three unadopted puppies left over from her last litter. I had pretty much saturated the Dover puppy market (in spite of having expanded my adoption services all the way to Bill Town) and was having trouble moving product. With three adolescent Freckles look-alikes left over, we now had seventeen dog-mouths to feed. In those days, most Dover moms did not have jobs (like raising their own kid-litters wasn't a job?), so the old man struggled just to keep his eight kids fed on one income. And now this. His thoughts were racing: *Holy shit…* (Whenever the old man's thoughts raced, they always began with that preamble.) *Time they get weaned, they'll inhale a whole sack of puppy chow ever day.*

Two weeks later—Wednesday morning—I was up early as usual. I don't know, was it possible for a little boy to have maternal instincts? Whenever there were newborn puppies squeaking and squirming in the backyard, it was like some sort of mommy-gene switched on and I went into protector mode. I liked to crawl out of bed before anyone got up and go outside to watch Freckles nurse her babies. I tiptoed down the stairs and eased the screen door open, thinking that I could somehow muffle the screech if I pushed slowly. It still sounded like a dying cat—just took longer. Usually they were already going at it, a scrum of puppies slurping their way through breakfast. I sat next to Freckles, still in my jammies, and stroked her head while her ravenous pups tugged on her tits. I wanted to be there to pull the fattest one away and shove the runt in. I had a special place in my heart for that pint-sized outlier. Mr. Stork misread the shipping label the angels stuck on my butt and bumped me up on his delivery schedule. I was born way too early and got tossed into an incubator where Doc Hansen's nurses watched over me much like I watched over that runt.

A swirl of smoke still hovered over the kitchen table. A half-Chesterfield smoldered next to a half-coffee. A greasy egg looked like it had been pushed around on his plate, like the Chesterfield—unfinished. That never happened, especially to the Chesterfield. I looked around—no Dad anywhere. The light in our new indoor bathroom was still on. The old man never left a light *burning*. He must have run out in a hurry. Probably some farmer waiting on a load of rock or dirt or something. I ran out to the backyard to check on Freckles. She had been struggling the last few days to keep her twelve tits filled with enough milk for thirteen babies.

She was gone! Her puppy nursey—empty. Just a scent of puppy sweat and mommy milk.

I searched the back yard thinking maybe she had moved them. She did that sometimes when they started getting crowded. Nothing. I stumbled back to the house to wake Mom up. She'd know. Mom knew everything.

My bare feet barely hit the bottom step when I heard something under the porch. I got down on my belly and pushed the weeds aside. Freckles! Thank God! She must have moved her family under there. I crawled in and waited for my eyes to adjust.

She was all alone, coiled up on the dirt floor. Her chest heaved.

I crept in next to her and cradled her head in my lap. Wet streaks matted the hair under her eyes.

I laid her head back down on the dirt and crawled out to go to the kitchen and get her some water.

As I walked across the porch—I saw it. Dad always had a gunny sack hanging in the corner for the hickory nuts we picked up on Grandpa's farm.

It was gone.

RIDE 'EM PIGBOY

You've no doubt read about cowboys. Watched cowboy movies. Played cowboys and Indians. Probably wore a cowboy hat and had cowboy six-shooters strapped to your fuzzy cowboy chaps.

We had that cowboy stuff in Dover too. Hats, guns, six-shooters. The whole shootin' match. But way more exciting than cowboys and Indians—we had *pigboys*. Let me explain:

You wanna live=You gotta eat. Pretty simple equation isn't it? Like 2+2=4. However, if you look around, it's obvious that we fat-ass Americans extrapolated that equation to absurd levels. We shifted our nutritional needs into obsessive overdrive. Try to shove in front of some fat bastard at your fat-bastard neighborhood smörgåsbord after church on Sunday and you might get trampled. But I digress.

Since we *gotta eat* to satisfy the first part of that equation, it just makes sense that while we're in consumption mode, we might as well shove in some stuff that tastes good. Most of us devour a lot of crap that's not necessarily the healthiest choice we could make. Piles of pasta, dozens of donuts, and mountains of meat. As red-blooded Americans we eat red-blooded meat. Way too much meat (if you believe my cardiologist). Fat-bastard smorgasbord-eating Americans put the *car* in carnivore. There are two basic meat categories: bacon and *other*. Most of us like makin' bacon our number one choice.

So, let's take another look at that simple equation (stay with me...we're almost there): 1. We gotta eat. 2. Red-blooded Americans eat red-blooded meat. 3. The meat to beat is bacon. So, solving our equation like a Pythagorean Theorem—somebody's got to come up with all that bacon.

As you know, bacon doesn't come from Kroger, it comes from pigs. And pigs come from farmers. So there we have it—the missing piece to our puzzle. Our basic meat-need (bacon) is filled by basic providers (farmers). And since our American economy is based on the capitalistic premise that wholesale is king; before all of us fat-bastard neighborhood smörgåsbord retail consumers can wrap our jaws around all that bacon, all those farmer suppliers gotta have a wholesale *middleman*.

Thus, we have our story (see, I told you we'd get there).

In Dover, the pig middleman was Ray, Jr. His father, Ray, Sr., taught him a damn good lesson in life: "Ray, Jr.," he said, "be a middleman." So Ray brokered bacon.

Ray owned the Dover Grain Elevator & Stockyards. When he was building his stockyards, he knew that they had to be adjacent to the Rock Island Railroad Line. You know—for shipping all those pigs to Chicago to be, err, *dispatched*. He shipped a carload of his porkers off to The Windy City every week or so where their destiny awaited: their quick (and mostly humane) conversion to bacon. Since the Rock Island Railroad Line ran right through the center of Dover, that's where Ray put his pig pens.

That centralized location worked out pretty good for Ray. But not so much for Dover folks. When the prevailing westerlies blew through our backyards and backdoors, we were blasted with essence of pig. You'll probably remember that old idiom: *One man's trash is another man's treasure.* Well, folks complained a lot about his lots: *Ray, the whole damn town smells like pig shit.* His comeback (and I swear this is true): *Smells like money to me.*

Over the years, Ray became very successful. His business expanded right along with his waist line and his hog lots. Hundreds of fully-fattened, market-ready hogs lounged around all day in the Dover Grain Elevator & Stockyards, Inc. (You catch that Inc.? Ray's wife thought of that while she was painting the new sign above his newly renovated office that had an inside toilet and everything. She saw that Inc. thing in the July issue of the *National Grain Elevator & Stockyards Journal* and thought it looked cute.)

They had nothing better to do but #1. Digest and #2. Defecate. Then, after they wallowed around in #2. for a while, get up, eat some more, and do 2. all over again. Pretty much an endless cycle. Every pig in Ray's pens was a self-contained digestion factory, perfectly designed to convert corn to poop. He held his pigs until market conditions were just *right*. Which meant that they stayed in Ray's shit salon until he squeezed every penny out of them that a middleman could squeeze.

For us, the Dover Grain Elevator & Stockyards, Inc became a major source of after-school and all-day-Saturday entertainment. Other kids played baseball and basketball. But Riker, the Deuter Brothers, Mickey, Gary the new guy, and I— the Dukes of Danger, the Emperors of Exploitation, the Pharaohs of Fun—we figured out a whole 'nother use for Ray's pigs.

PIG RODEO!!

We were dorkin' around the stockyards with our BB guns one Saturday morning shooting the blackbirds that always flocked in to feast on the lavish free lunch courtesy of Ray's grain spillage. Milo saw it first. One of the pigs, for no apparent reason (to us anyway), climbed up on the back of another one. We were still ignorant of the birds and bees stuff because our chicken-shit dads were too terrified to touch the subject.

After watching that pig wiggle around on top of the other one several times, it became obvious (to Milo anyway) that he must be trying to ride her. Peculiar, we thought, how the boy pig smiled when he finally got up there and hung on to the girl pig's back with his front legs. It looked like it was fun. Wait—did somebody say *fun*? Well, right there, that was all she wrote. BINGO! Pig Rodeo was born.

Arnie, as you might recall, was our risk taker. He always threw the first rock at a yet-unbroken window. Lit the first fart. Shot the first BB. So naturally he stepped up for the first ride. He and Milo had a pony that their dad claimed he had "found" in a road ditch on the way home after his day shift at the tractor plant. (The old man found puppies. Mr. Deuter "found" ponies.) Arnie rode that little pony everywhere, but his legs were longer than the little pony's, so he dragged his boots in the dirt. He reasoned that riding a pig couldn't be any harder than riding a pony. Little did he know that he was about to be taken to school by a 280-pound pissed-off porker.

He jumped down from the fence while we hung on the top rail to watch. He boxed his steed into a corner with the least amount of pig poop piled up. He stood his ground as he stared into her beady eyes. She stared into Arnie's beady eyes. She dared him to make a move. Arnie's boy-machismo kicked in as he exploded in a flurry of arms and legs and ran at her screaming like one of my sisters when I stuffed her dolly's head into our commode. When he had her cornered he threw an arm around her neck, straddled her back, and spurred her flanks. That sow squealed like the hound of hell breaking away from Santa. (No, wait!—*Satan*. Damn dyslexia.) In pig-speak it must have been sheer terror because the other 37 pigs in the pen squealed back. Mob mentality took over and they stampeded like some sort of pig apocalypse. Arnie wobbled like a rag doll atop that behemoth. He hung on for six or seven seconds until she decided that it was time for them to terminate their relationship. *Plop!*

Arnie laid there like a corpse. Nary a muscle twitched. Was he hurt? Did he break his neck? Did he have any loose change in his pockets? What I am sure was at most a minute seemed like hours. Finally, he popped up. A chocolate-covered champ, smiling from ear to ear. "Gotcha," he laughed at us.

We were laughing so hard, nobody heard him. *Ray, Jr.*! He bounded (well, as much as an old fat man could bound) from his office. He had heard his sows screaming and was coming for us; shaking his cane in the air, "You little shits get your butts outta there. You gonna kill my pigs."

We scrambled, leaving Arnie to fend for himself. We tumbled into the ditch alongside the Rock Island Railroad tracks and laughed until our sides hurt. Ray burned every ounce of energy he could muster to mount his blustery attack and only made it about half-way to the pens before he petered out. Satisfied that he scared the bejesus out of us, he wobbled back to the comfort of his newly renovated office (with an inside toilet and everything) and fell (literally) back into his three-wheeled office chair and opened his fourth morning bottle of Mountain Dew.

Like cockroaches after the basement light has been shut off, we scrambled back to the pens to see what had become of Arnie. We climbed to the top of the fence and scanned the pens.

Where the heck was he? We were about to climb down and probe the poop with some sharp sticks when, once again, he rose from the muck. It dawned on him that since he was already covered with pig poop anyway, he might as well close his eyes and lay back down. Ray never saw him.

After that incident, we fine-tuned our game plan. We gave Richie a tin whistle and posted him behind some feed sacks outside Ray's newly renovated office. If Ray so much as rattled the doorknob, Richie blew his whistle and scrambled back under the feed sacks while we scrambled like those cockroaches I was telling you about. Ray stepped outside his office door, wobbled a few seconds as he cocked his head towards the pens with his hands cupped behind his hard-of-hearing ears. When he saw that all was quiet in his pens, he retreated to the comfort of his three-wheeler and fell (again, literally) into it, satisfied that his pigs had probably been spooked by some tractor backfire.

Life was good. We rodeod three, sometimes four nights a week after school. Saturday afternoons were our favorite. Ray would be riveted to the radio listening to his favorite team, the Nebraska Cornhuskers, lose another football game. (The favorite football team of every Grain Elevator & Stockyards, Inc. operator from Minnesota to Missouri was, of course, the Cornhuskers. Everybody knows that.)

We got to be pretty darn good at it, too. Milo held the title of *Champeen Pig Rider of the World*. He could stick a ride like a PBR bronc buster. One Saturday he hung on for almost three whole minutes—his personal best. Three minutes! As far as I know, his record still stands. We never knew what Ray did with that sow. She sort of just laid there, blowing mud bubbles with her snot-covered snout.

I pretty much sucked at pig riding. I hung on for 15, sometimes 20 seconds. My personal best was 35. And that was only because she pinned my leg against the fence and I couldn't get off. That pig and I screamed in two-part harmony just like my sisters when I pissed off two of them and stuffed both of their dollies' heads into our commode.

Richie continued to watch and whistle and duck. We continued to ride and hoot and duck. The pigs continued to squeal and scream. And Ray—he continued to wobble and drink Mountain Dews. It got to where he knew we had him beat, so he'd just reach over and rattle his new door and mutter, "Get ch'asses outta there." Didn't even bother to shout anymore.

Everything was going along about as perfectly as anything we emperors of exploitation had ever exploited. Even better than when we scammed Mr. Robick for a three-cent pop bottle deposit five or six times with the same bottle. Pig Rodeo consumed our lives. All those endless hours in our fort, lighting farts and rifling through the brassier section in the JC Penney catalog became passé.

Life was good.

One sad day, it all came crashing down. Ray figured out that he could fetch higher prices for his hogs after we rode them to near-exhaustion. I know, that sounds counterintuitive as hell. But here's what happened: America was just beginning to go lean. Fat was out. In those days, before the advent of today's mega hog lots, with their ag-science approach to lean swine production, pigs pretty much ate whatever the farmer threw at them. Table scraps, dead chickens, after-birth (boy-talk for calf placenta). After those pigs lounged in the barnyard mud all day, eating after-birth and dead chickens, fat piled on in thick layers.

Their bacon was laced with the greasy white stuff. That's why it tasted so damn good.

Thanks to all of our riding and all of their screams and all their running around, Ray's hogs burned fat like a YMCA gym rat jacked up on steroids. Sitting there in his three-wheeler one afternoon, reading all about this emerging dietary trend in *National Grain Elevator & Stockyards Journal*, Ray, Jr. figured it all out. Dollar signs flashed in his eyes. His pigs would fetch a premium price if they were trimmed down to a relatively svelte 220 pounds. And so, there we have it. He hired us to be Professional Pigboys. That's what he called us—*Pigboys*. One word. He explained to us that if *cowboys* rode *cows* (which actually, they didn't, but we blindly bought into his false dichotomy anyway), then it only followed that boys who rode pigs should be called Pigboys.

After Ray's monumental insight we not only had access to unlimited riding, we were being *paid* to do it. Not much, mind you, but enough for a post-rodeo RC Cola and bag of Planters Peanuts. No more Richie with his whistle. No more getting run off by Ray with his hickory-stick cane. No more rolling in the Rock Island Railroad ditches. No more laughing 'til our ribs hurt. No more adventure. No more emperors of exploitation.

No more fun.

Alas, our pig party pretty much petered out. It was a hard lesson in life to learn but one I never forgot: *Gratification is inversely proportional to legitimacy.*

OUTHOUSES

Evolution is a funny thing. Slow as hell, but still...funny. Our ancestors weren't exactly the sharpest sticks in the jungle, but they somehow went from inscribing rudimentary scratches in the river mud to inscribing rudimentary communications on anything they could find. Their simple pictograms on smoky cave walls (the first graffiti) led to entire alphabets. By passing large hunks of roasted lizards around that newfangled thing they called *fire,* and actually sharing, they developed early forms of social skills. Animalistic grunts and groans eventually led to verbal skills. But the big daddy of all evolutionary achievements happened when mankind made the big leap forward and refined his toileting skills. Before all those written and social skills evolved, cavemen ran around doing pretty much whatever they wanted. They slept whenever they wanted. They procreated (usually with another hominid) whenever they wanted. And they ate dead, roasted lizards whenever they wanted. And when they over-gorged on way too much dead, roasted lizard and the urge hit them, they stopped their running around doing whatever they wanted and got down on their haunches. As they squatted in the river mud to read the latest news, they made a few animalistic grunts and groans and plopped their *stuff* right into the mud. It laid there for months like a booby trap. Finally, after a few millennia of reckless plopping and with all those booby traps piling up everywhere, he figured out a more salubrious means of *elimination.* Anthropologists and neurologists agree that it was about the same time that the piriform cortex developed in Neanderthals' brains and gave them an acute sense of smell (pretty obvious, right?). Had it not been for that evolutionary breakthrough, maybe our stop-drop-and-go behavior would have stuck with us (and stuck *to* us). Imagine the challenges we'd have today negotiating a maze of *"drop zones"* in malls, shopping centers, and city parks. To say nothing of having our olfactories overwhelmed.

As mankind evolved, various forms of sanitary facilities evolved right along with him. Arthroslogger Man (from the Greek ἄρθρον *arthro*-knuckle, and the Latin *sloggus*-to drag), or more commonly called Knuckle-Dragger Man, dug holes next to their cave entrance and invented the first pit toilet. Early villages built open-ditch sewer systems. And then, just when we thought we were doing pretty good, using those pit toilets and open-ditch sewers, along come the French to set us back a few generations. During the Renaissance, French folks evacuated their bladders and bowels in a corner of the room of some fancy palace. I shit you not.

It's only within the last generation or two that we democratized pooping for the masses and invented something we all take for granted today—the indoor toilet. But before we could have indoor toilets we had to have had commodes. The very first commode was invented by the 19th century British plumber, Sir Thomas (John) Crapper. I shit you not. It was his commode that begat the indoor toilet.

Before we get into this poop epistle, let's define a few terms. Somewhere in that evolutionary cycle, between Knuckle-Dragger Man's pit toilets and John Crapper's commodes, an intermediate technology was developed. In Dover, most folks called them outhouses. Some—shithouses. Still others simply dropped the "house" part and called them shitters. After WWII, GI's returning from the bare essentials of army life to the bare essentials of Dover life called them latrines. Most Dover Folks called them outhouses. Just one word thank you—outhouses.

Every home in Dover had a backyard, the splendor of which was testament to its owner's commitment to the preservation of vintage automobiles. Dover Men cherished their long-since "retired" family cars and parked them in archival rows behind their homes. No matter how neatly they positioned their tributes to Detroit, the owner was always careful to leave enough separation between them to provide an unobstructed, straightaway path to the outhouse. Winding paths were avoided at all costs in the event that some family member had a need that was, shall we say, of an urgent nature. Any impediment to his or her hastened steps was certain to result in catastrophe.

Back then, backyard outhouses were as common as today's front yard ornaments. Outhouses were certainly more functional than some cute concrete kid with his pants pulled down pissing on the petunias. In outhouses, real people with *their* pants pulled down could piss on whatever it was that was down there.

Milo, Arnie, Mickey, Riker, Richie and I, who you know as The Gang of Five (I know, that makes six but we rarely counted Richie), invented "opportunities" for mischief in everything from spitting to farting. Dover's outhouses were ripe (sorry) for exploitation, so we created a whole new *opportunity*—outhouse tipping.

Outhouses were not well engineered or, as far as that goes, very well built. The roofs leaked, the doors creaked, and wind blew in through the wall cracks and up the user cracks. But more than anything, the most critical reason that our newly-discovered exploitation worked so well—outhouses were not anchored to a foundation. Mostly because there was, well, no foundation to anchor them to. The simple wooden structure straddled over a hand-dug hole. Sometimes that hole was dug a little too large and, after a heavy rain, erosion made some of them tilt (not unlike the Leaning Tower of Pisa). Vacationers passing through Dover oftentimes stopped to take pictures.

Those were our favorite targets. The *leaners*. With minimal effort, we sent them toppling over in the starry, starry night like dominos. We got dang good at it too. Under the cover of darkness, we never got caught.

Then, one night…

Old Man Peters eventually got fed up with our shithouse shenanigans and decided to do something about it. On average, we tipped his outhouse once a month. Sometimes twice. It was such an easy target. Flimsy and wobbly at best. You have to understand that Old Man Peters wasn't much of a carpenter. In the hierarchy of Dover outhouses, his cobbled-together leaner wasn't much more than a half-rotted relic. It was so shabby even the rats wouldn't infest it.

It was a hot July night. Dover was suffering one of its annual summer heat waves, and the outhouses were percolating. Old Man Peters always went to bed early which made him even more vulnerable. We crouched in the bushes across the street waiting for the flickering black-and-white light from his flickering black & white 19-inch Philco to stop flickering. 8:30—*Gunsmoke* was over. Once again Marshall Dillon saved

Miss Kitty from the bad guys, and for his gallant efforts, all he got was a wink and a warm beer. You could see in Marshall Dillon's eyes that he was looking for something a lot warmer than just a warm beer from Miss Kitty. The old man always said it was just like real life. Mom always smacked his bald taterhead whenever he said that.

Reassured that Miss Kitty's chastity survived another episode and Marshall Dillon's pleasures were once again deferred (in his naiveté Old Man Peters never realized that the 1950's FCC censors pretty much guaranteed that no other outcome? was never gonna happen), he clicked off the Philco and crawled into bed. If we moved quickly we'd have his outhouse tipped, make a clean escape, and still have enough time for our post-tipping celebration with an RC Cola up at Tilleys before our nine o'clock curfew. Did you notice those two little words back there—*clean escape*? Remember them.

We approached our target in silence. Old Man Peters' coonhounds were half-blind and full-stupid; but they did one thing better than any other dog in Dover—they smelled *everything*. Staying downwind from them was crucial. Milo led the assault. His uncanny navigational skills were unaffected by darkness. *Or so we thought*. The coordinates of Old Man Peters potty were etched in his brain like a GPS. *Or so we thought*. We spread out like invading Huns across Old Man Peters backyard and rendezvoused behind Milo. Somehow, something just didn't feel right. Milo held up his hand and we halted. He sniffed the air like he had seen Old Man Peters coonhounds do. Where was it? That distinctive bouquet? That *eau de toilette*?

Nothing. Milo didn't detect so much as a whiff! He wondered if Old Man Peters had maybe hired Old Man Kowolski to bring his manure spreader into town for his shit-pit's annual cleaning. He took a few more steps and stopped. *Sniff.* Nope. Something wasn't right. Were his coordinates somehow screwed up? Was his step-count wrong? It should have been just a few more steps. Did he miss something? He waved his hand and motioned for us to proceed.

Then—he had it! The scent finally floated through the night air like a gypsy moth and fluttered around his nostrils. He figured it was only two, maybe three steps away. He gave the signal and we lined up in attack mode. Shoulder-to-shoulder.

One more step. Just one more…

Ker-Plop!! Actually *Ker-Plop* x 6. (Well 5, I forgot…we rarely counted Richie.)

After the initial shock wore off, we struggled to affect our extraction. I'll try to be delicate here, but if you have ever had your foot stuck in mud and tried to pull it out…that's what it sounded like. That sickening sucking sound. The more we squirmed…the more sucking. We wallowed until we were knee deep. Richie was up to his hips. Just when we thought there was no hope and we'd be stuck there until the sun came up, Arnie managed to pull himself free and jerked the rest of us out.

Mom, whose keen sense of smell was exceeded only by her keen sense of hearing, was hanging on the wall phone in her kitchen yacking about the upcoming Saint Boniface bazaar when she sniffed Richie and me trying to sneak in. She left the receiver dangling with Aunt Ev still ranting about Old Man Peters coonhounds and ran to the back door. She shoved us right back out onto the porch with her broom and locked the door. We spent the whole night out there. Freckles, who was already curled up on her rug, ran off into the woods after she caught a whiff of Richie as he tried to lay down next to her.

The next morning, like a prison guard sliding a food tray under a cell door, Mom shoved a couple bowls of oatmeal out the door. After we ate, we went out in the backyard and started to spray ourselves off with the garden hose. Mom yelled out the window and told us to do that over by her tomato plants. You know...fertilizer. After we finished fertilizing her tomatoes, we sloshed in our wet pants and shoes (we had tossed our tee shirts in the burn barrel) back to the crime scene to do a little reconnoitering. Maybe figure out what the heck went wrong.

Remember how I was telling you that Old Man Peters finally got fed up with our shenanigans and decided to do something about it? In an effort to thwart our efforts, he had moved his outhouse a few feet south and covered the pit with some rotten boards. Then he threw some dirt and weeds over his snare. Turns out that Milo's internal GPS really was spot-on.

That little fiasco pretty much brought our outhouse tipping to a halt. Riker had read in a magazine somewhere how we could do the same thing with cows.

****

Most of Dover's outhouses were two-holers. No one knows what bizarre logic led to their development. Taking a dump was not considered by most folks to be a social experience. Maybe for some aboriginal tribesmen squatting side-by side in the jungle posing for a National Geographic photographer. But not in Dover. The repugnance associated with excrement pretty much ensured that getting rid of it was a private affair. For all the years that I braved the horrors of our outhouse, I cannot remember ever sharing that second hole with anyone. Nor had I been invited to share it with anyone else. It was commonly accepted practice to dance around outside the door and risk a mishap rather than share that second hole. I mention all this by way of introduction because, as we get close to the end of this chapter, you'll want to remember it.

Eventually the march of modernity lifted Dover out of the plumbing Dark Ages. The Dawn of the Age of Indoor Toilets arrived. We added a new word to our lexicon: *Bathroom*! Koop, Dover's town mayor, hardware store proprietor, and only plumber, went off to a school somewhere to learn the ins-and-outs of indoor outhouses—err—*bathrooms*. Over the years folks came to trust him for all their plumbing needs. Everything from leaky pipes to seepy drains. So it was only natural that he monopolized the Dover indoor bathroom installations as well. He learned everything there was to know about *commodes*. Another new word. Koop soon cornered the Dover commode market and before long he was…err…*flush* with cash.

Everyone in town had to have one. And they had to have it, by god, *right now*. The icy winter winds, which added a whole 'nother dimension to outhouse pooping, were just around the corner. And folks were getting puckered up (literally) just thinking about it. The old man bribed Koop with a 12-pack of Schlitz to put us on the top of his waiting list. Koop even bumped us ahead of Old Lady Zimmerman. She wanted a pink commode for her bathroom to match her poodle, but the commode factory told Koop that they didn't get many calls for pink commodes so it was on backorder. So it really wasn't the old man's bribe that got us bumped up. Koop kept the 12-pack of Schlitz anyway.

Koop promised the old man we'd be installed by Thanksgiving. The only problem was that Koop promised *everyone* that he'd have them installed by Thanksgiving. He just didn't tell them *which* Thanksgiving.

Koop arrived that blustery November morning (the day before Thanksgiving) with his indoor bathroom installation manual, three tool boxes stuffed with his indoor bathroom plumbing tools that he drug across Mom's just-waxed linoleum floor, and our shiny-new porcelain *commode* still in its cardboard box. He and his hired man threw their coats on Mom's kitchen table and rolled up their sleeves *after* they fired up a couple of Chesterfields that they bummed off the old man. Fortified by the free smokes, they were ready to install our new indoor bathroom. But wait. "Hold yer horses there guys," mom shouted as she came from the kitchen with a fresh percolator of Folgers. "Not'll I pour ya's a couple a cups of Folgers." Nothing ever happened in Mom's house until folks were properly caffeinated with fresh Folgers. After a third "warm-up" (*insurance* Mom called it) and another free Chesterfield, the old man showed Koop and his hired man Mom's recently-vacated pantry that still reeked of onions and sauerkraut. "This room right here," he told them, "thisus where I want my inside outhouse." By now we had our new word memorized, so all of us kids shouted, "*Bathroom*, Dad. It's called a bathroom."

Dad was boneheaded. He said *traditionalist*. But truth was—he was boneheaded. Traditionalists like him, he said, couldn't be expected to abandon their traditional ways every time something new came rolling down the pike. Some things were sacred to him and deserved our respect. Things like wearing a gray suit and matching fedora to Mass on Sunday. Or not letting that new-fangled thing they called "pizza" on his supper table (said it was just a fad and would never last). Or public displays of affection. Getting all soft and mushy was *verboten* as his starch-stiff German mother insisted. He did screw up once however and actually kissed Mom in front of us kids.

The old man had stayed up most of the night. Apparently this strange new concept of an indoor outhouse intimidated the hell out of him. After spending a lifetime *doing his business* outside in a two-holer, this "hole" indoor toilet thing required some careful pondering. He pondered it all night. For the old man pondering and Chesterfields went hand-in-hand, so by sunup his bedside ashtray was overflowing. He had everything pretty well figured out by the time he led the well-caffeinated Koop and his hired man into what had been Mom's pantry,.

Mr. Traditionalist walked over to the back wall of what had been Mom's former pantry. He turned around and spread both of his arms wide like he was one of Bob Barker's babes on *The Price is Right*. He looked straight at Koop. This was important.

The old man grinned and pointed at two black X's he had marked on the floor when he jumped out of bed in the middle of the night. It was either the ninth or tenth Chesterfield that triggered his *Eureka!* inspiration.

"Right here and right here. Thisus where I want both of our *commodes*."

A TRAIN RUNS THROUGH IT

Just where the heck *is* Dover? You've probably figured out by now that it's not in Alaska or Hawaii. So that leaves 48 states where our not-quite-mythical town is parked. Well, make that 47. It's pretty obvious that it's not in Mississippi. Dover folks thought *y'all* was a small boat. Dover folks wouldn't know a *y'all*, (which can be expressed either as a second person singular or a second person plural pronoun) if they heard it. Everyone knows it's *youse guize*. So, here's the deal—Dover's map location really doesn't matter. It's a reflection of a time and place where I grew up. Give it a chance to grab a foothold in your mind and it will spring to life. If you help it to germinate in a few unused, but nonetheless fertile, neurons (you probably have a couple lying fallow), it'll take root. After you lay this book down and kick back in the old La-Z-Boy with two fingers of Jack to reflect on *your* life and *your* Dover, perhaps some of what you read here will resonate. Collectively, much of what we all experience—what we see, what we do, what we think—is universal. You say *tomato,* I say *two-mah-toe* and all that…

As you read and we find a common chord (which we surely will), maybe, if we're both lucky, we *will* work the whole thing out. And that will make both of us smile.

Take another look at that chapter title up there. Go ahead…I'll wait. Okay, in case your eyes won't make the trip, it says *A Train Runs Through It*. Just so you're not confused, let's get it out there: Dover is not in Montana. A *river* does not run through it. The title of Norman Maclean's magnificent novella, with its stunning scenery, colorful characters, and tragic plot sounds much more poetic than the title to this chapter. But don't let that deceive you into thinking that life in Dover was any less stunning, colorful, or tragic (<u>you</u> fall in up to <u>your</u> knees in an outhouse pit and tell me if that isn't tragic). So what if there's not a river rippling with icy water and teeming with trout running through Dover? So what if it's a Rock Island train running through it? So what if it's lumbering through, gasping for breath? Protesting as it scuttles over every *clickety-clack* rail with its judgement-day air-horns blasting, "Get the hell out of the way?" And its rusty boxcars bulging with hogs, corn, and freshly-built tractors? Just as Gramma appeared to be a chicken-slaughtering, murderous old woman—first impressions can be deceiving.

   The Rock Island Railroad locomotives ripped through Dover three times a day and twice on Sunday. Every baby sleeping in every crib in every home in Dover was jolted awake by those blasting horns as the diesel beast rampaged through town. The Rock Island Railroad dispatcher, howling with glee in his traffic control center somewhere in Hell, sent an extra one on Christmas just to piss folks off. Whenever a Dover mom heard one of those beasts approaching, she tip-toed into the nursery and folded her hands over her sleeping little angel's ears in a futile attempt to mitigate the impending disaster. She gazed heavenward imploring the Cosmic Commander of Everything: *Please Lord, just this once, don't let the little shit wake up.* Her supplications were futile.

Federal DOT regulations stipulated that the engineer was required to blast one loooooong and two short *audible signals* when approaching a road or street. It was obvious that the Rock Island Railroad dispatcher assigned the Dover route to his most sadistic engineers. They started blasting those *audible signals* a mile away, and continued, uninterrupted, until they shot out the other end of town. After 130 box cars, three diesel locomotives, and a caboose rumbled through, the ground stopped quaking and the Dover dogs stopped howling. But Dover moms did *not* stop cursing. And Dover babies did *not* stop screaming. They were just getting warmed up. An hour or so later, after all those little shits settled down, calm was restored. Loaded diapers were changed. The whole drama would play out again in less than three hours.

No one knew when the Rock Island Railroad started running through Dover. I asked Old Man Peters once and he just looked at me, spit downwind (thank God) and said, "Right after them tracks was laid, I 'spect." While Old Man Peters wasn't the sharpest knife in the drawer, his wit and wisdom had a way of cutting to the core of just about everything. While most of his responses consisted of one, sometimes two words, whenever he bothered to string together six or seven syllables, you needed to listen. A great truth was about to be revealed. Homespun philosophy that was equal parts revelation and bullshit. It was your job to sort it all out.

The best anyone can figure out, it was during the early part of the last century that the Rock Island Railroad Company bought up the right-of-way and laid down their tracks. It was probably on the edge of town back then, but folks being folks, they started building houses on both sides. Eventually, those shiny steel rails split the growing village right down the middle. The have-nots lived on one side. More have-nots on the other. Sadly (no…make that *fortunately*), bigger-house and shinier-car affluence never bothered with Dover Folks.

The Rock Island Railroad crews constructed the rail beds with such extreme engineering standards, they will probably endure until the end of time. They will stand as a testament to American ingenuity long after the Great Pyramids crumble, the Great Wall of China topples, and the McDonalds Golden Arches fall (I wonder…will they call them The Great Fallen Arches?) The rock-solid rail beds were constructed of, well—solid rock. Oak ties were laid and steel rails spiked. Have you ever notice how poets embellish those rails as *Ribbons of Steel*? Ribbons my ass. They were big-ass bars of Pittsburg steel forged in Hell. Trenches were trenched on both sides which the engineers called *drainage ditches*. Drainage ditches my ass. They were big-ass canyons deep enough to stop God from ever pulling off another stunt like He did to that guy in the Old Testament. Moses or Noah or something.

Those *drainage ditches* that paralleled the *ribbons* were—since we're getting all biblical here I'll put it in Dante-speak—*Paradiso*. Milo, Arnie, Riker, Mickey, and I played army in them like most other kids played baseball. We slaughtered entire civilizations, including their women and babies. Our ruthlessness did not discriminate. We left a path of destruction that would have left the Goths and Visigoths consumed with envy. But not the Huns. We never played Huns. We were Dover boys and we never, not ever, called each other Hun.

What would the Rock Island engineers have done without those majestic Grand Canyon ditches that shouldered their equally-majestic locomotives? More importantly, what would we have done without them? They fired our imaginations and drained our energy on Saturday afternoons as we mired in their mud, slaughtering babies and women. But more than just draining our Saturday afternoon energy, they also *drained* something else.

Let me explain:

Dover is flat. Kitchen-table flat. After the Pleistocene glaciers melted away, Dover had been scrapped as smooth as a dinner plate. (But not *my* dinner plate. Anything that smelled or looked like a vegetable always got left behind. Well...if I outlasted Mom.) The only topographical feature that could remotely be described as a hill was the Dover town dump next to Old Man Peters house. Since Dover was so damn flat, an infrastructure dilemma developed. Remember how Dover home owners paid Koop to install their new-fangled indoor toilets? Well, if you have a new-fangled indoor toilet you haftahave a new-fangled septic tank too. Being a bunch of cheap asses, Dover folks balked at shelling out yet more money for the new-fangled septic tanks. Most Dover residents regarded the septic tank as a frivolous expense. They told Koop to plumb the poop-chute pipes directly into their basement drains. Koop wouldn't have it. He stood firm and reminded everyone that state sanitary regulations had to be followed and he, by god, would put in their septics or no new-fangled indoor toilet.

Thus, we have that infrastructure dilemma I was talking about. In order for a septic tank to function properly, it needs a *properly* constructed drainage field. Well then (stay with me now), here we go. Those Pleistocene glaciers that scraped Dover flatter than a dinner plate left more clay than dirt behind after they melted. Koop said that all that clay wouldn't *perk* (whatever that meant). So enterprising (read: cheap) Dover home owners dreamed up an alternative solution (read: scheme) to their perkless drainage field issues. The Rock Island Railroad drainage ditches!

Trenches were trenched, ditches were dug, and channels were channeled. After the whole shootin' match was cobbled together, every home in Dover had their septic tank connected to that catacomb of culverts, pipes, and gutters. They ditched all of that septic tank discharge right into the Rock Island Railroad ditches.

After all those countless connections were completed and Dover's newly-minted commodes flushed all day and half the night, the Rock Island Railroad ditches filled to the brim with the homeowners' err...*byproducts*. Keep in mind that damn near every house in Dover was packed to the rafters with kids. A mere five or six offspring indicated that the parents of that household probably suffered from infertility. It was only after seven or eight little shits blessed their lives that most parents threw in the towel. What I'm trying to tell you here is that no matter how well Koop installed the septic tank, regardless of its capacity and factory-specified flow rate, it could not *digest* (that's what septic tanks do—they digest) all the byproducts from so many users. It doesn't require much of an imagination to visualize what happened to that undigested *byproduct* as it overflowed through the network of discharge pipes. After it meandered through subterranean Dover and emerged at its ultimate destination (I'll try to be delicate here), the bigger *chunks,* well, they bobbed around on the surface of the brim-full Rock Island Railroad ditches.

That pretty much put a halt to our war games.

It didn't take us long. We invented our next Big Thing. Coin Crush! Long before some Silicon Valley billionaire geek created Candy Crush, we created Coin Crush. We "borrowed" pennies and nickels from the jar the old man hid under his underwear in his dresser drawer. Whenever Richie and I heard an approaching train (remember the engineer started blasting a mile out, so we had a pretty good heads-up), we rushed to the old man's stash and borrowed just *one* nickel and *one* penny (so he wouldn't notice) and ran like hell down to the tracks. When we arrived, usually well ahead of the train, sometimes just in time if Richie dropped his penny, I got one of the *steel ribbons* and Richie got the other. We laid our penny and nickel on the rail. As the train approached with its engineer doing his best to get all those babies and mommies stirred up, we crouched among the cattails and copperheads. We wiped (what we hoped was) mud from our fingers and stuck them in our ears. Twenty or thirty minutes later, after 130 boxcars rumbled off into the sunset, we popped our fingers out of our ears and rushed back to the tracks to see who won. The Coin Crush winner was determined by whoever's penny or nickel stretched the longest or was smashed into the most unusual shape. Richie had the record—his penny stretched 6½ inches. My nickels didn't stretch so far. They usually squashed into some sort of glob. Apparently copper was stretchier.

If there was a Coin Crush Hall of Fame, what happened on that hot August afternoon would be nothing short of stellar. We heard the approaching train and copped our coins from the under the old man's underwear, and arrived in plenty of time to carefully position them on the rails (for once Richie didn't drop his penny). After the box cars rumbled into the sunset we popped our fingers out of our ears and ran to the tracks. We gasped as we looked down in amazement. *Holy Shit!* My nickel somehow survived the onslaught of those steel wheels with little, if any, globbiness. This happened occasionally. They would blend into the rail and take on the most peculiar shape. So, there it was. My nickel—shimmering in the sun. It...it looked just like the face of Jesus on the front page of our Baltimore Catechism!

Well, sort of...

We ran back home to show Mom. I laid it on the kitchen table while Richie ran out to the garden to get her. She walked in with her apron sagging with tomatoes. Well, that was all she wrote. She took one look at it and passed out. After Richie and I helped her get up off the floor dripping with tomato slime, she put a hankie on her head (like she did when she went to Mass), and made the sign of the cross. She was so overwhelmed with religious ecstasy that she ran to her bedroom and rifled through her dresser drawer to get her rosary from under *her* underwear. *It's a miracle*, she said. She told us not to touch it. *It's a holy relic*, she said. As she ran out the screen door she turned back and yelled at us to go upstairs and change our pants. You know—those railroad ditches.

She ran across the street to the Saint Boniface rectory and beat on Father Hempel's front door like some Holy Land pilgrim on fire with fervor for Jesus or some saint or something. Father Hemple was just sitting down to his supper with his housekeeper, Melinda. Mom, overcome like the holy rollers we watched on television eating snakes and jumping around like teenage girls at an Elvis concert, quivered on his doorstep. Her chest heaving. Panting. She fumbled for words and finally blurted: *Jesus...Miracle...Holy...* Father Hemple, who enjoyed eating even more than hearing confessions, did something totally out of character. He threw down his fork and abandoned his meat loaf and mashed potatoes. He and Melinda tripped over each other as they chased after Mom who had already broke and was running back across the street.

Richie and I were standing in the kitchen in our underwear (our other jeans were dirty too) staring at my Jesus-nickel. Mom rushed in with Father Hempel and Melinda in tow. When Mom ran out and warned us not to touch it, Richie, of course, fiddled around with it and accidentally pushed it into some ketchup still puddled on the table from last night's supper. He didn't have time to wipe Jesus' face.

Father Hempel took out his hankie and wiped off the precious blood, being careful not to touch it with his bare fingers. He held my Jesus-nickel up to the light bulb that dangled over our kitchen table. "Holy Mother of God!" he exclaimed. Melinda stepped up from behind him to have a look. "Holy Mother of God!" she exclaimed. By now Mom was cowering next to the fridge. Her chest heaving. Panting. Her fervor at fever pitch. Now she could go to her grave knowing that her two little boys would one day join her in heaven. Surely this was a sign from God himself. A miracle.

Eternal bliss was in the bag!

Oftentimes, railroad tracks have a cruel and prejudicial way of segregating communities. Social status, ethnicity, or skin color dictate on which side you belong. But not so in Dover. Our tracks were simply a place to play army, drain your septic tank, or find Jesus. It was a corridor through which the great wheels of commerce flowed, fueling vitality to a strong and vibrant nation. Dover was only too proud to do its part.

If only all those screaming babies would shut the hell up.

TWIN & TWIN

Twins. Nearly everyone knows one. Well, actually, two. Paired People. Binary Beings. Many are plain old garden-variety twins. They look different. They act different. Oftentimes, they're the opposite sex. The only thing they have in common is an egg. Or is it a sperm? Look, this isn't a zygote conference. If you need to know the ins and outs about how twins are made (pun intended), go to your Google machine and search *twins*. Depending upon what Google digs up, you might learn a whole lot more about a Minnesota baseball team than the reproductive process.

In addition to the garden-variety twins mentioned above, there are those *other* twins. Mirror-image twins. The ones commonly referred to as identical. Here's where things start to get a little freaky. Some crazy zygotic combination conjures them: one egg…two sperms, or two eggs…one sperm. Over easy. Scrambled. I don't know.

Not only do they look alike and act alike (just like Republicans), they even think alike. And when they want to really mess with you—they even dress alike. Sometimes right down to the underwear. We had twins in our family. A boy and a girl that we referred to as our brother and sister. They tried that. The dressing alike thing. Mom had to put a stop to it sometime around their sixteenth birthday when our brother got to liking his twin sister's dresses a little too much. We never told our sister, but her clothes looked better on him. Especially her color-coordinated blouse and skirt outfits with the cute little pumps.

Dover had its very own special set of identical twins. Well, they didn't exactly live in Dover. They had homes in a nearby village-ette about a mile or two west of our comparatively sprawling metroplex. By the time I knew them they were getting on up there in age. From the perspective of a twelve year-old, they were old men. But, as you shall see, they couldn't have been *that* old. They were *so* identical they even got cavities in the same tooth at the same time. Mother Nature called them to the outhouse that straddled the property line between their houses every morning at 8:15. They were the only two folks that ever used a two-holer simultaneously. And like a lot of twins (and us too-long married folks), they oftentimes completed each other's sentences. But the twins took it one step further—they completed each other's cussing too. If one said *son of a...* The other said *bitch*. If one of them said *ass...* The other said *hole*. If one said *mother...* Well, you get the idea.

It was said that they came into the world side-by-side, not one behind the other. It was as though they already knew they were twins and didn't want to upstage the other. Doc Hansen said it was the first time he had ever heard newborns cry in two-part harmony. After extensive reconstructive surgery, their mother sought revenge for their little delivery fiasco that would plague them for the rest of their lives. She gave the little boogers confusing names like Tim and Jim. Maybe Bob and Rob? Bill and Phil? No matter, no one in Dover could remember their names anyway. Since Dover Men had absolutely no clue if the twin they were talking to was Bob or Rob, Tim or Jim, or whatever, they defaulted to the safety of simplicity. They called both of them *Twin*. I am not making this up. As long as I knew Bob or Rob or Tim or Jim or whatever, they were both called Twin.

This arrangement proved to be mutually beneficial to the Dover Men as well as Twin and Twin. Dover Men didn't have to waste their time trying to figure out which one of these incredibly identical men they were addressing. If Twin or Twin stumbled into Tilleys for a beer (stumbling *into* Tilleys was an option—stumbling out was mandatory), some Dover Man would shout, "Hey Twin." Then Twin, or his brother Twin, would smile back at them and answer, "Yeah?"

This also proved to be a most agreeable solution for Twin and Twin. They were so identical in speech, appearance, mannerism, and thought that there was at least a 50/50 chance that, if some clueless Dover Man used their Christian name, he would have been dead wrong. So, rather than waste *their* time correcting that wild-ass guess, Twin and Twin were quite satisfied with just being called Twin. You getting all this?

You're probably asking yourselves, "What the heck did Dover Men do when Twin and Twin appeared together?" Dover Men despised duplicity. They lived in a mostly black and white world. Boy…girl. Democrat…Republican. Ford…Chevy. No gray areas please. So when Dover Men encountered ambiguity they defaulted to conflict avoidance. If Twin and Twin were seen together, Dover Men simply ignored them and went on about their business as though they were not even there. After suffering a few episodes of being ostracized, Twin and Twin decided that they'd never again be seen in Dover together. An elegant solution if there ever was one. A singular Twin was greeted warmly, slapped on the back, and most importantly, set up with a complimentary beer. Dover Men loved to shoot the shit with either one. The Twin *de jure* would just sit their sipping his free beer and when the Dover Man stopped his shit-shooting long enough to catch his breath, the Twin would just smile and say, "Yeah!"

About the time when they were in their forties, maybe fifties (I was nondiscriminatory twelve-year-old, so it could'a been thirties), loneliness was beginning to take a toll on the unmarried pair. Their sullenness betrayed them as they sat in Tilleys. They were less engaged. Mirthless. Their once-enthusiastic *yeah*, somehow hollow. Their iconic response less and less coupled with their iconic smile. During an afternoon shade-tree discussion in their backyard, sipping on a couple six-packs of Schlitz (which they actually bought themselves), they stumbled upon the source of their desolation: *bachelorhood*! They, by God, had been alone way too long and decided right then and there that they needed something more in their lives. Nothing as superficial as a newer used car or a bigger black n'white TV. They needed something that would add more focus to the mind-numbing routine of their day-to-day existence. Something to refresh their spirit. You know—something to light their fuse.

They had just started in on the second six-pack when Twin thought of it first and, of course, Twin agreed. They, by God, they needed a *woman*. Or so they thought. If they had a woman (well—women), all of their problems would be over. Their minds would be focused. Their spirits refreshed. Their fuses, errr…lit. Oh, if they had only realized what a complicated rabbit hole they were about to go down. Sometimes insights that accompany a second six-pack of Schlitz are best ignored.

Twin told the old man one night up at Tilleys in an uncharacteristic, damn-near full sentence, that his dagger had lost its swagger. He told the old man how he and his brother had reached a cathartic moment in their lives and they were pretty sure they wanted a woman. Then, when he thought about that dagger thing, he corrected himself and said that they actually *needed* a woman. The old man bought him another beer and shared his thoughts on women and sex. It was a pretty short conversation.

Incredibly, the next morning…they were *gone!* Twin and Twin! Just like that. They disappeared. Completely off the radar. Their '57 Chevy was not seen on Dover's main street with whoever's turn it was for the never-missed 7 a.m. coffee shop rendezvous. Whatever had happened to Twin and Twin? Dover's gossip-mongers lit up the party lines like a Christmas tree.

After he had his little sex-talk with the old man that night, Twin was too…err…*stimulated* to go to sleep so he sat at his kitchen table and read the paper. He saw an ad about a twin convention in, where else, the Twin Cities. Up there in Minnesota somewhere. Overcome with yet more *stimulation*, he ran next door and hauled his brother's ass out of bed to tell him about it. Right there, with both men bubbling with all that *stimulation*, they decided that, bright and early the next morning, they backed the Bel Air out of whose ever driveway it was parked in, filled it up with oil, check the gas, and drove up to the Twin Cities. Maybe, they thought, just maybe (please, God) they'd get lucky and come away with a couple of female women.

By the time they checked in late that afternoon, the Ramada Inn was already rockin'. The hotel manager, desperate for his year-end bonus that was tied to his budget, saved the thirty-two-foot canvas banner from last summer's American League playoffs that read: WELCOME TWINS FANS. He told the maintenance guy to take a spray can of black paint and X-out

FANS. The twins argued with the kid who tried to carry their shared suitcase to their shared hotel room that had (what else), shared twin beds. Twin was suspicious that the kid would run off with their shared suitcase when he caught the kid eyeballin' his expensive K-Mart rayon tie sticking out of the side. Even though it was only Friday night, Twin told Twin, "What the heck, they ain't no extra charge for a bath. And they got the hot water already heated up." They flipped to see who'd go first.

They cleaned up pretty good considering that the second Twin used the first Twin's hot water (*don't want them other folks runnin' out of hot water*). They admired themselves in the steamy Ramada Inn indoor toilet mirror, resplendent in their K-Mart black rayon sports jackets, black rayon slacks, black Sunday shoes, and white socks with cheap elastic that had pretty much given out when they wore them to church last Easter and caused them to bunch up around their ankles after a few steps. They walked in side-by-side and made a grand entrance to the grand *soiree* in the Ramada's grand ballroom. I didn't mention this earlier, but Twin and Twin were actually pretty good-looking men. Well, make that not-so-bad-looking men when they remembered to wash and comb their hair. Chiseled chins even—when they remembered to shave. As they walked in, tugging at their bunched-up white socks, they flashed their once-iconic smiles, which were already making a comeback. (Anticipation will do that to a man who's been single way too long.) Their pearly-whites sparkled—when they remembered to brush.

They spied a couple of gals standing alone next to the beer and little-weenie-on-a-toothpick table. Carrie and Sherrie Perry. That's what it said on their peel-'em-and-stick-'em *Hello, My Name Is* nametag. Under their names they scrawled, with impeccable cursive, *Yes...I'm single*. Even though that should have been quite obvious.

It was love at first and second sight. Twin and Twin took just one look (each) at Carrie and Sherrie and were smitten. Carrie claimed that she was swept off her feet. Sherrie later said that her sister was half-drunk and had tripped on some balloons.

Like Twin and Twin, Carrie and Sherrie were exact copies. And, just like Twin and Twin, they had mirror-image mannerisms. They laughed the same. Coughed the same. Even held their weenie-on-a-toothpick the same. Things really started clicking when they discovered that the four of them drank the same beer. Yes indeed, God himself would surely be smiling down on them from heaven tonight.

As luck would have it, the promoters of the Twin City Twin Convention had a Rent-A-Reverend all rented up and ready to go right there in the Ramada Inn Hotel grand ballroom. He was some non-denominational preacher that the cost-conscious hotel manager found for the promoters in the Twin City Yellow Pages. Apparently love at first and second sights was a pretty common occurrence at the Twin City Twin Convention, and on-the-spot marriages were a regular thing. After several dozen little-weenies-on-a-toothpick and at least that many cans of Hamm's that Twin and his brother Twin took turns fishing out of the ice water so Carrie and Sherrie Perry wouldn't have to get their dainty little hands cold; it was all over. The google-eyed foursome stumbled to the little room that the promoters fixed up like some cheesy Las Vegas wedding chapel, complete with blinking Christmas lights. Twin and Twin peeled five-spots from their billfolds and handed them to the Rent-A-Rev. When he asked if they would *"blah-blah-blah for better or worse until death do youse part,"* they responded (in harmony), *"Yeah."*

Initially, married life made quite a change in the boys. They were outgoing and engaged. They actually shaved. Not just on Saturday night either. Wednesday too! They went about town with a certain spring in their step. Dover Men chided them up at Tilleys, "Hey Twin, how's the little woman? Ya gittin' any?" The brothers' snickers suggested that everything was okay in their knickers. A little swagger was back in their little daggers.

But then, something changed... (Don't say that I didn't try warn you about second-six-pack insights.)

Six months into the marriage and even the pretty-much insensitive Dover Men sensed it. Twin and Twin were becoming quite sullen and were once again retreating from their social responsibilities.

The old man saw it too and decided that he, by God, would find out what the heck was going on. He pulled up a stool next to Twin up at Tilleys one Wednesday night and bought him a beer. He had spoken with the other Twin, at least he thought it was the other Twin, on the previous Tuesday night but didn't get much out of him. The old man hoped that Wednesday-Night Twin would open up.

Sure enough, two beers in and he spilled his guts. He told the old man how he and his brother, Tuesday-Night Twin, had started to regret their quickie marriages. With the promise of a third beer hanging in the air, Wednesday-Night Twin went on to say that they had maybe been a little too hasty. No, he said, it wasn't that they were disillusioned so much by the actual marriage thing. Marriage itself was just fine, thank you. It was the *selection* they each had made. Tuesday-Night Twin had taken Carrie for better and worse, while Wednesday-Night Twin had taken Sherrie. So here they were, only six months after taking their vows from the Rent-A-Rev and they realized that the *worse* part of the equation exceeded the *better* part. They had made a mutual mistake and began to covet the other's seemingly more compatible wife. If only they had taken time to get to know Carrie and Sherrie better. A few more weenies-on-a-toothpick. A few more Hamm's. Maybe they would have paired off differently.

Well, I got to hand it to the old man. Just like that, sitting there at Tilley's like some high-dollar marriage counselor, he worked out the perfect solution. Sometimes, not often mind you, but sometimes, lightning would strike the old man. He'd get an insight, a hunch, or a revelation that was damn near genius. (Maybe I was a little generous with that *genius* thing.)

He bought Twin that teaser third beer and laid out his lightning-strike insight. He told Twin to sneak across the backyard and tip-toe into his brother's bedroom the next morning and drag his ass out of bed. He cautioned him to be careful not to wake Carrie or Sherrie or whoever it was in bed with him. The old man told him to take his brother out for a ride in their '57 Chevy and while they were cruising around, tell him to pack his bags after supper that night while Carrie or Sherrie settled into her La-Z-Boy for an evening of *Hee-Haw* reruns. Meanwhile, he would do the same. Later that night, when the girls were sleeping and their snore-count hit a rhythmic three-per-minute, Twin and Twin would slide out of their beds and meet up in the woods out *behind* their adjacent houses. Right next to the outhouse that straddled the property line.

Okay, you ready for this? Stay with me. The most crucial part of old man's plan: he told Twin that he and his brother were to trade places. Flip-flop. The old switcheroo. He told Twin to take his packed bag and sneak into his brother's house. And his brother would, well, by now you get the idea. They were such exact copies, such clones, such mirror-images that Carrie and Sherrie wouldn't suspect a thing. *Nada*.

Voilà—problem solved.

Twin took a sip and looked at my damn-near-genius old man and grinned, "*Yeah.*"

Well, Tilley, remember Tilley? She was perched behind her bar eavesdropping on Twin and the old man, pretending to ponder 37 down in her crossword puzzle. Just as their conversation was getting to that crucial part about the old switcheroo, a bunch of *dammits* and *sombitches* came from the back room and she had to get up and waddle back to the pool table and knock a couple of heads together. Two well-oiled Dover Men were cussin' about scratching on the eight-ball. Well, before she waddled off, the last thing she heard was Twin whining about his incompatibility issue with Carrie or Sherrie.

After she opened for business the next morning she couldn't stop thinking about the part she actually *did* overhear about Twin's fading affections for Carrie or Sherrie. It bothered her so much she stayed awake half the night worrying about it and working on that damn crossword puzzle (she never did figure out *37 down*). So, Tilley being Tilley, she couldn't let things like that go without offering assistance (*sticking her fat ass in*, the old man always said). So later, after the *Price is Right* was over and she had the newspaper properly rifled, she reached around and fumbled for the telephone next to the jar of pickled pigs' feet and called Carrie first.

In her well-rehearsed lines, Tilley told Carrie how distraught Twin was and how he was beginning to have, umm...*designs* on her sister Sherrie. She told Carrie how she had *accidentally* heard Twin telling the old man that maybe they had rushed things a little too much. How he and his brother enjoyed their marital bliss; but it was just that, looking back, well, that maybe they should have selected their spouses with a little more discretion.

Well, you can imagine the shock on Tilley's face when Carrie told her that she and Sherrie were having the same doubts. They too were questioning the compatibility thing and were beginning to covet each other's "Twinie."

Apparently lightning can strike twice. Right there—in the middle of that conversation—it ripped through the clouds and struck Tilley like it had struck the old man. **BAM!** Tilley came up with the same plan that the old man had revealed to Twin the night before. The part she didn't hear.

Like some unfolding Greek drama, the plot, as they say, thickened. Tilley told Carrie to meet Sherrie that night with all their stuff packed. But not out *behind* the house…out in *front*. Tilley didn't want the defenseless girls (even though their corpulence overwhelmed their scrawny-ass "Twinies") getting bit in the ass by some roving Dover dog pilfering their garbage.

Several weeks later, Friday night rolled around and the regulars were getting a head start on the weekend up at Tilleys. Twin was being well attended to as he sat on his stool down at the end of the bar. It was pretty obvious that his swagger was back in his dagger. His iconic grin attended every slap on the back as Dover Men stacked cans of Hamm's in front of him. Yes indeed, Twin, and it's probably safe to assume that the other brother Twin, were back. Life was good.

After Dad went through his Ford, Chevy, and liberal Democrat rants with a couple of Dover Men, he walked down a few stools and sat next to Twin. He fired up a Chesterfield and, as he blew that first drag into the overhead cloud, asked Twin, "Everything going okay with the (wink, wink) *new* wife?"

Twin grinned at the old man, "*Yeah!*"

NO ONE KNEW...

Memories are lifeboats that float across our bows as we plow through the sea of life. Often we bob up and down in swells of joy. Happy little waves of recollections. But sometimes we cling to our little lifeboats with unease, swept up in a swirling vortex of anxiety. Suffering some past misdeeds or misspoken words that were not carefully considered. Tangled films of adult sagas, adolescent angst, and childhood tales replay in the swing and swirl of our neurons like some vandalized Hollywood movie vault.

My favorite memories, and yours too I suspect, are those that we conjure from our childhood. Early-time reflections of innocence and virtue. I carry mine around in my noggin like a Holloway's All-Day Sucker and take them out from time to time and relish a few licks. Those honeyed remains of my little-boy past renew my *joie de vivre*. Life's sweetness savored and cherished.

Sometimes that sweetness gets a little sticky. What's this—a little dirt? Some grit stuck on my sugary recollection? Neuropsychologists tell us that our brains have the ability to mitigate the raw emotions associated with our more troublesome memories and stuff them in our brain's backlot where they stay dormant for years. It's called suppression. It allows us to bob up and down in our happy little lifeboats unfettered by certain *uncomfortable* realities. But occasionally, something shakes lose. Dirt, grit, and all. As I strolled through my warehouse of memories, taking inventory in preparation for the telling of my lavishly-embellished recollections, this not-so-pleasant fragment surfaced, demanding to be dusted off and confessed.

No one likes to do this.

Where the hell did they come from? Those words echoed all around Dover. Up at Tilleys, the gas stations, Clete's barber shop, and both grocery stores. Even after church, those words were mumbled with a fresh Chesterfield in one hand and a bible in the other. They fell from lips that were not smiling. Inflected with scorn more than inquiry. *You see 'em all hangin' on that truck? They don't look like us. Don't even sound like us.*

They were different.

They were Mexicans.

No one knew where they came from. I suppose most folks *assumed* that they migrated from Mexico. Pretty logical, right? That, I am sure now, is exactly what Dover folks did. They *assumed*. (Why ask when assuming is so easy?) Their assumption was no more correct than supposing that Dover folks came from Germany, or Poland, or Ireland. After all, big chunks of our DNA testify to those origins. Never mind that our migrations took place generations ago. Never mind that theirs might have too. Right?

No one knew how many there were. Like backyard mushrooms that sprouted in the spring, they popped up overnight. Thirty? Fifty? *Must be a hunnert*, some thought. It really didn't matter. Even if it had been only four or five, the reaction would have been the same. They were different. Suspicion was in order. They needed to be watched.

No one knew how they happened to settle into the abandoned schoolhouse up on the hill. Consolidation had cleaned out its classrooms years ago. The old wreck of a building stood in a weedy field, looking all Bates Hotel-like. It was too big and too expensive to demolish for the school board's budget. Half of the windows had been reduced to shards by rock-throwing little bastards like me. So it just stood there for years, waiting…waiting. The city fathers took a crack at it, but it was too much of a money pit to be repurposed as a community center for a handful of forgetful seniors to argue over poorly-played hands of euchre and drink free coffee all day. But yet somehow, that abandoned schoolhouse proved to be just right for thirty, forty, *prob'ly a hunnert Mess-kuns.*

No one knew what they did. One thing was certain however, they were not Steinbeck's migrant farm laborers. This was not the dust bowl days of the '30's. And it sure the hell wasn't Salinas. Our farms were pretty much mechanized. Tractors, plows, combines. Big steel implements to plant, cultivate, and harvest our crops. Backbreaking manual labor had long ago been supplanted by the engineering marvels of John Deere and International Harvester. But they all piled into the back of that truck every morning (*you see 'em hangin' all over the sides of it?*) to go off and do *something* to support their families that stayed behind, crowded into those empty classrooms all day. It was *assumed* (there's that word again) that they worked in some factory somewhere.

No one knew that Mexico was the Ivory Soap of Catholicism—99 and 44/100% pure faith in Jesus. No mention of that in our Baltimore Catechism. It had been that way since the Jesuit missionaries waded ashore in the 1500's to convert those hungry souls to the Catholic Church (whether they needed it or not). Our half-empty Saint Boniface pews should have been simmering with smiling brown faces at Sunday morning Mass. We should have been inspired by their devotional humility. We should have been moved by their spiritual dedication to our faith. We should have embraced their prayerfulness. We should have welcomed them into our church family. (Our silent stares didn't offer much of an incentive for them to return.) We should have opened our hearts to them in celebration of Jesus. We should have... We should have...

Here's where my memory gets a little sticky. Accurate or not, this is how I remember that place: I befriended a boy about my age. Name? Don't know. I remember being invited into his home and being shocked. Shocked because it wasn't what everyone assumed it was. Even I had preconceived notions about the shit hole I was sure I would find. But it *wasn't* overflowing with garbage. There *weren't* piles of rotting food everywhere. *They* said that the rooms were teaming with snotty babies. They weren't. *They* said the place was crawling with vermin. But it wasn't that way at all. It was clean. I remember that. Everything in its place. Dirty brown faces didn't stare at me with starving eyes and runny noses. They were not living in some sort of third-world squalor. It was peaceful and it was happy and it was simmering with joyful life. I was taken in with warmth and acceptance. Exotic aromas swirled through the halls, the likes of which this meat-and-taters blue-eyed German boy had never experienced.

No one knew how the hell it happened. Or so the story goes. Somehow it burned down one rainy night in October. Rumors raced through Dover: *Probably one of them little gas cook stoves. More likely a rat chewed the cord on a record player that bellered that La Cucaracha racket every night.* Some said they did it to themselves. *Drank too much tequila and burned it down*, some said, eyes darting around seeking reassurance. *Pretty damn sure. They all got out (didn't they?). Nobody got hurt(did they?).*

Next morning they all cleared out. *Poof!* They had nowhere else to go. Not in Dover. Closed minds and closed hearts hid behind closed (and lately—locked) doors. So…they left.

No one knew where they came from. *No one knew* where they went.

No one knew…
No one cared.

ALL-DAY SUCKER

> *Tinker, tailor, soldier, sailor,*
> *rich man, poor man, beggar man, thief.*
> Old English Nursery Rhyme

Whoever you are. Whatever you do. Whether you are a tinker, tailor, or even a sailor, that old English nursery rhyme speaks to the universal nature of man. We share common beliefs and truths no matter our culture, religion, or race. But somehow *Competition* hitched a ride on that cosmic force that binds us together. Maybe it was never intended for us to go there. Seems like it's a misplaced mote that tends to separate all of us tinkers, tailors, and sailors rather than join. Divides rather than unifies.

But I, like many, think that it's good for us: *Competition*. Everybody loves a contest. It's just in us. Something in our DNA drives us to see how we measure up. I can sew a suit better or sail a boat better than you. We love nothing more than to take up the gauntlet and sally forth to engage our rivals.

Competition takes many forms: sports—score the most points. Education—earn the most A's. Careers—make the most money.

Politics—get the most PAC money, err...votes. Or sex—get the most...! Whoa, you're on your own with that one.

Competitiveness is a collective expression of the ego. Old Joe Stalin and Vlad Lenin tried to drive society down the road of collectivism but kicked folks' competitive spirits off the bus. You see how that pretty much fizzled. When our cutthroat spirit is suppressed, we as a society wallow in the *shallows and miseries.* I think Roger Bacon penned that. (Or was it Kevin?)

So, whether we are climb-highers, or run-fasters; just beating that other bastard is what drives us down that road. No one enjoyed that ride more than me. For me, competing was easy. It was the winning part that was hard. As you already know, Milo Deuter was my best buddy in the entire galaxy. Because he was *not* an actual brother, we were actual friends. But, as you will see, competition wedged between us one time and I battled my brother from another mother. Problem was—I sucked more than him.

Formal competition jumped into my life at a very tender age. Before it showed up I was already competing for not-so-formal things: being first in line for the bathroom, jumping into bed first so I wouldn't have to sleep in the middle, or rolling up in my blanket on the floor closest to the Philco to watch cartoons on Saturday morning. However, none of these experiences would prepare me for my ultimate challenge in the summer of my eighth year.

As I mentioned in an earlier chapter, Mr. Robick stocked an entire section of his three-aisle grocery store with candy. Beautiful, sugar-soaked, cavity-causing candy. Dover mothers suspected that he received kickbacks from Doctor Mohlar, his brother-in-law dentist in Bill Town. For Dover boys, the two most feared events in our lives were trembling in Doctor

Mohlar's dentist chair on Saturday afternoons and trembling in Father Hemple's confessional on Saturday nights. In spite of all that trembling, we didn't stop eating all that candy and we sure as hell didn't stop sinning (as much as eight-year-olds can actually sin).

Mr. Robick was highly regarded by the Midwest Regional Candy Distributor, Inc. in Chicago. Over the years his enviable candy sales earned him their prestigious five-star rating. They further honored him by naming one of their warehouses after him. Route salesman competed to have his store in their territory. Over the years countless sales reps had their kids' college degrees financed by the commissions they earned from the Dover kids' candy consumption.

Mr. Robick's candy sales were lagging during the summer of '55. The UAW called for a strike at the tractor factory where many Dover Men were wage-slaves. High on the list of their grievances was their dinner breaks. (Remember…in Dover there was no such thing as "lunch." What you ate at noon was dinner. Everybody knows that.) The workers, for whatever reason, had the notion that they should be entitled to actually stop building tractors at noon and eat their dinner. Apparently management didn't see it that way. "Let 'em eat on their own time," the plant manager was quoted in the newspaper. So they struck. With substantially reduced family incomes, Dover mothers were hard-pressed to stretch their strike-pay budgets to cover the weekly essentials like beer and cigarettes. There was barely enough left over for meat and potatoes. Candy got reduced from a major food group to a rare treat.

As the UAW strike continued, management hunkered down. The union hunkered back. The tractor factory plant manager said that he'd stay hunkered until he broke the union's back. Well, as you can imagine, the Midwest Regional Candy Distributor, Inc. suffered a corresponding loss of revenue brought about by all that hunkering and Dover's economic austerity program. For the first time in the history of the company, the candy folks faced cutbacks. Mr. Robick shuddered when his sales rep pulled up in his new Mercedes one day and walked in to tell him that the 25,000-square-foot Robick Warehouse # Five might have to be shuttered.

Things eventually got so grim that the CEO of the Midwest Regional Candy Distributor, Inc. was forced to sell his six-bedroom "cottage" on an island off the coast of Florida that his wife and kids used for their vacation home. But not the six-bedroom "beach bungalow" on an island off the coast of Bangor, Maine that his girlfriend and her kids used for their vacations. (Whenever the CEO took unexpected trips away from the office, he told his staff he was *going to Bangor*. They never caught on that Bangor was a transitive verb.) In a last-ditch effort to rescue Robick Warehouse # Five from being shuttered, the desperate Midwest Regional Candy Distributor, Inc. CEO did what all desperate CEO's do when they're in panic mode. He called a staff meeting.

Midway through the meeting, after the sales guy who worked the Omaha route snarfed the last Long John, the CEO read a suggestion he had plagiarized from the employee cafeteria suggestion box. He stood up next to the now-empty donut box and proudly announced that he had come up with a plan to rescue their sagging candy sales. According to the pilfered plan the Midwest Regional Candy Distributor, Inc. would sponsor a contest. The grand prize winner would be awarded a giant-ass sucker (he thought calling it *giant-ass* was cute and would erase any doubts about the originality of his plan). And not just any giant-ass sucker mind you, but the ever-popular, much-coveted, American Dental Association award-winning single largest cavity generator in the whole world—Holloway's All-Day Sucker! And by *giant-ass* he meant canoe-paddle humongous.

The company's accounting supervisor, perhaps a little too enthusiastically rubbing the thigh of the Accounting Department's secretary under the table in the back of the board room, raised his other not-so-busy hand to challenge the CEO's plagiarized plan. He was the only employee at the Midwest Regional Candy Distributor, Inc. who didn't kiss the CEO's ass because he had actual photos of the CEO in a rather compromising position in the executive restroom with the Customer Service Department's secretary. (Apparently The Mid Midwest Regional Candy Distributor, Inc.'s personnel office hired a lot of loose Department secretaries.) He was about to enlighten the CEO that his plan pretty much sucked given the current financial status of the broke-ass Dover families. And when families are broke-ass, big-ass suckers are the last thing on their list of priorities. He was about to let go of his secretary's thigh so she could lay a transparency on the overhead projector showing the dismal quarterly sales results when some other department flunky rushed in from the company cafeteria shouting the breaking news he had just heard on Channel 7. Dover's UAW strike was finally over. The tractor factory plant manager unhunkered first and threw in the towel. The Dover Men would get their damn dinner break.

With fresh paychecks on the horizon for all the Dover dads, the company's accounting supervisor sat down and went back to work on that thigh. The contest was on.

I know you've been waiting for this, so let's get right to it. Here, at last, is where I enter the picture. Remember how I started out this chapter telling you how this would be the first *formal* competition in my life? I had already demonstrated how much I sucked at such trivial competitions like baseball, spelling, and collecting Kellogg's cereal box tops for the starving pagans in China. Or was it Africa? No matter, all that was meaningless crap compared to this. This was big. This was a major competitive event that would capture the attention of everyone in Dover. And most importantly, now, at last, I would shine! Maybe.

Mr. Robick cleared half of aisle three (the candy aisle) to make room for the special contest display that the marketing folks at the Midwest Regional Candy Distributor, Inc. designed. It was resplendent with blinking lights and loudspeakers that blasted music and public service announcements all day long about the Holloway's All-Day Sucker contest. And right there in the middle of the display, cradled on a custom-built stainless-steel rack that the Midwest Regional Candy Distributor, Inc. industrial engineers had welded together, was *The Sucker*. The Holloway's All-Day Sucker. Secured with cables, chains and padlocks (so it wouldn't, you know, somehow walk off). One look—that's all it took—one look and I knew that *The Sucker* would be mine. I coveted that thing with every ounce of my being. I had confession-grade covetousness. As I gazed upon that caramel canoe paddle I dreamed of how it would take me months of sucking to finish it off. I planned to suck on that thing everywhere I went. At the supper table, watching cartoons on Saturday morning curled up on the linoleum floor in front of the Philco, and lying in bed at night as I and another brother (I forget his name) jammed jammie-clad Richie in the middle. As Richie wiggled around watching me, I wouldn't give that little shit so much as a lick.

I made up my mind right there that I would be the Dover kid who'd take it home. Negotiating a trade agreement with Satan was not out of the question. I visualized my picture on the cover of the August issue of the Journal of the National Confectioners Association, and maybe (dream big Dad always said), maybe even Life Magazine.

The contest rules were pretty simple, really. Competition would extend for one month. At the end of that time, the Dover kid who had collected more Holloway's All-Day Sucker wrappers than any other Dover kid would win. That's it. No posters to color, no essays to write, and no stupid questions to memorize. Just bring in the most wrappers. And therein was the genius of the Midwest Regional Candy Distributor, Inc. CEO's plagiarized plan: by the end of the contest we Dover kids would have purchased enough Holloway's All-Day Suckers to finance not only *The Sucker,* but also keep the bankers from foreclosing on his girlfriend's beach bungalow off the coast of Bangor. I walked out of Robicks with the resolve of Nixon. I, by God, would win. I wasn't sure how I'd do it; but I was going to win. It was my destiny.

It all started out innocently enough. I gathered my pop bottle money, my meager house-chore money, and the money I got from selling my Kellogg's cereal box tops to the Dueter brothers so they'd get a pissy little gold star behind their names on Sister Mary Larry's *Save the Starving China Kids* cardboard tally poster. (She wouldn't work on the Africa Kids until first we had all the China Kids fattened up.) I walked into Robicks and bought however many Holloway All-Day Suckers my pocketful of pennies and nickels would afford. The contest was only into its second week when I experienced a financial windfall. I crawled through the weeds under the bleachers at the softball park one hot afternoon scrounging for more pennies and nickels. I pushed a rusty beer can aside and there it was—a whole quarter! To an eight-year-old Dover boy, a whole quarter was a butt-load of money. It was heavy and weighed way more than a dime. And it could buy so many wonderful things. That quarter, if my math was right, would net me five Holloway's

All-Day Suckers. Maybe six if Mr. Robick gave me a volume discount.

I kept my wrapper-stash in the bedroom closet that I shared with my brothers. Three of them (I forget their names), including Richie, were my hated competitors. The other brother was too little to compete. He had only recently been evicted from the crib that Mom and Dad had permanently set up in their bedroom until the day (thank God) when Mom would hit menopause. It (we assumed it was a boy but wasn't no way any of us would look under that diaper) was transferred upstairs to our barracks. The diaper-clad little shit was always getting into my stuff, so I had to hide everything.

I made a treasure chest out of an old shoe box and took a Magic Marker and scrawled *Bill's Trezshur Chess —Keep Out* on the top. After I sucked my suckers, I licked the sticky off the wrappers and stuffed them inside. I wasn't sure that the "Keep Out" part would stop my snoopy brothers if they found it so I hid my *Trezshur Chess* under the one thing that I knew would scare the bejesus out of them—a stack of school books. It couldn't have been more secure if it had been locked up in Fort Knox.

Three weeks into the competition and my treasure chest wasn't so much as half-full. Just one week remained and I had only ten and a half wrappers. Yes, you read that right—ten and a *half*. I found half of a wrapper in the Dover town dump behind Old Man Peters house. I almost tossed it back, but at the last minute , licked off the sticky residue and kept it, thinking that the other half would somehow show up. And when the winds of fate blew it my way, I'd stick the two halves together with a little scotch tape and have me a whole wrapper. It might even be the one that would carry me on to victory. And if that other half never showed up? Well, anyone who had entertained the notion of holding trade negotiations with Satan certainly was not opposed to lying. Pretty pathetic, but even at that tender age I had already been introduced to the fine art of deception. I would tell Mr. Robick at the counting ceremony with all the newspaper and magazine photographers milling about, that my dog ate the other half. How could he not allow that? Surely some photographer from the National Journal of Candy Distributor, Inc.'s magazine, waiting to snap his Pulitzer Prize-winning cover shot for the August edition, would shout at Mr. Robick, "Hey asshole, give the kid a break." Surely that would shame him into letting me include it. Surely.

I was beginning to get nervous about my odds of winning. I waited until my brothers wore themselves out playing grab-ass under our *eau de piss* sheets and had fallen asleep. I crawled out of bed and went to the closet and slammed the door behind me. (Crap! I forgot. This wasn't one of my scare-the-shit-out-of-Richie nights.) I flicked on my flashlight and inventoried my dismal wrapper-stash and realized that I had to do something or I'd be eating Milo's dust—again. Earlier that day, during afternoon recess at Saint Boniface, I overheard him bragging to Riker and Mickey that he was already up to twenty-one wrappers. *Twenty-one? How could that be? Twenty-effing-one!* (I wasn't even allowed to *think* the f-word. Effing was all I got). *How did he buy that effing many? Did his effing grandpa die and leave his dad an effing fortune? Did his mom win the effing Publishers Clearing House Sweepstakes? No effing kid in Dover got that effing much allowance.* Whenever I got really effing nervous I did a lot of effing.

I fell asleep and dreamed that Milo was standing at the podium with Mr. Robick. He was wearing his little-boy suit, little-boy black tie, and little-boy black wingtips. His ruby-red cuff links sparkled in the exploding flashbulbs. A sea of reporters were shouting questions: *What was your winning strategy? How did you ever collect so many Holloway's All-Day Sucker Wrappers and beat Billy Rausch? Did your grandpa die and leave your dad an effing fortune? What will you do with your grand prize? Do you plan to share it with your brothers and sisters?* Milo looked at them batting his curly eyelashes as his ruby-cuff links sparkled and answered, "Yes." BAM. Right there I knew it was a dream. *No* kid in Dover ever shared anything with their brothers and sisters.

The next morning as I lay in bed wide awake…lightning struck. Was it my incredible genius? Nocturnal inspiration driven by desperation? Essence of pee? No matter. Right there in the early-morning tangle of sheets and pillows I spawned my grand strategy. *Gramma*!

Grandmothers come in various degrees of benevolence. One gramma might be a warm, loving, Rockwellian matriarch who'd give you anything. Even the shirt off her back. Except real grammas don't wear shirts. Everybody knows that. The other gramma is a Wicked Witch of the East gramma who'd rather feast on Toto's liver than give her grandkids even a stale cracker. My gramma was the former. And she was a pushover. All I had to do was comb my hair, wash my face, and put on a mostly-clean shirt before I went to see her. If I smelled sweaty enough, blinked my *oh-gosh-Gramma* baby blues enough, and contorted my face into something that resembled those little plastic angels nested at the little plastic feet of the Blessed Virgin Mary that Gramma kept on her hallway table, she'd shove me between her gramma-boobs down by her belly button and smother me with hugs and kisses. With her Listerine-and-coffee breath, she'd coo into my ears. Then, after she released me from her braless hug, she'd look me right in the eye and ask, "What you want this time, kid?"

I rode my bike over to her house later that morning and pounced on her porch. I waited until *The Price Is Right* was over. Hell hath no fury like a gramma without her morning Bob Barker fix. I banged on her door hoping to catch her while she was still on her Barker-high. After we dispensed with our social niceties over an RC Cola and a Moon Pie, I explained my dilemma. I concluded with a well-embellished sense of urgency (intoning what I thought was just the right balance of sincerity and whine). Risking ten extra Hail Mary's from Father Hemple, I lied and told her that I had recently been entertaining suicidal thoughts whenever I contemplated that I might not win *The Sucker*. That got her. I knew how much she hated getting all dressed up in her black dress and putting on a damned bra just to go to a funeral. So she pulled me in close to her well-concealed belly button and asked, "What can I do to help this time, kid?"

I pushed the right-sided one over and looked up, straight into her eyes (like the old man taught me to do whenever I was talking to an adult) and laid it out: "Gramma, you know how you always give us some cheesy card on our birthday with a dollar bill wadded up inside?" I realized immediately that I shouldn't have said "cheesy." Recycled would probably have been better. It was Gramma's practice to take her birthday card back after we opened it and use it for the next grandkid. It wasn't uncommon to get one with at least a dozen scratched-out names on it.

"Uh-huh," she said, ignoring my ill-chosen adjective.

"Well...could you...maybe, you know, sort of give me my wadded-up dollar now?" My heart was racing and I had trouble breathing (the right-side one flopped back). I swallowed hard and went on, "I know my birthday is still ten months away, but...well...I sure could use it now. To win that contest up at

Robicks. I need twenty more Holloway's All-Day Suckers in less than a week to be sure I crush that little shit Milo." That was one word Gramma understood…*crush*. She was the only old lady in the Saint Boniface Old Peoples' Card Club who played for keeps. Cutthroat Euchre she called it. Nobody wanted to be her partner. If someone played the wrong card and caused her to lose a hand, they might lose a hand.

Gramma pondered my words a few seconds and started making motions like she was going to try to stand up. I *HAD* her! I rushed to her side and grabbed her arm and pulled and jerked until she transitioned to a relatively erect posture.

"Let go my arm, kid. Ya tryin' to jerk it off?" she yelled at me. She hobbled into her bedroom to find THE PURSE. The vessel of all things good. A veritable Ark of the Covenant. Deep within its dark and seldom-explored depths, lying there amongst the detritus from four Presidential administrations, she retrieved a crumbly dollar bill the consistency of a dish rag.

She gripped it with clenched fingers. I tugged on it, being careful not to rip it in half. She was still mumbling something when she finally released her iron grip. Before she could stash THE PURSE back under her bed, while it was still in her hands, I decided to go all in. *Nothin' ventured, nothin' got* the old man always said.

"I was wondering, *Dearest Gramma* (was that a little over the top?), how 'bout *we* (the collective pronoun was premeditated), give me next year's dollar too? By then you'll probably have seven or eight brand new grandkids, and *my* dollar won't put such a dent on your fixed income." (Gramma was on Social S'curity. She adored Roosevelt. *Ruse-velt*).

She thought for a moment. My fingers were crossed so hard behind my back, I heard a knuckle crack. *Please Lord*, I whispered to myself, *please, please, please.* I think I even promised Him that I would stop looking at the big-ladies bra section of the JC Penney catalog. I didn't mention the regular-ladies bra section.

She went for it! My cockeyed plan somehow made sense to her as she pondered her long-term financial planning. A future capital expense deferred. Why not?

Her fishing expedition took a little longer this time. She pricked her finger on an *I LIKE IKE* button. She muttered a *sonofabitch* that I wasn't supposed to hear and stuck it in her mouth…her finger, not the button. Undaunted, she continued searching with her unpricked fingers. She finally came up with another dollar bill in a similar condition to its predecessor. I easily ripped it from her now-weakened pricked finger. I bounced off her bed, toppling the seven or eight dolls she had propped against her pillows and ran out like a thief. I was about to jump off her porch steps when I remembered my manners. I stopped, embarrassed at my behavior, and went back into her hallway and shouted past the statue of the Blessed Virgin Mary with the angels nested at her feet—"Thanks."

"Never mind, Sweetie," she shouted back. My name still hadn't come to her. "You go out there and crush that little shit Milo and win that sucker."

I smiled to myself as I rode straightaway to Robicks.

Those two whole dollars netted me forty suckers. Forty yellow and brown wrappers added to my stash of ten and a half. I took out a pad and pencil and wrote the numbers down in a column like Sister Mary Larry taught us in arithmetic class and added them up. *Holy shit!* I said to myself when I saw the total under the little line like Sister Mary Larry had taught us in arithmetic class. That made fifty and a half wrappers! Eat my shorts Milo Deuter. Fifty and a half. Even if you say a dozen Hail Marys you'll never beat that. I could already feel myself basking in the warm glow of the exploding flash bulbs. All those reporters shouting their questions at *me* like they had been taught in journalism school.

It took me the rest of that week to suck those forty Holloway's All-Day Suckers down to their sticks. If I had let them lay around, Richie and those other brothers would have helped themselves. I got up in the pre-dawn darkness and stood on the back porch with the old man. Him sucking on Chesterfields. Me—Holloway's. Every morning I'd have one half-sucked before breakfast. I started back in right after school, took a suck-break while we ate supper, and then got right back on it until the old man shouted at us to get our butts to bed. I laid down Friday night with a bit (okay—hell-of-a) gut ache. But I made my deadline.

It was a glorious Saturday morning. Some of us Dover kids had been lined up since midnight in front of Mr. Robick's store, waiting for him to unlock the screen door. By the time he arrived we were curled up on the sidewalk in eerie silence. Holding our shoe boxes, treasure chests, bread sacks, and rubber-banded bundles of wrappers. 8:37. Right on time. He rattled the little hook on his door and we rallied. We shoved in around him like vultures jockeying for road kill. I caught a couple of sharp elbows in my ribs. I was pretty sure it was Milo. Competition does that. (Remember all that stuff about competition we were talking about way back there in the very first paragraph of this story?) It affects (infects?) adults even more than kids. Best friends are reduced to slaughtering whoever or whatever stands between them and victory.

After we settled down, Mr. and Mrs. Robick started counting wrappers. Some of the little kids had eight, some ten. Richie had four. *Amateurs*, I thought. It would be years before they were ready for the big leagues.

Riker had thirty-one wrappers. Mikey—thirty-six. They stood there grinning like a jackass eating a cactus. Little did they know that the smug expressions on their faces were about to evaporate.

"Fifty wrappers for Milo Deuter," Mr. Robick shouted toward his wife behind the counter. She marked everyone's total with a black Magic Marker on a cardboard scoreboard propped up next to the cash register. Milo hung around the scorecard sniffing his freshly scrawled score until Mrs. Robick kicked him away. We never figured out what the folks at the Black Magic Marker factory put in those things. All we knew was that we liked the way they made our heads buzz.

"Beat that, idiot," Milo mumbled as he strutted by and popped me in the ribs again. "*Fifty!*"

I gritted my teeth and looked him straight in the eye. *Oh, don't you worry about that*, I thought to myself. I knew exactly how many wrappers I had. Counted them twice last night before I crawled into bed and once this morning. I knew. But more than that I knew what was coming. *Controversy*. I was sure of it.

I started to sweat.

Like always, I was last. Mr. Robick opened my Trezshur Chess and started counting. His lips were moving. Some kid sneezed and he lost his count and had to start over. Thought I was gonna die. My sweat went from rivulets to rivers.

Finally, Mr. Robick looked up, his lips stopped moving, "Fifty. Billy Rausch has fifty wrappers," he shouted as he stuck a pencil under his white paper hat to scratch his comb-over. His comb-over always itched whenever he got nervous. Like when some Dover mom would catch him with his thumb on the scales. "Folks, it looks like we have us a tie."

My world exploded like the nuclear bombs we watched in those 16mm Civil Defense movies Sister Mary Larry got from the folks at Time-Life. My ten minutes of fame were ripped away in an instant. The cover of the Journal of National Candy Distributor, Inc.s would be—what? Shared? Shithead Milo's toothy grin out-toothing mine as we posed side-by-side for the photographers? The Holloway's All-Day Sucker canoe paddle cut in half by Mr. Robick's meat saw? My knees buckled. My ears sizzled like a hornet's nest.

Even with all that buzzing in my ears, I somehow heard Mr. Robick, "Wait…wait, folks. I didn't see this one. It was stuck to the bottom of the shoebox." (Apparently Mr. Robick couldn't tell a treasure chest from a shoebox.)

"WHAT'S THIS?" He held up my half-wrapper. "Well, I certainly didn't see this coming," Mr. Robick was flummoxed. "Mrs. Robick," he shouted, "I'm flummoxed (see…I told you). Does this count? A half-wrapper?"

Everyone turned to stare at Mrs. Robick who had dropped her black Magic Marker when she saw Mr. Robick itch his comb-over. With everyone starring at her, she got flummoxed too. But then again, Mrs. Robick spent a large part of everyday flummoxed.

Folks' focus shifted from Mrs. Robick back to Mr. Robick who was standing there like some forensic investigator holding up a strand of hair at a crime scene on *Perry Mason*. My pathetic half-wrapper flapped between his thumb and forefinger. Then heads swiveled back to the still-flummoxed Mrs. Robick. Bated breaths waited—bated—for her response. It was her turn. Cow-eyed, *she* started to sweat.

The crowd-buzz died. My ear-buzz didn't. The store was as solemn as a Saint Boniface funeral mass. With all eyes on her, Mrs. Robick rifled through the pages of the official Holloway's All-Day Sucker Competition Rule Book and was about to lick her finger for the 67th time when she stopped on page 68. There it was. She heaved a sigh of relief. The crowd un-bated their breaths and gasped a collective sigh. The formerly-flummoxed but now enlightened Mrs. Robick shouted back, "Right here, Mr. Robick. It's right here on page 68. Rule 163, Paragraph 3-C: *Portions of any Holloway's All-Day Sucker wrapper measuring in excess of four-inches shall be considered eligible in calculating the contestant's total.*"

Their verbal volley continued. Dover heads pivoted back and forth. Mr.—Mrs.—Mr.—Mrs. Mr. Robick finally comprehended the subtleties of Rule 163, Paragraph 3-C. The word *eligible* threw him a curve. He though his wife was saying *edible. Why the heck would any of these little shits wanna eat a Holloway's All-Day Sucker wrapper?* He thought. Mr. Robick reached into his back pocket and pulled out the tape measure he used when he dispensed licorice (the Midwest Regional Candy Distributor, Inc. packaged licorice on cardboard reels and it was sold by the inch). He laid my half-wrapper on the factory-made display, its lights and loudspeakers darkened and silenced. He stretched out his tape. His hands quivered like my aunt's before she had her first pot of coffee in the morning. He began to measure. One inch. Two…three. My half-wrapper slipped. He started over. I was dying. The crowd was back in funeral-mass mode. Thought I was gonna puke. (I did that a lot when I got nervous.)

"Four! That's it! Four inches! Now, how did that rule read again, Mrs. Robick?" He volleyed.

All heads shifted back to Mrs. Robick. She still had the rule book opened to page 68 which was a good thing—she was out of spit. "Let me see, Mr. Robick," she shouted back. "Rule 163, Paragraph 3C says that portions of a Holloway's All-Day Sucker wrapper measuring in excess of four-inches shall be considered eligible in calculating the contestant's total count."

Mr. Robick: "You say in *excess* of four-inches?"

Mrs. Robick: "Errr…yes, Mr. Robick. Excess."

Mr. Robick: "What do you mean, *excess*?"

Mrs. Robick: "Mean's you gotta have more than four inches."

"Can't it just be equal to four inches."

"Nope. Ya gotta have more than four inches."

This was beginning to sound like bedroom talk.

Back to him: "Well, then, it looks like we *do* have a tie. Ain't no *excess* here. Milo Deuter and Billy Rausch will have to…" Suddenly Mr. Robick went silent. I saw it first. His left hand let go of my wrapper ever so slightly. He had reflexively twisted it with his well-practiced palming technique that, over the years, netted him thousands of dollars when he shorted us as he measured our licorice. My half-wrapper was now fully exposed. Another quarter-inch came into view.

"Well, I'll be dipped." His voice cracked just like mine did whenever I actually talked to a girl. He was nervous. Oh, the embarrassment! Oh, the shame! "Well then…looks like we do have us a winner. My fingers must have, umm…slipped. Billy Rausch has fifty and little-more-than-a-half wrappers! Young man, step up here and claim your prize."

He scanned the audience, where the hell was his winner? "Errr—Billy Rausch? Anybody see him? The little shit was standing right over there a minute ago."

The buzzing throng parted like the Red Sea in a Cecil B. DeMille movie.

"Give the little shit some air," someone shouted.

"What's that on his mouth?" somebody else yelled.

Women waved their hankies in my face as I came around. Mom rushed in with a roll of paper towels that Mrs. Robick gave her to clean up my face. Yup. I puked just before I passed out.

Needless to say, it was a pretty inauspicious victory.

Mommies stormed off, swearing "My kid shoulda won."

Kids stormed off, swearing "I ain't never talkin' to him again."

Old Man Peters just stood there, swearing for no apparent reason like he liked to do.

Mrs. Robick tossed her cardboard scoreboard in the trash, never stopping to consider that someday I might want it to tape it on my college dorm room wall next to my posters of Farrah Fawcett and Bart Starr. Even Milo wouldn't shake my hand. Mom was the *only* photographer in the entire crowd. She spit some spit in her hands and pasted my hair down before she snapped my picture with her Kodak. Apparently that sea of reporters had other events to cover. It would be weeks before Milo and I would speak to each other.

Monday morning. I went to school and handed my canoe-paddle Holloway's All-Day Sucker to Sister Mary Larry who shipped it off to the starving China kids. After sucking forty suckers all week I sorta lost my taste.

BADDER UP

Sports is big business. Before we get going on this one, indulge me for a moment. Look again at that lead sentence. You hear it all the time. Stop and think, could I write: *Cars is big business* or *Movies is big business*? Of course not. What we have here is number disagreement, as Sister Mary Larry taught us in fourth-grade grammar. A plural noun such as movies, cars, cheeseburgers etc., requires a verb that agrees in number. So it's obvious, we need us a plural verb. Thus: cars *are* big business, and cheeseburgers *are* delicious. But sports somehow gets a pass. Listen to the talking heads tonight on *Live at Five* when you flop in your La-z-Boy and fire up the flat screen with a cannaHamm's in your hand, "…*sports is up next*." Go figure.

As I was saying, sports *is* big business. Multimillion dollar players play for multimillion dollar franchises in cities from Los Angeles to Miami. Wealthy owners get all duded up in their Giorgio Armani suits to perch in their lavish sky boxes with their multimillion dollar trophy wives flaunting knuckle-bustin' store-bought diamond rings and button-bustin' store-bought tits. Every time you buy a hot dog and a beer in their multimillion dollar parks, remember that you're helping to pay for all that.

Especially those store-bought tits. They were damn expensive, so have two hot dogs. One for each.

Our fly-over state never boasted a multimillion dollar sports franchise. Dover never had multi-anything unless you count kids. But, as unlikely as it might seem, even Dover had a sports team. We competed in a sport which showcased the athletic skills of every male who ever grew up there. The only requirement to land a spot on the team roster was that he could walk and chew gum without tripping over his cleats (shoes...not the barber).

We played the quintessential king of all sports—Softball. Or more specifically—Fast Pitch Softball.

Every small town had a team. From Dover to Bill Town it was a big deal. A town's softball team was a source of community pride that defended its honor. Their team gave them something to cheer for. Dover folks did what psychologists call *transference* when they focused all of their hopes and aspirations onto those nine almost-jocks. It elevated their collective spirits and animated their *joie de vivre*. But more than all that—it gave them something to do on Wednesday nights besides sit home and watch another *Gunsmoke* rerun.

Usually the town merchant who had somehow managed to generate a positive cash flow that year stepped up to shell out a few bucks for the team shirts. Not whole uniforms, mind you. Just shirts. The team's name was never displayed on the shirts. Nothing like the teams we watched on TV like the Cardinals or Blue Jays. Although Mrs. Old Man Peters volunteered once to embroider *Dover Parakeets* on them. She thought it sounded cute. The only thing embroidered across the back of our shirts was the name of the merchant who shelled out the money for them. The shirts were a sort of a warm-blooded billboard and helped the merchant justify his capital outlay. In Dover that buisness was (almost always) Robicks Grocery. My dad and Uncle Ralph volunteered to spring for the shirts the year that they realized windfall profits from the contract the Dover town council awarded them to haul the trash from the Dover town dump and dump it in the river. But alas, they were soundly rejected by the team manager. He told them that if the back of their shirts were embroidered with *Rausch Brothers Trucking, Excavating, and Lime Spreading, Incorporated*, all those warm-blooded billboards would wag like a flag in a thunderstorm. Their fielding and batting skills sucked hard enough without wrapping them in a voluminous team shirt.

Mr. Robick's marketing strategy was nothing short of genius. Since he was one of the few positive cash flow merchants actually willing to spring for the shirts, those warm-blooded billboards gave him free advertising for three, sometimes four seasons. It depended on two things: First—how fast the colors bleached out, and second—how fast the bellies filled out. Players' beer guts were always in a dynamic state of flux. Most leveled-off at *bulging*, but the truly exceptional made it all the way to *pendulous*.

On any given Wednesday night a grocery store, think *Robicks*, might play a hardware store. Or a funeral home might battle a gas station. But the real crowd pleaser, the most well-attended game of the season was when the ladies lingerie store, *Pam's Panties,* played *Dick's*, the men's clothing store. The bleachers would be filled to overflowing. Fans packed the seats, not so much to watch the game, but to shout their suggestive, near-erotic jeers. *Dick's* actually was a pretty good team and frequently fielded several heavily-recruited, relatively sober powerhouse hitters. It was not uncommon that, at some point in the game, those heavily-recruited, relatively sober powerhouse hitters would have the bases loaded. The next batter would dribble one out to the shortstop who'd make a play for the runner advancing to home plate. The runner would make a diving attempt to score and collide with the catcher in a cloud of dust. Five or six half-drunk Dover Men (full-drunk being reserved for the later innings) would stand up and shout: *...and another Dick slides into Pam's Panties.* The half-drunk Dover Men would all go crazy if, say, the runner was a hulking farm kid. Some six-foot-three, 240-pound gorilla with raw knuckles. There'd be a riot in the stands when they added an adjective to describe the lumbering runner: *...ooooohh...a big Dick slides into Pam's Panties.* And if some batter hit a double, and two Dicks scored...well, let's just let it go at that.

Mr. Robick's real motivation to spring for the team shirts wasn't just the free advertising. As the shirt-provider he got the holy grail of Dover's retail market: exclusive rights to the concession stand. Every game day, he loaded up the trunk of his car with wooden cases of pop in real *glass* bottles. Our 60-million-plastic-bottles-a-day society hadn't yet come up with those landfill-busting throw-aways. RC Cola, Nesbitt Orange, Grapette, Seven-Up, Hires Root Beer, and Dodger Cream Soda. And of course—Pepsi and Coke. All of them destined for a nice long ice-water bath. He filled his back seat with boxes of Baby Ruths, Snickers, Old Dutch Potato Chips, Cheetos, Dots, Boston Baked Beans, Sugar Daddies, and Milk Duds. And of course—Holloway's All-Day Suckers. Iconic ballpark hot dogs were not mentioned on his hand-printed sign (they were reserved for tournaments only), but Mrs. Robick could pop a mean bag of popcorn with their popcorn contraption thing.

Here's where his marketing genius really shined: that exclusivity clause in the concession stand contract eliminated any competition from his nemesis across the street—B&D Grocery. And since he had sole access to all those captive customers, he did what any red-blooded American entrepreneur would do with an exclusive contract—he price gouged. Pop that sold for a dime at the Dover gas stations and taverns was fifteen cents. Three-cent candy bars were a nickel. And nickel candy bars were a dime. Fifteen-cent potato chips that had a whopping fifteen potato chips crushed to bits in a bag that bulged with more air than taters, were a whopping twenty cents. *Twenty cents*! But nobody bitched. Fans were so caught up in the frenzy of the game that it didn't seem to matter. Enthusiasm was, as they say, contagious. For a few hours during those Wednesday night home games Dover folks escaped the bone-crushing reality of plowing corn, changing diapers, or threading bolt A into slot C at the tractor factory. Everyone, players and fans, moms and dads, aunts and uncles, was a kid again. Laughing, backslapping, and carrying-on. Heckling the Dicks as they slid into the Panties.

The Deuter Brothers, Riker, Mickey, and I rarely sat in the bleachers to actually watch a game. We were *at* the game, but never *saw* the game. We were engaged in wealth accumulation. Let me explain:

Mr. Robick paid us a three-cent bounty for every pop bottle that we hunted down and returned to the clapboard concession shack during the game. As I mentioned earlier, back then, before billions of throwaway plastic bottles choked our nation's landfills, glass *beverage* bottles were reused over and over again. Pop bottles, milk bottles, and beer bottles. They were rinsed out (more or less) to remove the dead crickets and mouse turds and put back on the assembly line to be refilled. However, (and I swear this is true), sometimes the bottling plant pressure washers missed a few. It was not uncommon to hear about some guy in Peoria who took a swig of RC Cola and gagged on a mouse foot. Or worse...*a finger*!

The regional beverage distributor charged Mr. Robick a nickel for every unreturned bottle. After he shelled out enough nickels, Mr. Robick's price-gouging profit margins suffered dearly. Mrs. Robick took out her pencil and paper one night after supper and showed him that after you subtract three cents from five cents you have two cents left over that went right to the bottom line. She actually said that—*bottom line*. She was no accountant or anything. It's just that by the time she scrawled all those figures on her note pad so Mr. Robick could understand them, she was down to the bottom line of the page. After that eye-opening financial insight, he was only too eager to hire us bounty hunters.

We spent every minute of every home game crawling like commandos under bleachers, benches, and cars. We kicked through weeds and dug in garbage cans searching for the rich veins of bottle ore.

I may have mentioned this earlier, but small towns like Dover were like isolated medieval villages. Social interaction (and marriages) with folks in far-away villages was rare. As a result of this *relative* isolationism, everyone was someone's relative. Somebody's distant aunt or distant uncle, cousin twice-removed, niece or nephew, or shirttail whoever. Some were so far out on the branch tip of a family tree that only the most astute aunt or grandmother could make any sense out of our jumbled genetics. As all those distant relatives sat in the bleachers yelling at the Funeral Homes, Grocery Stores, Dicks, and Panties, sipping fifteen-cent RC Colas and munching potato chip slivers, we had them squarely in our cross-hairs. When they had their bottle nearly sucked dry, the Deuter brothers, Riker, Mickey, or I would swoop down on the unsuspecting aunt or uncle or something, and demand family allegiance for that three-cent bottle. Surely one of us was a far-flung nephew or grandson or something. Many nights I went home exhausted after the game. Not from scrounging for all those bottles but from all the arguing over lineage.

Multitasking. That's what social scientists call our self-imposed git'er done pace of life nowadays. In today's world you're doomed to wallow in professional failure if you cannot write a report, talk to a client, eat your lunch, and plan your five-day, six-night vacation to Wally World with your kids at the same time that you're sitting in a meeting with your boss discussing why your department's productivity for the last quarter is in the shitter. Well, that's what we did. We multitasked. We developed a dual revenue stream by simultaneously collecting pop bottles *and* foul balls. Before we go on, you need to understand a thing or two about foul balls. Foul balls (no…not dancing chicken testicles) were wonderful, glorious, revenue-generating things. Money in the bank. Pocket-bulging, rainy-day-fund cash reserves. Except for Dick's, most team rosters were filled with (and I'll be kind here), *mediocre* hitters. Strike-outs outnumbered hits three to one. But before they'd suffer the humiliation of yet another strike-out, desperate hitters swatted at damn near anything that came within five or six feet of the plate. Their swings were usually too late, too early, too high, or too low because they were too tired. After plowing corn or bolting tractors together all day, they struggled to actually see, let alone hit the ball. With all those too-late, too-early, too-high and too-low swings, foul balls rained down like manna from the heaven.

We negotiated our foul ball territorial boundaries like the spoils of war. The Deuter Brothers got the bleachers on the third base side. Riker got the right field line. Mickey—the bleachers on the first base side. I claimed the gold mine—the bleachers behind home plate. It didn't take a statistician to figure out that, like so many things in their lives, Dover batters were always too late. Their too-slow swings sent the ball sailing overhead, drifting back…back…back directly into my waiting glove. Since I sucked at just about everything sports related, I almost always dropped it. Somehow I snatched it up before Mickey or the Deuter Brothers swooped in like a squadron of German Messerschmitts.

Now the best part—the money. The home team was responsible for providing the so-called *game ball*. A game ball had to be relatively unused, relatively unblemished, and relatively white. Oh—and relatively round. No beat-up practice balls that were lumpy and more gray than white. Only fresh, out-of-the-box softballs could be used as game balls. Well, fresh out-of-the-box game balls were expensive and, as such, highly coveted. We had heard that they cost $2.79 from some supplier in Chicago. Every time a farmer or tractor factory worker sent the ball flying into foul territory, fans were eligible to catch and *keep* the ball like Cardinal and Blue Jay fans did on TV. So that's where we stepped in to fill a critical financial void and assist the team with their cash flow issues. Team managers loved us. They knew that greedy little bastards like us valued the bounty they paid us way more than some stupid game ball. After we caught one of those dazzling-white $2.79 babies, we ran to the Dover bench (snagging a stray pop bottle or two along the way) and held it hostage until the team manager coughed up a quarter. A whole quarter. Applying the principles of return on investment, this was one of the purest forms of win-win negotiations ever devised. The team saved almost three bucks (when you added in the cost of taxes, shipping, and of course, *handling charges*—whatever they were) and the Deuter Brothers, Riker, Mickey, and I went home with all those quarters jingling in our pockets.

One of the best seats in the park to watch the teams battle it out for nine innings was from the comfort of your very own car. Softball parks were usually located on the edge of town where they had been carved from a former corn field. Sort of the *Build It and They Will Come* thing. Construction budgets were tight, so until a few years of revenue generated a little profit, the nascent parks had no fences to keep fans and wandering cows off the field. Indiscriminate chalk lines (more or less) defined the field of play. Motorists were allowed to park their rusty Fords and beat-up Buicks anywhere outside the chalk line. It was the umpire's responsibility to police any driver found to be in violation. That game umpire was usually some unfortunate fan shamed into service by the home-team manager. There were only two prerequisites for being selected for this dubious honor: the candidate had to have relatively good eyesight and, just like the players themselves, had to be relatively sober. It wasn't unusual for the so-called umpire to suspend a game when some *not-so-sober* driver inched his car past the indiscriminate chalk line so as to afford a better view. Seasoned umpires recognized that an inharmonious relationship existed between outfielders' kneecaps and Buick bumpers.

Fans leaned back in the front-seat comfort of their Fords and Buicks to watch the game. Cold six-packs of Schlitz were never far out of reach. Some even brought blankets to spread on the hood so the kids could climb up and do their kicking, scratching, and fighting outside and let mom and dad and their Schlitz the hell alone. Car hoods in those days were sheet-metal monstrosities. Roughly the size of a front porch. Detroit engineers still hadn't figured out the principles of reinforcement. Hell, they were still trying to figure out how to make a V-8 last longer than a Briggs & Stratton lawnmower. So, when six or seven kids climbed up on the hood with toys, blankets, pillows, and the sacks of pirated snacks that their moms and dads smuggled into the park to avoid Mr. Robick's price gouging, it was just a matter of time before the whole thing caved in. That ass-over-tea-kettle scrum put a whole new meaning on family togetherness.

If the stars in the heavens were aligned just right and the batter squinted his eyes just right…sometimes…somehow…he actually hit the ball. And if he got *really* lucky…a home run. It was then that all hell broke loose. The Ford and Buick drivers, in various stages of sobriety, honked their horns in a celebratory salute. Horns back then were not the cartoonish *beep-beep* horns we have on our little Hyundais and Kias today. They were mighty Union Pacific, dual-tone, twenty-four inch trumpets capable of splitting eardrums with their Judgement Day blasts. The honking cacophony echoed into the night, long after the hitter—still in a state of shock—crossed home plate. The umpire had to suspend the game until relative order was restored. Or the pissy little six-volt batteries petered-out.

Every summer every team in every town sponsored a tournament. Theoretically, tournaments were held to showcase the athletic skills of the farmers and tractor builders. However, that was not the *real* reason for the tournaments at all. It was simple economics. Tournaments made money.

There was no admission charge for the regular season Wednesday night games. Meager athletic talent would not have attracted much of a crowd if those fans had to actually pay. But by God, you put something in front of Dover folks for *free*, and they'd jump on it like ticks on a dog. That's what the old man, the crown prince of cliché, always said—ticks on a dog.

Tournaments, though, were a whole 'nother ball game. Tournaments required the payment of an actual admission fee.

In spite of that, Dover folks came anyway. Even if they had to water down their cans of Campbell's Tomato Soup for a couple of suppers or take a pass on Father Hemple's collection plate for a couple of Sundays. Dover Moms were quite skilled at end-of-the-month creative financing. This was theater. A Barnum-and-Bailey spectacle. An entire weekend-long event that was not to be missed.

Early two-day tournament arrivals staked out the best spots. They parked their cars door-handle-to-door-handle around the entire field and walked home after the last batter struck out on Saturday night. They left their family ride behind to hold their spot until the last batter struck out on Sunday night. The latecomers who missed out on the primo parking along the baselines parked out in the outfield by the bisexual outhouse. Hoping to avoid shattered windshields from unlikely home runs, seasoned latecomers spread an extra blanket or two over their windshields and made their kids (or any kid who happen to be wandering by) sit on them. You know—to shield the windshield. Sometimes, if the kid was old enough, he or she might actually catch the homerun ball as it screamed toward them. If the kid was too young (say one or two-years-old) and hadn't developed the motor skills required to actually catch the ball—well, let's just say it wasn't pretty. *Windshields are damn expensive* was the most frequently heard excuse when the emergency room doctor chewed out the mom or dad.

With our Wednesday-night nickels, dimes, and quarters beginning to show promise of supporting our winter-long candy needs, the Deuter Brothers, Riker, Mickey, and I were not about to part with so much as a penny of it and pay some stupid admission charge. Stupid admission charges were for losers. Let them file through the baler twine "front gate" with little red flags tied to it and fork out their fifty cents. Or (gasp!) a buck for the whole weekend. No sir. We, by God, we would do what every red-blooded American kid would do. Sneak in.

Over the years we developed some pretty sneaky ways to crash the gate. The easiest method was to run up to the gatekeeper/money collector seemingly out of breath and gasp that our Mom (or Dad) had a long-distance phone call. Long-distance phone calls were as sacred to Dover Folks as the dusty family bible. Not because long-distance phone calls might bear bad news from some long-distant relative about somebody—you know—dying or something. But they were damn expensive. Everybody knows that. Another method was to simply circumvent that tangle of baler twine and red flags, walk a mile out of town, crawl into Johnny Klotschky's corn field, and infiltrate through the outfield under cover of the Fords and Buicks. I, more lazy than devious, was not about to hike through those mosquitoey corn rows. I walked right up to the "gate" and pretended to bend over to tie my shoe. Sometimes it would take half an hour to tie that shoe. I waited until the man selling tickets got tied up arguing with some cheap bastard about how it was genetically impossible for all *eight* of his back-seat brats to be under *five* years old and qualify for free admission. Even if the cheap bastard countered with, "Three of em's twins," the ticket seller (who had counted on his fingers behind his back) knew better. He shouted back at the cheap bastard, "Ain't no Dover woman can have eight kids in five years. Five's all. Maybe six. But not eight." So while they while they were engaged arguing about human gestational periods, I just breezed through. Piece of cake.

Then, one summer—POW—I got busted. I had been fiddling with my shoelaces for *only* ten or fifteen minutes when an old Ford drove up. It looked to me like it was packed with aunts and uncles, kids and coolers. My glasses must have been dirty or greasy or something, because I didn't see it. It was Old Man Peters and his coonhounds. They were jumping around in the back seat just like a bunch of kids. As Old Man Peters took his sweet-ass time counting his handful of pennies, nickels, and dimes, the ticket man spied me crouching along the side of the car and shouted, "Halt, you little shit!" That was all she took. Old man Peters coonhounds started barking, cars in line started honking, and I started running. Old Man Peters caught a glimpse of me in his side-view mirror and shouted over his coonhounds, "Hey, ain't that one of them Rausch kids trying to sneak in?"

The ticket man ran around the car and knocked me to the ground like I was some sort of felon. He cuffed me by the ear and took me to the only authority in the park—the Dover team manager.

By now it was nearly noon. The first game was ready to start and the team manager still had not scared up an umpire.. There were only one or two sober adult males still left in the bleachers, but neither of them was from Dover (it always helped to have a Dover umpire umpiring Dover games). So for my sentence, the Dover team manager gave me a padded chest protector (which was way too big for me) and a padded face mask (which also was way too big for me) and made me the umpire. Just before the game started he took me aside and winked at me as he whispered in my ear, "You know what to do."

I missed a lot of calls that afternoon. A lot of calls. I was booed like Nixon at a VFW convention. It was the first time in tournament history that the Dover team lost the tournament. Some of my bad calls were probably the result of my glasses sliding down my sweaty nose. But I made most of them because

I got pissed off watching Riker. He stepped in to claim my gold mine behind home plate.

All I thought about was "my" lost quarters.

I wrote this chapter to give you a nostalgic look back at pop-bottle bounties, foul-ball quarters, crushed car hoods, and sobriety-challenged horn honkers. Yes indeed, sports is big business. And even after all these years, my memories *is* great.

WORLD'S GREATEST PORK TENDERLOIN

It wasn't much of a truck, really. Not by today's 500-horsepower, supercharged, triple-axle standards. Just a 1957 yellow Ford F-600 dump truck. Affectionately named "The Palomino" by the old man. That is—when it ran. At least once every week, when it went all haywire on him, he called down Satan's fury on the poor thing with saliva-sprayed vehemence. Mom rushed out to the driveway and jerked on his boots as he sprawled under the grease-caked crankcase exhausting enough expletives to make a merchant marine proud. "What if Father Hempel drove by?" she shouted at him. "You'd be in confession for a month and sayin' Hail Marys 'til Christmas."

Mom gave him a cannaHamm's to settle him down and smeared his bloody knuckles with Mercurochrome. With the threat of confession looming large, the sullen old man would finally get The Palomino chompin' at the bit again. Rearin' to run another day. He grabbed the last Hamm's from Mom's fridge and jumped in behind the steering wheel while she was still running (The Palomino—not Mom) and headed for the quarry. He loaded her up with eight, sometimes nine tons of dirt, gravel, or crushed rock and hauled it to some broke-ass farmer who might, if the old man was lucky, *actually* pay for it after the crops were out the next fall.

That's how the old man made his living. How he put groceries on the table and a roof over our buzz-cut towheads. Dark-to-dark, six days a week. Grabbin' gears, eatin' dust, and keepin' a cannaHamm's nestled between his legs. All the while doing his best to dodge the *scale boys*—the much-feared and brutally-cursed DOT Weight and Measurements enforcement *assholes* who pulled *his* ass over if they suspected his load of dirt, gravel, or crushed rock was so much as a pound over the legal limit.

As I mentioned above, at least once a week Dad and The Palomino limped home early. He stomped into Mom's kitchen. She turned *Stella Dallas* down on the radio, hoping that he'd give her the short version of all the sonofabitches and f-bombs he'd have to confess on Saturday night so she could get back to Stella to see if she was going to leave her no-account bastard husband and run off with that shoe salesman from Peoria. He cussed the carburetor, the distributor, and the radio. Then he cussed the rear end (the Palomino's—not Mom's). He cussed the Democrats who usually caught hell for anything that didn't go right. Satisfied that everything had been properly dispatched to eternal damnation, he grabbed a Hamm's and walked out to confront his demons. On his way out, he kicked the dog, the screen door, and, if I was anywhere in the vicinity, well…you get the picture. He laid down on the driveway and crawled under the grease-caked crankcase where he once again tried to work his magic.

At least once a year even the old man couldn't pull a rabbit out of his hat. His mechanical magic was useless when the busted part involved the *fouled-up* hydraulics. Apparently *fouled-up* hydraulics were way too specialized. Way too complicated. And way too expensive to get *fouled-up* even more by the old man. (Okay, by now you know the old man didn't say *fouled-up*.)

The old man's disabled dump trucks were useless if they weren't, you know, dumping. With that *fouled-up* expensive hydraulic cylinder not working—the Palomino was not dumping. And if it was not dumping, the old man wasn't putting groceries on the table. And so, with everything else operating relatively well and a brand new set of recapped tires on the front end, the old man would once again take off for the only industrial-strength, heavy-duty, expensive hydraulic shop in the state—Wilkins Industrial-Strength Heavy-Duty Expensive Hydraulic Shop, Inc. where he'd fork over lots of money to the rich bastard who owned the shop. He was probably a Democrat. The old man was sure.

Problem was it was located way down at the state capitol. But the old man's all-day-drive logistical nightmare turned out to be pure heaven for me.

You know how some things get burned into your brain and stay stuck in there forever? Like your first communion, your first kiss, your first beer? And of course, your first piece of—Ha! Gotcha!—your first piece of pepperoni pizza? Well, one infamous day (when once again the Palomino packed it in) got burned into my brain like an old Beatles song. The old man stomped in from the driveway after exhausting his mechanical and vocabulary skills. As he scrubbed Palomino gunk from his bloody knuckles with a bar of Lava he shouted over *Stella Dallas* at Mom, "Any money in yer checking account?"

The expression in her eyes betrayed her: *Maybe a hundred bucks*. She understood that the old man needed that money because hydraulics was something that only the industrial-strength, heavy-duty, expensive hydraulic shop could work on. But no—*Hell No*—she wasn't about to give her hundred bucks to him. She had a nest of mouths to feed.

Then…finally, "Yes," Mom could never lie to the old man. "But you can't have it. You know my budget's about as tight as a Republican's underpants."

Oh, how the old man got himself all worked up when Mom, who stood on the other side of the political fence, disparaged his Republicans. He bit his tongue (he really needed her hundred bucks) and just stood there at the sink working that bar of Lava into a sudsy frenzy. Finally, when he couldn't contain his rage any longer, he put down the Lava and railed about the Democrat sonsabitches. Mom reminded him that there were kid-ears standing around, so the sonsabitches got downgraded to mere bastards.

When he finished scouring his knuckles, he wiped most of the grease and blood on Mom's dish towel and walked over to Mom. He put his hands around her still-skinny-after-six-kids waist, and looked at her with his baby blues. The baby blues she got hooked on the first time she saw him at her girlfriend's wedding dance. The baby blues that she would wait for while he went half way around the world to kill Japs. The baby blues that had just sucked her in like a Hoover vacuum cleaner. Like always, she surrendered. (*What was I 'sposta do?* she always told her sister.) She gave him her checkbook (with her hundred bucks in it) and a kiss (with her tongue in it).

He stuffed her checkbook into his shirt pocket and looked down at me, standing there with my ears cocked at him like the RCA Victor dog on Gramma's Victrola. I was trying my best to look nonchalant. You know, as if I just happened to be passing through. Actually though, I had strategically prepositioned myself next to his ashtray knowing he'd fire up a Chesterfield after he finished with the Lava. I stood there, hoping my nonchalant expression didn't betray my *chalantness*. Praying and pleading. Actually bartering with God Himself: *Please Lord...just this once.* Then...then...holy criminy, God actually heard me and put just the right words in the old man's mouth.

"You wanna ride along with me to go see the rich bastard?"

There it was. The phrase I had yearned to hear since I had grown from a snotty-nosed toddler to a snotty-nosed eight-year-old. He actually said it. All I had to say was one little word, and it would be a done deal. Just one little word...

"Well?" the old man was getting testy. I saw Richie out of the corner of my eye, already making his way in from watching Mighty Mouse on the Philco. The little shit smelled opportunity and was poised to exploit my reticence.

My voice wouldn't work. I was overwhelmed by the shock and awe of my longtime dream about to be fulfilled. My brain refused to process what was being played out in front of me. That little voice in my head was screaming: *Say it, idiot. Tell him—tell him yes. Say YES before he changes his mind. You see that little bastard Richie comin' don't you?*

"Earth to Bill," the old man said. "You wanna go or not?"

Dang it Bill, do something. I willed my hand to slap my left cheek. Then my right. Finally two words tripped from my tongue, "Uh-huh."

The old man tiptoed into our bedroom and poked me as I lay there in a knot of brothers. Absolute silence was paramount. If Richie woke up and saw what was going down, he'd stand in the hallway in his pissed-up jammies and wail like the Hound of Hell because he was not going. The only thing that would shut Richie up would be for the old man to renege on his promise and tell me to stay home. He'd once again drive down to the industrial-strength, heavy-duty, expensive hydraulic shop at the state capitol alone. I'd be left to wallow in in my misery, living out another impossibly long summer day with every other kid in Dover. Throwing rocks at windows that needed breakin' and kicking dogs that needed kickin'.

We arrived at the state capitol sometime around mid-morning. I knew that it was not yet noon because *Polka Party Time* with Frankie Yankovik and The Six Fat Dutchmen had not yet played on the Palomino's radio. Mom listened to *Polka Party Time* every noon at home. The lively polkas helped relieve the existential angst that distressed her after thirty minutes of listening to *Stella Dallas* and her no-account bastard husband. I think she secretly had a thing for Frankie Yankovik. Maybe even The Six Fat Dutchmen, but I didn't want to think about that.

We parked the Palomino in front of a brick and glass building and walked into one of the cleanest shops I had ever seen. It wasn't at all like the grease-crusted floors in my Uncle Pete's gas station in Dover. These floors sparkled even more than the floors on the Spic & Span TV commercials with those cartoon sparkly things that fooled housewives into thinking how nice it would look if those little sparkly things danced across *their* floors. An equally clean and sparkly man was sitting behind the shop's counter with a name patch embroidered above his shirt pocket that read: *Assistant Rich Bastard—Wilkins Industrial-Strength Heavy-Duty Expensive Hydraulic Shop, Inc.* A sinister smile tilted the outside edges of his handlebar moustache at a cockeyed angle. "Well, hello again, Old Man (I'm sure he said that...*Old Man*. Everyone called my old man Old Man). "How ya doin' today? Ya bring the old lady's checkbook?"

When the old man whipped out Mom's check book with the pink plastic cover with yellow daisies, the Assistant Rich Bastard smiled even more. So much that he poked himself in his right eye with the tip of his well-waxed handlebar. A little drool dripped onto his name patch. He knew. He knew the old man was using Mom's grocery budget and that he was taking food right out of the mouths of what would soon be starving babies. "Alrighty then," he said. "Palimino's expensive hydraulics again?"

"Yup," the old man snapped. He did not like the Democrat Assistant Rich Bastard.

"Alrighty then. Guys'll have her done by three. Three-thirty at the latest. Free coffee over there in the corner by them trucker magazines. And free ice water for yer little man there."

My eight-year-old unblemished heart skipped a beat. That was exactly what I wanted to hear. Not the smartass thing about the free ice water for yer *little man* thing, but the three o'clock thing. The maybe three-thirty thing. That meant we'd be having dinner (what they called *lunch* down there at the state capitol). And if we were actually having dinner; that spelled just one thing: P-O-R-K-T-E-N-D-E-R-L-I-O-N! ...whoops! L-O-I-N!

In order for the rest of this story to make any sense at all, you need to make a pretty sizable suspension of your disbelief and trust me. I promise you that what I am about to relate is only mildly embellished and for the most part true.

While we were growing up in our big-ass Catholic family (of ten), eating supper somewhere that was *not* in Mom's kitchen, was an event as rare as, and equally miraculous as, the birth of the baby Jesus. Unlike the eat-out-three-times-a-day society we live in nowadays, stepping out to eat a meal prepared by the hands of someone other than Mom—well that was dang near insane. And *when* our family did go out for a meal, that right there was a news article for page three in next week's Wednesday newspaper. And if it was a slow news week—

maybe the front page. Our eat-out supper would be reported with the names and ages of everyone in the dining party, a detailed account of what got ordered from the menu, including the entrée and dessert. And just like a page-turner mystery, with sub-plots and nefarious characters, the reporter would build tension and conclude with The Cost! *Get's 'em every time*, the editor always boasted.

The Pork Tenderloin Sandwich had long ago achieved near-celebrity status in our home. Right up there with Elvis, Ed Sullivan, and the Pope. Mom had their pictures on the living room wall...exactly in that order. Whenever the old man returned from one of his runs to the state capitol, Mom would be waiting for him at the door. A Hollywood sun would be setting in a purple haze behind his bald head. She had a cold cannaHamm's waiting on the table with two triangle holes punched in the top. Frosty sweat beads shimmered in the candlelight (on the cold cannaHamm's...not the old man's bald head). She took him by the hand and, and like Ginger Rogers dancing on the silver screen with Fred Astaire, waltzed him to her Formica kitchen table and lit his Chesterfield for him.

"Didja...didja have one?" she trembled.

The old man relished moments like that. He took a long suck from his cannaHamm's and another long suck from his Chesterfield. He blew the smoke into the bulb hanging over our Formica kitchen table and threw his squinty-eyed gaze into her dancing eyes.

Then, after a significant dramatic pause, "Yup."

Mom swooned. When she finished swooning she yelled, "Kids...get out here. The old man's gonna tell us about the Pork Tenderloin Sandwich again."

We tore ourselves away from another *Gunsmoke* rerun and ran out to her Formica kitchen table, squealing in our jammies. We never tired of his well-embellished Pork Tenderloin

Sandwich stories. We gathered around him in our age-determined stair-step formation like medieval courtesans paying homage to the monarch.

The old man launched into his dissertation about the Pork Tenderloin Sandwich. He summoned every superlative he knew to describe its rich meaty texture, its fried-to-perfection-with-whatever-it-was-they-put-on-it crispy coating, and, of course, its generous topping of onions and yellow mustard.

By now Mom listed heavily to the right, nearly toppling onto the dirty supper dishes as he went on to describe the sheer size of that porcine patty. "Bigger than the back of my hand," he'd say. "Hell, damn near as big as that silk pillow that Gramma and Grandpa brought back from Mount Rushmore," he winked at us. As he was winding down Mom turned to us, and in her motherly lilt said, "Okay kids, story's over, get ch'asses up to bed."

We gave her a kiss and then climbed up on the old man. He braced for what he knew was coming. We kissed him good night right on the lips! Not as a display of affection, but on the outside chance that we'd get a whiff or maybe even a lick of some Pork Tenderloin Sandwich morsel still stuck in his five-day stubble.

Okay, nuffa dat, let's get back to the state capitol. The old man exercised uncharacteristic restraint and decided to forgo the pleasure of giving the Assistant Rich Bastard the finger after his wise crack about "the old lady's checkbook." We turned toward the door and walked out. "Piss on their free coffee and ice water," I heard him mumble. He took my hand as we bobbed and weaved across the street through the state capitol traffic snarl.

We stepped up on an actual curb and onto the sidewalk on the other side of the street. "Look up, Bill," the old man already had his head cocked towards the sky. "I don't want you to ever forget this." I tilted my head back until my neck bones cracked like knuckles and looked up. A flashing red and orange sign boasted for all the world to see (if the world bothered to look up until its neck bones cracked like knuckles). One of the most magnificent testaments to mankind's culinary accomplishments. Ever. THE WORLD'S BEST EVER PORK TENDERLOIN SANDWICH SHOPPE. The letters were bigger than a Buick. I whispered a prayer to Baby Jesus, *You can take me now, I'm ready.*

The old man pulled open the heavy glass door. Inside, a strawberry-blonde waitress greeted us, "Welcome to the World's Best Tenderloin Sandwich Shoppe. Ever." She pronounced *shoppe* like *copy*. "Kin I getcha's a table?" She had what looked like a paper peanut-and-mint-cup thingy (like they used at the Big-Ass Dover wedding receptions you'll read about later) bobby-pinned to the top of her hay-stack of sorta red hair. Defying traditional fashion standards (and modesty), she had somehow squeezed herself into a robin-egg-blue dress. Her bulging blouse pockets were trimmed with white lace. The source of those bulges did not escape the old man's assessment.

"We'll take one of them boobs, err—booths—over there by the window," his voice cracked. Sounded just like mine at recess.

After we were seated, she tossed two plastic-covered cards in front of us, "Look 'em over and see whatcha's want. I'll be right back." She went off somewhere and got us each a big glass of water with—*what's this?*—ice? They put ice in the water? I guessed that they liked to waste ice at the state capitol. I wasn't sure, but I guessed that they probably even put it in their Cokes. The old man was going to have her take the ice out and take it back, but after she reassured him that it was free, he settled down and grinned at her chest.

"Okay men...whatcha's havin' today?" (I liked the way she referred to me as a *man*). I could read some of the words on the plastic-covered card, but *au gratin* and *soufflé* baffled me. I knew that whatever that was, I surely didn't want any. I mustered my self-control and sat quietly and watched the old man's lips moving. I was so filled with anxiety that I had to close my eyes. *Can this actually be happening? Me? Here with the old man? About to consume what mere Dover mortals could only dream of?* As she pulled a pencil out of that gravity-defying stack of sorta red hair with the nut-cup thingy bobby-pinned on top, she said, "We've added double cheeseburgers to the menu, ya know. Folks been sayin' how they're pretty damn good."

I cringed when the old man faltered for a moment as though he would even dare entertain the notion of (gasp!) actually ordering one. "Pretty good, then?" he asked.

She leaned ever so slightly toward the old man and revealed what I had heard some of the older boys in the Saint Boniface boys lavatory call *cleavage*. Even I, a mere eight-year-old, could see that she was trolling for a big tip with her free peep-show. The old man sat there and took it all in. Both of them.

How could he? I thought to myself. Sweat beads popped out on my forehead like a fresh crop of pimples. I shivered a little, like at the end of a good pee. *Don't you dare do this to me. Dad... Dad...*

The old man looked over at me and then back at the peep show which by now had relocated to only a few inches from his also-sweating face. "Well, in that case then, why don'tcha bring us..." (He looked at me again. Was he teasing? Please be teasing.) "Why don'tcha bring us *men* two of the World's Best

Pork Tenderloin Sandwiches." Then he rubbed my buzz-cut, "Gotcha!"

Tears of joy flowed down my cheeks.

The waitress scribbled something on her notepad, "Well then, there ya go, two of the World's Best comin' up. Youse want something to drink?"

"Bring me a cannaHamm's," the old man said. "And bring my hired man here one of those chocolate milk shakes. With whipped cream on top."

What? Did I hear that right? A chocolate milkshake? A real chocolate milkshake! With whipped cream on top? Nobody's going to believe this. Father Hemple was surely going to accuse me of lying. *A chocolate milkshake!*

She turned to leave, but not before winking at the old man (tip insurance). She was only a step or two away when he yelled, "And don't be afraid to get real generous with them onions and mustard…*Sweetie.*" I liked the way he added the sweetie thing. He looked at me to be sure that I understood: Mom didn't need to hear that part.

We waited for what more than likely was not much more than five or six minutes. It seemed like hours to a mouth-foaming eight-year-old. Sweetie finally pushed her bountiful self through the swinging kitchen doors that had little round windows in the middle.

"Here you go, men," she said as she bent over in front of the old man to put our plates down, lingering a little longer than necessary. "Two of the World's Best Tenderloin Sandwiches ever with (she nodded at the old man) *extra* onions." Then quickly added, "No charge."

"And right here's yer chocolate shake, Mr. Man. And tell ya what, when yer done, you can keep the straw and take it home." She didn't have to tell the old man there was no charge for the straw. He somehow knew. Then she grabbed a glass mug that was so cold it had frost on it. I saw two little bumps pop up on her pockets. "And here ya go, Hon. The world's coldest Hamm's. I already poured it outta the can for ya, Hon." She was good. *Hon.* Twice.

I sat there staring at my little red plastic basket with the wax paper lining. It was my turn to take it all in. The masterpiece lying in my very own red plastic basket. And my very own chocolate shake with whipped cream on top and the red straw I'd be taking home. The old man was absolutely right all those nights he sat at Mom's kitchen table and described this with every superlative he could summon. It really was *awesome, massive, gorgeous, and amazing.* And his favorite…*a piece of resistance.* I watched his nicotine-stained fingers as he fumbled, trying to wrap them around his sandwich. In my eyes it really was bigger than Gramma's Mount Rushmore pillow.

I'm not sure how long it took. Hours? In my karmic state of ecstasy, I was unaware of the passage of time. For the first time in my life, I actually chewed my food. I didn't want to diminish the experience of tasting every bite. Every morsel. Every crumb. By the time we finished my eight-year-old belly stretched like a python swallowing a six-pack of lab rats.

As we got up to leave, the old man stopped by the cash register where our waitress was waiting for us. Her eyes were as wide as mine were on Christmas morning, filled with expectation of the financial windfall she was about to receive. She leaned back a bit, arching her blouse pockets more than a *bit.*

"What's the damage?" Dad said as he winked and reached for his billfold.

"Let's see…two World's Best, a chocolate milk shake with whipped cream, and an ice cold cannaHamm's. Right?" She winked, as if she didn't know.

"Yup," the old man said. I saw the wink.

She looked up at the ceiling for a bit. I saw her lips move. "Comes to $2.90 with tax."

The old man pulled three bucks from his brick-thick billfold that had old parts receipts, little notes about stuff he wasn't supposed to forget, and five or six pictures of the Palomino. He never carried pictures of us kids. Or Mom.

There ya go, Sweetie," He winked at her again. She winked back. This was getting to be a regular wink-a-thon.

She pushed some buttons on the cash register. It dinged three or four times and the drawer flew open on her little apron.

She winked and took a dime out of the little section for coins and pushed it across the counter at the old man. He shoved it right back.

"That's for you, Sweetie."

That pretty much ended the wink-a-thon.

We bobbed and weaved our way back across the street to the Industrial-Strength Heavy-Duty Expensive Hydraulic Shop, Inc. where Dad paid the grinning Assistant Rich Bastard. As we walked out the door to the parking lot, the old man faked a cough punctuated with a not-so-subtle f-bomb. The old man was cool that way. He always got the last punch.

We scanned the parking lot and there she sat in the back corner—The Palomino. Good as new. The expensive shop specialist (the Assistant Rich Bastard's nephew) who did the work was standing next to her wiping the greasy door handle with his greasy shop rag. He jumped into the cab and started the engine. He pulled the lever to raise the dump box all the way up so the old man could see that she was all fixed up and that our depleted grocery budget was worth it.

I flopped over and fell asleep on the seat on the way home. The Palomino was having a good day. Hitting on all eight cylinders.

Its grease-caked crankcase played a symphony of hums and knocks that lulled me and my tenderloin-tummy to sleep. I gripped my free straw in my left hand. My right hand rested on the old man's leg. He grinned as he rubbed my sweaty buzz-cut. I saw him wink.

Probably thinking about Sweetie.

DISCOVERY

Man is happiest when he confidently awaits the fulfillment of his highest dream. Thomas Wolfe, considered by many to be one of the most influential novelists of the 20th century, wrote those words or something pretty darn close to them. Go back and examine them and you'll see what a splendid insight he had to the human condition. My old man was an unwitting philosopher of sorts, and occasionally stumbled upon little nuggets like Mr. Wolfe's. I assure you that his were more accidental than inspirational. But regardless of how he came up with them, they more or less guided me as I ambled down this tortuous path we call life. His discernments were not expressed in carefully couched phrases like those that Mr. Wolfe no doubt labored over. The old man's quips serendipitously tripped off his tongue without warning or premeditation. His observation about life went something like this: *It don't make no difference where you're headed, Bill. It's how you get there that counts.*

So, let me show you where I was headed and how I finally got here and you can decide if I let him down or not.

Discovery is a helluva thing. Really important discoveries like the internal combustion engine, internal medicine, and the Internal Revenue Service will get a passing mention in this book. There...that's done. Consider them mentioned.

The discoveries I'm talking about are not the *Eureka!* insights of Archimedes and other great thinkers who advanced civilizations, built nations, and made the world a better place for mankind. No, I'm talking about personal discovery that's not so much *society-shaping* as character-shaping. Perhaps my discoveries didn't make the universe a better place to live, but it sure as heck made my world a better place to live. And way more fun.

Discovery is evolutionary. One insight oftentimes leads to another, more advanced hypothesis. Our brains are better at making incremental steps rather than giant leaps. The basics of any body of knowledge must be pondered and comprehended before advancing to a higher plane. Let me illustrate: Sister Mary Larry couldn't pound long division into our hayseed heads until first she beat simple addition and subtraction into our hayseed heads. We didn't develop our later-in-life discerning tastes attuned to the culinary delights of fine cuisine until we first figured out how to suck the creamy stuff out of Long Johns. Like boys everywhere, we Dover boys went down the road of discovery in a more or less progressive fashion. Comic books preceded Playboys. BB guns led to .22's. And inhaling secondhand smoke led to firsthand smoke.

Eventually, we stumbled upon The Mother of All Discoveries. It was not the result of collaboration or team effort. We each arrived at our own pace. We eventually found ourselves tangled up in that awkward emotional jungle known as *Girls*!

However, we didn't complete the journey without a few, shall we say, *little bumps* along the way. Let me explain:

There I was, horsing around in my happy little life, shrouded in a cloud of sexual uncertainty. My rich stew of hormones was just beginning to bubble. The Deuter Brothers and I had recently advanced from Mickey Mouse, Donald Duck, and Spiderman to the ladies underwear section of the JC Penney catalog. Satin nighties and panties. And seemingly endless pages of various sizes and shapes of beautiful bras. Low-cut bras. Under-wire bras. Lacy bras. That alphabet of cup sizes from triple A to double D (especially the double D's) eventually spiked our curiosity and got the best of us. We wanted to know what lurked beneath all those beautiful bras. We put JC Penney down the day we discovered Riker's old man's *Playboys*. Even pilfered a *Penthouse* or two from Clete's barbershop.

It wasn't long after that and, as little boys often do, we stumbled upon the next big thing in our lives—masturbation. Our first experience was innocent enough—nocturnal emission. *Wet dreams*. After we came through our first one (pun intended), whenever we knelt down with our Moms to say our prayers at night, we secretly petitioned God that whatever that thing was last night, could we please have another one. It was the Saint Boniface high school boys who eventually revealed masturbation's forbidden secrets to us when they let us hang out with them on the school playground. Or sometimes hang out with them at the urinals (again...pun intended). We'd cock our little ears and listen intently, hoping not to be noticed as they snickered. After a few of those infomercial urinal sessions, we pretty much had the situation, err...well in hand.

Apparently masturbation changed something else in us. Was there some telltale behavior or little gleam in our eyes? Maybe it was the subtle stir of those just-beginning-to-bubble hormones. Whatever it was, *something* betrayed us. Sister Mary Larry saw it and suspected that something was, err...*up*. With her keen sense of Sister-insight, she did what she had been taught to do years ago in Nun School—she ran to the rectory and told Father Hempel.

A few days later he walked into the classroom to teach our weekly catechism class. We had already gone through the Ten Commandments and he was beginning to explore the vast guilt-universe of venial sins. Mortal sins were reserved for fifth graders, it being commonly believed that third and fourth graders were incapable of acts that would pretty much ensure they'd wind up in the fires of Hell. But fifth graders could. When he walked in that morning he looked, well, somehow different. Like a death row inmate who had just finished his last meal. All serious and solemn-like. Sister Mary Larry already knew what was coming, so she had the girls filing out the door as he shuffled in. Janet Beemer, the first girl in our class to sport a training bra, stuck her tongue out at me as she walked past my desk. She always assumed her facial taunts would piss me off, but in fact her protruding tongue only heightened my prepubescent lust. I heard her say as she walked out the door holding Luanne Gray's hand, "We're going down to the lunch room for a little *girl-talk*."

Riker and I looked at each other as they marched out. Clueless. For us that was pretty much a common condition. We couldn't see the Deuter Brothers to tell what their reaction was. They always sat in the back of the room. Sister Mary Larry bucked the commonly accepted educational practice of seating "slow learners" down front where they could receive more focused instruction. She parked them in the back of the room where, according to her teaching philosophy, they wouldn't impede the progress of the rest of us intellectual giants. (Truth be known, all of us should have been in the back of the room.) Arnie was already preoccupied with rolling spitballs for his daily target practice at the back of my neck. He was even more clueless than me and Riker. But unlike us, he didn't care. Arnie was cool that way.

Father Hempel waited for the girls to leave before he closed the door. That was our second clue that something was up. He was wearing his long black skirt-thing like priests did sometimes in those days. Along with his black tricorn cap with the fuzzy black ball on top. He gathered the folds about his legs like Gramma did when she sat on Mom's couch after our Sunday fried chicken dinner. He plopped down on Sister Mary Larry's desk chair and looked down at his hands and picked away at his fingernails in eerie silence. Riker and I saw his lips moving. He cleared his throat ten or fifteen times. We didn't know what to do. So, in a sort of Mexican standoff, we squirmed in silence, fidgeting with whatever was lying on our desks. Pencils, spit balls, paper clips. I found a weeks-old wad of Wrigley's Spearmint stuck under my desk top so I picked it loose and popped it into my mouth. Surprisingly, whoever stuck it under there left a little of the flavor behind. It was difficult to determine who was more nervous, him or us. But judging by the sweat stains on his Roman collar, Father Hempel was the bigger basket case.

"Now boys…," he began. *That was it*! Right there we knew this was going to be serious. That expression, *now boys*, was reserved for one thing and one thing only. Our most egregious offenses. Not really sins, not even venial sins, but about as close as we could get without stepping over the line to eternal damnation. The last time we had heard one of his *now boys* was that Saturday morning when we dug in his garbage can during one of our pop bottle roundups and found it brimming with beer bottles. "*Now boys*, you keep your big fat mouths shut," he warned. To seal the deal he played the confession card: "You boys have any idea how long it takes to say a thousand Hail Marys?"

"*Now boys...*" he went on. "It has come to my attention that some of you (he was staring at his hands again) have reached a certain stage in your lives where you have discovered some things that are not, err...shall we say...umm...not appropriate for young boys."

He stopped there, apparently satisfied that his opening volley was successful. He wiped the sweat from his bifocals with his priest hankie. He shoved his glasses back on his nose and his priest hankie up his sleeve (whenever priests wore their skirt-thing, they always had their hankies shoved up their sleeves. Apparently it would suggest immodesty to undo one's skirt-thing to get at one's back pocket). He went on: "*Now boys*, without getting too specific—because, well, most of you already know what I'm talking about here..."

We looked around at each other. I was relieved. Even Mickey looked as confused as the rest of us. Mickey was always a step or two ahead of us in everything. Like rolling up the pant legs of his blue jeans into little cuffs like James Dean so his white socks would show. Even rolling up the sleeves of his tee shirt like James Dean so his skinny arms would show. Sex stuff was no different. He boasted that he actually touched one of Janet Beemer's tits once. *What's this? Touched...one?* For little boys on the cusp of sexual awareness, that was like winning the lottery, except we didn't have a lottery. All we had was Ed McMahon on TV. We demanded to know exactly which *one* (as if that made a difference). We shoved him around between us until he finally admitted that it was an accident. He was reaching across the table in the Saint Boniface lunchroom for some ketchup when he, you know, sorta *brushed* it. I glanced to the back of the room. Arnie had hunkered down. The morning target range was open for business. I don't think he even heard what Father Hempel was mumbling about.

Father Hempel continued to ramble in some sort of semi-lucid lingo, his words offering no promise of coherence. It seemed like hours later, but it finally sounded as though he was making his closing argument. We had heard so many of his Sunday sermons that we knew when he was winding down. His last sentence trailed off with, "...so then, you see, boys, God gave all of you wonderful bodies as a sign of his unconditional love. And he expects you to keep them in tiptop shape just like Billy Rausch's dad does when he lays out there in their driveway keeping the Palomino in shape, cursing and taking the Lord's name in vain (he gave me a cold stare). And knowing that, I'm sure that you all realize that you, umm—you must stop abusing yourselves."

The room fell into even deeper silence (if you can quantify silence). Deeper confusion (which is quantifiable). We looked around at each other with slow-motion head-swivels. Clueless once again as to what the hell this man of the cloth was talking about.

Arnie, having spent his arsenal on the back of my neck was getting bored. He broke the ice and raised his hand.

"Yes," Father Hemple looked at Arnie with anxious eyes, relieved that his stilted dissertation would maybe lighten up a little with some audience participation. A little give-and-take. *Quid pro quo* like he always said with his priest Latin. *Ive-gay and ake-tay* like we said with our pig Latin. Little did he know what Arnie was about to hit him up with. "Errr...you there...way in the back. Yer one of those Deuter boys, ain't you?"

"Yup."

"So, you gotta question *youngman*?" (Father Hemple only knew the names of two or three of us. Of course, I had to be one of them. Everyone else was *youngman*. Pronounced *yungmun*.)

"Err...Father Hempel...what's that mean?"

"What's what mean?"

"That part at the end where you said abuse. We hurtin' ourselves or somethin'?"

Father Hempel opened his mouth to answer and stopped. Lost for words again. Saint Boniface parishioners were pretty sure that Father Hempel had graduated 23rd in his seminary class of 23. It's not that anyone ever questioned his piety or being called to the priesthood by the Lord, but let's just say, as I had heard the old man mention several times, "They can't all be popes." Sometimes though, the Holy Spirit moved him, and up there in his Sunday morning pulpit, right on the spot, no notes or anything, he'd tear into some good old-time Bible thumping. His *altar* ego kicked in and his sermons sizzled with brimstone and hellfire. But what he did best, the sermon he preached with more gusto than anything else, was his money sermon. He railed about how our moms and dads weren't stepping up to the *plate* (he always paused there to chuckle at his own pun). One hot August Sunday, in one of his bi-monthly money sermons when the church coffers were, according to him, lower than Satan's belly button, he remarked how the parishioners proved, without a doubt, that Saint Boniface was indeed a nonprofit organization. That even made a few other folks chuckle. Most didn't get it. Several were sleeping.

So...where was I? Oh yeah—rather than explain to Arnie that, according to Catholic doxology, we were spilling the seeds of life that were intended for reproductive copulation, he threw his arms in the air and gave up. He dropped his abuse charges and mumbled, "*Now boys...*"

Before our boy-or-girl hormones kicked in sometime in the seventh or eighth grade, whenever we sang in Sister Mary Larry's Christmas programs, our voices sounded the same.

After the girls beat us at kick ball (again!) at recess, we marched back into our stuffy classroom smelling the same. We read the same stupid *Dick and Jane* books, wrote the same *What I Did On My Stupid Summer Vacation* assignment, and screwed up the same long division arithmetic homework. Whenever we put on our shirts or blouses, our chests looked pretty much the same. We had no idea of what the heck went on behind that door marked GIRLS LAVATORY down at the end of the corridor. We imagined that the girls elbowed each other around the urinal to tell poop jokes and pee just like we did. We figured we all had pretty much the same plumbing. Not that I ever looked, but Ken and Barbie's featureless crotches didn't help.

Then—it happened. The Great Awakening. Rivers of secretions from our heretofore dormant endocrine glands coursed through our veins. Our voices started to sound different. Some of us got moved to the back of the chorus. To what Sister Mary Larry called the alto section. And the girls—were they getting smarter? They read *Dick and Jane* with passion and tonal inflections. They didn't stumble over the hard words like *Mother* and *see Spot run*. They practically raced to the blackboard to divide 789 by 13. We woke up one morning, surprised as much as alarmed by the sudden sprouting of pubic hair. And what's this—sundry forms of follicles springing up on legs, arms, and…ugh…arm pits? By seventh grade, Arnie had facial hair. By the eighth grade his moustache was thicker than his mom's. But none of us really cared. We started beating the girls at kick ball pretty consistently. We actually slaughtered them once a month on the days that Billy Jean Kowolski's mom made her stay home from school.

A few girls, those whose endocrine glands woke up early and opened the flood gates for all those secretions I was telling you about, popped little bud thingys on their chests. By the time they were twelve some started wearing *training bras*. It was right about then that the bolder girls began to experiment with makeup. They tiptoed into their bathrooms before school and kicked their little brothers out. While their moms yelled at their little brothers get their butts back in their bedrooms and put on some clean underwear, they smeared lipstick mostly on their lips and brushed on some blush. It stayed on their faces until 8:15 when Sister Mary Larry, always on alert for Satan, spied them sneaking into school and shoved them into the lavatory where she scrubbed their faces with Lava and steel wool. We looked over at the girls' pew during Mass to see which ones had been busted that morning. Skin abrasions were a dead giveaway.

While we were in our hormonally-triggered sexual transition, we were confused as much by girls as long division. We masked our bravado by teasing anyone caught making overtures towards the *opposite sex*. If some unfortunate soul was caught actually talking to one of them at recess, he'd be laughed right out of the lunch room. And if he held hands with one of them at recess, well, he might as well have come down with leprosy.

Fourth grade was finally over. None of us ever got the hang of long division, but Sister Mary Larry passed us anyway. Next year we'd be Sister Mary Arnold's problem. School was out for the summer which meant we had way too much free time on our hands. We were in that developmental sweet spot that comes around only once in a boy's life. We weren't quite big boys yet, all serious and worldly and stuff. Too young for serious summer jobs. (Maybe mowing some old lady's yard for a quarter or two when the pop bottle crop dried up.) And too old to while away our afternoons around a campfire roasting weenies, debating Old Man Peters stupid coonhounds, or arguing about which one tasted better—RC Cola or Pepsi. We were just big enough that our moms cut us some slack and allowed us to roam free-range around Dover. Even as far away as the quarry to skinny-dip and skip stones. But not so big that, by God, we better not be late for supper.

It was either Riker or Gary the new guy…I don't remember which. School was only out a week and one of them claimed that he actually *kissed* a girl. I'm pretty sure it was Riker. He was so excited that his still-changing voice chirped like a cricket when he told us. He said it was nothing at all like the cheek-kisses we got from our cheap-perfumed aunts on Christmas with lips so tight you couldn't shove a toothpick in. All Listerene-and-Polident-smelling. Apparently, according to Riker anyway, a real girl-kiss was a whole 'nother thing. We were stymied as he struggled for words. Confused not so much by his emotional recounting of the event, but by *our* reactions. Strangely, we didn't even make fun of him! Not so much as a snicker. Something stirred in our groins.

By the middle of that summer, even the Deuter brothers joined Riker at that sexual summit. Mickey assumed that a kiss on the cheek satisfied the requirement and it automatically made him a member of that exclusive club. His application was rejected and he got sent back until he got it right.

Like always, I would be the last. It was the middle of August and I still had not cut that notch in my belt along with the rest of the guys. However, moral corruption was lurking just around the corner. Well…down the street. I had Luanne Gray squarely in my sights.

That would be my last summer of innocence.

By the end of June, Mickey made a bold announcement that made us question his credibility. He bragged that he had advanced from mere kissing and had been exploring other regions of the opposite sex girl-universe. He actually touched *two* training bras. Not just accidentally this time, but for real. Actually touched them with full intent and forethought. For the first one his hand was on the outside of the blouse. We told him that one didn't count (like *we* knew). But for his second (it was Janet Beemer in case you were wondering), he had fumbled his way through the lose-fitting summer dress and actually felt it. Smooth and lacey, he said. But kind of lumpy, he said. Misshapen even. We later discovered that in the competitive world of embryonic boob-budding, some girls supplemented their emerging attributes with a Kleenex or two. When Mother Nature didn't step up, Kimberly-Clark rode to the rescue.

Not to be outdone, Gary the new guy exceeded even Riker. None of us ever gave Billy Jean Kowolski (remember Billy Jean?) a second look, let alone actually talked to her. Gary was the first one to notice them with his good eye. Apparently when her mom kept her home from school once a month, she was busy growing up. I mean really growing up. She jumped at his invitation for a sort of date. They were drinking RC Colas out at the quarry one afternoon and copped three or four actual "feels". That's what we called it when there was *flesh* contact. We later learned at the Saint Boniface urinal buzz that the proper term was *feel her up*. Tenth graders were gods!

August 12th. The summer was nearly shot. A few days earlier I had finally crossed the threshold with Luanne Gray and scored my first kiss. I was now (finally) able to enjoy the benefits of membership to the club. She apparently enjoyed that kiss as much as I had and started meeting up with me pretty regularly in the weeds behind Nick Jacoby's barn. We started out innocently enough. Just horsing around. Our eyes were wide open, but our mouths were tight shut. Dry kisses—that was all. Spit was still high up on the yuck scale in our minds.

But that August 12th was destined to be different. We were just getting into it and had progressed to *heavy petting*—a tenth-grader term that made no sense to us (wasn't that what you did with a dog or cat or something?). Luanne was breathing heavy. She sounded like she had just played kick ball for an hour or two. Her chest heaved rhythmically. Her eyes were closed. It was like she was in a trance or something so I figured *What the heck…I'm goin' in*. Gary the new guy…move over. I fumbled (pathetically I might add) with her blouse (her favorite—the one with little sunflowers). I finally had two buttons unbuttoned. Well, okay—one. The second one popped off when I yanked. Holy shit! Was that what I thought it was? A bra? I saw it! Unobstructed visual confirmation. *Houston—we have a bra*. An actual bra. *Okay Bill*, I thought to myself, *take it easy. You can do this*. I was aiming to shatter Gary's exclusive domain. I, by God, was going in to feel her up.

What the hell are you two doing? I froze. Crap! What the heck? It was MOM! She was standing behind us with her hands on her hips wearing an expression on her face that she reserved for the old man when he really pissed her off. How the hell did she get here? Apparently the radio announcer had broken into a Frankie Yankovic song and told the listening audience that Billy Rausch and Luanne Gray were doing some pretty *heavy petting* behind Nick Jacoby's barn. (Well, that's what flashed into my mind anyway.) I discovered later that my little shit-brother Richie had been stalking us. He got scared when he saw Luanne go all trance-like and ran home to tell Mom that she sounded like she was getting sick. Really sick.

She told Luanne to go her house and wait there. As Luanne walked off, still a little dizzy, Mom shouted, "*Young lady* (that always meant Mom was really pissed), you tell your mother to get off the damn party line so I can call her later." Then she pulled me up by my left ear, her favorite form of apprehension, and jerked me all the way home like a puppy on a leash. She kicked the screen door and propped me on a kitchen chair and proceeded to rip me a new one. But get this—she had no concern for our heavy petting. Or Luanne's open sunflower blouse. Or the busted button. Or even the fact that I was about to cop a feel. None of that made Mom's moral compass so much as quiver. She was chewing me out because Luanne was my *second-cousin*. Now how the hell was I supposed to know that? In Dover, where everyone was related to everyone else through our gnarly family trees, I didn't have a clue. With my hormone-hazy head buzzing with confusion, I figured we had to be somehow exempt.

Before the afternoon was over Luanne and I were sentenced to a mandatory cooling-off period. Mom grounded me for a week. Luanne didn't fare so well. She got a month. Luanne's mom believed everything she read in the Old Testament. After that big screw-up in the Garden of Eden, where the woman was the evil temptress, it was them who had to bear the burden of guilt. So naturally, Luanne got a month.

As part of my sentence, in addition to no Mighty Mouse and no desserts, I had sit on a kitchen chair and sprinkle starch water from a Coke bottle on the shirts, pants, and hankies while mom ironed. Mean, hateful Mom made me sprinkle extra starch on my underwear, you know, just to make a point. While I sprinkled I was forced to listen to that stupid Frankie Yankovik and his stupid polka music on her stupid radio. Richie glared at me from outside the window, picking his nose as he twirled in our tire swing.

Mom (sweet, loving, kind-hearted Mom) commuted the last two days of my sentence for good behavior. All those glowing comments I made about how nice her ironed hankies looked didn't hurt. After I swore that I'd keep my hands off Luanne, she untied my ankles from the chair legs. I busted through the screen door and, after I kicked Richie out of the tire swing, ran straightaway to Gary the new guy's house to cut a deal. I swapped my second-cousin Luanne for Billy Jean Kowolski.

He jumped on it. Word was getting around town that my second-cousin's training bra was Kleenex-free.

Remember that destination thing that the old man was talking about when we started this chapter and how he said: *It don't make no difference where you're headed, Bill. It's how you get there that counts.* It would take me many more years to finally figure out where I was truly headed; but Luanne and Billy Jean got me started down a pretty exciting path. Maybe not exactly the *right* path, but a joyful path.

They taught me a lot that summer. As I grew from being a relatively innocent Dover boy to the man I am today, I never forgot those early discoveries about the *feminine mystique*. For the past 47 years I have celebrated life with Joanne, my *feminine* wife. She is kind, gentle, and loving. She teaches me about that feminine mystique every day.

And I have the scars to prove it.

MR. OUTDOOR MOVIE MAN

Groceries, beer, and gas. These are the retail hubs around which small towns spin and swirl. You won't find day spas, nail salons, or organic *ristorantes*. Groceries, beer, and gas. Life's essentials. Local merchants, Mom&Pops. Bodegas. Neighborhood Shops. Call 'em what you will, but they're the ones who fill our needs. Provide those *Life Essentials*. All too sadly, trigger points are reached when local folks stop throwing their paychecks at the local merchants. Fickle consumers, owing allegiance to nothing but a buck, succumb to the lure of bright lights, big cities, and big box stores that offer endless aisles of cheap crap. Walmart, Dollar General, and other discount vampires suck the cash (and life) from small town retailers. *Poof!* Like a Houdini hat trick—Mom&Pops disappear. Neighborhood Shops croak. Another nail in the coffin. The town teeters on the brink of obscurity. Another so-called bedroom community supplants what was once a vibrant home town.

When Dover's retail hub was still spinning, our grocery, beer, and gas merchants were its spokes. You already know a lot of this, but in those days, we had three peddlers of *each*. Nine spokes. They were the core of our commercial infrastructure and nurtured our village vitality. It still amazes me how those nine merchants and their nine families survived. Had it not been for the marketing genius of Mr. Outdoor Movie Man, perhaps our Mom & Pops would have ended up like James Dean and Buddy Holly. Dead before their time.

Before I tell you about Mr. Outdoor Movie Man, here's a quick snapshot of our storekeepers, barkeepers, and, gaskeepers.

First—the grocery stores. Robicks, to which I have already devoted considerable ink, had the most charm, most colorful characters, and the most candy. It continued to operate as a Mom&Pop for most of my boyhood. Eventually the owner/operators, Mom and Pop Robick, went tits-up. Their business failure was not caused by the economic pressures I was talking about in that opening paragraph. More likely it was bad management. As he aged Mr. Robick couldn't keep up with the newfangled retail tools like cash registers and newspaper advertising. He relied instead on simple cyphering with a pencil and paper. Jot down the 4, carry the 2…. When his wholesale distributor set up a system of supply order forms and just-in-time inventory to assist with their cash flow, Mr. Robick refused to play. He remembered what was running out, the bare spots on his shelves, and told the delivery man what to bring next week. Combine that with the sales pressure applied by his competitor across the street, D&B Grocery, and that was all she wrote. Seriously. That's what Mr. Robick told his loyal customers on his last day of operations, *that's all she wrote*. I am deeply indebted to him for giving me so much fodder for these stories. So, in a way, it wasn't *all she wrote*.

As I was saying, D&B was Robick's cross-street rival and represented a more, shall we say, *progressive* retail philosophy. D&B was Dover's only new post-war store (with the exception of my uncle's gas station). It was a majestic edifice that was *constructed,* not just slapped together by a bunch of part-time carpenters. In an otherwise drab downtown with its drab turn-of-the-century cluster of never-painted stores, D&B stood out like the new kid on the block. Its street-facing façade included (gasp!) bricks and mortar. And (double gasp! gasp!) plate glass windows so colossal that folks drove by just to watch themselves wave back at themselves. With its "modish" arched Quonset hut architecture, D&B gave Dover residents a glimmer of hope that maybe, just maybe, their little town was alive and growing.

And lastly, Rodiwalds. I doubt that very many former Dover Folks remember Rodiwalds. Maybe a few who are having this read to them by one of their great grandkids at their nursing home bedside. Rodiwalds was established at the turn of the century when Dover was just a one-horse town. It stayed in operation until we became a *sophisticated* two-horse town and outgrew our old-fashioned ways. But that was long enough to fill me with some of my very earliest childhood memories. Take another look at that distinctive name—*Rodiwalds*. Three whole syllables. Quite a mouthful in a town where most of us had monosyllabic Germanic monikers. It was almost foreign-sounding; perhaps taking its origins from some balkanized minority.

Rodiwald's was a nose-carnival. Pockets of pungency swirled around the store as shoppers navigated *both* aisles. A rich mix of fruit here. Fresh garden vegetables there. And spices and meat back there. Piles of Mrs. Rodiwald's homemade, unsliced breads left naked in a wicker basket on the counter.

The bouquet of aromas that attacked my nose with never-to-be forgotten delight is gone forever. Rodiwald's was an old-world bazaar lacking only hijabs and whiskered Pashtuns sitting cross-legged beside their goods. I miss that. Always will.

Today, the FDA and the Department of Agriculture has reduced our shopping experience to plastic-wrapped everything.

Some will question my recollection of Dover's *three* gas stations. *Bill, there's always been just two*, they will insist. But for a handful of us—we know. Those two, the remembered two, still stand today—one (more or less) still in business. It functions as a kind if mini-mart. If your mini-mart needs are limited to milk, bread, and cigarettes. Maybe a couple of cans of Campbell's. Gone are the days when you could drive in, buy a new set of snow tires, have your oil changed, and get your car tuned-up. You had to go to Tilleys for *your* tune-up.

Down the street, the other station is in its death throes. More falling over than standing. It's not much more than a clutter of crap scattered from the front door to the street, leading the casual observer to speculate: is it a flea market or a plain old eye-sore? Opinions lean toward the latter. Its old-timey pumps have been long since snapped up by some antique dealer and are probably sitting in some man cave today. The glass dome radiating ambient room light while the Cowboys trounce the Vikings.

Finally, the long-forgotten third *filling station.* That anachronistic term defines what used to be the primary—and sometimes *only*—function of the early entrepreneurs who took a chance on those new-fangled horseless carriages and risked their life's savings just to *fill* their tanks with the gasoline that the Phillips brothers squeezed out of the Oklahoma crude.

It was housed in an iconic yellow-and-red clapboard building that stood at Dover's crossroads. Yup, *that* crossroads. The one that witnessed Dover's first traffic fatality (Old Man Peters coonhound) back in Chapter Whatever. It had a service bay of sorts, its dimensions clearly intended to accommodate vehicles not much larger than Henry Ford's T's and A's. And finally, (you ready for this?), it even had an ice house. The *only* ice house in old Dover. And while I don't remember the slabs of winter-cut river ice being stored inside, I do remember the thick walls and leftover sawdust that was packed between those winter-cut slabs to prevent them from sticking together. That old ice house stood for years as a testament to a past when the convenience of Norges and Frigidaires could only be dreamed of.

Okay, we have already pretty much explored (beat to death, actually) Dover's three beer taverns: Tilleys, Bonfigs, and Charlies. So many good-time, beer-guzzling factory workers, farmers, and old farts allocated disproportionate amounts of their income to them (read: pissed away their paychecks). They flourished for years but eventually yielded to the pressures of a more sophisticated, actually—more sober, society. Only one survives today.

So there you have it, the primary Dover merchants (the Big Nine) that provided those three essential commodities—groceries, beer, and gas. Thanks to them, Dover folks had access to the Life Essentials that helped them provide their families with the rich cultural experiences so critical to the development of a vibrant community.

Oh…almost forgot. We had a library too.

Dover's retail merchants cut out their cut-throat competition and joined together on the first Monday night of every month to discuss ways they could cooperate to sustain the town's long-term viability. More importantly, to discuss ways they could sustain *their* long-term viability. They formulated new strategies (wild-ass guesses, actually) that might lure customers into their gas, beer, and grocery stores. They called themselves the Dover Commercial Club, a forerunner of today's Chambers of Commerce. Their mission, as stated on the poster they hung up in the town hall before every meeting was simple: "Make More Money."

Enter *Mr. Outdoor Movie Man*.

When most of you think of outdoor movies, you probably harken back to that iconic American institution known as the *Drive-In Movie*. Bastion of the Back Seat Boogie. Drive-ins reached their height of popularity when all those horny GI's came home after WWII. It doesn't take a rocket scientist to figure out that Drive-In Movies put the *boom* in Baby Boom.

Dover folks wallowed in pre-television radio land tedium. We were starved for entertainment. Radio nights filled our darkened parlors with Fibber McGee and Molly, The Lone Range, and Amos n' Andy. We were bored listening to Molly's crap crashing out of her over-stuffed closet. A masked man galloping on his silver stallion while the *William Tell Overture* echoed across the Western plains. And two fake black guys uttering subtle racial slurs to an unsuspecting audience. We wanted pictures. Things that actually *did* prance around on a screen like we saw during our once-a-year visits to the *thee-ay-a-ter* up at the county seat. Since we lived in Technicolor, by God, we wanted Technicolor images projected on a screen right here in Dover. Images that would not only entertain, but images that would expand our philosophical horizons and broaden our intellect. Images like Bugs Bunny and Porky Pig.

The Outdoor Movie Man would make that happen. No one remembers who he was or where he came from, but after he pitched his idea to the Commercial Club, Dover's outdoor movie night was born.

Dover's town park was stuck between the two commercial giants that dominated the south side of Main Street: Tilleys and Bonfigs. Besides being a home to chiggers and rusty beer cans, the park provided a natural venue for his "giant" screen. Its strategic location was perfect for luring shoppers to Dover's retail hub and was large enough to accommodate crowds that oftentimes swelled to as many as 30 or 40 folks. The Deuter Brothers, Riker, Mickey, and I had our butts parked in the park long before Mr. Outdoor Movie Man showed up on the first Saturday night of every summer month. We arrived early to stake out our front row "seats" with blankets, tarps, and rugs. That's how folks divvied up the seating space. Blankets, tarps, and rugs. Once in place, they defined the territorial border that was not to be violated by so much as an overlapping pillow or bare foot. When border disputes flared up, they were waged with a back-and-forth *Get ch'asses over* until the weaker party retreated.

As the dusty sun went down behind the dusty fields that surrounded Dover, Mr. Outdoor Movie Man arrived in his '53 Plymouth with trailer in tow. The first order of business was to tie his giant screen to the rickety 2x4 frame that the Commercial Club members threw up every spring. His giant screen was IMAXian (to a fourth-grader anyway). In reality, it was nothing more than a couple cotton sheets that Mrs. Outdoor Movie Man sewed together. He wobbled on his ladder as he weaved twine through the little rings that Mrs. Outdoor Movie Man sewed along the edges of their repurposed, mostly-unstained sheets. We sat on our blankets, tarps, and rugs, fascinated by the shimmies and shakes of his rickety ladder leaning on the rickety frame. Waiting…waiting…hoping. Somehow, he never fell.

His sheet-screen was not without a few battle scars. One year, mid-July I think, we were well into our summer ritual movie, when some pissed-off patron in Tilleys was well into *his* summer ritual of getting pissed-up. The pissed-off, pissed-up patron apparently didn't like the way Clark Gable winked at Betty Grable, so he hurled his half-empty bottle of Schlitz at the sheet-screen. It ripped a hole through Mr. Gable's right eye. Or was it Miss Grable's left eye? (I get my Gables and Grables garbled.) Anyway, for the remainder of that season we suffered the consequences of that pissed-off patron's Gable/Grable fiasco and watched the movies with huge chunks missing. Have you ever tried to watch Marilyn Monroe with one of her, umm...*attributes* projected into the void? Apparently Mrs. Outdoor Movie Man was too busy to repair the repurposed, mostly-unstained sheets.

After Mr. Outdoor Movie Man had his screen secured he climbed down off his rickety ladder and went back to his trailer to haul out the Rube Goldberg contraption that he called a *projector*. It was bigger than a Buick, complete with gears, belts, and pulleys. On the side it had little knobs that he constantly twisted and turned during the movie. We never enjoyed more than ten or fifteen seconds of viewing pleasure without the image fading in and out of focus. Mrs. Outdoor Movie Man finally convinced him to go see the eye doctor when she got up one morning and caught him getting dressed in their closet and wearing one of her dresses. He blamed it on his eyesight. After that he pretty much left those little knobs alone. But not her dresses.

Mr. Robick was the next to arrive. The owner of D&B Grocery, Mr. Divorak (who claimed to be a great-great nephew of Antonin Dvořák—sans the funny lines and squiggles), negotiated a truce with Mr. Robick that they would provide the refreshments for the captive audience on alternate summers. Like Dover's fast-pitch softball park, their exclusivity allowed them to operate their retail snack trade unfettered by competition. Once again unfettered price gouging ensued.

By mid-July, Dover Saturday nights were hotter than a firecracker. One sausage-sizzling Saturday night, Dover's outdoor movie era came to an abrupt end. Something awful happened. So awful that the Commercial Club pulled the plug on Dover's last picture show. That "something awful" was so scandalous it got burned into my brain forever.

That last night looked like it was going to play out pretty much like every other outdoor movie night. Blankets, tarps, and rugs had been deployed and territorial borders had been established. Mr. Outdoor Movie Man had his screen tied in place and his Buick-sized projector all fired up. Mr. Robick's popcorn was popping. The picture-show's pitcher of butter had a nice moth-scum fluttering on top. Mommies with endlessly squalling brats lined up along the back where they suffered endless shouts of "Shut that kid the hell up."

Darkness fell. Mr. Outdoor Movie Man clicked the switch on his projector. Belts, gears, and pulleys whirred to life. The lights inside Bonfigs and Tilleys dimmed when the power-sucking Buick-thing sapped Dover's electrical grid. We settled down into the comfort of our blankets, tarps, and rugs waiting for the Technicolor stars and starlets to flash across the sheet-screen. The sweltering July heat swirled and simmered. The first "shut that kid the hell up" had already been fired off. Popcorn crunched in the night. Buttered-lips and greasy cheeks shimmered in the moonlight. Moth wings were spat across territorial borders onto adjacent blankets and tarps. Hank Williams choked in the middle of *Your Cheatin' Heart* when Tilley pulled the plug on her jukebox in deference to the movie crowd.

Slowly the screen flickered to life. Fade-in the opening scene with *film noir* fuzziness. *What's this?* Some artsy-fartsy

European émigré director showing off what he learned in artsy-fartsy film director school? Mumbled voices? Moaning? *Really...was that moaning*? We looked at each other. Where the hell's Bugs Bunny? Or Mickey Mouse? We always got a Looney Tune or two before the movie. Confusion. Where were the David O. Selznick Technicolor titles and orchestral sound track? Where was John Wayne? Clark Gable? Betty Grable?

ZZZZAP...the fuzziness focused to life with burning brilliance. The images jumped off the screen at us. The source of all that moaning was suddenly revealed in a twisting tangle of arms and legs. Two men...one woman? Two women...one man? That part of my recollection is a little foggy. Regardless of the ratio, I *do* remember that the man (or both men?) was wearing a Zorro mask. Just a Zorro mask. That was all! All three of them...the entire *ménage à trois*...they were...they were...*neked*!! Mothers screamed. Brats screamed louder. Men hooted. (They had busted out of Tilleys when they heard those opening moans, apparently having heard moans like that somewhere before.) Mr. Robick, jockeying for a better look-see, spilled moth-wing-butter all over his pants as he tripped over a blanketful of kids.

The Deuter Brothers, Riker, Mickey, Gary, and I were frozen to our blankets and tarps. Mesmerized as the masked man (or men) proceeded to educate us in ways that our chicken-shit dads couldn't touch.

The lust lingered for several minutes which, to us, seemed like hours. Finally (alas), out of the back row, some screaming mommy rushed up, tossed her screaming brat to Mr. Outdoor Movie Man, grabbed a bottle of RC Cola from Mr. Robick's tub of ice, and went postal on the projector. The sizzling industrial-strength projector bulb exploded. Sparks showered the night sky.

The following week Mr. Outdoor Movie Man was summoned by the acting-president of Dover's Commercial Club. All those righteous mommies in the back row demanded and got the former Commercial Club president's resignation. The acting-president invited Father Hempel to the meeting to provide moral ballast. Mr. Outdoor Movie Man cowered as he stood before them, mumbling something about how he and Mrs. Outdoor Movie Man had been arguing about her disappearing dresses and things got, well, a little heated. He ran out the back door as her rage escalated and, in his panic to dodge her dinner plates, he grabbed the wrong film. He mistakenly snatched one from the stack he reserved for his Thursday night gig at the Bill Town Elks Lodge.

Mr. Outdoor Movie Man was banned from ever showing another film. Dover's golden era of outdoor movies came to an end. Our Saturday nights would never be the same.

Many of us Dover boys would never be the same either. Those shocking images were burned forever into our brains.

Thank you, Mr. Outdoor Movie Man.

Thank you.

LUNCHROOM LEGUMES

Nowadays colleges have cafeterias, private boarding schools have dining halls (Harry Potter supped in the Great Hall at Hogwarts), and the tonier Junior Highs have a campus *café*. These upscale eateries are replete with soft lighting, soft seating, and soft rock. They even have alternative menus dished up at satellite serving stations offering entrées that the Michelin folks would award their much-coveted three-star rating. Nutrition? Hah! Nutrition has nothing to do with it. For today's everybody-gets-a-trophy generation, it's all about making the little bastards feel good.

At Saint Boniface we had a *Lunchroom*. No cafeteria. No campus *café*. A Lunchroom. And there was no mistaking the lunchroom's function. It was a spartan facility where clean-your-plate compliance was compulsory. Picky eaters were known to spend entire days in the Lunchroom; shackled to a table leg until their plastic plate-tray thing was scrapped clean. (In those days the rudimentary plastic was flimsy at best, so in order to reinforce its rigidity, the plastic factory added asbestos fibers.) It was the unchallenged realm of Sister Mary Larry, a.k.a. Lord of the Lunchroom. She ruled her ptomaine palace like a fascist.

Deep in the bowels of the Saint Boniface basement there were three rooms: 1. The coal room—where they (duh!) dumped the coal down the (double-duh!) coal chute to heat the school and church. 2. The kitchen—where they *sort of* cooked the food. 3. The lunchroom—where we stuffed that *sort-of* cooked food down our throats. As we entered the lunchroom, dimly-lit to make it impossible to identify the food-like fare, there was no doubt that we were about to descend into Sister Mary Larry's sanctum sanctorum. A plaque above the door revealed Dante's classic inscription: **ABANDON ALL HOPE, YE WHO ENTER HERE**. After the pupils' pupils dilated, the Lunchroom Rules carved into the concrete walls behind the serving line came into focus: 1. Sit down. 2. Shut up. 3. Eat. That was all we needed to know. Resistance was futile. Comply and twelve allotted minutes later, you might escape with your freedom. Violate any one of the rules and that **ABANDON ALL HOPE** part would be your fate. According to Saint Boniface student lore, buried somewhere in the dusty depths of that adjacent coal room, lay the skeletal remains of those who challenged S.M. Larry's rules.

The meats that were flopped on our plastic plate-tray things added a whole 'nother definition to the word mystery. The thin soups were colored water with flotsam and jetsam skittering across the surface like thin water bugs. The sandwiches—nothing more than oily butter on white Wonder Bread—were Dickensian by today's pizza, cheeseburger, and you-want-fries-with-that school cafés. None of us thought it unusual that the near-zero nutritional value Wonder Bread butter sandwiches qualified as an entrée. We mindlessly tossed them down our throats as we raced against the clock to comply with Rule 3.

There was one menu item that shook the very foundations of our souls. Trepidation stewed in our gut juice as we descended those dark stairs into gastronomic hell.

When would it be this week? Tuesday? Thursday?" She guarded her target day ferociously. None of us knew when she would foist them on us. Once a week, every week, Sister Mary Larry commanded the cooks to cook them. They were foul-smelling. They were evil-tasting. They were vomit-inducing. They were *Lima Beans*.

The cooks soaked the legumes all night until they swelled to the size of the two-for-a-penny jaw breakers at Robicks. Then they were boiled. *Boiled hard* in ten-gallon pots until the inedible pebbles morphed into inedible mush. Then the cooks took them from their military-grade twelve-burner stove and tossed in a concoction of tomato paste, tomato sauce, and tomato ketchup until the resulting mélange resembled some medieval gruel. Sister Mary Larry always took the first taste. She swirled it around in her mouth like a wine connoisseur swishing a fine Bordeaux. Satisfied, she spit it out on the floor and pronounced the barely recognizable legumes ready. Notice she did not pronounce them palatable. Just *ready*.

We filed past the servers (eighth graders who were sorta like prison trustees) and held our plastic plate-trays up until we heard the conformational *plop* (our pupils were still not dilated). We pivoted and proceeded to our assigned table where, in compliance with rule number two, stared in silence at our three-section plastic plate. On most days the three neatly divided sections isolated our various vittles. Meat in one, potatoes in another, and veggies in the third. Dessert was never an option. The starving China kids never got dessert—so why should we? But on Lime Bean Day—yup, you guessed it—we stared at a heaping three-section trinity of Lima Beans. I cupped my hands over my mouth to stifle a gag reflex. Sixteen third-graders with sixteen cupped mouths gaped with death-row eyes at each other. We knew. Eat or join the class of '53 for a coal-nap.

In addition to us third-graders, the other tables were lined with other-graders in various degrees of retching. All of us except for one little boy. One precious, wonderful little boy seated at the far end of (thank you Jesus) *our* table. Jerry Brumgart, my second cousin. He was—how do I say this and not offend—he was *different*. He played with the girls at recess. Parted his hair in the middle and wore pastel sweaters. Sometimes argyle socks. But the most beautiful thing about him—the weirdest part—he actually *liked* lima beans. He craved them and consumed them with gusto. On Lima Bean Day, Jerry was everybody's best friend. There was just one not-so-subtle problem. *Her*.

Sister Mary Larry patrolled around the linoleum floors like a junkyard dog, her nun-shoe heels clicking in the eerie silence that was broken only by the rhythmic clatter of tin spoons scraping on three-section plastic plate-trays. She put the fear of God in us with the steady *clap-clap-clap* of her ruler smacking her palm. With muscles quivering just beneath her cheek skin, her clenched jaws made it obvious that, with the slightest provocation, she'd lash out at any kid who dared to violate rule number two. We pretended to eat, really just shoving the gruel around with our tin spoons, as we waited for her to waddle over to patrol the far side of the lunchroom. Then, when we were out of view, we rushed to offload our plate-trays onto Jerry's. He ate as fast as we shoveled. Oh, how every third-grader loved my second cousin. Pastel sweaters and all.

It was one of those dreary February Thursdays. Warm enough to melt the dirty snow from Dover's dirty sidewalks, but cold enough that we still need our cheap JC Penney rayon parkas. We hadn't seen sunshine since October 12th. It was cold and it was bleak and…it was Lima Bean Day. But this was not to be just *any* Lima Bean Day. It would be the Lima Bean Day from hell. Lunchroom Lima Bean Day as we knew it would be changed forever.

Our table got busted.

Gina Lekenberg was a little slow on the draw that day as she was shoveling section three of her plate-tray onto Jerry's when Sister Mary Larry caught her red-handed. Literally—*red* handed. To expedite the bean transfer, she threw down her tin spoon and shoved the mush with her hand. Jerry didn't mind. He was a booger eater, so a little palm scum was no big deal. When the Lord of the Lunchroom spied Gina's hand dripping with tomato paste, well, it was game over! From that day forward, SML sequestered Jerry on Lima Bean Day at a corner table set up just for him. To keep him isolated, she had Nick Jacoby, the school janitor, come in on Lima Bean Day and tip some tables around him like the pioneers did when they circled the wagons.

With my second cousin Jerry now pretty much out of the picture; we scrambled for an alternative solution to our dilemma. We had to do something before SML's 12-inch ruler permanently injured someone's knuckles. We might have had a future concert pianist in our midst. Turns out we didn't. But we coulda'.

So…here's what we did:

Every Friday evening after the blackboards were scrubbed, the erasers pounded clean, and the cloakroom swept, Sister

Mary Larry cut us loose for the weekend. After we were gone and the doors were locked, SML met with my Aunt Amelia. (Everyone called her Hub. Go figure. But then again, if my name was Amelia, I guess I'd prefer everyone call me Hub too.) Hub was the head-cook at Saint Boniface. Larry (we dropped the *Sister Mary* thing a lot) and Hub huddled in the office to organize next week's lunch menu. Friday was always a no-brainer—fish sticks. It was a Catholic thing. Larry always reserved at least one day for our white Wonder Bread butter sandwiches. The only criteria that she had for Lima Bean Day was that it be randomly rotated on any day except, of course, Friday. Oh, and the same day could not be repeated from one week to the next. And under *no* circumstances, never not ever, were the students allowed to know which day. "We can't have the little bastards committing an act of espionage," SML told Aunt Amelia...err...Hub.

So, after they agreed on the next week's menu, Aunt Amelia, dangit...Hub, jotted it down on a napkin, stuck it in her bra for safe keeping, and went home for a weekend of well-deserved rest. Larry went back to the convent where she climbed up to the attic and hug upside-down on a rafter until Monday morning.

Aunt Hub was actually my *Great*-Aunt, so (here we go with all that gnarly Dover DNA again) her daughter was my *second* cousin. Like everyone else, she hated lima beans. So, with minimal persuasion from me, she agreed to sneak into her mom's bedroom during the *Gunsmoke* rerun on Saturday night, shake her bra (her mom's, not her trainer) until the napkin fell out (the one with the menu, not the four or five stuffed in her trainer). Then she copied down next week's menu. She slipped it to me after Mass on Sunday morning. Defying our second-cousin DNA, I kissed her anyway. And just in case anyone was looking—on the cheek.

Later that night, during *The Ed Sullivan Show,* I was supposed to be doing my homework while Mom and the old man were laughing their asses off at Señor Wences and his talking hand with its lipsticked lips (when I got to be a teenager I did that to my hand when I locked myself in the bathroom and got Mom's lipstick out of the medicine cabinet). I tore a sheet of paper from my Big Chief tablet and wrote 47 notes with Lima Bean Day identified in my secret code. Monday was *Nun-day.* Tuesday was *Dues-day.* Wednesday—*Wets-day.* You get the idea. I worked weeks to develop that code and was certain it was uncrackable.

The next day, *Nun-day* morning after Mass, I passed out my uncrackable coded notes to everyone.

As the days rolled by, reassured by our secret knowledge of Larry's *secret* menu, we paraded into the lunchroom with complete confidence. A bit of a bounce in our step. A sense of anticipation was in the air. Larry suspected that something was up. It was angst-written all over her face. With delicious pleasure, we watched her get all jittery with suspicion: *Why the hell are the little bastards smiling in my lunchroom?* No one ever smiled in her lunchroom.

Lima Bean Day finally arrived. I'm pretty sure it was *Wets-Day* that week. We crawled from our beds in the misty dawn to put our plan into motion. Every Catholic kid in Dover sat in jammies at their kitchen table and complained about their bowels over bowls of Cheerios. Stomach cramps and diarrhea—one of the easiest maladies to fake. For those of us more accomplished in the art of deception, we actually puked. Didn't even need the old finger-down-the-throat thing. Just thinking of lima beans produced puke. Within minutes Dover's party lines lit up like a Christmas tree as our disgusted mothers telephoned Sister Mary Larry. Our sick-in was on.

One kid actually showed up at school that morning. You can probably guess who.

HOT DOGS

Our life stories are filled with character-defining chapters that bubble up from time to time. They put fire in our spirits, love in our hearts, and ants in our pants. Those character-defining episodes are called by various names: Milestones. Rites of passage. My old man, arm-chair philosopher and shameless fatalist, said it better than anyone—*Shit Happens*.

Sometimes those events fetch smiles. Sometimes—tears. We never know *when* they'll pull up a chair and join us at our banquet of life. It might be when we're "*...flyin' high in April or shot down in May*," as ol' Blue Eyes crooned. Are they part of some cosmic plan? Or are they serendipitous? Unforeseen? Who knows? Forget those philosophical implications; we don't even know when they'll happen or what they'll be. They just happen and we don't even recognize it until we examine them in hindsight with the clarity of 20/20 retrospection.

While writing these look-back crazy gazes at my life, I got to thinking about several of *my* character-defining episodes. Some still have such hurtful sharp edges, I'll take a moment and give them a passing mention here: When Freckles chased one car too many and I carried her broken body home to lay her in her smelly dog house for the last time. When Uncle Louie crashed his airplane in a thunderstorm out in the Dakota prairies and they brought him home in a box. How my sister's life was changed forever after the 1950's polio epidemic swept through Dover. And that fuckin' Vietnam mess.

Okay, got those serious issues off my chest. Let's not linger. Would you like to enjoy one of my *unserious* ponderings? Alrighty then. There was another time when (paraphrasing the old man) *feces occurred* in my life that I want you to know about. Let me explain:

The Deuter brothers and I were on one of our pop bottle safaris with my little brother Richie in tow. Mom always made me take him with us. We redeemed our bottles at Robicks for three cents and divvied up the booty 3½ ways (little shit Richie got half a share). Occasionally though, Richie came in handy. He was small enough that we hoisted him up and flipped him into some of the more promising trash barrels to pilfer the pop bottles we couldn't reach. We always stopped at Old Lady Hoffman's barrel to toss him in. She had the wonderfully wasteful habit of throwing out Old Man Hoffman's empty pop bottles. Apparently three cents was no big deal to her. Doc Hansen warned Old Man Hoffman that his two-six-pack-a-day addiction to RC Cola would spike his diabetes. Some men hid their whiskey. Some—*Playboys*. Old Man Hoffman stashed RC Cola. Every Saturday morning when he was out mowing the lawn, Old Lady Hoffman searched the house looking for the stockpiles squirreled away in his all-too-familiar hidey-holes. But like an exasperated wife of an incurable alcoholic, she finally gave up. Said the fightin' wasn't worth it.

At the graveside service, when it was his turn to offer a few words about the deceased, Doc Hansen, more concerned about his professional reputation than Old Man Hoffman's demise, offered up a few somber words, "I tried to warn him, but the stubborn old fart just wouldn't listen." Old Lady Hoffman donated his entire bib overall wardrobe to Sister Mary Larry for the African Missions (apparently neither she nor SML stopped to think how the heck some skinny-ass African tribesman was going to fit into 8XL bib overalls). She had just finished cleaning out all those hidey-holes the Saturday morning after his funeral as we stumbled down the alley. We ran toward her post-mortem trash barrel when we saw that it was erupting like Mount Vesuvius. After the Deuter brothers raked off the easy pickins' we tossed Richie in. He surfaced several times, popping up between last night's spaghetti and an amorphous scum of creamed *something*. Maybe chipped beef. When he surfaced for air he was cradling in his arms as many still-unbroken bottles as he could hold. By the time we finished with Old Lady Hoffman's windfall our wagon was overflowing, so we cut our safari short and rushed straightaway for Robicks. We bought sacksful of stuff: Snickers, Planters Peanuts, Jaw Breakers, Red Hots, Milk Duds, Boston Baked Beans, and Holloway All-Day Suckers. We never, not once, deferred our hedonic pleasures by doing something so stupid like saving our money. We were on the leading edge of the social behavior known today as instant gratification.

We were barely halfway home when we heard it. The unmistakable rumble of a Ford flathead V-8. If you ever heard one of those 65-horsepower, eight-cylinder marvels, you'd never forget it. So of course, right away we knew who it was. Didn't even have to look. Jesse Riker and Mickey Green barreled around the corner in Riker's '54 Crown Victoria.

Let me tell you a little about Jesse Riker—we called him Riker. Not sure why. I think he told us to. Maybe thought it made him sound like one of those guys in his old man's Soldier of Fortune magazines (which back then had pictures of girls that real Soldiers of Fortune apparently like to fool around with). He was the first, and at that point the *only* one of us that had his own car. Here's how he got those wheels: Like many other Dover Men, his old man was a wage-slave at the tractor plant. Against all odds, Riker's old man finagled his way to get promoted to shop foreman. Local gossip had it that Riker's dad walked into his boss's office one lunch hour to complain about the men smoking in the foundry (go figure) and caught him behind the filing cabinets going at it with Gladys Bonner (the factory guys called her Gladys *Boner*). Gladys worked in the personnel office and always found an excuse to visit his office at lunchtime for a little, shall we say…*dic-tation*. Well, the pissed-off shop foreman secured Riker's old man's silence with a bribe: "Ya keep yer damn mouth shut and I'll see to it ya get a cushy foreman's job just like mine. AND…a nice pay bump. Not to mention a parking space up on the front row."

I'm telling you all this because in Dover's social hierarchy, Riker's folks were considered to be in the upper crust. That ranking was based solely on the financial shot in the arm that came with that "nice pay bump." Education, family lineage, or culture had nothing to do with being in Dover's upper crust. In those days, the only metric used to determine class distinction was money. (Pretty much just like it is today.) So, with his much-envied pay-bump, Riker's old man, who by now had cultivated the cock-sure presumption that comes with being a shop foreman, bought his son the Crown Vic. After all, what good is money if you can't flaunt it?

"Hey, you guys wanna have some fun?" Mickey Green rolled down his window and shouted as Riker screeched the Crown Vic to a stop.

"Heck yeah," half-share Richie piped up somewhere behind us, sucking on a Holloway's All-Day Sucker.

"Shut up, Richie. Mickey wasn't talkin' to you," I said. Then I said to Mickey, who was by now half-hanging out the window, "Heck yeah."

"Jump in," Riker yelled from behind the wheel where he was fiddling with the fuzzy dice dangling from his rear-view mirror that always got knotted up whenever he slammed on the brakes. "Old Man Peters got his leaves raked out to the street and we're gonna roast a little dinner and raise a little hell." That was all he had to say. We squeezed into the back seat. When he finally finished dickin' with his tangled fuzzy dice, Riker reached for the radio and turned Hank Williams down from DEFCON-3 so he wouldn't have to shout. "We're goin' to Robicks for some weenies. You guys got money?"

"Heck, yeah," Richie said.

"Shut up, Richie," Arnie said. "He ain't talkin' to you." He looked back at Riker and said, "Heck, yeah."

Milo chimed in, "We still got 28¢ left over. (Even little hedonic bastards like us could eat just so much candy.) We'll get the buns."

As we left Robicks with our buns and wienies, Mickey shouted over Hank Williams (who was once again booming), "We'll stop by Old Lady Hoffman's front yard and cut some sticks from her hydrangeas for the weenies." Our pop-bottle benefactor was by now probably sitting at the kitchen table celebrating with a glass of Chardonnay with her bachelor milkman (who smelled opportunity) and wouldn't notice us out in her front yard hacking away at her hydrangeas.

Old Man Peters—I swear that was his Christian name—*Old Man*. No one ever called him any other name. I'd bet a six-pack of still-unbroken pop bottles that his birth certificate read *O.M. Peters*. Anyway, Old Man Peters was Dover's official cranky bastard. Like Old Man Hoffman he wore way-big OshKosh B'Gosh bib overalls that were pretty much *de rigueur* for anyone over 50. Mostly old men…but some old women too. A lot of them (the old men) went shirtless all summer, providing anyone who came close enough a free (and much unwanted) anatomical revelation.

Old Man Peters owned two lots on the south side of town next to the town dump. His big house (and four lesser coonhound houses) squatted in the middle of seldom-cut undergrowth and a jungle of trees. He had finished raking his annual harvest of oak, piss elm, and box elder leaves and heaped them in the street all along his double-lot. Every year he soaked an old rag in kerosene and stuck it on a pitch fork to set them ablaze. Some years his blazes were epic. The fall of '55 was an unusually dry autumn that kept the old farts up at Tilleys talking half the winter about how it was the driest since '38. Just as his blaze grew to biblical proportions, a south wind gusted in and the entire town dump shot up in flames. It smoldered for weeks, reeking of old tires and asbestos. That gave them enough conversational fodder to keep them busy the rest of the winter.

"What about Old Man Peters' coonhounds?" I shouted. "They'll be all over us while we're standin' by the fire. They'll eat the weenie right off our stick."

"You *ijit*," Mickey shouted (the guys called me that a lot). "We ain't gettin' outa the car. Riker'll park at the end of the block, in front of Johnny Miller's rent house and we'll wait for

Old Man Peters to fire off his leaves. When she's throwin' flames real good, we'll roll down the windows and shove our weenie sticks out. Riker'll go like a bat outa hell next to the fire and time we get to the other end—we got dinner. Burnt perfection."

As I listened to Mickey I started getting a little nervous. Actually, a *lot* nervous. Riker's Crown Vic always reeked of gas fumes. The rust on the Vic's fenders was exceeded only by the rust on its gas tank. We had "patched" that gas tank more than once by rubbing it with a bar of Ivory Soap.

But even more than those gas fumes, I smelled something else. Disaster!

One thing we never ever did in front of each other was display weakness. Especially if Arnie was around. Remember Arnie? He'd pick a fight for something as simple as the color of your underwear (which in those pre-boxer days was always *more or less* white). So, knowing that discretion was the better part of valor (and way better than getting kicked in the balls by Arnie), I stifled my reservations and pussied out.

"Heck, yeah," my voice cracked again. "Let's do this."

Riker stopped the Crown Vic in front of Johnny Miller's rent house as planned. We sat there and waited. The flathead rumbled. I looked through the windshield past the fuzzy dice, trying to mask my pussiness. There he was. Off in the distance I watched Old Man Peters touch his Zippo to the kerosene-soaked rags. Even a block away we heard the *Whoooomph*. After he finished slapping his scorched whiskers, he looked at his torch and saw that it was ready and wobbled toward the leaf pile.

He started at the end of the leafbank nearest us and walked the line, torching his piss elm and oak leaves like some arsonist on Channel 7 News at 6. The sun was beginning to set as the raging inferno lit up the street all the way to the by now replenished city dump. Sparks spiraled upward like drunken fireflies.

Riker dropped the shifter into first. "Let's roll," Mickey shouted.

The flathead roared.

The tires squealed.

Richie screamed.

Patsy Cline raged.

I pussied in silence.

We had had our sticks wienered-up and poked them out of the widows of the screaming Crown Vic. Mickey had two sticks. One for himself. The other for Riker. Arnie's stick was double-wienered. He had the appetite of a lumberjack and could eat half his old man's paycheck in two days. Richie just sat back. He already ate his wiener. Raw.

We looked like slaves on a lopsided Roman Galley with our wiener oars sticking out.

Smoke billowed.

Eyes watered.

Wieners sizzled.

Riker swerved.

I pussied in silence.

Hot sparks sucked in through the windows as the Crown Vic zipped closer. Old Man Peters scrambled to get the hell out of the way. Coonhounds wailed. Flames shot higher. Riker steered even closer, his tires knee-deep in hell.

Riker finally slammed the Crown Vic to a stop at the other end, his fuzzy dice all gnarly again. Our eyes watered in the back-seat haze as we hacked like three-pack-a-dayers. The Crown Vic's paint was blistered.

Doors flew open and we piled out like circus clowns. Somehow we managed to hold on to our weenies. I broke out the buns and Milo unscrewed the ketchup bottle. We stood behind the car, giggling like girls as we savored our culinary achievement.

"Let's do it again," Richie squealed.

Five wiener-bun muffled mouths shouted, "Shut up, Richie."

Remember the beginning of this chapter? Where I said this was one of those life-changing events for me? Well, even to this day, whenever I'm driving home after work on some cool October evening in our quiet suburban neighborhood and see folks out violating the city code and burning their leaves, I *almost* turn around to go back to Safeway for a package of...

But then...I pussy out.

BIG-ASS WEDDINGS

In order for evolutionary events to move things along, a natural sequence must take place. The Grand Cosmic Design of Everything is driven by a dynamic protocol which dictates just how things can proceed. You want a Universe? First, you need a Big Bang. You want a chicken? Not until you first have an egg (or is it the other way around?). You want a few friends over for steaks tonight? First, you need a cow.

Okay, hang on—this is what you call the *set-up*—you want babies? First you have to go out and get a girlfriend (or boyfriend), date 'em, kiss 'em, marry 'em, and then—well, you know the rest. By today's loosey-goosey marital standards, that evolutionary sequence of events is a novel concept. But that's how it was in Dover. Let's take a look at how this all worked out:

Marriage was a sacred institution back then. Mr. & Mrs. Married Couple were not at all like today's slippery singles whose slippery marital relationships way-to-often terminate in court battles where child custody is challenged as the litigants shout: *You take em'… No, you take em'*. The divorce rate in

Dover was roughly zero. Zip. Nada. Due in large part to the sanctity of the institution (and a little thing called love). *Till death do you part* was taken seriously. Today, according to the last statistic I read, over half of the marriages in United States wind up busted. Got that? More than half.

Happy beginnings make happy endings. Gramma said that a lot. It was her standard answer when we asked her, "How'd you stay married to Grandpa so long?" As cute as Gramma's homespun logic sounded, she didn't mention the hard part: the *gittin' along* stuff that follows the *happy beginnings* stuff. Mr. & Mrs. Married Couple stuck together through good times and bad. Sickness and health. When love was a critical component in the relationship, the missus missed her mister if they were apart more than a day. Did the mister miss his missus? You better believe it. Just read my old man's WWII tear-stained love letters soaked with jungle sweat.

Marriage is hard. Marriage can be not-fun. It requires dedication and trust. Marriage is more about understanding and sacrifice than bunny-rabbit sex. My old man, the crown prince of homespunsterisms, put it like this: "If Mom ain't havin' fun…ain't none of us havin' fun." Most of us guys *get* that. We better.

Courtship was alive and well in Dover. Perhaps not as courtshippy as the prudish Victorians. A Victorian young man pursued the affections of a Victorian lady for decades. If he was lucky (and persistent as hell), he might win her hand in marriage about the time she stopped menstruating. Which, come to think of it, is probably why Victorian marriages were so successful. Hell hath no fury like sayin' the wrong thing to the wrong woman at the wrong time of the month.

Dover courtships, while not of Victorian extremes, usually ran a respectable one or two years. There was no such thing as a whirlwind romance. No *quickies*. If a Dover courtship ever ran less than a year, the gossip mongers fired up the party lines; whispering words like *knocked up* and *pg* (a common euphemism back then...pronounced pee-gee if you need help). The old man, never one to rush things, courted my mom for five years. But then, that little adventure out in the Pacific jungles kinda got in the way.

Following the courtship came the down-on-one-knee engagement. And finally, hot on the heels of the down-on-one-knee—the Big-Ass Wedding. Gramma's *happy beginnings* part. I'm not talking about your average justice-of-the-peace, do-you-I-do...do-you-me-too, fitty-dollar wedding. I'm talking about a Big-Ass Dover Catholic Wedding where the storybook bride and groom were bookended by no less than *eight* bridesmaids and *eight more* best men. So many that the wedding photographer needed a Panavision lens. The pews got packed butt-to-butt with three or four hundred relatives and best-friends-ever all dressed up in their Sunday clothes. Father Hempel always said that nothing put feets under the seats like a wedding. He stood before the giddy bride and groom wearing a wistful expression on his priestly face as he gazed at the assembled masses; oftentimes shedding a telltale tear. He wasn't so much contemplative of the blessed event he was about to celebrate as he was for the missed opportunity to take up what surely would have been a sizable collection. Passing the collection plate at Big-Ass Dover Catholic Weddings was frowned upon by the bishop. The bishop figured that the bride's family had already shelled out enough for the grand *soirée*. And all those guests? Well, the guests (except for a couple of cheap-ass uncles) shelled out three or four hours pay on some cheesy blanket or toaster. But not to worry, they'd more than recover their cheesy-toaster costs with all the free-flowing beer and ample ham sandwiches waiting for them at the reception.

Following the taking of the vows (not the taking of the collection), the newly minted Mr. & Mrs. paraded down the aisle behind their 16-member entourage. Sister Mary Augustine, (Sister Mary Larry's sister sister), was nestled somewhere amongst a forest of organ pipes up in the choir loft where she blasted the only secular song she knew—*Here Comes the Bride*. The stained glass window behind the altar shook so hard it looked like Jesus really was rising from the holy sepulcher.

The bride and groom, still not even out of the church, were about to experience their first test of marital tolerance. Three or four hundred relatives and best-friends-ever slathered them with sweaty hugs and wet kisses as the couple stood in the vestibule. Lusty uncles held their kisses maybe a little too long. A sharp elbow and not-so-subtle *Behave yourself dammit, folks are lookin'* uttered by a not-so-subtle aunt was usually all it took to get them back in line.

With the slathering done and the lascivious uncles still grinning, next up—The Gauntlet. Folks shuffled out the door and lined up on the steps where little nieces and nephews decked out in big peoples' dresses and suits passed among them carrying buckets of rice. They reached in and filled their fists. After the bride wiped the all the uncle-drool off her face, the freshly-minted Mr. and Mrs. ventured from the vestibule. They braced themselves knowing what was coming. As they walked down the steps, hundreds of flailing fists pummeled them with a thunderstorm of rice.

After the rice deluge, the bride and groom were swept away by whichever groomsman had the newest used car. Its two-tone paint job, scrawled from hood to trunk with white shoe polish with quips like: *Just Married, Hot Springs Tonight,* and of course, the ever-popular, *Suckers*. They were chauffeured through Dover in a tin-can-dragging, horn-honking parade of used cars and yelping dogs.

They returned (sometimes hours later) after they stopped at all three of Dover's taverns to be toasted by the semi-sober well-wishers who had been inexplicably omitted on the near-universal invitation list. True friendship was directly proportional to inclusion on the wedding invitation list. The couple was escorted down to the church basement reception hall, festooned with cheesy crepe paper ribbons and cheesy crepe paper wedding bells. Rows of tables were well embellished with little paper cups spilling over with pink and yellow mints and salted peanuts. The couple went virtually unnoticed as they entered; the room already abuzz with three or four hundred relatives and best-friends-ever already well into their third plastic cup of Schlitz. The actual event, the wedding, was by now a sideshow. Everyone was there for one thing and one thing only: their *pay-back* beer buzz. Actually a *free* beer-buzz for the cheap bastards who didn't bother to bring a cheesy toaster or blanket.

After the bride and groom fought their way through the throng of beer-sloshing best-friends-ever, some Saint Boniface altar society lady, usually the one with the biggest set of, err, *lungs*, shouted: *Dinner!* (My God!—it was nearly noon!) 300 heads swiveled. 600 ears bristled. And 259 plastic cups bottomed-up (Father Hemple abstained. You know…appearances). Then it was every man, woman, and child for him and herself. The Running of the Bulls in Pamplona paled by comparison. Chairs got kicked. Kids got trampled. Elbows got jabbed. Eventually the ravenous crowd formed a line in front of the serving table. A lavish *two-course* dinner had been prepared by the big-lung altar society woman and her squad of big-lung altar society church ladies: Ham sandwiches and potato chips. And if the bride's father had worked a little overtime or sold an extra hog or two, maybe a few gallons of Van Camp's Pork n' Beans to complement the *haute cuisine*.

The diners' dinners, which included three or four free ham sandwiches (cost recovery, ya know) got interrupted when *it* started. Some tradition-bound aunt presiding in the back row usually got it going: Clink...clink...clink...**clink**. Before long the entire room rang out with 257 spoons clanging on 257 water glasses (Mr. & Mrs. *and* Father Hemple abstained). Everyone knew what that meant. Folks waited for it. Expected it, actually. The bride and groom, faking reluctance like a couple of bad actors, eventually stood up for the clinking crescendo and kissed. Not some tight-lipped altar-kiss that Father Hemple had earlier enjoined them to perform with his "You may now...", but a back-seat-at-the-drive-in tongue-thruster. The clinking faded when the red-faced Father Hemple started jerking on the bride's dress. A few minutes later some other aunt presiding in some other back corner would get the whole thing going all over again.

Things didn't always go quite that smoothly at every Big-Ass Dover Catholic Wedding reception. I remember one where, in spite of all wet uncle-kisses, cheesy toasters, and water-glass clinking, the groom *did not* kiss his bride. Let me explain:

Jimmy Kowolski met Ludmella Kavinski at the tractor factory where they both worked. She had recently moved to Dover from Kansas or Canada or sommers. Might have been Kentucky. Anyway, when they spied each other across the second-shift assembly line one night, it was love at first sight according to Jimmy. Both of them were welders, and the first time he saw her with her helmet flipped up, he flipped out. Something about those bloodshot eyes he said. Ludmella lived in the apartment above Old Lady Koski's garage. Old Lady Koski was Jimmy's aunt. Remember that. Jimmy's aunt.

They courted for almost two years (social protocol you know). As Jimmy dropped Ludmella off at her apartment after their Wednesday night bowling league, he popped the big question, "What'cha doin' next weekend?" Ludmella gushed, "Nuthin'." Well, things just kind of took off from there. Apparently those were enough words to imply a marriage proposal. Before anyone knew it, Dover's party-lines bristled with the news of Dover's next Big-Ass Catholic Wedding. Ludmella called *her* aunt, Emma Kavinski (you gettin' all this?), in Canada or Kansas or sommers to invite her to the big-ass affair. She checked her social calendar and said right there on that long-distance phone call that she could *maybe* cancel her crochet club (she was right in the middle of crocheting some wicked doilies) and that she'd *try* to make the long drive up for the big event. However, when Ludmella told her there would be three or four kegs of free beer at the reception, a resounding *HELL YES!* boomed over the long-distance lines. Later, after they hung up (before the long distance call exceeded the much-feared three-minute limit), Ludmella's aunt felt somewhat guilty about her initial reluctance.

There they stood at the altar, all gussied up in their bride and groom outfits. Ludmella, just a journeyman welder at the tractor factory, couldn't afford a real wedding dress, so she bought an off-white (the party-line called it beige) summer dress at JC Penney. Only problem: it was sleeveless, low cut, and rigged up with one of those uplifting bra-things that are capable of making mountains out of molehills. Well, Ludmella, like her aunt Emma Kavinski, was pretty well-stacked and had more than a little trouble keeping her *girls* corralled. Father Hempel had more than a little trouble too; trying to keep his eyes off the girls and on the page of his *Big Book of Catholic Wedding Stuff*.

Lucky for him (he thanked Jesus) he had officiated at so many weddings that he could recite the entire ritual even with his stack-gazing eyes diverted from the page.

Father Hemple gazed out at the congregation and took a mental inventory of the pews, coveting those heaping collection plates that coulda, shoulda, woulda been gathered had not the bishop stuck his big fat nose in and laid down his no-wedding-collection policy. He was watching Ludmella slap one of her escapees back into her uplifting bra-thing when a ruckus arose from one of the back pews not far from the confessional. Ludmella's aunt, Emma Kavinski had had a flat tire in Missouri and was late. While Ludmella shoehorned the errant girl back into relative concealment, Aunt Emma was trying to shoehorn herself into the back pew between two unyielding parishioners. (Church people are funny that way. They sit in the exact same spot every Sunday for decades and, by God, don't you even try to make 'em move.) After a few sharp elbows and shoulder-shoves, she wiggled her way in. Which was the source of the ruckus. It's not easy squeezing a double-wide bottom into a single-wide pew.

As fate would have it, one of the don't-shove-*me*-over parishioners was Jimmy's aunt, Old Lady Koski.

Well, those two old women fumed at each other eyeball-to-eyeball, daring the other to blink first. Then, something clicked and, just like that, it was all over. You would have thought they won the Publisher's Clearinghouse Sweepstakes with all their carrying-on and such. The squeals, the hugs, the crying, the laughter, the all-consonant-nary-a-vowel Polish gibberish. Or was it Yiddish gibberish? (Who could tell?) 400 heads swiveled 180-degrees to see what the hell was all that back-pew squalling.

A flummoxed Father Hempel just stood there. *This...this never happened before. Weddings are solemn things. Staid, even*. He thumbed through his dog-eared *Big Book of Catholic Wedding Stuff* and found nothing. No canonical guidance. So he did what every priest in every parish did when confronted with a situation for which there was no canonical guidance. He just stood there and glared. He had all day. He could wait.

Things finally settled down when the two women broke their Polish or Yiddish (who could tell?) bear-hug. Father Hemple dialed his glare down a notch or two and asked them, well, shouted at them, "What *are* you two ladies doing?"

Okay, pay attention. This next paragraph is gonna get gnarly. Father Hemple stopped the wedding and told the two women to meet him in the sacristy along with Jimmy's sister for a little "conference." Emma Kavinski told him that she had moved to Kansas or Canada or sommers 40 years ago when her husband, Karl Kavinski, landed a job welding for the Kincaid Oil Company on their oil rigs. While they were in that back pew, locked eyeball-to-eyeball, she saw it. Old Lady Koski was her nearly-forgotten cousin. And since Old Lady Koski was Jimmy Kowolski's aunt, and since she and Emma Kavinski were long-lost cousins, that made Jimmy and Ludmella second cousins—or something.

That was all Father Hemple had to hear. He walked back out into the sanctuary—alone—and bluntly announced, "This wedding is suspended."

Confusion washed over the church basement crowd in waves. *This never happened before. Can Father Hemple really do that? Cancel a Big-Ass Wedding?* Well, by God, if they had all bothered to dress up in their Sunday clothes and haggle with the check-out clerk in the K-Mart up at the county seat over the cost of that cheesy toaster or fuzzy blanket, they were not to be denied. Heck, the ham sandwiches were already made up anyway. The potato chip bags were ripped open and the store wouldn't take them back now. But more than that, more than the chips and sandwiches, three or four kegs of Schlitz were iced down, tapped, and ready to go. No need to let a Big-Ass Canceled Catholic Wedding go to waste.

And that right there, to get this train-wreck of a story back on the tracks, is why at the free ham sandwich, chips, and beer big-ass wedding dinner in the church basement, Jimmy Kowolski and Ludmella Kavinski did *not* kiss when the water glasses cascaded with clinks. However, several did shatter. Frustrations can run high when age-old aunts are denied their *age-old* traditions. But thanks to the efforts of Jimmy's sister (who scurried around the room whispering her lips dry), all those frustrations were mitigated. After she explained the Kavinski-Koski thing, folks finally figured it out. Everybody knows that second cousins can't kiss. Let alone get married! So Jimmy and Ludmella just sat there and pouted at the head table with Father Hempel seated firmly between them.

Now here's the really weird part. After the third keg floated, Jimmy Kowolski and Ludmella Kavinski sneaked out of the reception and departed for the motel anyway. The honeymoon suite at the Dew Drop Inn Motel and Laundromat was already bought and paid for and Dewey Ludwig, the 37-year Dew Drop's proprietor, had a strict no-refund policy. Before they left, Ludmella cornered Father Hemple, and with a little assistance from the unruly *girls* (which she had years ago trained to jiggle on command), convinced him to allow them to use Dewey's no-refund honeymoon suite. But not until he gave her some strict instructions—*absolutely no sleeping together, ya hear?* So when they arrived at the Dew Drop Inn Motel and Laundromat, Ludmella argued with poor Dewey until he agreed to switch them from the more expensive honeymoon suite to the ten-dollar room with two single beds. His no-refund policy didn't count discounts off that super-king that was waiting for them. After Ludmella pried herself and the girls out of her wedding dress behind a *locked* bathroom door (like Father Hemple said), she shoved those two single beds to opposite sides of the room (like Father Hemple said) and put the dresser with the TV between them. Jimmy said later that he didn't know that Channel 7 aired *Gunsmoke* reruns all night long. He had to crank up the volume pretty much all the way in order to hear Miss Kitty and Marshall Dillon over Ludmella's snoring.

The following Monday morning Father Hempel called the courthouse and straightened out the whole mess. Turns out Old Lady Koski and Emma Kavinski weren't cousins. They were *second* cousins. That made Jimmy Kowolski and Ludmella Kavinski *third* cousins. Father Hempel consulted his *Big Book of Catholic Wedding Stuff* and there it was. On page 1136 it clearly stated: *Third cousins shall be allowed to enter into the holy sacrament of matrimony providing that one of them is a woman.*

Here (at last!) is our happy ending. Nine months later and, whoops! There it was! Ludmella Kowolski-Kavinski (turns out Ludmella was one of those "libbers" and stuck a dash between his n' her last names) gave birth to little Karl Kowolski–Kavinski (named in honor of her dead uncle). You catch that? *Nine months*! That sent the Dover party-line gossip-mongers flipping through their calendars just to make sure. They remembered what Jimmy had said about watching Channel 7's *Gunsmoke* reruns rerunning all night, but they checked anyway.

Jimmy and Ludmella would go on to have six more little Kowolski-Kavinski kids (which included a set of cuddly Kowolski-Kavinski twins). They named their brood Karl, Kenny, Kathy, Kyle, Karen, Kent, and Bobby. Jimmy put his foot down after the sixth triple-K.

Happy beginnings make happy endings. Remember how Gramma said that at the beginning of this chapter? Now you know that she was talking about the Big-Ass Dover Catholic weddings. After all the confusion with this *happy beginning,* let's just close with a Big-Ass Happy Ending.

BIG-ASS WEDDING DANCES

No recollection of Dover's Big-Ass Weddings would be complete without weaving in a few stitches about Dover's Big-Ass Wedding Dances. My embellished past, much like yours I suspect, was no lavish Renaissance tapestry (Really…whose is? Eventually and frequently we all succumb to the mundane.) But this chapter pretty much rings true. Big-Ass Wedding Dances were as much a part of the fabric of my crazy-quilt heritage as beer taverns, outhouses, and Old Man Peters. Like all of the chapters in this book, I have shot a little adrenaline into my recollections. Sometimes (as you are well aware of by now) a LOT of adrenaline. So hold on to my sweaty hand and let's go dancing. But you have to lead.

Dover's Big-Ass Wedding Dances gave Dover folks just another excuse to demonstrate their spirited conversational skills (read: shoot off their big mouths). By the time they made it to the dance hall, most of them had belted down enough plastic cups of Schlitz at the Big-Ass Wedding reception (that we just left), that everything they said was pound-the-table funny. By their own estimation, they *shoulda been on television*. Lubricated lips fluttered like just-washed Monday morning boxer shorts flapping on the clothesline. Meager dancing skills were complemented—no, make that *overshadowed*—by those spirited conversational skills. There was so much shouting and carrying on out on the dance floor, the band might as well have taken a permanent intermission and bellied up to the bar. But more than all their jaw-flapping and knee-slapping, it was their drinking skills that really shined. By the end of the night the band *oompah'd* their last Frankie Yankovic polka and walked off the stage. The house lights glared like a solar-flare and revealed a scrum of back-slapping, sweat-soaked folks reaffirming their universal love for *everyone*.

At one time wedding dances were held in the Saint Boniface church hall. Which, as you already know from the Kowolski-Kavinski fiasco, was in the church basement. Eventually Father Hempel put the kibosh to those cotillions. He didn't think it was proper for the upstairs part of the church—the sanctuary, confessional, and pews—to smell like the downstairs part during Sunday morning masses. Cigarette smoke filtered up through the floor registers overnight and infused the church with essence of Camels and Chesterfields. Even the incense couldn't camouflage it. And let's not forget about the beer. Wherever Catholics have a Big-Ass Wedding Dance, there will be beer. Lots of beer. And wherever Catholics drink and dance, there will be spillage. *Lots* of spillage. Sometimes, after a really *big* Big-Ass dance the stale-beer bouquet on the basement floor, in spite of the big-lung church ladies' scrubbing, wouldn't be Lysoled away for weeks.

So one Sunday morning Father Hemple, after he had squandered most of his sermon on a mostly inattentive, mostly hung-over crowd, announced that Big-Ass Wedding Dances would no longer be permitted in the Saint Boniface church basement. Years later, at his retirement reception, he lamented to the big-lung church ladies that it was one of the dumbest decisions he ever made during his 63-year priesthood. The lost revenue from all those church basement rental fees put a pretty good dent in his Florida retirement plans.

From that Sunday morning forward, wedding dances got relocated to various dance halls around the county. Those dance halls were not fancy affairs. If you're thinking "ballroom" ratchet your expectations down a little. They were gymnasium-sized buildings (one was a converted barn) where the most prominent feature was, what else—the bar. They also had relatively flat floors that were *relatively* free of obstacles. I mention *relatively* free of obstacles because some of the dance halls had satellite bars out in the middle of the floor for folks who needed to re-beer in the middle of a polka. Most were built with open-studded walls; no sheetrock or cheesy imitation wood paneling. The perimeter was lined with booths that were designed to hold six normal-sized people. If their cabooses were double-wides, three or four folks *might* squeeze in. By the end of the evening however, most booths were jammed with eight or ten pretty cozy, pretty drunk cabooses.

The little-ass bands that played at the Big-Ass Wedding Dances didn't have much of a repertoire. The only thing smaller than their playlist was their assortment of instruments. Usually a pair of dueling accordions and a set of drums. Sometimes a tuba. A tuba? Yup—a tuba. If you know polkas, you know you gotta have a tuba. Sometimes the more innovative bands stretched their musical talents and played a schottische or a waltz. Then—back to polkas.

Dover dancers were, if nothing else, adaptable. What they lacked in finesse they more or less made up for with their *moves*. Rather than dance the same old rhythm to the same old polkas, they changed up their steps to shake like Quakers at a prayer meeting. They pranced around the dance floor doing their made-up *moves*, pretty much ignoring the accordions, drum, and sometimes-tuba. With all that hip-gyratin' and foot-stompin' they looked like circus poodles on steroids. An actual dance partner was optional.

Dover dancers were not decked out like the dancers you may have watched on Lawrence Welk reruns on Saturday nights. Lawrence Welk dancers dressed up in actual dresses and suits. Suited gentleman sashayed skirted ladies across the television studio dance floor in graceful elegance while Myron Floren serenaded them with his accordion. High fashion had no place at Dover dances. Folks went home after the Big-Ass Wedding reception for a quick wardrobe change. After they dabbed the beer spills off their Sunday clothes they hung them back in the closet so they'd be ready for Mass the next morning. They arrived at the dance hall resplendent in their every-day blue jeans and every-day shirts. Sunday shoes with bunched-up white socks stayed on.

Dover wedding dances were a rite of passage for us hormone-raging, pimply-faced adolescent boys. My dancing skills pretty much sucked. My polka looked like I was trying to stomp out a grass fire. My schottische—like girls playing hopscotch but with more hopping than scotching. When I waltzed I wobbled and never drifted with my less-than-enthusiastic partner more than two or three steps from where I started. Oh, I almost forgot—my two-step! My two-step was where I shined! I tip-toed through a two-step like a ballerina. For us hormone-raging, pimply-faced, adolescent Dover boys, two-steps were an opportunistic grope-fest. Outside of the chance recess encounter at Saint Boniface, usually when we kicked our dodgeball ball into the middle of their silly hopscotch, the two-step was the only time we had actual physical contact with girls of the opposite sex.

When the band struck up a two-step, my inhibitions evaporated as my alter ego kicked in. I made a beeline to claim my next *gropee*. I stood in front of some girl of the opposite sex, wiped my sweaty palms on my already sweaty pants, stared straight at her chest, and cleared my throat praying that my voice wouldn't betray me. *Crap!*—it cracked again. The girl of the opposite sex laughed.

I remember the night that I got the jump on the other pimply-faced Dover boys and ran over to the opposite sexes all lined up on the other side of the floor. There she stood—Janet Beemer. She was a goddess. Ranking right up there with Marilyn Monroe, Liz Taylor, and Miss Kitty on *Gunsmoke*. She was the *first* girl I wanted to spend the rest of my life with. The *first* thought in my head every morning. The *first* real love I had. The *first* non-cousin infatuation. Dover's *first* girl with a training bra! I saw her face once.

I slid to a stop right in front of Janet, stared deeply into her training bra and crackled, "Would you guys like to dance?"

I nearly fell over. They—I mean *she*—said yes.

My ears stopped buzzing about halfway through the polka. I was so buzzed-up delirious that I never heard the music. I was swaying to and fro doing—what else—my two-step. As the buzzing faded and my thoughts cleared it finally dawned on me: *Holy shit, I'm doing the two-step to a polka.* But that was no big deal (not to me anyway). Then something else dawned on me: *Holy shit, I'm doing the two-step with Janet Beemer.* Reality gripped me and I got down to business. There was really just *one* reason any of us wanted to dance with Janet Beemer. Well, make that *two* reasons. And they were nestled somewhere down inside that training bra.

I pulled her closer. She squirmed. So, I pulled even closer. She submitted, realizing that resistance was futile. I tightened my embrace. Suddenly, she swayed to just as I swayed fro. *Whoa! What was that*! Substantial buds, firm as leftover jelly beans from Easter, brushed my heaving chest. I couldn't breathe. My vision blurred. We…we were nipple-to-nipple!

Then—it happened.

You know how sometimes, like at a church bazaar or family reunion, you stack your sandwich with ham, cheese, pickles, lettuce, and mustard so high that you have to smash it down to get your mouth around it? Then, as you go to take that first bite, it plumps right back up?

My head was spinning as the accordions accorded and the tuba tubed. I reeled Janet Beemer in like a pond carp. Tighter and tighter.

Cozier. Closer. Tighter.

Woooosh—

Huh?

Ham sandwiches plump up. Kleenex…not so much.

SLEEPING WITH DAD

"Bill, getch'ass up," my old man's Chesterfield morning-voice growled in my ears. "C'mon, we don't wanna be late."

I rolled over and stretched, being extra careful not to stick my elbow in my brother's eye. Normally I didn't care, but this morning was special. I didn't want him to wake up and mess up my plans.

My toes poked through my socks like whack-a-moles as I stumbled down the stairs. Our upstairs bedrooms were stuffed to the studs with seven—soon to be eight—sibs, so I had to tread lightly. I stumbled into the kitchen and saw the clock. *4:30! My God—it's only 4:30.* I was halfway to the stove when my nose bristled—*Dad's breakfast!* The old man didn't do a lot of cooking so it was a rare event when he practiced his limited culinary skills. This was back when chauvinism trumped chivalry. Cooking, as everyone knew, was *women's* work. But by God, whenever he unshackled those sexist chains and found Mom's bucket of lard, the old man could fry up one hell of a breakfast.

His favorite recipe, passed on to him by his German mother, was an amorphous mess that he called *kneadles* (pronounced *kuh-NEE-dulls)*. It more resembled wallpaper paste gone bad than fare fit for human consumption. It was simply a few fists of buckwheat flour and a little salt tossed into a pot of boiling water. He stirred it around until the spoon stood on its own. He pried it from the pan and plopped it onto our plates. Then he grabbed the frying pan filled with chunks of side-pork sizzling in knee-deep grease and poured it—hot grease and all—over the aforementioned amorphous mess. A little more salt and pepper, and it was a breakfast fit for any low-country German. None were lower than us Rauschs.

This morning the old man was in a hurry, so he didn't have time to mess with his *kneadles*. So he fried the only other breakfast he knew how to fry: fried eggs, fried potatoes, and fried fish. If the old man could have found a way to do it, he would have fried the toast too. We sat in silence, "Don't want the other little shits waking up," the old man said as we stared out the window into the pre-dawn darkness, exchanging fish-and-egg-yolk yawns.

Oh, speaking of fish (nice segue, huh?), they were the reason we were awake at this ungodly hour. The old man and I, his first-born male child, his biggest boy, the one he loved most, just the two of us and nobody else—*we* were going fishing.

Just the two of us. That might not sound like a big deal to you if you were fortunate (or unfortunate—it's all a matter of perspective) to be born into in a statistically average American family with 1.93 kids. For those of us reared in Midwestern Catholic families with a statistical average of 8.69 sibs, going one-on-one with either parent was a rarity. We fought for Mom and Dad's affections like a litter of pups. The only time Dad and I went one-on-one was when I got my ass chewed for something like *accidentally* spilling a glass of milk on my sister's dress. Or *accidentally* hitting my brother in the head with a hammer. Or getting sent home from school because I *accidentally* said shit at recess.

"Leave the dishes for Mom," Dad said as we pushed back from the table. "We gotta get movin'. Johnny and them'll be waitin' on us."

I didn't argue. I did, however, make at least token effort to clear the table. Not so much because I was the obedient one, always eager to help. Nope. It was subterfuge. A selfish attempt to gain a few more brownie points with Mom since I was planning to ask for a transistor radio that Christmas. A 7-transistor RCA beauty that I circled in early August edition of the Sears Christmas catalog and left flopped open on her dresser. I put my plate into the sink still filled with last night's supper dishes and, just to be sure that my token effort scored a point or two, stuck a note on the smeared yolks: *This was my plate, Mom.*

Dad went outside to double-check everything. Before we went to bed the previous evening, he packed the Studebaker with fishing essentials like beer, rods, reels, tackle box, beer, stringer, dip net, and of course, a couple cartons of Chesterfields. And a last minute afterthought—a box of groceries. I tossed in my duffel bag that I packed with *my* fishing essentials: my cleanest dirty sweatshirt, comic books, and a flashlight. Then *my* last minute afterthought—a bar of soap and an extra pair of underpants. Before I went to bed Mom yelled up at me, "In the morning, be sure you leave *the* toothbrush for your brothers." That was fine with me.

I grabbed a last gulp of milk and ran out the screen door. The old man was already sucking the life out of his third Chesterfield as he paced in the driveway. The Studebaker was warming up and it smoked right along with him.

I jumped in the front seat and the old man backed out of the driveway. He kept the headlights off until we were out in the street so that their pissy six-volt glimmer wouldn't wake my brothers. I smiled through his haze of Chesterfield smoke as we drove off, *Look at me, riding in the Studebaker with the old man. Right up here on the front seat...actually alone.* I glanced at the backseat. Something felt strange. Then it hit me. It was (gasp) *empty*! The Studebaker never went anywhere without five hip-to-hip brats waging war in the back seat. Mom's two smallest brats shared the front seat with her and the old man. Usually one cuddled up on her lap because, more likely than not, it was still a baby. Remember—we were Catholics. Damn good Catholics. Even if they didn't need another one, Mom and Dad always had a baby or two crawling around somewhere. I asked the old man once where all those dang babies kept coming from. He chickened out and fed me the standard Catholic line: *They're a blessing from Jesus or something. Hey, how 'bout them Yankees?*

So there we were, our sleep-creased father-and-son faces reflecting the warm glow of the dashboard lights long since yellowed by Chesterfields. This was July, so Dad had his window cranked down to coax the cool morning air into the rancid back seat. Kid-spit, pissed-up diapers, A&W Root Beer, and cigarettes were as much a part of the Studebaker's character as its pointy nose. Rolling the widows down to cleanse that *character* was an exercise in futility.

"Uncle Ralph be there?" I asked.

"S'posta' be," Dad said.

"Bob?" (My cousin.)

"I 'magin," he said.

"Who else's goin'?" I asked, even though I already knew. I overheard him talking on the kitchen phone the night before. Uncle Johnny's distinct cough came from the other end. He and the old man punctuated their coughs—Camels v. Chesterfields—with snippets of conversation.

"Your Uncle John's goin'. Said he's bringin' Allen."

Allen? Did he just say Allen? I didn't hear him mention Allen on the phone. My heart jumped for joy. Al was my favorite cousin. One of my best buds. Only two months separated our births, so our world view was remarkably similar. We hated girls and school and loved RC Cola with Planter's Peanuts floating on top (he's the one taught me that culinary quirk). We hated Sunday shoes and loved Keds. We hated *Archie* and *Dick Tracey* but loved *Super Woman* (especially Super Woman's pointy cartoon tits). But more than anything else, Al and I loved to go fishing.

Before we were half way to Uncle Johnny's house the rising sun was jockeying for position above the misty rows of just-busted-out corn tassels. When the old man pulled the Studebaker into Uncle Johnny's driveway, Uncle Ralph and Bob were already milling around. Dad and I, having to drive the farthest, had a lock on being last.

"Well, well, look what the cat dragged in," Uncle Johnny messed with Dad as they shook nicotine-stained hands. "I was just sayin' to Ralph that I was gonna yell at Margaret to call over and wake yer ass up. Hell, it's damn near time for dinner."

Dad took a drag off his Chesterfield and squirted the smoke out between his teeth like he always did when he was trying to look cool. Something smart-ass was about to fall from his lips. He glanced over Uncle Johnny's shoulder to be sure I was out of earshot, "Well, the Old Lady was feeling a little frisky so…"

"You old dog. Ain't she five months along?" Johnny jabbed.

"So…?" the old man grinned.

They huddled behind Johnny's Oldsmobile in the dawn's-early-light cigarette cloud and leaned into its open trunk to take inventory. Fishing gear—check. Worms—check. Extra pants—check. Extra underwear—optional. Beans and soup—check. Wonder Bread and baloney—check. Beer and cigarettes—

check. Wait...go back. Beer and cigarettes—double check. Toilet paper—check. Satisfied that they had missed nothing, Johnny gave the expedition his blessing and pronounced our mission worthy of departure. The caravan was organized with Dad and me (as always) leading the way. Wise cracks about the Studebaker's aerodynamic pointy nose followed us even as we slammed the doors shut. As we backed out, Aunt Margaret ran from her kitchen. Actually, she walked. Yup, you guessed it—four months along. She had a sack bulging with baloney sandwiches for our dinner. An accomplished angler herself, she chided Johnny and the old man, "You guys better come home with more than headaches. Those ice chests best be full. And I don't mean empty beer cans either."

Three hours later we arrived at the foot of the old iron bridge. Its arch soared over the muddy Mississippi, stitching two states together like a rusty thread. Dad down-shifted the PRNDL to L and let the Studebaker's V-8 ease us down the steep grade like a jake brake. We pulled up in front of our "cabin" perched under the bridge. As Dad killed the engine, the sun took a time-out and ducked under the gathering clouds.

   About that cabin. Firmly fixed in the mind of every ten-year-old boy who grew up reading about Paul Bunyan and Laura Ingalls, the word *cabin* conjures visions of hand-hewn logs chiseled from lofty balsam firs by pioneers with chiseled chins. And a mossy-bearded shake-shingle roof with a stone chimney curling oak smoke into the forever-blue sky. It goes without saying that it was nestled in some aromatic pine forest with squirrels and bunnies frolicking on the porch while mama bears frolicked with their cubs in the bushes. All of them in Disneyesque Bambi-harmony. And, of course, it would be surrounded on three sides by sky-blue waters (even bluer than the aforementioned forever-blue sky) lapping at the shore a few shoeless steps away. Inside, our ten-year-old boy, fresh from his morning swim in the brisk water, would be bathed in the warmth of spark-spitting embers of a forever-roaring fireplace wafting its aromatic smoke high in that forever-blue sky we were just talking about. A fuzzy bearskin rug on the rough plank floor would tickle his toes (and other stuff) as he lay naked before the blazing fire. An overhead loft would complete the vision, with beds neatly arranged along the railing, covered with Grandma Moses quilts. Essence of pine would permeate its interior tinged with a hint of breakfast bacon crackling in the cast-iron skillet, and a hearty venison stew bubbling in the forever-roaring fireplace. Oh, almost forgot, the yeasty essence of fresh-baked bread wafted from the oven. Ten-year-old boy dreams about aromatic cabins, aromatic fires, and aromatic squirrels, bunnies, and bears must have fresh-baked bread wafting in them somewhere. The old man's k*neadles*? They had no place here.

Well...that's pretty much what my naïve imagination conjured during our drive.

Shit! My vision busted like I always did to Richie's birthday balloons as the Studebaker rocked to a stop (Studebaker suspension sucked). Right there before us, squatting in mounds of mud was the crappiest clapboard "cabin" ever. It looked like the pictures of the Appalachian shanties Sister Mary Larry showed us in a book she got from the folks at Time-Life. Its foundation—crumbly concrete blocks. Its front porch—half rotted. Its windows—mostly busted. My aromatic pinewood forest was nowhere to be seen or smelled. In its place was a weed-infested yard littered with beer cans and dog shit. Those *mere steps* from the pristine lake were *mere steps* from a potholed street also littered with abandoned cars. You want aromatic? I'll give you aromatic: the boat docks across the street reeked of aromatic fish guts and oily outboard motors.

"Grab that box of groceries and your duffel bag," Dad said as he unlocked the trunk. "I'll get the fishing poles and coolers."

"Okay," I yelled back. The cans of beans and soup had rolled around in the box and crushed the Wonder Bread. Luckily Dad's cartons of Chesterfields escaped harm. If the old man spent more than fifteen minutes without a fresh fag dangling from his lips he'd be jonesing.

I was so preoccupied balancing the food box in one arm and my duffel bag in the other that I side stepped off the sidewalk and slipped on the muddy slope. As I struggled to stand back up, I thrashed around like a Channel 7 fake rassler in a fake full nelson. By the time I got my feet back under me, my jeans were slimed from cuff to crotch with more dog shit than mud. When I finally stumbled into our "cabin" my eyes glazed over. (Okay—I cried like a little girl.) As I looked around at our home for the next three days my jeans didn't seem to matter so much anymore. *You gotta be shittin' me*, I mumbled to myself. The floor was patched with scabs of linoleum. The walls were road maps of spider-webbed cracks. The ceilings sagged. The floors bounced. The roof leaked. Two windows were covered with plywood. If anyone had the mistaken notion to tidy the place up a little, a shovel would have worked better than a broom. A pair of couches squatted in the middle of the room like bloated cows. A crate between them served as a coffee table of sorts, but judging from the previous renters' piles of beer cans, it hadn't seen a coffee cup in decades. I walked into our "kitchen" and flicked on the lights. It was only noon, but the sky was darkening. A bare bulb that hung on a twisted cord above the stove flickered to life. Speaking of the stove, it was crusted with some sort of crap that looked like the lava flowing from the Kilauea volcano in Hawaii that Sister Mary Larry showed us in a book she got from the folks at Time-Life. Our *bathroom* was located out back. A two-holer.

Meanwhile, Dad already made his way up the stairs to the bedrooms. Make that *bedroom*. I heard him clomping around up there like the monsters that clomped around after midnight in our bedroom back home. (I'm kidding about the monster-clomping thing. It was me. I did that when I got up to pee just to scare the shit out of Richie.)

"Bill," he shouted down the stairs. "Git up here. We gotta talk."

I walked out of the kitchen to the "living room" where my uncles and cousins were just making their way through the front door.

"You gotta be shittin' me," my cousin Al said as he walked in.

"You gotta be shittin' me," cousin Bob repeated.

"Not too bad," Uncle Johnny said behind them.

"Hey Bill," Al smiled. "Where's the kitchen?" He was carrying their box of groceries loaded down with Wonder Bread and uncrushed Camels.

"Right through there," I cringed. "Watch out for that stove."

I grabbed my duffel bag and took off. I topped the stairs where a whole 'nother shock waited for me. Just when I thought that things couldn't possibly get any worse…

The upstairs bedroom was a barracks kinda thing with head-banger ceilings covered with stained wallpaper (that leaky roof). There were three so-called *beds*.

"Which bed you want?" Dad asked. He bounced his hands up and down on the so-called mattresses on the so-called beds.

"Err…Dad?" I was puzzled. "Where will the others sleep?"

"These all we got, Bill. So which one we gonna sleep in?"

"We?"

"Yup—*we*," he smiled back. "Pick one."

"But, err, how are two of us gonna sleep in one of...*these*?"

"We'll be fine," he said. "When I was in *Dubya Dubya Eye Eye* (old-man-speak for WWII) we slept in a lot worse over in the Philippines."

By now I was so overwhelmed—dog-shitted yard, plywooded windows, and lava-crusted stove—I was incapable of making a decision, so Dad grabbed the middle cot and kicked it against the wall. "There. See! You sleep up against the wall and I'll sleep on the outside. That way, if I get to rollin' around, I won't shove ya on the floor. We'll be snug as a bug in a blanket."

"Rug," I said.

"Huh?"

"Rug, Dad. It's rug. Snug as a bug in a rug."

"Whatever."

Lacking any reasonable sleeping alternative, I tossed my duffel bag onto the so-called blankets.

"What the hell's that?" Dad said as he got a whiff of me. "Cripes, yer pants stink like dog shit. You better change."

I grabbed my duffel bag. Even before I got it unzipped, it hit me: *I am so screwed.* In my dumb-ass ten-year-old eagerness, I forgot to pack an extra pair of jeans. Since we were going to be gone for only three days, I didn't see the need. Extra underwear—maybe. But that was just to keep Mom from yelling at me when we got back home.

I stomped down to the kitchen where the others were busy stacking their cans of soup and beans on the kitchen table. That sad little thing lost its will to stand when Uncle Johnny tossed his coolers of Schlitz on top.

"Holy shit!" Johnny said as I walked in. He was on his hands and knees chasing runaway beer cans. "What's that godawful stink?"

"Me," I fessed up.

"Dang—you smell like dog shit."

"It's not *me*—it's my jeans."

"Well then, your *jeans* smell like dog shit."

"Yeah. I know. Don't rub it in."

"Rub it in?" he was smiling now. "Hell, I ain't even gonna touch it, let alone rub it in."

That one hurt.

I peeled my pants off and threw them in the kitchen sink along with a handful of 20 Mule Team Borax I found in one of the cupboards. I turned on what I hoped would be hot water. Several minutes later, tepid water spit from the faucet. Whiffs of dog-shit drifted from my pants as I swished them in the brown suds. There was no way to dry them, so I wrung them out as best I could and put them back on. The toasty July sun would finish the job when I sat in the boat.

KAAA-BOOM! Doors shook, windows rattled, and soup cans rolled off the table. Al, Bob, and I ran to the front porch where our dads had already gathered. Forget that toasty July sun thing. Inky clouds swarmed overhead.

"Sonofabitch!" One word was all Uncle Johnny needed to sum up the situation. "I thought the weatherman said it was gonna be partly cloudy."

"Probably is back home," the old man said. Back then weather forecast accuracy was optional.

"You never know what it's gonna do on this old river," Uncle Ralph chimed in with his good-natured demeanor. I always admired that about him. Most folks developed crow's feet from squinting, but Uncle Ralph got his from his near-perpetual smile. If you look up the word *pleasant* in the dictionary, you'll see a picture of my Uncle Ralph. Crow's feet and all.

"Well, we better go get that stuff we piled in the boat before it gets soaked," Dad said. "My new Zebco was five bucks and I sure as hell don't want it ruin't." We made a run for it across the street to the dock. Just as we grabbed our fishing poles, tackle boxes, and worms, the fuzzy-bellied clouds ruptured. By the time we got back to the porch everyone's jeans were soaked. Seeing them in their drippy britches, I didn't feel so stupid. But after we got back inside, *they* changed into dry pants that *they* remembered to pack. I felt stupid all over again.

Looks like an all-dayer," Uncle Johnny prognosticated, doing his best to mask his delight. "Might as well go down the street."

Down the street. That was always music to our ears. It was an expression that we generally heard around five o'clock. It seemed a little strange (to us boys anyway) to hear him invoke it this early in the day. *Down the street* was Uncle Johnny's euphemism for beer joint; an institution that was far from unfamiliar to our world-class beer-drinker dads. If the Olympics included competitive beer drinking, our dads would be loaded down with gold medals. If there were a Beer World Series, they'd trounce the Yankees. The Cardinals—maybe. They could belly up to the bar with the best of them. And indeed, such majestic bellies they were.

With the fish slaughter suspended for the rest of the day, we piled into Uncle Johnny's big-ass Oldsmobile Rocket 88 and set out to find a beer joint worthy of our patronage (which left the field pretty much wide open). I called *shotgun* as my cousins and I piled into the couch-sized tuck & roll rayon back seat. Oldsmobiles, with their iconic "Body by Fisher" interiors were pretty fancy when you compared them to Fords and Chevys. Even Studebakers. Tuck & roll rayon seat pleats were complemented by back window speakers. You haven't heard anything until you've cruised down the road with the hardtop windows cranked down and radio cranked up with Buddy Holly wailing *Peggy Sue* in those speakers. Just thinking about it today makes me want to tuck a pack of Luckies in my rolled-up tee shirt sleeves, jam a cannaHamm's between my legs, and comb my Ducktail back. (Well, everything but that Ducktail thing. Maybe comb my combover over.) There were chrome-plated strips sparkling in the ceiling fabric and chrome-plated ashtrays in the armrests. Uncle Ralph heard me call shotgun so he shouted his own shotgun as the men piled into the tuck & roll front seat. Even though the mere utterance of *shotgun* gave him undisputed rights to a window seat with its own chrome-plated ashtray embedded in the armrest, he sat in the middle anyway, not having a clue what it meant. Johnny fired up his road-boat and we blasted off in the downpour.

Three blocks. "There's one" the old man pointed through the steamed-up windows. Uncle Johnny cranked the steering wheel, stomped the brakes, and cut a U-ee like the cops did on TV. The land-yacht slid perfectly into a curb-side berth. We jumped out and splashed to the door.

The place was practically deserted (remember, it was barely dinner time, aka: noon). We had the joint to ourselves except for a couple of laid-off low-lifes. Every small town has them—the chronically unemployed. Do they wallow in un-productive existence due to a lack of opportunity—unlikely. A lack of skills—nope. Surely somebody somewhere had some sort of honest work that didn't require much more than a strong back. So maybe (I'm just guessing here), that chronic unemployment was due to their lack of ambition. Bingo! (Now who sounds like a Republican?)

Okay—off my soapbox and back to our story. The pair of ne'er-do-wells nursed their hangovers with twelve-ounce drafts mixed with tomato juice, a well-known remedy that was more mythical than medicinal. Their buddies—let me rephrase that—their *employed* buddies were still bustin' their balls at work.

Any other hapless fishermen that we hoped would already be in there to share their favorite fishing holes and lies about that big muskie that got away still hadn't made it in off the rainy river.

I was the first one in the door (remember I called shotgun) and stood there spellbound by the sheer majesty that was spread out before me. Rob's Place had all the requisites of a bona fide beer tavern. Neon beer signs glowed in the window: Blue Ribbon, Hamm's, and Schmidt. Some smartass had taken a marker and blacked out every other letter on the Schmidt sign (think about it…think. You can do this. Got it? Okay, feel free to read on). Chrome legs sparkled on the orange Naugahyde bar stools lined up all along the brass foot-rail. Some of the orange Naugahyde seats weren't even ripped. Rob's mirrored bar was festooned with hand-carved embellishments. His floors hadn't seen a broom in days, maybe weeks. They were richly carpeted with cigarette butts and peanut shells. The lights, smeared with years of nicotine and cheeseburger grease, were muted to just the right level of luminescence, providing an ambiance that begged *just one more round.* A jukebox glimmered on the back wall, radiating a carnival of pastel light. It coaxed nickels and dimes from broke-ass beer drinkers hell-bent to drown their sorrows with overdoses of Tammy Wynette and Conway Twitty.

Out there on the floor, right in the middle of everything—*it* sat in majestic solitude! Dominating what little open space Rob allotted from his revenue-generating card tables. Glowing green beneath a stained-glass lamp was a slate-top, solid-oak, ivory-inlaid, leather-pocket pool table. Not your Sears and Roebuck $149.99 stock-reduction, close-out special, but an honest-to-God slate-top, solid-oak, ivory-inlaid, leather-pocket Brunswick (not quite in the same league with Charlies billiard behemoth back in Dover—but close). It beckoned. Beckoned bad.

Complementing Rob's blue-collar beer-joint bouquet was a fragrance found in every tavern from Savannah to Sacramento.

After my nose sorted through the ambrosial fragrances of stale beer, cigarettes, and cheeseburgers, there it was—essence of urinal. A rarely-flushed, butt-plugged, urine-soaked urinal. In the center of that butt-plugged drain was a little pink cake that stank. Not so much like Ponderosa pine, but more like mothballs. For target shooters like me (c'mon guys, most of us are), our piss runoff chased the butts away and burrowed a neat little hole into its center.

As Dad and my uncles pushed in behind me, they were equally awe-struck. This was a whole 'nother thing. Nothing like the shit-kicker beer joints back in Dover. This was brewski bliss. As they drank in the scene before them, they knew that, in spite of the rain, (actually, *thanks* to the rain), this day would have purpose.

Never comfortable sitting in a booth (booths were for women) they went straight away for the *unripped* orange Naugahyde stools at the far end of the bar. The stools they picked were not the random selection that beer drinkers of a lesser caliber might have made. Theirs was a premeditated, well-thought-out seat selection made with one very important criteria: mere steps from the john.

"Cute," Dad said as he noticed the hand-painted sign on the door that read *Robbers* with Yosemite Sam painted below it. The sign on the women's door read *Robins* with red-breasted robins fluttering below it. Apparently Rob had a creative streak in him. More likely it was Mrs. Rob.

My cousins and I settled in and went right to work. We had long ago fine-tuned the fine art of finagling. Our capacity for beer tavern pleasure was directly proportional to our ability to finagle nickels and dimes and the occasional quarter out of our dads. They were softies. Patriarchal admonishments always got checked at the door in beer joints. The unspoken price for this behavioral latitude: *Don't tell ma*. It was a beautiful arrangement. Cash infusions became more generous as the hours and the beers took their toll. (None of us would ever forget that night in Tilleys when Al actually got a whole dollar from Uncle Johnny). What was only a beer joint to our dads was an amusement park to us. But our complicity didn't come cheap. It took a butt-load of nickels and dimes and the occasional quarter to finance our eight-ball games, Elvis and Buddy Holly (much to the consternation of the Conway Twitty and Tammy Wynette crowd), RC Cola, Snickers, and Planters Peanuts. But best of all, Mrs. Rob's amazing cheeseburgers. Blackened bits of ground beef crusted around the edges of a cheese-topped masterpiece, crowned with an inch-thick onion slice. She tossed on a few pickles and plastered the whole thing with mustard. Holy crap! Could life possibly get any better?

It was nearly midnight when, after the third last round, our dads decided to call it quits while they could still stand. Outside, the clouds had emptied their fuzzy bellies and crawled back across the river, leaving in their wake a clear and cool night sky. Stars danced like fireflies across the heavens. Fireflies danced like stars in the shadows. Frogs the size of dinner plates croaked in three-part harmony.

Thud…thud…thud…*sonofabitch*! (Yup…Uncle Johnny's thumb). Four Rocket 88 doors slammed in sequence just prior to blast-off. A harrowing two minutes later we arrived at our shit-palace and bailed out, thanking God for once again providing safe passage and, in his almighty benevolence, allowing us to survive Uncle Johnny's Schlitz Driving Academy skills. We stumbled up the slope to our shack, kicking off our muddy boots on the porch, leaving them to fend for themselves out there in those dog-infested streets. In just a few hours the mangy curs would slink onto our front yard to make their nocturnal deposits. We trudged up the stairs in stocking feet and got ready for bed. Or more correctly—got ready for cot. No tooth brushing or face washing for us. Mom was miles away. Besides that…we were men. Face-washing and teeth-brushing was for all those booth-sitting women back in Rob's. Al and Bob fumbled around downstairs where they set up camp on the floor. *They* remembered to bring their sleeping bags while I didn't even remember to bring an extra pair of jeans let alone my Roy Rogers sleeping bag.

The rain-chilled air gave me goosebumps as I stripped down to my underpants and jumped into our cot. I scrunched next to the wall as Dad and I had previously agreed. He crawled in beside me—his boozy breath seasoned with onions and Hamm's. He was nice and toasty.

"G'night, Bill," he slurred.

"'Night, Dad."

"Shorry 'bout the rain," he apologized. "We'll schlaughter 'em tomorrow."

"S'okay, Dad. We're still having a good time…"

"Yup. Schleep tight. We're rollin' out at five."

"Okay."

We laid there in the darkness for a minute or two. "Hey…," he rolled over and faced me.

"Yeah?"

"Snug as a bug…"

"In a blanket," I grinned.

In a blanket.

I woke up a few hours later. Uncles' beer farts swirled. I tried to fan them away and brushed the back of dad's bald head shimmering in the moonlight. He rolled over and we were face-to-face in the silver-blue glint. A splash of yesterday's Old

Spice lingered on his stubble as he flopped his meaty arm across my chest. As uncles farted in their cots and mice scratched in their walls, I smiled and thought to myself, *Look at me…sleeping with Dad.* I squirmed closer to see him better. As I studied his face in the moonglow, I thought of how every day, I looked at my dad but never really *saw* him. In that quiet moment, with snores, beer farts, and scratchy mice, I saw serenity in his face. The peacefulness of a good man living a good life.

Oh, there is one thing I almost forgot to tell you. The real reason we took that trip—the fishing part—we actually wet our lines the next day.

And we did not disappoint Aunt Margaret.

****

Oftentimes, I look back at that nostalgic summer of 1957. Dad's no longer here to share fishing trips, cheeseburgers, and gnarly cots. But that trip. That summer. It still makes me feel as snug as a bug.

EASY (GOING) RIDER

Most of the recollections that I have shared with you have dealt with episodes of my not-so-innocent *early* boyhood. However, for this episode we'll need to borrow a chapter from Chairman Mao's program to modernize the Chinese society. We need to take a Great Leap Forward, leaving behind my yesteryears of virtue, innocence, and sweetness. (Hey, a little self-delusional therapy is always good. Right?). Let's leave the dancing chickens, Harry, and big-ass weddings behind for now and push forward to a time in my life where I had accumulated near-infinite intellectual insight and radiated with the wisdom of ancient philosophers. You know…when I was a teenager.

I flunked the State Department of Motor Vehicles driver's license exam twice. We didn't have a traffic light in Dover and since I had never seen one, I thought red meant "go" like it did for Grandpa's bull. After I got my reds and greens straightened out (but not that yellow one; even today I think it means "hurry"), I passed with, err, flying colors. It was like the old man always said: *third time's a charm*. Finally, I could drive to any damn place any damn time I wanted to. Now that I was seventeen and fully certified by the state to operate a motor vehicle—the universe was mine. Boundless. Timeless. As long as I was back home by 7:30.

While I was growing up I had always heard rumors that there were other towns out there beyond the Dover city limits. Not just towns, but big-ass cities. Some reported to be more that ten times Dover's size. Ten times! Sister Mary Larry told us there were entire civilizations even. As far as I knew, it was pure speculation. To appreciate my limited world view, you have to understand that to a nine-year-old, Dover was a self-sufficient economic, social, and spiritual microcosm. While it was not much more than a fly speck on the map, it was *my* fly speck. *My* universe. Venturing out to Grandma's farm was the equivalent of today's interstate road trip. Surely, I thought, leaving Chickasaw county must have required a passport. But to actually summon the courage to cross the state line? Well…only Superman or Buck Rogers could do that. The point I'm trying to emphasize here is that we Dover Boys lived quite sheltered lives. But having now advanced into my late-teens, I was on the cusp of tearing down that social barrier. But first—I needed to find me some wheels.

I dug under the dirty underwear pile in our closet and found my Smucker's jelly jar filled with my life savings. That near-perpetual pile of skid-marked JC Penney tighty whities provided five-brother-proof security equal to the old man's safety deposit box up at the First Commercial Bank and Trust where he kept all of his important papers like his fishing license and hunting license. He was going to put his marriage license and last will and testament in there with them…but they got lost. I had my Smucker's jelly jar stuffed with lawn-mowing money, pop-bottle money, foul-ball money, and Perfumy-Aunt birthday card money. With only $118.73, an actual car was well beyond my financial means. But it wasn't a car I wanted anyway. I would get me a motorcycle. A James Dean terror machine that I would rumble through the streets of Dover looking for something to run over or rape. Just like Mr. Dean and Heck's Angels (seventeen and I still wasn't allowed to say...you know...cuss words). It took nearly three weeks of actually volunteering to do the dishes, mow the lawn, clean our bedroom, and whining, lots of whining, that, if I was allowed to have a motorcycle, I would ride it like a girl. After Mom's *Oh hell no, people get killed on those things ever day* reaction mellowed to her reluctant permission, I set out to buy one. Providing of course that it cost $118.73 or less.

Hondas were too expensive and Harleys were too big. Then one morning I spied a Suzuki in the *Penny Saver*. The guy was asking $117.00 for it. That was within my budget. And with $1.73 cents left over, heck, I could buy enough gas to ride to one of those distant civilizations Sister Mary Larry was talking about. So I called the number. An old man's voice answered. Bingo! He said he only used it to ride to church on Sunday but decided to quit *since folks was getting killed on 'em ever day*. (Crimeny! Mom was right!) We dickered a few minutes. With him all paranoid about those dead folks, convincing him to knock off twenty bucks was way too easy. I hung up the phone and let out a scream like a little girl (yes...my voice cracked). She was mine.

After supper that night the old man and I drove up to the county seat where the old man lived to pick her up. Since I had no idea how to shift it, I rode all the way home in first gear. I parked it in the garage and rubbed, and polished, and shined, and all but made to love to her. She really was...she was mine! A little after midnight Mom yelled out into the garage that whatever it was I was rubbing on, I needed to stop and get my ass up to bed.

Even though *Sue-zoo-key* sounded like a girl's motorcycle, it was perfect for an undersized, skinny-ass seventeen-year-old like me. It was just like the papa bear-mama bear thing. Not too big—not too small. Not too fast—not too slow. But most importantly, not too expensive. She would be my ticket out of Dover. The vehicle that would rocket me to those distant horizons I ached to explore. It took Mom a few weeks to overcome her lingering anxiety, but after she watched me riding it like a girl like I promised (I wasn't even trying. My riding skills sucked that much), she eventually allowed me to ride it past the end of the block. And before you know it—all the way to the Union Pacific railroad tracks. Eventually, as far away as Tilleys. After that, if I didn't screw up and come back late for supper, Mom promised me the universe. Well, as far away as the county line. Which was okay with me since I didn't have a passport.

My first rides outside the Dover city limits were exploratory. A mile or so this way. Five miles that way. Then, feeling a little cocky one afternoon—I rode up to the county seat to tell that old man how much I like his Suzuki. As I turned onto his street I saw him standing out in his yard shaking a pitchfork at me. Apparently some of his old fart buddies told him at coffee one morning how bad I had screwed him on the price.

With my confidence and riding skills steadily improving, I decided that I was ready for a road trip. You know, one of those Kerouac On-The-Road adventures where I'd aimlessly wander America's byways in search of my soul and cheap cheese burgers. With the sun in my face, wind at my back, and bugs in my teeth; I'd cast my fate to the wind and twist the throttle. And just like Jack, fly with those winds upon which I had just cast my fate and let my mind drift in Zen-like bliss.

Kerouac had the balls to serendipity be his only guiding star, but me...not so much. I made a few precautionary plans. I had already discovered how those open-road things could be treacherous when one of Old Man Peter's coonhounds darted out in front of me. Full disclosure: I goosed the Suzuki so I could hit the yelping bastard. I was rewarded with my first road rash. My visit to Doc Hansen's office for a few stitches taught me three very important lessons. First: don't goose the Suzuki to try and run over yelping-bastard coonhounds. Second: Run over Chihuahuas instead (like old Lady Zimmerman's) if they weren't too fat from being stuffed with Doggie Yum-Yums and Twinkies by their overindulgent old-lady owners. Third: *Be prepared*. I had learned that in the Boy Scouts before I quit over a squabble with the troop leader about some merit badge. Knot tying I think.

With the remembered Boy Scout Motto in mind, I packed...err...a *few things*. I wasn't sure how long I'd be gone or how far out into the universe I'd venture, so packing was a logistical challenge. Especially for a seventeen-year-old on the threshold of omniscience who couldn't even remember to pack an extra pair of jeans for a fishing trip. I backed the old man's Studebaker out of the garage and parked the Suzuki right on top of the perpetual oil puddle. I gathered all of my stuff and started tying it onto my two-cycle pack-mule. My yellow and red Roy Rogers two-man pup tent, my equally yellow and red Roy Rogers sleeping bag with Dale Evans face printed on the fuzzy liner where she gave me funny ideas when I crawled in, a fry pan, fork, spoon, plate, cup, salt and pepper, canteen, a can opener (real adventurers eat lots of beans just like Roy Rogers and Dale Evans. I am still amazed at how none of us Dover Boys ever question why Roy Roger's wife or girlfriend or whatever she was had a boy's name), a blanket, five *Playboys* that I "borrowed" from our Boy Scout paper drive pile before I quit (I thought they might help me, you know, fall asleep). A flashlight with extra batteries, five pairs of socks, five pairs of jeans, five shirts, and one pair of underwear. At the last minute, I dumped out the old man's tackle box and filled it with a few tools in case I'd have some, you know, *mechanical issues.* Pliers, screw driver, and a hammer. Tools that were essential for mechanics like me.

I stepped back to admire my 250 cc Suzuki smothered somewhere under that mélange of crap. I felt confident that I could survive anything short of a thermo-nuclear war or coonhounds. Even over-stuffed Chihuahuas. I ran into the house to brush my teeth and wash my face knowing that I wouldn't be doing either of those things for the next couple of weeks. Maybe a year. Then I did something that proved fearlessness: I left my pimple cream in the medicine cabinet. I ran back to the garage and fired up the 'zuki and took off; an intrepid warrior on an amazing mission. Universe—prepare to be conquered.

Two minutes and four blocks later. I turned around at Tilleys and went back home. The universe-conquering intrepid warrior forgot to kiss his mommy goodbye.

I was less than twenty minutes into my Zen-like adventure when the perfectly-aligned stars collided. All planetary motion ceased when I found myself stranded at the side of the road. My smoking steed suddenly stopped rocketing me down the road and wheezed herself to death. Now, you have to understand one thing about growing up under the constant scrutiny of a Catholic mom: I wasn't allowed to unleash the f-bomb when I was in our house or anywhere within a two-block radius of her preternatural hearing. I don't know why, but I looked around to be sure she wasn't lurking in the ditch or crouched behind some fence post. Nope. No Mom. So I blasted one. *FUCK*! Okay—a couple. An earsplitting enunciation of the forbidden noun, adjective, and verb (the f-bomb is incredibly versatile) followed by a cascade of lesser expletives that I never bothered to confess. I felt morally obliged to rip that f-bomb to ensure that my rotten luck was properly acknowledged. Again, I'd deal with Father Hemple later. Maybe.

Sitting there, wallowing in the middle of my pity-party—it dawned on me. *My tool kit*! That's it! My tool kit. For mechanics like me it was just a matter of twist this, screw that, pound on those thingamajigs…whatever they are. But there was just one problem—my tool kit (aka: the old man's tackle box) was buried somewhere in that mountain of crap.

I was so pissed that I couldn't focus enough to untie my tangle of knots (Our troop leader was probably justified when he ripped my merit badge off my left sleeve and burned it. But he didn't have to do it in front of all the guys.) I finally gave up and flipped open my jackknife and started shredding. I put all my crap on the ground. Threw it, actually. Violently. My yellow and red Roy Rogers two-man pup tent, my equally yellow and red Roy Rogers sleeping bag with Dale Evans' face on the fuzzy liner where she gave me funny ideas when I crawled in, a fry pan, fork, spoon, plate, cup, salt and pepper, canteen, and the can opener. Everything. It looked like a yard sale.

There it was—at the very bottom—the old man's tackle box filled with a few extra tools. Pliers, screw drivers, various wrenches. And of course—my trusty hammer. Wait a minute. *What the *%$@#**! (yup…I used it as a noun. Actually a direct object). *Where was my *%#@**! hammer? (an adjective). *Well, #*&%* me*! (and a verb). The most important tool in my arsenal was not there. Then I remembered, *Bill, you dumb ass—it's strapped to your handlebars*. I had decided that I wanted it within arm's reach, you know, in case I ran into a band of Heck's Angels or something. I had considered sawing off the barrel on my Daisy BB gun, but I figured it would prove pretty much useless in close combat since I'd have to cock it after every shot. But a hammer in the hands of a pimply-faced, Zen-like, 126-pound seventeen-year-old? Well, that would surely make any band of Heck's Angels pause to reconsider their mortality.

I went to work twisting, screwing, and pounding any thingamajig within reach. The carburetor came off first. Not so much because I understood what it did or how to work on it, but because it was easy to get at. Sitting there all by itself on top of the motor. I looked at it in my hands and turned it over a few times. It smelled like gas. That was a good thing—right? I tossed it on the ground. Next up—the greasy chain and back wheel. Not sure why, but, yup—you guessed it—easy to get at. After I got them ripped lose, I convinced myself that they were the source of my problems and climbed back on the bike and tried to start it. *Danggit...nothing.* (I had depleted my f-bomb arsenal. For now.) Then I had a flash of mechanical insight (this must be how Archimedes felt)—*Eureka!—electrical! The damn problem's gotta be electrical.* (I had heard the old man say that once when he was f-bombing his truck.) Something probably got shorted out so I cut the wires to the horn, headlight, and those damn orange turn signals that I always forgot to turn off. That *had* to be the problem. Not even close. Still wouldn't start. I kicked my frypan and heard it splash in the ditch water. I sat down on Dale Evans' face on the liner of my red and yellow Roy Rogers sleeping bag and, keeping part of my promise to Mom, cried like a little girl.

I wiped my tears away and was screwing in my fifth spare sparkplug when I heard it. It sounded like a lawnmower. He rode up behind me and shut it off.

Dale.

Dale would eventually become my first not-Dover-Boy buddy. He grew up in Gassett (pronounced like the hound dog—*Basset*), another wide spot in the road about half-way between Dover and Bill Town. Their town slogan (painted on a sign by the road—they couldn't afford nor did they need a water tower) was: *Welcome to Gassett—Stop In—Don't Pass It*. Incredibly, it was even smaller than Dover. If Dover was an atom, Gassett would have been an electron or neutron or something. When the United States Postal Service assigned their new-fangled five-digit zip codes to every town in America, Gassett only got two digits.

Dale was riding a Honda Trail 90. Next to my mighty 250cc Suzuki it looked like a toy. Sissy little seat and sissy little handlebars. It made about as much noise as Mom's Sunbeam mixer. I muffled my laugh. Everyone knew that REAL motorcycle riders like Heck's Angels and James Dean riding around looking for something to run over or rape had 250cc "big irons" like me. This *thing* he was sitting on with his folded arms and smug grin was obviously beneath me, so I ignored him and kept screwing the sparkplug.

I jumped back on the seat and tried to start it again. Of course it didn't start. Of course, I let go with a bunch of fresh f-bombs. Of course I didn't really need all of them, I was just showing off in front of the stranger. I started digging through Dad's tackle box again, clawing around for the factory-provided universal fits-all wrench. I, by God, would rip off those fucking (adjective) handlebars. I wasn't sure why. Surely they had to be the cause of my problem.

"You check the gas tank?"

The stranger spoke? I pretended not to hear him. How dare some pimply-faced scooter rider presume to actually speak to some equally-pimply-faced motorcycle rider? Like *he* understood the complex mechanics that enabled REAL motorcycles to fly down the road, rocketing forth on some cosmic quest, leaving girlie scooters like his in their dust?

As I mashed my last not-yet-bleeding knuckle with the factory-provided fits-all wrench, the stranger dared to speak again, "Seriously, dude. You check the gas tank?"

I wheeled around to confront my nemesis perched on his padded girlie seat with his arms still folded across his chest. He smiled smuggier. A damn Cheshire cat, shit-eatin' f-bomb smile.

I fake-smiled back. "You got nothin' better to do?" I scowled. He didn't budge. Didn't he know that there was nothing for him here? It was pretty obvious that I had a handle on this. Which ironically, I pretty much did. I was cradling the handlebars in my bloody knuckles.

He just sat there on his girlie seat with that stupid smile. Did he know something that I didn't? Surely not. Anyone could clearly see that I was on the threshold of finding the problem. I'd be straddling my seat and conquering the cosmos in no time.

I threw the handlebars on the growing pile of parts: the carburetor-thing, the chain and sprocket, the back wheel and tire, five fouled sparkplugs, and of course—the horn. That last one made me feel pretty stupid when I thought about it. I mean, a horn has nothing to do with a real motorcycle's ability to start. Does it?

Then, just to add insult to injury, the damn battery went dead. Cranking the motor 20 or 30 times every time I screwed in a fresh sparkplug drained the life from its clear plastic see-thru cells. So I threw my leg over the seat and flipped the pedal down on the kick-starter. *Those handlebars*, I thought. *Those handlebars have got to be the problem. Got to be. This sonofabitchin' Suzuki was going to start now.* (Take note Father Hemple: that was not an f-bomb). I'd show him. I'd get the last laugh on the shit-grinning stranger. I stiffened my right leg and kicked the kicker with every ounce of muscle in my still-hairless calf. *What's this?* The motor...it...it actually turned over.

Quick—another kick.

Nothing.

Again—KICK.

Sputter! *What?* Was that a primordial spark of life? Did it just try to start?

KICK.

SNAP! The sound was sickening. I was sure that I had broken something. Surely not the Suzuki. It was Jap. Everyone knew Jap stuff didn't break. Maybe it wouldn't start, but it never *broke*. Harleys broke. Fords broke. And 19" Philco black&white televisions broke. But not Jap stuff. It never broke. *Oh Shit*! That **SNAP**... it was my knee. Mechanical genius that I was, I had forgotten to tighten the last sparkplug and the third time I kicked down, it popped out like a pimple on my forehead. With no compression to counter my 126-pound kick, my knee hyperextended and snapped like a pretzel.

As I rolled around on the road, rocking back and forth and crying (again) like a little girl, the smiling stranger walked over to me and stuck out his hand. He helped me limp over to my yard sale and sat me down on Dale Evans' face. He went to my stripped-down REAL motorcycle and unscrewed the gas cap.

"Should'a checked the gas," he smiled.

He climbed back on his scooter-thing and started it up. He told me to stay right there; he'd be back in about 20 minutes. I wanted to drop an f-bomb on him and say something like, "Where the #@%&* ya think I'm gonna go?" But after considering my present position I mumbled a pathetic, "Okay." As he rode off, I laid there and surveyed all that I had accomplished. Or, more correctly, all that I had screwed up.

Dammit! He was right all along. It *was* the gas. I had been in such a hurry to leave. In my Zen-like yearning for open-road bliss, I forgot to fill it up. What I smelled in that carburetor-thing was nothing but fumes. It was going to take a miracle to get this pile of parts running again.

My miracle arrived in a '59 Ford pickup. Dale's dad climbed out from behind the wheel. He stuck out his forefinger and pointed it right between his eyes to push his glasses back up on his nose. He took one look at my yard sale and shook his head. I saw right away where Dale got his shit-eatin'grin.

He looked over at me, "Should'a checked the gas." No *Hello…how'ya doin'*? Or, *Kin I help ya?* Nothing. Just *Shoulda checked the gas.*

Dale and his old man worked on my Suzuki in their garage for a couple of hours. Like Humpty Dumpty, they put her back together again. Dale's dad even carried the carburetor-thing over to his shop bench and took it apart like a Swiss watch and cleaned it (it was pretty much caked with road dust after I slammed it on the ground). A couple of Camels and Cokes later, he bolted it back onto the top of the motor.

"Try her now," Dale's old man said as he sat on the tail gate of his Ford sucking on another Camel. By now my knee felt much better thanks to the amazing recuperative powers of the Coke and Moon Pie that Dale's mom brought out. I walked over to my bike nearly limp-less and straddled the seat. I barely touched the little red starter button and she jumped to life. Now it was my turn to smile. The horn even sounded better.

Dale and his dad smiled back. Without even looking at each other they said, in almost-perfect, father-and-son two-part harmony, "Should'a checked the gas."

During the course of our senior year in high school, Dale and I bonded in that very special way that only adolescent boys can do. Narrow-minded opinions had not yet cluttered our lives. We said stuff without even thinking about it, unfiltered by the social protocol that sometimes causes adults (at least those with a filter) to pause before staking out a position on some inane topic. We shared formative experiences that helped make us the men that we are today. Cathartic events shaped our character, fortified our spirit, and formed the basis of our personalities. Of course, I'm talking about *girls, tits*, and *beer*.

But there was one thing (not included in that list) that set us apart from all the other boys—our shared passion for motorcycles.

It was the summer after we graduated from high school. Vietnam was raging. The draft was raging. Protesters were raging. The military-industrial complex that I heard McNamara lying about to Walter Cronkite on TV was hungry and needed more cannon fodder. I was about to celebrate my 18th birthday and, in a matter of months, would be low-hanging fruit for the county draft board. Uneducated middle-class expendables (like us) filled their quotas. In my naiveté, I had come to subscribe to the widely-held misconception that men somehow controlled their own destinies. That we could make life-changing decisions that would shape events and alter our futures. (Cynicism has long since supplanted my naiveté.) But lacking the political will to shape my future and control my destiny by burning my draft card like so-many like-minded and stronger-willed boys were doing, I took the low road. As badly as I wanted to tell Nixon, McNamara, and the military-industrial complex to stick that war up their asses…I took the road more frequently travelled. I enlisted in the Air Force. I was scheduled to leave for basic training at the end of the summer.

Dale and I rode out to the quarry one moon-lit night after yet another unsuccessful character-defining *girls, tits, and beer* quest that I was telling you about earlier. As usual, we scored a triple strike-out. For graduation Dale's old man had rewarded him with a factory-fresh Honda 305 Scrambler which now reduced *me* to girlie-bike status. Oh, how the mighty fall. We shut off our bikes and sat on the limestone cliff that overlooked the shimmering water below and talked about all those things that preoccupy pubescent boys. Yup—*girls, tits and beer.* (You startin' to see a pattern here?)

After we got ourselves all worked up, our discussion (and testosterone levels) settled down and we focused on something that was closer to reality. The one thing we did know a little something about. The only certainty in our lives—*motorcycles*. Within minutes it was decided. As we rode back into the night, we had it completely planned out. Before Uncle Sam signed us up, straightened us out, and shipped us off, we, by God—*we* were going on a road trip. A Thelma-and-Louise-Peter-Fonda-and-Dennis-Hopper Road Trip.

Destination—Canada!

I located that ensemble of crap that I had strapped on my Suzuki for my failed expedition the previous summer. Most of it was still piled up in the corner of the old man's garage. Thankfully the old man hadn't conducted one of his five-year purges. Everything was still there except for my Roy Rogers sleeping bag. I liked to lay it on top of my bed and sleep in it every night (Mom never could figure out why). So I grabbed some rope and started tying all of it back on again.

After I checked the gas (I actually remembered), I ran into the house and kissed mom goodbye (remembered that too). I was sure that my departure would trigger one of those emotional

Mother-Son Moments, fraught with tears and *be careful sweetheart* things. Alas, it was not to be. She looked up at the kitchen clock and said, "My, you better get going. We don't wanna keep Dale waiting now, do we?" As I turned to go she added, "Ya check the gas?"

Dale and his dad were pacing in their driveway. A trail of Camels told me they had probably been out there since dawn. As I climbed off the Suzuki they smiled at me, "Ya check the gas?" I had anticipated that and responded with one finger. We double-checked everything. Once again I made sure that my hammer was easily accessible. No…this time I would use it to pound in the stakes for my Roy Rogers two-man pup tent. Over the course of the next week Dale and I would ride together, eat together, shoot the shit around the camp fire together and yes—even sleep together. I don't know if you have ever slept in a Roy Rogers two-man pup tent with anyone, but suffice to say, it's a bit, err…*cozy*. Maybe a little too cozy.

Initially the ride went pretty well. Dale would be our navigator so he packed a map. He signaled me to pull over every six or seven miles so he could locate our whereabouts. He got off his bike, untied his pack, and dug around for the map. After he confirmed our location, he pointed to one of the red or blue lines to show me where we were headed. I nodded my head as though I understood. My navigational skills were roughly equivalent to my mechanical skills. He refolded his origami map-puzzle a few times and stuffed it back in his stack where it would remain until we pulled over six or seven miles later.

As you look back on your life, have you ever noticed that many times when you tested fate, it somehow taught you a lesson that you never saw coming? It did that to us. We forgot to pack two things that even Peter Fonda probably forgot:

matches and rain gear. Every afternoon black clouds banked in around us and we rode through an Old Testament downpour not unlike the one suffered by Moses or Noah or some other bible guy. Well, here's something you're probably not aware of unless you're a Weather Channel nerd: Northern Minnesota has only two seasons—July and winter. This was August. Summer had already come and gone. Our daily deluge was roughly the same temperature as a Popsicle.

I don't know if it was the every-eight-mile map stops, the uncooked-wiener-breath intimacy of a pup tent partner, or the well-worn and no longer cute *ya-check-the-gas?*, but our road trip, not yet fully into its third day, spiraled into an exercise of conflict avoidance. Cold-stone silence and indifferent glares. I sat on one side of the wet logs to chew on a cold weenie while Dale sulked on the other. Friendly evening chats were reduced to wiener belches and bean farts. We slept back-to-back with our faces facing away from each other (just like married folks).

Three weeks after we arrived home, we finally started talking to each other again. Clumsy at first. Eventually we got around to full sentences. I don't think either of us apologized or even mumbled *I'm sorry*. We moved on as though nothing ever happened. Again, just like married folks. Well, husbands anyway. Wives—they never forget *anything*. I'm just sayin'.

Through the years, Dale and I have remained best friends. We strayed for a while as we lived our lives, raised our kids, and endured the mind-numbing motions of jobs and careers. But like whack-a-moles, we popped up in each other's world from time to time. We yacked on the phone regularly and recollected some of our adventures. We got getting pretty good with that embellishment thing. Especially when we got around to talking about *all* the girls we had and *all* those six-packs we guzzled.

We'd long-since forgotten about the tits thing. (Oh, hell no—I'm just checkin' to see if you're paying attention.) Our intentionally distorted memories had no regard for something so silly as truth.

Every boy, in every age, in every part of the world should experience a summer like that. A summer of Last Hurrahs. Youthful innocence savored before the harsh reality of life intrudes. Dale fought for his life as a ground-pounder in the jungles of 'Nam. I *braved* four years of being an Air Force frat-boy, somehow surviving in the jungle of girlie bars in downtown Taipei. Two motorcycle boys departed Dover on that cold January day to do our patriotic duty. Two men returned.

Today, Dale is gone. He died recently. The first of our Gang of Five (expanded to six to accommodate him). The last thing I told him was how much I loved him. I hope the first thing he tells me when her rides up to the pearly gates to greet me on his Honda is, "You check the gas?"

MY OLD MAN

The Old Man. You've seen that idiom countless times throughout this book. You've probably noticed that I always expressed it with capital letters when used in reference to some Dover Old Man. You probably asked yourself, *Huh? He used capital letters for Old Man.* I did that because *Old Man* was essentially a proper name back in Dover. Well okay, maybe it wasn't really a *nom de guerre*, but for sure it was an expression of honor. The French have their *Monsieur*. Hispanics—*Señor*. Most Americans—*Mister*. Dover folks had *Old Man*. Old Man Peters and Old Man Green were more than just fictional characters; they were my stand-ins. Surrogates for genuine, honest men. Contentious—yes. Crusty—of course. But they had within them a noble sense of honor and integrity that frankly, is just plain hard to find nowadays. Not once, in all the years that I knew Old Man Peters and Old Man Green, did they compromise that honor. Old Man Peters (the real one) said to me one day as we shared a beer up at Tilleys (the real one), "Bill, don't ever try to be somebody you ain't." Go ahead and Google Philosophy 101 and try to find something—anything—that beats that. Even Kant can't come close.

Now you know why Old Man is not old man.

My dad—my old man—was an exception. I did not capitalize it. Did you notice it? My editor sure did. Took some heat for it, too. The same rules that apply to *Father* apply to *Old Man*. Since this is not a grammar book (that should be abundantly clear by now), I won't go into all the details.

So then, with that probably unnecessary clarification, let's dig into what this chapter is really about. My old man.

When Mom was still alert, *still with us* (as they say), I went to spend a week with her for what we laughingly referred to as *Bill and Rita's Big Adventure*. It was our last day together and it was raining. Hard. "Looks like an all-dayer." Mom surmised. "We got all the time in the world," she said. Our last day's adventure would be confined to her never-used-'cept-for-Christmas dining room table. She sat me down and poured the Folgers from her never-empty coffee pot and told me to sit still (just like when I was her Dover Boy) while she went to her bedroom to get something from her closet. I heard her fumbling around back there and waited for that Fibber McGee and Molly thing, but two cups later she came back carrying a shoebox. She had a strangely familiar look in her eye that I hadn't seen since I was twelve. *The Look* normally preceded a much-deserved ass-chewin'. But today it was somehow…different. Soft. Wistful.

She put her shoebox on the table in front of me and told me to open it. I blew the dust away and looked inside. You have probably already gathered this about our harried Mom…she was old school. Neat and tidy surrounded everything she touched. But organized…not so much. So you can imagine my astonishment when I looked inside and saw them all stacked in neat rows like files in some anal-retentive office secretary's file cabinet. She had them tied with faded silk ribbons in little bundles. Her love letters. She said she wanted me to read them. Wanted me to see what Vince and Rita were like before they became Mom and Dad. I grabbed a bundle and before I had the ribbon untied, she started telling me how, back then, they lived in a different world before eight of us (somehow) popped up. She chuckled a little as she remembered their naïve family planning skills (yup…that Catholic thing again). *Poke & Hope* she snickered. They were two love birds living one day at a time; unfettered by the sequential banalities of life.

As those letters would soon reveal, they *were* quite the item. That's what she said…*quite the item.* Dad poured his guts out in some of them. War was tough. Dead buddies deserved a lot more of his ink, but he just couldn't. But more than that, he always reserved the last paragraphs to pour his heart out too. As I opened the first envelope postmarked July 7, 1943 I looked over at mom and saw her gazing out the rain-drenched window. The memories still echoed in her heart. Joy and Laughter. Sorrow and Tears.

As I started reading I tried to imagine the 22-year-old homesick Private First Class sitting in his sweltering tent in the jungles of New Guinea. With pen in hand and air-mail onionskin tablet balanced on his knees, he poured his heart out to his hometown beauty. For all men in all wars, the dead-serious business of soldiering was counterbalanced by hours (and days) of boredom and bullshit. His letters reflected that. A lot. He captured the camp tedium with incredible detail; searching, I'm sure, for something—anything—to fill the page. While the fighting was hard and combat intense, ennui was ever-present. Those empty hours provided the young lover with more than enough time to compose his emotions.

He warmed up by reporting on the routine of camp life— ordinance inventory, weapons maintenance, and latrine duty.

Yup—latrine duty in a *love letter*. That must have brought a smile to Mom's face. And of course—chow hall complaints. No soldier was worth his gunpowder if he didn't bellyache about the food. Dad was a *meat-and-taters* man and didn't much care for the swill they served. That's what he called it—*swill*. Farm mothers spoiled their sons. After working endless hours in the fields, their famished farm boys came to the table expecting culinary perfection. And they got it. Maybe just meat and taters...but they got it.

After he finished with the routine crap (err...literally), he summoned his courage and, without getting specific (the Army censors would have redacted it anyway) forced a few nervous passages from his pen. Soldiers were not permitted (nor did they have the desire) to detail their battlefield horrors. Many would repress them for years; some with not very nice outcomes. So, with as much bravado as bullshit, he wrote how they were *gonna get them Japs* and how the *little yellow bastards* didn't have a chance.

Saving the hard part for the end, he filled the last onionskin page with romance. Not necessarily a Shakespearian sonnet or Jane Austen elegy; some of his faltering attempts were (sorry, Dad), quite cliché. He used 1940's jargon that seems innocent by today's standards. Movie dialogue he had probably heard Bogie whisper into Ingrid Bergman's ear in *Casablanca* at one of their outdoor jungle movies. But at times he was quite the romantic, lyrical even, with his farm-boy phrases. I'll respect their privacy and not share them here. Reading them gave me an insight into a man that I never *really* knew. There was (quite obviously) a tender spot deep in his heart that cried out for *his gal*. Sadly, that tenderness would not be shared in the relationships that he'd one day have with his children.

August 6, 1945. Brigadier General Paul Tibbets and his intrepid B-29 crew dropped the bomb on Hiroshima and the

Japanese conflict was nearly over. So did Dad's love letters. He was shipped back to the states, discharged, and returned home; *apparently* unscathed by the ravages of war. The young lovers made up for all their lost time (obviously) pretty quickly. In less than a year they were married. A newspaper clipping that announced their soon-to-be wedding was tucked under one of the bundles in Mom's shoebox. It was the only document I have ever seen that fills even a small part of the post love-letter void. There were a few faded black-and-white photos that gave a glimpse of their honeymoon bliss. I have them in my own shoebox.

They settled into a rent house in Dover and the old man went to work driving a truck. He (quite) obviously was home long enough to make babies. Fat, pink, squalling, Catholic babies. By the time the countin' was over…EIGHT. Mom and the old man pushed the envelope (even by Catholic standards) when they made me. Less than eleven months separate me and my sister. Hippity-hop, hippity-hop.

They struggled. Dad with his broke-ass trucks and staying one step ahead of the bill collectors. Mom frazzled by floor-crawling ankle biters and dirty diapers. Both of them trying to keep enough groceries on the table for eight always-empty bellies. So of course the flames of romance faded. When it came to *amoré*, apparently The Greatest Generation was just The Okay Generation.

There is no doubt that my old man was his father's son. Unassuming and reserved. Always guarding his inner feelings. Dad sprang from damn-near pure Germanic stock and learned his paternal skills in a home where the outward expression of emotions was discouraged. Our reclusive grandfather, *when* he was present in his five son's lives, was a demanding taskmaster. Maybe not the rigidity (and certainly not the abuse…let's be clear on that) of The Great Santini, but expectations had to be met. Affections were abandoned in deference to cultural compliance.

The best I can do here is offer my carefully considered assumptions gathered from subtle inferences. None of my grandfather's children—my uncles and aunts—ever spoke of their father with affection. I have never heard them share stories about him. His legacy was doomed when, in a final act of desperation, he took his own life. No one rose to defend his final desperation. I was much too young to remember his funeral or eulogy (if one was even offered), but I cannot imagine it being very pretty. I'm sure, in his own way, Grandpa did his best. But something snapped. Something bad.

Apparently my disciplinarian grandfather was not repressive. His detachment in some ways proved to be an advantage for Dad and his brothers. They were a tribe of crazy bastards. They drove hot cars and hot motorcycles. They plowed corn by day and sewed wild oats by night. The wild oats thing is probably more braggadocio than fact given their staunch Catholicism. I heard more than one uncle recalling his escapades on Sunday afternoons when they gathered around a tub of iced-down Hamm's in our backyard and were safely out of earshot of Mom and my aunts.

Those rowdy Rausch boys. That was the oft-heard expression repeated in church halls and beer joints all around Chickasaw county. Like the old man, all five of them backed up that reputation and fought bravely in WWII. Miraculously, all five of them returned to perpetuate the legend. I only wish that they would have shared some of their adventures with us. The conversational snippets that I gleaned as they stood around that tubaHamm's in the backyard were but a teasing glimpse.

They're all dead now. One of the old man's brothers learned to fly and was a regular Wiley Post. He plowed headlong into a violent thunderstorm somewhere out in the Dakotas and met his death fighting the controls of his Cessna when the weather conditions exceeded his aviation skills. Two more died tragically. (One was the old man. I don't want to talk about it.) Two "passed on" naturally.

All of their amazing stories should have been shouted, argued, and laughed over. Handed down for *us* to shout and argue and laugh over. Sadly, they took most of their yarns with them to the grave. They would have made one hell of a book.

We need to take a little time-out here. We are about to walk into some pretty tough territory. This next part is more about feelings than facts and will necessarily be brief. This stuff is not easy to write. Besides that, no one likes to listen to some sentimental fool whining about his disadvantaged past, bereft of emotional warmth or paternal reassurance. *Oh, poor me* and all that. We writers are all too good at that. So allow me one brief interjection here: the following paragraphs won't sound like much of a love letter. And there will be no embellishments here. No absurdities cunningly crafted to help me duck and run. As you read, don't you go climbing up on your high horse of moral certitude and chastise me for writing another show-and-tell exposé. Reserve your judgement until you finish this thing. If your first reaction is to kick my ass—get in line. But if your take-away inspires you to give me a hug—get in the other line. I pray that one is considerably longer.

Up to this point in the book, I have dealt with my old man's beer drinking in a light-hearted, oftentimes comical way. His cannaHamm's up at Tilleys. His late-night escapades whispering into Furlan's ear in the corner booth. But that wasn't always necessarily so. Sometimes maybe, but not always. In later years he was plagued by the menacing draw of alcohol that took him into places—dark places—that a simple cannaHamm's never intended. Back in those years we all blindly bought into the myth that his *problem*, his goddam drinking, was just a character flaw. No worse than overeating or oversmoking. As Oscar Wilde, himself no stranger to the bottle, put it, "Work is the curse of the drinking class." But it was more than a simple snag in his willpower. It was a disease, a goddam *physical* disease, every bit as physical and devastating as his emphysema or what might have been his two-pack-a-day cancer (we never knew). So we conveniently dismissed it as just being a part of our dad and gave him a get-out-of-jail-free card. He and all those men *up at Tilleys* simply had Oscar Wilde's working man's curse. Men like Dad were never characterized as alcoholics. Polite expressions like "heavy drinker" and "he likes his likker" were common. In those days, at least around Dover, there were no clinical programs to help victims like Dad who were haunted by this monster. So lacking any moral incentive to do otherwise, Dover Men banded together up at Tilleys in a confederacy of enablers: *Buy another round. Tell another joke.*

When Good Dad showed up, we competed for his affections like a litter of sweaty puppies. We devoured him. He'd *rassle* on the floor with us and rub whisker burns on our kid-cheeks. We'd laugh till our sides hurt from his tickle-fights. But on the frightful nights, long after we ate yet another supper without him (a not uncommon occurrence), when Bad Dad stumbled through the door, we ran for cover. Dishes got thrown. Doors slammed. Shouts raged. Expletives echoed down the hall until they found our bedrooms. Underneath our pillow-covered heads, tears flowed. We cowered...Mom struggled.

Even Good Dad, in spite of his well-intentioned rasslin' and whisker-rubbin,' wasn't equipped to step up to the emotional plate that came with parenthood. He was the only role model we had, so with nothing else to compare it to, we assumed that this was what dad-behavior was like. He didn't know how to kiss. How to hug. How to put his arm around a shoulder and beam with pride at a Cub Scout merit badge or a hard-fought A in history. How to soothe, much less kiss, an *owie*. How to console a son or daughter when hurtful things happened. How to take a private moment to teach his children.

Don't you dare say it. Because I'm certainly not. It wasn't that our dad didn't love us. He loved us deeply. He loved us with the same heart that he poured out to Mom in all those love letters. All eight towheaded little critters he helped to create. Sadly, we accepted his reticence as a kind of *normal*.

Life is filled with opportunities that might lead us on to success…or failure. Sometimes, in our bone-crushing routines, we lose sight of our win/loss ratio. Our successes arrive in stubborn bits and pieces. We cling to them. Celebrate them. Thank God for them. But sadly, so many of our failures occur without even being recognized until it's too damn late. Hindsight is so damn perfect. All of us, if we are honest with ourselves, have private moments of *shoulda' coulda'* reflections. Mom shoulda fought back and not just surrendered. We coulda been stronger. We shoulda been braver. We coulda been smarter. We shoulda helped the old man cry out for help.

One damn thing I know is absolutely certain. There is One Truth I shall forever carry in my heart as long as I live: My old man did his best.

I suppose one day my sons might express similar feelings about my inadequacies. My failures. How I let them down. How sometimes I wasn't there. But one damn thing is absolutely certain. There is One Truth I shall forever carry in my heart as long as I live: I'm doing my best.

EPILOGUE

Past is Prologue. Or so they say. I'm not sure that I agree with it. But I still like to say it. Makes me sound smart. But I'm not sure it's true.

The folks that proffer that philosophy would have you believe that as individuals or as a society, we are the culmination of everything that preceded us. And according to their certain knowledge, we are destined to do it all over again. As Old Man Peters might have put it, *You are what you were.*

Dover is a fictional name, but it is not a fictional place. It's a very real place. It's still out there; still alive. Still kickin'. Sure, it was no cultural mecca or commercial beehive. No New York City or Chicago by any stretch of even my wild-ass imagination. But even though Dover is no *l'Amerique profonde*, it still deserves to be acknowledged. And in many ways—admired.

This was my tribute to all of the Dover Men, the Dover Women, and perhaps more than any of them, all my Dover Boys. They were the weavers of the fabric of my life, wrapping me in rich and vibrant threads. The Deuter Brothers, Riker, Mickey, the new kid Gary, Dale, and my little brother Richie animate my Dover memories. They will always be with me.

Memories are ephemeral things. Puffs of smoke that swirl through our lives defying clear definition. What good are our memories if they are not cloaked in hope? Our triumphs survive pretty much intact and we conjure them often. But our sorrows, for the most part, become muted over time. Some get swept under our cerebral carpets. Retrospection comes equipped with its own Delete Key that mercifully masks the painful. I didn't even attempt to strike a balance with these tales. I am quite aware that I recalled and celebrated—with *lavish embellishment*—far more carnivals than cries. I'll let you be the judge whether or not that was fair.

I hope that you enjoyed my recollections. They were slippery little things and I wrestled with them mightily. They pinned me to the mat a few times during our late night bouts; but with enough ink, perspiration, and a cannaHamm's (or two), I persevered. I pray that, lurking somewhere between the lines, I threw enough light on my town, my people, and my Dover Boys to give you a peep show. And maybe, if I got lucky—that light warmed your heart.

Please let it be true that I made you laugh a time or two. That you chuckled when you heard Old Man Peters' coonhounds yelping on the porch, smelled the Pigboys rodeoing in Ray's stockyards, and watched the chickens dance as you trembled with me behind gramma's apron.

And if you did—if you laughed—well then, as the old man always said, "That's just frosting on the cake."

Made in the USA
Coppell, TX
30 July 2020